FLORIDA KILLS

A NOVEL

ANN KENNA

CHELONIA
PRESS

Printed in the United States of America

Paperback book: ISBN 979-8-9915917-0-6

Hardcover Book: ISBN: 979-8-9915917-2-0

eBook: ISBN 979-8-9915917-1-3

An imprint of Chelonia Press, LLC

Website: AnnKenna.com

Cover design and illustration design by Noah Scheiner

INCREDIBLE PRAISE FOR FLORIDA KILLS FROM REGULAR PEOPLE

"Ann Kenna's sharp-witted writing is a joy to read! Nuanced characters, laugh-out-loud humor and intelligent plot twists keep the reader engaged and entertained from start to finish. I loved every page."

– Theresa Morgan- Vero Beach, FL

"Get ready for the unexpected! Ann Kenna's *Florida Kills* mixes comic mobsters, steamy romances, and a dedicated detective in the dangerous environment of Florida's swamplands. Terrifying and hilarious at the turn of every page!

Florida Kills is a riveting book full of suspense, colorful characters, and vivid imagery and satisfies the appetite for mysteries only the vibrant, untamed Florida environment can conjure. Kenna is masterful at bringing the nuances of Florida alive...she keeps her readers riveted on every page."

—Susan Lovelace, Editor

"With *Florida Kills*, Ann Kenna delivers a gripping, darkly humorous ride through Florida's wild heart. Her compelling storytelling captures the spirit of Carl Hiaasen while crafting a thrilling tale of crime, redemption, and the hidden dangers lurking beneath paradise."

—John DiMenna, FL

"Ann Kenna's debut novel *Florida Kills* brings the Florida Everglades to life with vivid scenery, swampland residents, humor, and shocking mysteries that hook readers from the first chapter. If you've been there, you'll feel at home. If not, you'll feel like you're visiting for the first time. Florida Kills is a must read."

—Elaine Spooner, Sebastian, FL

"*Florida Kills* is a riveting book full of suspense, colorful characters, and vivid imagery. Ann Kenna is masterful at bringing the nuances of Florida alive for all to marvel at."

Kelly Marker, Florida

"In the Sunshine State...who knew there were so many ways to meet your demise? Prepare for a wild and wacky ride-along with Ann Kenna's debut novel, *Florida Kills.* Along the way you'll meet a cast of quirky characters and fierce predators...get ready to laugh-out-loud."

—Patti Sorrentino-Port St. Lucie, FL

"*Florida Kills*...covers all the bases: crime, redemption, action, humor, and of course relationships. The diverse characters including a burnt-out detective, wanna be wise guys and a fearless, beautiful herpetologist, create an exciting recipe of events only possible in the Sunshine State. Ann Kenna's very entertaining story is enhanced by the author's firsthand knowledge of the area and her vivid imagination making it a truly "Florida" adventure...looking forward to her next book."

—George Bolton, FL

"*Florida Kills* is a gritty thriller with cleverly crafted characters. Twists and turns, and laugh-out-loud humor, make Ann Kenna's debut novel the ultimate gripping crime read."

—Jayne Potter, New York

"Debut author, Ann Kenna has masterfully blended rich characters and romantic intrigue with murder and suspense - while bringing the setting of the Everglades and 'old Florida' to life in *Florida Kills*. The well-developed characters, and the author's vivid descriptions of the Everglades and a small Florida town are spot on. The novel opens with a startling scene and then follows our protagonist, Pete Landry, a rugged detective, who tackles the dangers of murder, the wilds of the Everglades and the complications of romantic relationships. I found myself eagerly turning the pages, anticipating what would happen next.

Mystery lovers and Florida aficionados alike will find much to enjoy in this atmospheric, character-driven thriller."

—Amy Morgan- Vero Beach, FL

Dedication

To John, sitting by the sea, you and me,

making dreams come true.

FLORIDA KILLS

CHAPTER 1

January 30 – Big Cypress National Park, FL

David Andruzzi didn't see the alligator until he jabbed it with the pole. The large reptile had been motionless beneath the boat, its color blending with the algae filled swamp. The agitated beast, jaws open, jagged teeth dripping scum, swam to the starboard side. David stood still and held his breath until it swam off into the mangroves.

The pole boat remained stable. Its narrow beam and flat hull were designed for the meandering streams and shallow bottom of the Everglades. Stability was the only plus David could see—the sides from water line to rail were maybe eighteen inches. A small gator would be onboard in seconds; a large one could flip it over in a heartbeat. *Fuck my life. I'm from Queens. I got no business being out here.*

As the creature slid out of sight, David's forearms pimpled, his ragged breath revealed a deep fear not experienced since night terrors stalked his childhood dreams. He summoned his wise-guy swagger. "This is exactly why I'm in this boat," he spoke aloud. "Keep your eye on the goddamn ball, Davey." The tough words fell flat. He inhaled sharply as he realized there would be no echo in the depths of hell. The Everglades were hell on earth.

He patted his pocket; glad he had a weapon. The nine-millimeter pistol had been taped under the boat's rear bench along with a new cell phone and a navigational chart with a route into the Everglades highlighted. Unfolding the chart, he checked he was still headed in the right direction. Everything around him looked the same. His efforts to calm himself failed. He couldn't pretend he was paddling through the canals back home with a six-pack and a fishing rod.

Sweat stung his eyes as he searched the vegetation that rose up from all sides. The green wall surrounding him was alive with the buzz of insects, the whine of distant airboats, frog croaks, and screeching birds. A branch cracked to close. *I should have done some homework on this god-forsaken place, insisted on one of those airboats. This piece of shit is worthless.* He became aware of a deep odor of rot. *What is that smell?* He mopped his brow and applied bug-spray. A soupy mist discolored the morning light. The treetop canopy was so thick no direct sun punctured the gloom. He reached for a water bottle. Despite the dampness, his mouth was parched, his body dehydrated.

He poled further into the swamp, scanned for signs of predators. *This was a huge mistake. I'm outta my league here.* His hands shook as he pulled the pole out of the water. The steady drips from the pole drummed and shivered the mercury-colored surface, ratcheting his tension. David tightened his arm motion and prayed he could be silent as he drifted forward. He thought he heard the reeds whisper as he passed.

A vibration on his right thigh startled him. His panicky jolt sent ripples splashing against the nearby mangrove roots. Hissing sounds emerged from behind the closest tree. Between the twisted roots a handful of baby gators, their bodies writhing over each other, snapped their perfect miniature jaws. *Oh shit, can this get any worse?* He pushed past the nursery and floated down the center of the channel. The phone continued to vibrate and now emitted a quiet ping. Removing it from his pocket, he checked the GPS app was activated, then silenced the device. He was getting close. Placing it back in his pocket, he surveyed the area. The vibration continued until it became one long hum.

David pulled the boat up to an area of higher ground, tied the bowline to a rotted tree stump, then stepped onto the soggy hillock. In the murky light he could see a box about forty feet away. *Bingo!* The two-foot square box was lying beneath a giant cypress. Its heavy, leafed arms extended far overhead; an army of knotty roots protruded up from the ground. *This place is fucking creepy.* He took a deep breath...*You got this. Just get in and out quick.* He checked the gun one more time.

His cautious approach revealed no signs of danger. His anxiety lessened as he reached the package. Nudging the box with his foot, he noticed it had been damaged. The oilskin wrapping was torn. The GPS transmitter was attached to the cord, but the cord was loose and frayed. It appeared to have been chewed.

Bending to pick it up, there was a change in the air around him. The persistent insect buzz and squawking bird sounds had been replaced with an unnerving silence. A deep musky scent infused the dank air. David wheezed. He pulled the pistol from his pocket and surveyed the perimeter of the small clearing. Seeing no threat, he relaxed and smiled at his good fortune. *Halfway home, baby, this is going to be a major league payday.*

He never looked up, never saw the monster as it slid from its tree top perch. Something solid brushed David's shoulder. He turned his head. A massive python, its mouth wide open, dangled inches from his face. Immobilized by heart-stopping terror, David's bladder let loose as the nightmare's curved teeth bit deeply into his shoulder. The snake, its skin cold and smooth, coiled around his torso from shoulders to knees. He was trapped. The python took no notice of the screams that ripped open the silence or the explosion of bullets fired off into the ground. The cracking of his rib cage was the last sound David heard as the life was squeezed out of him.

CHAPTER 2

Goodland, Florida

Detective Pete Landry sauntered into his favorite dive, the Buoy Bar, at 12:30 p.m. His personal hurricane hole was an oasis of calm and a three-minute walk from his canal-front trailer on Papaya Street. A cup of coffee, biscuits and gravy or a cold beer and steamers awaited him, depending on the time he woke up. Today, a beer appeared in front of him as he settled on the cracked wooden bar stool. The place was quiet. Wednesday afternoons were relegated to drunks and locals.

He stared at the countdown clock above the bottles. The number 137 leered back. An unseen weight pressed down on him as his broad shoulders slumped, his head dropped, and a deep sigh escaped his lips.

"Donna, hit me with a Jack chaser."

"This is early, even for you." With hands on hips, she questioned him. "Aren't you still working?"

"I'm signed out for lunch, a very long one." He took another swallow of beer.

"Well, I'm going to have to deny my favorite customer. How about I get you a plate of conch fritters? Real fresh, I just made them."

"No, I'm not hungry."

"I insist," she said.

Pete watched her as she served an older couple at the end of the bar. She was smiling and offering suggestions on airboat rides. Her blue eyes lit up as she described the beauty of the Everglades. She glanced his way and winked as she walked into the kitchen.

He swallowed to clear the painful lump in his throat. This was something he needed to fix. Donna had always been his willing bedmate. Through years of sex and dead-end conversations about someday, he knew he couldn't give her more and worse; she knew it. His hand shook as he raised the beer to his lips and sipped the liquid gold, hoping to fill the holes in his heart.

Donna placed the steaming platter of fritters in front of him. "On the house." She stepped back and squinted at him. "What's going on with you? You've been MIA for a week."

He ignored the question. "Why'd you put that clock up there? It's not the apocalypse approaching. I'm retiring. It's not like it's a national holiday."

She wiped down the counter in front of him and smiled. "Everyone around here is watching that clock close. There's even a betting pool saying you're not going through with it." She grimaced. "Maybe I shouldn't have given that up. You knowing about it could affect the outcome."

"It's going to happen. Tell them not to waste their money."

"Really, I'm serious. What's wrong? You've been hanging your head and complaining about work for two years now. If it's not your back, it's the tourists, or the poachers, or a kid shooting up the sofa on his mama's porch. You always joked and shrugged it off. But now, I don't know. Smiles are rare from you lately."

He gave her a lop-sided grin as he tried to shake off his funk. "Ah, honey, just thinking about that sexy boat ride to Dry Tortugas puts a huge smile on my face. By the way," he pointed up at the clock, "you're going to have to change that number."

"What are you talking about?" Her eyes widened. "You gave yourself one year from your birthday. What happened? You get hurt? Fired?"

"No, nothing like that." He looked at her shocked expression. Aware she could see the pain in his eyes, he studied the bar coaster as he continued in a soft voice. "I made a death notification yesterday. I told two very nice people their honor roll son was dead. He was found in his car parked near the beach. He had a needle in his arm. From the official time of death, he was watching the sunset as he died." He let out a ragged breath. "He was seventeen." He paused. "I left another family broken and sobbing—walked out of their home feeling like the god-damned angel of death."

"Oh my God, I'm so sorry. Your job, sometimes it's terrible."

"Lately, it's always bad and it never ends. I'm done, Donna. Twenty-five years and I only see the world getting darker." He sniffed and shook his head, defeat draped over him like a shroud. "I woke up today with a bad feeling in my gut. Something's coming, and it's not going to be good." Pete drained his glass and pushed it towards her.

"Maybe it was bad clams." She stood up tall, hands on the bar that separated them. "You are the best detective on the force. Everybody knows it. I...we all love you." She hesitated before she dropped a second beer in front of him. She reached over and squeezed his clenched fist. "You're just going through a rough patch."

"Yeah, well, sometimes those premonitions? They mean something. Just do it. The number, as of today, is officially thirty." His hands shook as he rubbed his forehead. He looked at Donna's stunned expression.

"For real? I never thought you were serious about this."

"When I went into the office this morning, I stopped in Human Resources, did what I should have done a year ago. I put in my papers."

As if on cue, Pete's cell phone let out a blood-curdling scream.

Donna jumped. "Will you change that ring tone, for god's sakes? It's a nightmare."

He reached for his phone, glad for the distraction. "No can do, sweetie. That's Charlie's ring." He rolled his eyes. "It always means bad news."

"Does Charlie know that's how you think of him? Does he know you're breaking up with him? And what does my ring sound like?"

Pete took in the strained smile on her face. "He knows. He gets it, and your ring. Nothing but sexy talk when your calls come in, babe."

"You are such a bullshitter, Pete."

⊰⊱

As Pete walked away from the bar, Donna could hear the familiar tone he used when he answered Charlie's call.

Charlie Hernandez was Pete's best friend. Partners for fifteen years, they were both promoted to the Collier County Sheriff's Department Detective Division on the same day and were assigned to a small case that blossomed into a huge one. They closed it out with cameras rolling and "Atta-boys" all around. They'd been together ever since.

"Hey, man, what's up?"

Donna watched as the smile on Pete's face turned down, and deep lines creased his brow. She could see he was upset. He was pacing like a caged panther. Tense and edgy, he was a magnificent sight to behold. His tousled dark brown hair was flecked with grey. His sexy stubble that felt so good against her skin, was always the right degree of rough. His eyes were the color of the ocean on a cloudy day. Those eyes could see through the lie she was satisfied with the small part of him he gave her. All that hotness was draped on a trim six-foot frame. She shook her head and blushed at the thought of his other qualities.

"You're shitting me, really?" he spoke softly into the phone. "Yeah, I got it, about forty-five minutes. A herpetologist? It's those goddamn python hunters, right? I'm calm, okay? You get ID on the deceased?" A long pause and a troubled expression crossed Pete's face. "I got it. Sure, I'm breathing. … I'm good. Donna will give me some Joe to go." Another long pause. He turned and walked towards her. "Yeah, no problem, I'll meet you at the dock."

Pete hung up and shook his head.

"What did I tell you, Donna? Bad news."

Donna didn't ask the obvious; Pete was a professional. She would hear about this on the news before he would confide in her or anyone for that matter. He's not about to start sharing with me now. It's one of the things I like best about him…strong, silent, and great in bed.

"Just be safe, Pete, I'll be closing up late if you want to swing by for some pillow talk." She knew Pete's form of therapy always ended up with her clothes on the floor. She wanted more, but he had trouble letting her in. She wondered if things would be different when he retired.

"Love your offer, babe, but it sounds like this case could be a bitch, probably going to tie me up for a while. I'll stop by if I get a break."

Donna sighed. Their hot nights were becoming less frequent. Maybe she should think about moving on. She always liked Tortola, and she had a friend opening a beach bar down there. She gazed over at an envelope leaning against the register. Pete was right. Changes were coming. She watched as his Jeep pulled out of the sandy lot and thought about sailing south to Cane Garden Bay.

CHAPTER 3

Everglades - Crime Scene

Pete heard the roar of Charlie's airboat as he pulled into the lot of the Big Cypress National Preserve Visitors Center located in Ochopee on Route 41. A school bus was idling out front, and Ranger Sue Meyers was waiting for a load of eight-year-olds to board the bus and return the center to its state of obscurity. Passing the phalanx of tykes, he overheard the ranger ask how they enjoyed the Everglades. A little girl in a watermelon print sundress rocketed her hand skyward. "My daddy says rednecks and dopers hang out in the glades and they should all be eaten by the gators."

The ranger, without missing a beat, retorted, "Gators prefer watermelon. Have a great day, kids! Come on back anytime." She smiled at the wise-ass child climbing into the bus, "Don't forget to bring your parents."

"Hey, Sue, you can really hold your own with those kids."

"Thanks, Pete. I hate the little shits."

Walking around to the back of the center, Pete spotted Charlie Hernandez coiling the lines by the floating dock set aside for the Park Service boats. His airboat, the *Miranda,* named after his deceased wife, looked old, but that was deceiving. Miranda was fully tricked out and Charlie spent all his spare time working on her. She was equipped with high-powered searchlights, GPS, depth gauges, and state of the art headsets. Beneath her seats he had compartments custom built for an assortment of weaponry. Charlie also kept a fishing pole handy, just in case.

Handing the headset to Pete, he signaled for him to get in. Within seconds they were speeding off into a narrow channel. Branches whipped Pete's bare arms as the intense airstream caused his face to quiver.

"Hey, buddy," Charlie's voice came through loud and clear. The headset filtered all sounds but Charlie's gruff words.

"Hey, Captain, where we are heading?" Pete spoke, turning his head away from the brunt of the wind.

"Due south, about twenty minutes."

"What are we looking at?"

Charlie shrugged. "I got a call from Bees Smithens. He was out of control, couldn't understand him. You know how calm that guy is, right? A bomb goes off next to him and he doesn't flinch. Well, I'm telling you he was screaming into the phone."

"He and his kids have been working out here for years looking for signs of extraterrestrial life or some shit." Pete laughed. "Maybe he found something."

Charlie continued. "He was looking for one of his pole boats. He was going out to do research this morning, and the boat was gone. He thought maybe the older one took it to do some night hunting, but the kid was home in bed dead drunk. Bees took his other boat out looking for some signs of life or the boat thief and came across a nasty scene. He never got out of the boat. Got back to the dock, called me, and then the Rangers."

"You go out there yet?"

"No, the Feds are ahead of us, but not by more than ten minutes. They had just pulled away as I arrived at the dock."

"Who was in their boat?"

"The rangers, Rosa Martinez and Christopher Willows, Bees and some chick decked out in designer khakis complete with mosquito netting."

"Reporter?"

"No, I'm guessing the herpetologist. When I called it in, HQ said a consultant would be joining us at the scene."

"You going to tell me what we are heading into? The suspense is killing me."

"A car was located off 41 about a hundred yards up a dirt track near a small dock and boat ramp. Some birders found it. They spotted it yesterday. It was still there today. They thought it was weird and called it in. A unit was in Everglades City; they checked it out. The car had no VIN numbers and switched tags."

"Stolen."

"Yep, looks that way, a 2000 Dodge Caravan. They popped the car and found maps of the glades, also receipts from the Walgreens on San Marco Boulevard for bug spray and water bottles purchased yesterday—cash. Smithens boat went missing from that dock."

"Foul play?"

"It was foul alright. M.E.'s report will tell us more. We're here. You can see it for yourself." Charlie shut off the giant fan and expertly glided *Miranda* between Bees Smithens' missing pole boat and the immaculate Park Service airboat.

As they climbed out, the sight of Willows and Martinez doing a tandem vomit assaulted them. The retching sounded deep and painful.

"Hey, guys, what's going on?" Pete coughed. "Tough call?"

Rosa Martinez stood up, wiped the puke from her face with her sleeve. She gave Pete the finger and a wan smile. "No, it's all good: another day in paradise."

Charlie walked up beside Pete. "Man, Willows, that's gross. Looks like you got some on your pretty boat."

"Funny, Charlie, eat this." Christopher Willows tossed a scummy towel at Charlie's head. Willows nodded towards the cypress grove. "It's over there, hope you had a light lunch."

Pete and Charlie walked into the grove. On the ground ahead of them was a very large python. Hanging out of the reptile's mouth were a pair of legs and feet. The feet were decked out in new Sperry Topsiders.

"Wow, that sucks for him," Pete said out of the side of his mouth.

"At least he was dead before the python started eating." Charlie offered. "Pythons crush their prey before they ingest them. He was spared the horror of watching his head being swallowed."

Standing beside the python was what seemed to be a woman covered head to toe in netting, waders, and elbow-length thick rubber gloves. In her left hand was a long sharp knife. The python's head, though still clamped down on the victim's thighs, was sliced completely around.

She pulled her pith helmet off with her right hand and a tumble of thick brunette curls cascaded down her shoulders. Pete and Charlie were speechless.

"I'm Doctor Vanessa Treehorn, Herpetologist, Florida Fish and Wildlife."

"Detectives Landry and Hernandez, Collier County Sheriff's Department." Pete extended his hand and quickly pulled it back.

"Hmm." Looking back down at the python, she continued. "The snake, a Python Bivittatus, more commonly known as the Burmese Python, was in a feeding state. It was important to try and stop the digestion process to preserve what was left of the victim. I severed the snake's head while keeping the corpse intact within its jaws. Feeding makes them docile."

Charlie leaned in for a closer look. "I wouldn't put my fingers near its mouth." Doctor Treehorn pointed at the snake's jaw still pulsing on the victim. "It will take approximately an hour for the snake to expire."

The snake twitched, and Pete jumped back. Vanessa pointed at the huge bulge. "Absorption should continue until the chemicals that have already been introduced into the process have dissipated. Though to be honest, I'm not sure this is going to work... a python this size?" she smirked. "I wouldn't bet on it."

"Wow!" Pete and Charlie mouths agape, exhaled in unison.

Bees walked up still shaking. "That thing dead?"

"Almost, Wonder Woman sliced it a new smile." Pete made a slicing movement across his throat with his hand. "Hey, Bees, speaking of superpowers, how are those orchids you been growing on your back fence? Word is the white ones have magical powers." Pete smacked him on the back. "Relax, just lightening things up."

Bees shook his head. "I heard big pythons could swallow a full-grown deer; never knew they could gobble down a man."

Vanessa looked up. "It is rare, but it has happened before. The victim, if you look at his legs, well, he was not a large man. I would guess he was maybe five foot five or six inches. Look at how small his shoes are. This snake looks to be about twenty feet long."

Pete handed his cell phone to Bees. "I think we need a commemorative photo of this event."

Dr. Treehorn stood up and moved alongside Pete, giving him a sly smile and a wink as she pressed in close to him. Turning to face Bees for the shot, she held up her blood-soaked blade and grinned. Pete looked over at her beaming face and knew he was in trouble. Charlie, on the other side of her, leaned forward, and winked.

"You guys are sick fucks, you know that?" Bees said.

Pete laughed. "Yeah, tell me you don't want a copy of this."

"Send it to my email. The wife's been checking my phone lately."

Bees took the photo moments before the two pale park rangers showed up.

"M.E. is on his way, Doctor." Chris Willows announced in a raspy voice. Looking down at the python now in two pieces, he gasped. "You cut its head off?" Gagging, he pushed past the pasty face of Rosa Martinez standing behind him.

"What the fuck scared him off? Oh shit!" Martinez held her ground and stared up into the trees.

"They are going to be no help," Charlie growled.

"Give them something to concentrate on. Have them secure the scene and set markers out on the evidence. There are spent casings, and who knows what else." Pete eyed Doctor Treehorn as she wiped blood off her blade and slid it back into the sheath on her thigh. "I need to speak to the doctor about transporting the victim."

Charlie stepped in front of him. "She's not your type, Pete, way too smart for you."

"Will you look where we are, Charlie? This is a crime scene, not a bar. Just let me do my job here. Anyway, I got plenty of time to get to know the doctor." The sound of airboats heading towards them sent a flock of herons aloft. "And a shit storm is fast approaching, my friend."

CHAPTER 4

Eight Months Earlier- Havana, Cuba

Raul Garcia Jr. powered up the MacBook Pro. His orders for the day were to clean up his father's inbox and spam folders. Raul shook his head in disgust. The pornography the old guy was watching had caused the computer to be swamped with spam. An unbidden image arose in his mind. He pictured his ninety-two-year-old father, grabbing his chest with a massive heart attack while deep in the middle of a marathon porn session.

Raul felt lost. He was thirty-two years old, the product of the marriage between his mother, who was a nineteen-year gold-digging whore and his father, a fifty-four-year-old widower. Don Garcia was a lonely man who believed the moans from the collagen-plumped lips of a bottle blond from the barrio. Raul knew he should be glad they met. He sighed. Having a young wife and child only increased his father's swagger, and his addiction to sex and power grew.

Raul deleted more porn and cringed. My father still thinks of himself as the macho stud from sixty years ago. Raul hit delete as a pair of enormous boobs appeared on the screen. This is all he cares about. My mother is now a fifty-two-year-old shopaholic; all she cares about is spending money. Boxes arrived daily and were piled in the front foyer. Her lavish shopping habit had intensified now that his father's corrupt patronage to the Castro regime gave them the luxury of the internet.

Raul looked at the time on the computer screen—four p.m. He wanted to be done and out of the house by five. Tonight, he would grab a bite at the food cart down the street. He no longer dined with his parents.

Raul wanted no part of his father's obscene dinner show. Each evening, before dinner was served, his father demanded his mother pour her round ass and fake boobs into a spandex dress. Her feet, knobbed with bunions, were crammed into stiletto heels. This ritual had been going on for as long as he could remember. She would hobble around the house avoiding the old man's groping hands. When he was a child, his mother would sit with him in his walk-in closet. That was always their special time together. She kept a flashlight and picture book in a shoebox tucked behind his stuffed animals. He would strain to hear her whispered words as she to read to him. She told him it was important to stay hidden and quiet in case the house was attacked by banditos. Not banditos, he thought. We were hiding from Papa.

He was twelve on the night they were discovered. His father dragged his mother out of the closet. She was screaming, "No, please, don't let him see." The thick mahogany wardrobe door slammed. He fell asleep to the sound of his father grunting like a pig and his mother's sobs.

He kept deleting and remembering. He was a teenager sitting in this very room when his father would brag of the nights he would accompany Raul's "slut of a mother" to the dance clubs in Vedado. Sitting in his over-stuffed leather chair, he would sip his single malt scotch and Raul would watch his weathered face come alive as he spoke of tequila and his Cecilia dancing. She would grind her body against the young men that earned their living seducing the rich women at the bar. His father would cackle with glee as he spoke "The young men wore tight pants, their bulges, I think not so real, straining against the cheap fabric. When they dance with my Cecilia, my cock is like Lazarus. One pill and he rise from the dead." His father's trusted bodyguard, Miguel, would whisper to Cecilia that Don Garcia was ready and would meet her in the car. Sometimes, if the young man seemed exceptionally endowed, he would be invited back to Casa Garcia. Raul gagged at the memories of the moans coming from the salon below his perch on the balcony.

Don Garcia had been an ambitious young man and built a fortune through legitimate agricultural endeavors and a more lucrative drug smuggling operation. He began his journey with a handcart laden with coconuts. He would sell them to tourists coming off the yachts weekending from Miami. He befriended the deck hands and soon realized sending them back to the States with more than coconuts might provide him and his young wife, Nadia, a better life.

The business grew and thrived, expanding to legitimate coconut groves and even more lucrative smuggling operations. Don Garcia passed the day-to-day operations of the family's true business to his older sons, Raul's half-brothers, Nelson, and Tito. They were in their sixties and hated Don Garcia as much as young Raul. They blamed their father for their mother, Nadia's, death. Lung cancer had taken her in nineteen eighty-two. Their father had smoked unfiltered cigarettes and custom rolled cigars every waking minute of his day, even in their bedroom. Nadia was stricken with lung cancer; Don Garcia was healthy as a horse.

When Cecelia arrived and Raul was born, his brothers could not tolerate the sight of her and verbally abused young Raul every chance they got.

All major business decisions and new ventures needed Don Garcia's approval. Even at his advanced age, he was still a formidable presence. The business maintained its 1950's posture. Most payments were made in cash, contracts always verbal with a handshake. His brothers were distrustful of the internet. It had recently arrived on the island and only elite "friends of the regime" had access. They put young Raul in charge of the web presence of the legitimate side of Garcia Enterprises.

The coconut groves in the eastern provinces provided the family a modest but steady income. More important was the unique cover it furnished for the transport and funding for the darker, more lucrative side of Garcia Enterprises. Coconuts had a myriad of uses, and Don Garcia availed the business of all of them.

On his eighteenth birthday, young Raul was given the official position as Vice President of Grove Operations. He was charged with keeping the groves healthy and profitable. He was forward-thinking with his introduction of drone technology.

Large, agricultural drones now sprayed the groves. This advancement was appreciated by the laborers who had developed physical ailments from hand-spraying toxic chemicals from trucks. When not spraying, the drones would ferry in fresh meals and water to the workers. Raul had developed a bond with the crews for his efforts at keeping them safe and healthy. By showing he cared about their plight, he knew he would have their loyalty when he called upon them in the future.

Raul was happy left alone to run things. No one watched his activities. If he kept the company secure and visible, the millions from the darker side of the business would continue unencumbered by scrutiny. He was not invited to be part of that venture. His brothers convinced Papa that he was still too young and needed to prove himself in the groves before he could be trusted with the family's true mission.

Nelson and Tito seemed oblivious to the possibilities the American awakening could have on their business. They kept their wives and mistresses happy with lavish gifts. They hoarded piles of cash and drank expensive martinis at the rooftop bars of the best hotels. They were at the top of the Cuban food chain. The Garcia Family was well-known and feared. They had greased every government palm in Castro's regime. But the old guard was fading fast.

Raul saw global expansion as the route the business needed to take. Americans were flooding the streets with products. Investors were handing out business cards in every lounge and beachside bar. His brothers hated the Americans. Raul knew those loathsome salesmen were the new reality. He would have to be choosy. He had already decided to make a move behind the backs of his brothers. When his deal hit gold, he would show them he was one of them— no— that he would be the new Don Garcia. The old ways were dead. He needed to be patient, find the right opportunity, and set the future of Garcia Empires on a rocket ship headed to the heart of America.

The tedious chore of unsubscribing and blocking porn websites had Raul's eyes glazing over. He shook himself awake and got up to make a triple espresso from the elegant machine on the sideboard in Don Garcia's office.

Sitting once again in front of the Mac, he leaned back and sipped. The rich velvety texture and strong aroma were direct evidence of the joys of wealth. Drip coffee out of Styrofoam cups would never be in his future.

The websites and subject lines made him laugh—*Maximum Boob, 52 Hook-up, Get Horney*. It seemed the internet picked up on his father's love of noir crime fiction. The next email stopped his deletion frenzy. "A lucrative business opportunity awaits you, Don Garcia; America is open for business."

"*Ay, Dios Mio!*" Raul clicked on the link and was directed to a business in Howard Beach, New York: Ferraro Salvage and Carting.

Don Garcia,

I believe our thoughts are like-minded. We are much more than a carting and salvage business. Please contact me at your earliest convenience.

Leonard Horowitz, Esq.
Solicitor, Ferraro Salvage Corp.
Raul the younger began typing. *Papa will never know.*

CHAPTER 5

June - Howard Beach, NY

Leonard Horowitz, Attorney at Law, tapped in a code on the small box at the end of Salvatore Ferraro's driveway. The oversized wrought iron gates, instead of sweeping inwards, slid behind the faux stonewall. This dramatic entrance would have been perfect guarding the winding drives of rural estates in the English countryside. Here in Howard Beach, a predominately Italian community in Queens County, New York, these metal gates symbolized his boss's position at the top of the mob-connected hierarchy. The gates fronted a twenty-five-foot triple wide driveway at the end of the cul-de-sac where Sal Ferraro and his second wife, Alexis, lived. These gates also punctuated the fact Sal Ferraro liked a grand entrance.

The Ferraro manse towered above the neighboring homes. Big Sal and Lexie had their home raised up twice the necessary height after superstorm Sandy destroyed their expanded ranch home and submerged the matching red Ferraris, which resided in the custom temperature-controlled garage. The new garage, with room for six luxury vehicles, was now located below the living area, six feet above the roadbed. Sal Ferraro loved his cars. This abundance of weather-related caution insured no one in the neighborhood had a view of Jamaica Bay, located directly behind the glassed-in, three-story lanai covering the second-story infinity pool adjacent to the Ferraro's bedroom.

The entrance to the house was impressively gaudy. Two life-size sandstone lions reclined beside Corinthian columns supporting a massive portico. Beneath the portico were formidable marble steps leading to imported, oversized, cherry-wood front doors adorned with bas-relief cupids. As creepy as the lions and cupids were, pressing the doorbell was far worse for Leonard Horowitz. Instead of chimes or a normal ring, the haunting melody from *The Godfather* played through Bose speakers secreted in the copper-coffered ceiling of the portico.

The door opened to a smiling Sal wiping his hands on a dishtowel tucked into the front of his worn, black sweatpants. "Lenny, come on in. Lexie is trying out her pasta maker. Fresh ravioli! Can you believe it? Been married four years, never seen her cook. Out of nowhere, she's getting domestic, must be angling for a kid. I'm too fucking old for that. Told her when we got married, she could have anything she wants, but no kids. Did you write that in the pre-nup?"

"Uh, no." Lenny stuttered. "That was never part of the contract."

"Must have been a discussion between me and Lexie. You know, when we were between the sheets. That count?"

"Not unless you got it in writing or recorded it."

"Man, we got some great video; with her ass and tits, we could be famous. Not a lot of conversation going on though." Sal looked over his shoulder at the kitchen. He signaled for Lenny to move in closer. "I had the big V. It was right before I met Lexie. I made sure my soldiers are out of harm's way," Sal winked. "No one's going AWOL—you know what I mean. That's just between you and me. I got to say she is hot-to-trot all the time. She's wearing me out. You can't die from fucking too much can you?"

"No, I don't think so, unless your ticker gives out."

"What a way to go." Sal slapped Lenny on the back.

Lenny followed Sal into the large circular foyer. He'd been in this house a hundred times and it still took his breath away. Everything was white, the marble floor and split staircase, the balustrades. The large round center table was custom bleached white mahogany. The flowers in the white vase on the table were white orchids.

Sal walked ahead of him; the sweat suit he wore stretched tight over his bull-like torso. The monk's patch atop his head was becoming more pronounced. His thighs made swishing sounds as they rubbed together.

Lenny cringed at the dichotomy of Sal living in all this virginal whiteness. Past the foyer, the great room had floor-to-ceiling windows facing the bay. The white theme continued into the open kitchen. Sunblock and sunglasses would be a great idea for anyone spending time in here.

"Hey, Babe," Sal called out to Lexie. "Look who showed up on a Sunday!"

Lexie turned from the counter. Her bright smile blinded Lenny and outshone the gleaming rays of afternoon sun. She was wearing an artfully ripped tee shirt, her cleavage revealed in a particularly opportune tear. Yoga pants, a fashion faux pas on most women, hugged her smooth curves, leaving nothing hidden. She was barefoot; her toes seemed completely edible in hell-fire red polish. Her blonde hair was swept up into a loose ponytail that hung down her back. She was of medium height, yet here amid the opulence of steel restaurant-sized appliances and double height cabinets, Lexie, holding a whisk and a small white Pyrex bowl, seemed tiny and vulnerable.

Sal walked up behind her and enveloped her in his arms. He was a big man, well over six feet, more than three hundred pounds. She disappeared in his embrace. His gold chains blended with her gleaming hair. Lenny watched this display and offered a smile. "Well, look at you two all lovey and doing the Sunday dinner thing. Domesticity looks good on you, Lexie."

"Hey, I'm way more than a pretty face. Stay for dinner. I'm making ravioli and Sal is going to grill some fish, he says in case the pasta doesn't work out. He should have some faith in me. I got this." Lexie's laughed tinkled like crystal pendants in the wind. She walked over to the sink, giving Lenny a great view of her perfect ass.

"So how do you stay in shape, eating pasta and all?" Lenny said as he gulped for air.

"Spin class."

"That's one lucky bike, right?" Sal laughed and smacked Lexie's butt. "Lenny, come into the den. I got something for you."

The television was tuned to a Mets game. Sal reached for the remote. "Those fucking Mets—break my heart every year."

Lenny sank into a white, winged armchair. The soft leather cushions molded to his body. He marveled that he was sitting on a cloud.

"Wow, this is something else." Lenny caressed the chair's curved arms.

"That's Lexie's favorite chair. It was just delivered. I had it custom made from down and memory foam. Cost me a fortune. She sits there every night drinking green tea and reading books." He sat down on the couch across from Lenny. "Don't get that girl. Man, just looking at her drives me wild. I'd do anything to keep her happy, and I'd fucking kill anybody who tried to mess with her. That reminds me."

Sal's abrupt change startled Lenny. "What?"

"I got something for you. Lexie picked it out; it was her idea. She says I never show appreciation for people who do shit for me. She's trying to make me a better man, more aware of people's feelings. So, I got this for you."

Sal dropped a box on the coffee table.

"This wasn't necessary, Sal."

"I know. That's what I told her. She insisted."

Lenny opened the small rectangular box. Nestled inside was a solid gold Mont Blanc pen. He carefully picked it up and read the inscription: "To L.H. thanks S.F."

"I came up with the inscription. Lexie wanted a fucking speech on it. It's a pen, you got to get to the point." Sal laughed at his joke.

Lenny smiled as he softly stroked the gift.

Sal poured two tumblers of Johnny Walker Blue and handed one to Lenny. "So, what's so important you show up on a Sunday?"

"We need to talk about diversifying and possibly relocating your real estate ventures."

"Why? What's the problem?" Sal leaned forward. "Diversifying? Re-locating? We got a nice set-up going here. Why do we got to mess with it?"

"I foresee major transportation problems, as well as competition from local startup companies in California, Washington, and Colorado."

"They're our biggest markets. Always been reliable."

"Our product has been legalized."

"Fucking hippies." Sal downed his scotch and walked over to the bar. "How's a hard-working guy like me supposed to survive in that environment? So, what other bad news you got? What's the deal with transporting?"

"If the border gets tightened up, and it looks like that's going to happen, we won't be able to move our product."

"Shit! We are getting screwed from both sides. What the fuck we going to do? You're the brains guy. You must have a plan."

"In fact, I do. It's going to involve a temporary move to Southwest Florida, just until we get things up and running. I think it would be important for you and Lexie to be present in the area while we negotiate with some partners I lined up."

"I just got this place fixed up from the fucking storm, now we got to move. Where in Florida?"

"Marco Island, south of Naples."

"What's the time frame?"

"That's the best part. You would be spending the winter in Southwest Florida. Palm trees and beaches."

Sal sat back on the couch and took a sip of scotch. "I heard Naples was the Ferrari capital of North America." He slapped his knee, startling Lenny. "Lexie is going to fucking love this. She is going to buy a shitload of thong bikinis to show off her tight body and forget about the baby thing. This is perfect. So, the new partners, Naples guys?"

"No, they are from outside the states."

"South America?"

"No, closer."

"Puerto Rico? Dominican Republic?"

"No, Sal, I want you to keep an open mind here. They're Cuban. You know, the ban on travel has been lifted, so a whole new market has opened. It's lucky for us, right? Good timing."

"Ah, Lenny, Lenny, life used to be so simple back when you knew who your enemies were. Nothing mattered back then, a little payola and you were on your way. Everybody was looking for a little scratch. How the hell are we supposed to deal with the Cubans? Who do we know who even speaks Spanish?"

"Sal, I speak Spanish. Who do you think has been taking care of the southwest end of things?"

"What you got for me?"

"There's this guy, Raul Garcia, a businessman with experience in transporting difficult cargo. I reached out to him with a business idea, and he has responded with a welcoming hand. He is very interested in the emerging Cuban export market. I've been working out a scenario that would mitigate the cash flow problems we have recently encountered and address our new friend's desire to infiltrate the U.S. market. We have been in contact about transportation. He has a guy in Miami who specializes in untraceable cars."

"I got a whole salvage yard full of cars nobody wants. How much is that going to cost?"

"Yes, but they are in New York." Lenny sighed. He also has a way to move product to the east coast."

"So, why does he need us?"

"He wants an American connection. The operation is going to be small at first. Cuba is not a big supplier. Garcia sends the cargo over, and our crew retrieves it from the Everglades. The product gets stashed in a hangar near the drop point. Garcia's guy switches cars inside the hangar, drops off the cash and heads east with the new shipment."

"Do our guys have to be worried about the cartels?" Sal poured himself another scotch, ignoring Lenny's empty glass.

"We will be competing with the Columbians. They are in a different league. They use big ships and huge amounts of cocaine. But like I said, we are kind of dipping our toes in. Nobody is going to suspect Ferraro Salvage. And the Cuban, Garcia, is a big deal down there."

"Lexie can't find out about this. She doesn't ask many questions, but I'm sure hard drugs would be a real problem for her."

"Sal, she'll never find out. She never questioned anything that happened at the yard, right?"

"Shut the fuck up about that, Lenny. Wait, did you say they were going to stash and switch in a hangar? What hangar?"

"Sal, let me explain the plan. This joint venture would require that locational adjustment I mentioned for you and Lexie and a small crew to bull through the swamp." Lenny opened his briefcase, removed a sheaf of legal looking documents, and set them on the white marble coffee table. I found an airstrip near Marco Island. Doesn't see much traffic: private jets, couple of prop planes, and a corporate helicopter. The owner has incentive to sell one of his hangars. He's in some bad legal shit. I helped him out. And here's the beauty part. He's willing to let go of his jet, not new, but well-taken care of. The whole package is a steal. He wants to sell fast. It won't look suspicious since you already own a couple of hangars in Jersey and the Hamptons, a good investment on all sides. I got some paperwork for you to sign to get the ball rolling."

Lenny slid the pile of legal-looking documents in front of Sal and handed him the gold Mont Blanc pen. "I found a penthouse for you in a luxury building on Marco Island, gulf front. It's completely renovated. It's quiet, residential, and mostly old people live there. I got a place there, too, overlooking the pool. You and Lexie are going to love spending the winter in Florida. Once we get this paperwork in order you can start planning your trip."

"No more commercial flights? This is amazing! Good thing I trust you, Lenny."

CHAPTER 6

September- Howard Beach, NY

Dominic, Louis, and David Andruzzi sat on petite-filigreed metal chairs outside the Sicilian Sons Men's Social Club on Cross Bay Boulevard in Howard Beach, New York. Early morning traffic was light south of the Belt Parkway. The summer, not ready to give up, offered a breeze off the bay that freshened the air with a salty tang. The oversized Dominic and Louis squirmed uncomfortably in package-creased double X dress shirts picked up the day before from the Kings County Mall. Wedged between his large brothers, the diminutive David appeared relaxed in in a Lacoste polo shirt and stonewashed jeans. Dominic and Louis held freshly brewed espressos in delicate cups between their massive sausage fingers. David drank a glass of Perrier with a splash of prosecco. Fresh bread and biscotti were hand-delivered to their table by the bakery down the block. The scent wafting from the silver basket was redolent of anisette and warm yeast. The three of them looked uncomfortable as they tried hard to fit in.

Dominic squirmed trying to find a comfortable position. "This chair barely fits one of my ass-cheeks."

"You guys shouldn't move around so much." David snickered. "I think you exceed the maximum load capacity."

"Fuck you, David." Dominic muttered, "How about we sit on you instead?"

"Stop your bickering. Look how far we've come from our usual booth in the diner." Louis smiled, pleased to be the peacemaker.

"We didn't come so far. It's right down the road." Dominic shook his head.

"You guys are idiots. Let's all just enjoy this moment." David picked up his prosecco "Let's toast to our good fortune, Cin Cin!"

Things were looking up for the brothers. Their minor roles within Sal Ferraro's carting and sanitation operation seemed to have been noticed by the big man himself. They had performed every task without question. Lenny Horowitz, Sal's right-hand man, asked the three underlings to meet Big Sal here this morning. They were to sit at his table and enjoy a simple breakfast on him.

Louis, double dipping his biscotti, grimaced as it fell apart dripping onto his lap and the freshly washed cement sidewalk.

"Lou, you're making a fucking mess."

"Shut up, Dom."

David shook his head in disgust. "Clean yourself up! We need to make a good impression."

"This feels weird, right? I mean we never been asked to come here before," Dom whispered looking over his shoulder to see if anyone was in earshot.

"Yeah, hope we walk away from this meeting in one piece. Remember what happened to Ricky?" Louis smirked. "They still haven't found all of him."

"Shut up, Lou. We've been good soldiers. I got a feeling this could work out sweet for us," Dominic retorted. "We took care of that Cacciatore job really good."

Louis shook his head from side to side and tilted it towards David, who was busy on his phone.

David looked up at his brothers. "What are you talking about?"

"Nothing, some fishing boat thing, a dinner cruise, chicken cacciatore on the menu." Louis knows a captain who rents his boat out, right, Lou? You remember, his brother is a great chef. His cacciatore is famous. Big Sal was appreciative. That might be why they thought of us for this job."

"Look! That's him! Dominic don't say anything stupid to mess this up," David whispered out of the side of his mouth.

The three of them, smiling broadly, looked at the street in front of them.

A low-slung, dark grey Mercedes sedan trolled slowly past the Andruzzi brothers seated at the small, wrought iron bistro table. The car continued down the boulevard and turned at the next corner. A few moments later, a black Suburban decked out with wide rims and low-profile tires glided up to the curb in front of the club. The blacked-out windows were impenetrable to prying eyes.

Dominic, Louis, and David straightened their backs even further and donned serious expressions for their audience with Big Sal. The car's back door swung open, and the boss emerged.

A woman's voice called out from the SUV. "Sal! Maria and I are going to head to Nordstrom's in the city. There is a huge sale on designer shoes. Do you need the car? Can the boys around the corner take you home?"

"Lexie, please! Why not tell the world my whereabouts? Yeah, take the car."

Sal slammed the door, shifted his bulk, and walked towards the three men sitting around his personal table. Their dour expressions confirmed they were in awe of meeting him.

The brothers jumped up in unison, causing two out of three wrought iron chairs to flip over. A startled rat in a nearby trash bin jumped out and ran between Big Sal's hand-stitched, dove grey Bruno Magli tasseled loafers. Sal automatically made the sign of the cross.

A waiter appeared with a padded oversized chair and the brothers shifted so Big Sal could join them around the table. A moment later a triple shot of espresso in a gold-rimmed cup and a china plate bearing a gigantic cannoli oozing fresh cream was ceremoniously placed in front of Big Sal. .The four of them shoulder-to-shoulder obscured the table.

Sal slowly raised the cup to his lips appraising the men around him. Lenny had chosen the right guys. They were primed and ready: the perfect tools. He was looking at three loaded pistols with their safeties off.

"Did Lenny tell you anything about why you're here?" Sal placed the cup on the saucer and reached for the cannoli.

"No, sir. Mr. Horowitz called and said to be here at 10 a.m. this morning and to wait for you." Louis fidgeted.

"So, boys, I got a big problem." Sal placed the unbitten cannoli back on the plate, signaling the importance of this conversation.

There was silence from the Andruzzi's.

"You know, I don't give shit about politics one way or the other."

Still nothing.

"This guy, running again, is spouting some crazy ideas. You know, he's hometown and all. He grew up in Bayside. I dated a girl from there. Real snob. Great tits. Her parents never knew their precious Ashley was banging a hood from the beach."

The expressions around him alternated between half smiles and tight-lipped fear.

"Ah, calm down! I'm just messing with you."

Polite laughter. "Yeah, we got that, Boss." Dominic seemed to shrink.

"I'm talking about what happens if the border shuts down tighter than Ashley's twat."

Louis piped in, "That ain't going to happen."

Sal stared at him. "The street is talking, and I been listening. And I'm thinking this is going to be a big problem for me and that means for everybody who works for me including you mooks."

Confused expressions all around when David echoed, "Yeah, that's a big fucking problem."

Dominic and Louis stared at their brother.

Sal leaned in, so the Andruzzi's did, too. Four heads hovered over the tiny bistro table. "I'm going to let you guys in on a little secret. I've been bringing in real estate over the border for years."

Dominic looked confused, "Real estate?"

"Yeah, you know, grass?"

"You mean sod, like out on Long Island." Louis smiled, appearing to make a connection.

Sal looked at the three assholes in front of him. He was now questioning Leonard Horowitz's competency as his consigliere.

Sal took a deep breath; he didn't want to spook them. "No, not sod. Pot, marijuana."

"Oh." The Andruzzi's simultaneously formed fish-like expressions.

"My empire crosses into many areas. Carting and sanitation are my official businesses. The information I'm about to lay on you doesn't leave this table. I need to trust you guys. *Capisce*?"

The three of them leaned even closer to Big Sal.

"You have been chosen, from among all of the Ferraro Carting and Salvage family, to take part in a new business venture." Six bulging eyeballs and three gaping pie holes floated inches in front of Sal's face. He added the kicker, "In Florida."

The brothers, who had never been farther than the Jersey Shore, sat back stunned. One of them farted.

"I just got one more question. You guys all good with the law? You been keeping your noses clean?"

Dominic took the lead "No, sir...I mean yes, sir, our noses, definitely clean. We knew our big moment would come. Stayed completely off the radar, so to speak."

"That's great, just what I needed to hear. Can I trust you guys to be discreet and do your best to ensure the success of this new enterprise?"

"Fuck yeah, Boss," Louis blurted.

Dominic smacked Louis on the side of the head, "Yes sir, Mr. Ferraro, you can count on us. The Andruzzi brothers are here to serve."

"Mr. Horowitz will be contacting you shortly with further instructions. I suggest you do some shopping and buy some clothes for your trip. It's hot as hell down there." Sal laughed, "You're going to be snowbirds, just like the old ladies from the Five Towns." Sal dropped a wrapped pack of hundreds on the table, moved his chair back, got up, and walked to the curb. The Mercedes slid up alongside him and the back door opened. In seconds, Sal was gone.

"Whoa," the brothers exhaled in unison.

"We made it," said Louis, looking around the table at his brothers.

Dominic feeling an itch on the tops of his sockless feet, reached down to brush away the annoyance. A parade of ants marched over his bare skin and swarmed the biscotti puddled on the ground.

"I hate bugs."

David leaned back and smiled, "Get used to it, brother. Florida's full of them."

CHAPTER 7

October - Ozone Park, NY

The Andruzzi brothers couldn't believe their good fortune. Lenny Horowitz filled in all the details in a phone call after their meeting with Big Sal.

David would be heading down first. A trial run was scheduled for late January. The brothers were tasked with staying low-key and out of trouble until then. They had made it to the big time. They were trusted soldiers given a serious job to do.

As the move came closer, David's jumpy behavior was noticeable to his brothers.

"What's your problem, David? You been weird since breakfast with Big Sal." Louis opened three cans of Budweiser, handing David his beer, "You good with this deal?"

"Yeah, yeah, I'm all in. It's just... remember when Sal asked about being arrested?"

"What the fuck did you do?" Dominic smacked his beer can on the table.

"I didn't do anything. When I was up Boston College, you guys knew I was a business major, right?"

"Yeah, go on." Louis said as he opened a bag of Doritos.

"So, I got an idea to, you know, run a game on Friday nights. There were a lot of rich kids with dough in their pockets. It was going good."

Dominic sneered, "Get to the point."

"Well, they kicked me out."

"Oh fuck, David." Louis shook his head. "Wait, you told us you were homesick."

Dominic pushed his beer away. "We thought you were the smart one. Did you get arrested?"

"No, no, nothing like that. But it's on my school records, and if anybody checks…"

Louis shoved a handful of chips in his mouth and pointed one at David. "Okay, what's done is done, and you need to watch your ass, so this won't be a problem. Hey, on a positive note, you don't need a degree to get rich. You're headed for bigger things."

Dominic raised his can, "To babes, booze, and big bucks. Salute!"

The first order of business was clothing that would help them blend in. Dominic went online and did a search for popular Florida stores. Tommy Bahamas was the top hit, so he went with that. Salmon-colored shorts, cotton shirts decorated with tiny palm trees, khaki slacks, a stack of golf shirts in bright pastel colors, straw fedoras, boat shoes, flip flops, and board short bathing suits all went in his cart. He ordered three sets of everything, two sets in XXXL and one set in small.

Louis, looking over Dom's shoulder as he completed the purchases, smacked him on the back. "We're going to fit right in. Nobody's gonna know we're from New York."

"Yeah, assimilate with the locals," David shook his head and snorted, "like that's going to happen."

Lenny sent an email explaining he had found them suitable accommodations. David would be in a motel on Tamiami Trail, a transient place catering to business types and short stays. Dominic and Louis would be staying in Chokoloskee, a small town off Highway 41, an east/west route between Tampa and Miami. He attached the website for the rental complex. It was very close to the Everglades. The online brochure mentioned the Everglades is a national park and a famous tourist destination. The trailer was in a community that boasted water views, a fire pit, boat slips, and kayak rentals.

"Wow, this place is waterfront!" Dominic hooted.

"Lenny mentioned the job might require some wet work." Louis enlarged the photo on the screen.

"You guys are fucking idiots." David headed towards the kitchen. "Wet work doesn't mean boats."

"Ignore him, Louis. He's just jealous cause we're staying in a resort and he's staying in a flunky motel."

The black and white pictures on the website were grainy and appeared to have classic cars beside each of the aluminum-sided trailers. They would be staying in a two bedroom with a pullout couch. A Google Earth search showed its location on a dead-end south of town. The long, rural road appeared to be unpaved. The trailer was set up just feet from a water access that fed into a larger canal that ultimately led into the Gulf of Mexico.

"This place is perfect!" the brothers shouted in unison.

"We should send Lenny a thank you note for finding us a great place to stay," Dominic suggested. "Wait, I don't think we have his address."

"Why send a thank you note? It's a job." Louis grumbled.

"No note," David walked in drinking a Tab and rolled his eyes. "We send a reply to his email that we have the address and are getting ready for the trip. That's it."

"Like I always said, David, you're the smart one."

"Thanks, Louis."

CHAPTER 8

November - Howard Beach, NY

Lenny paced the hallway outside his bedroom. Sonja, his Russian flight attendant neighbor, was peacefully snoring in his bed.

On her return last night, Sonja had stopped by with some top-shelf vodka made in her brother's distillery. Lenny suspected it was a tub in a stone cellar somewhere in Eastern Europe. They toasted her job, her brother, and Lenny's impending move to Florida. That required another shot to celebrate Aeroflot's nonstop from Moscow to Miami, which led to a toast to her switching her JFK flight to Miami where she would take a brief sojourn to Marco Island to fuck Lenny and work on her tan.

"I'll be leaving the beginning of January. I'm staying at the Albatross Condominiums on Marco Island, Apartment 1003."

"Lenny, you know that Albatross bird is no good luck. You should find another place to stay. I am not comfortable staying in that place."

"You can't stay with me. I'll book you a suite at the M Spa down the beach. You need to know something; I've found someone." He paused. "She's, uh, unavailable right now. If it works out, I won't be fucking anyone but her." He watched her face closely.

Lenny knew that Sonja would never consider settling down with him. At thirty-eight years old, she was satisfied with her life, unencumbered by commitments, she flew around the world landing in comfortable beds with men willing to take whatever she gave them. She always had the upper hand. When he mentioned he was in love with someone else, there was no crying, no sobs of indignation, no bottles thrown at his head. He knew she would just move on.

"I am glad you have dream, my brave lion. If she does come to you, that is no problem. Douglas, who lives downstairs, will be happy to do me. So, no worry."

Lenny winced. Turning from Sonja, he removed his Three Dog Night t-shirt and grey sweatpants; he paused as he saw his reflection in the full-length mirrored closet doors. He had them installed so he could watch his romps with Sonja from a different angle. That always excited him, but when he looked at his body in full view, a schlubby middle-aged Jew with thinning mouse brown hair, a puffy gut, and un-muscled legs, he cringed with the thought he had sunk to being a human dildo. Any guy would give his left nut to spend one night with her. One thing was certain: she got off on him. He would have been thrown aside a year ago if that wasn't true. He should be grateful for all Sonja has taught him. When he finally gets Lexie in the sack, he's going to give her the ride of her life. He looked down as he felt a familiar urge. He would teach her all she needs to know; she'll be begging for more. Turning to the side and sucking in his paunch, he looked over his silhouette. Not perfect, he thought, but Lexie has sex with Sal and he's a fat slob. At least he wouldn't crush her on the rare occasions when they went missionary. His eyes glazed over as he thought about Lexie rolling and wriggling beneath him.

Sonja stood up, moved in front of Lenny, and pushed him down on the edge of the bed. Removing her flame red uniform blazer, she moved even closer. Her butt-hugging pencil skirt dropped to the floor.

Lenny thought he knew Sonja, but this…she goes to work like this? Is that allowed? Aren't undergarments required?

"Your new friend will be on Marco Island?" Sonja whispered as she reached up and removed a single pin from her required Aeroflot bun. Her long, black hair fell in waves over her shoulders and dangled seductively. Her catlike, brown eyes followed his hand that had wandered down to his official *Mets* briefs with the team logo on the butt.

"Err... yes." Lenny's eyes traveled from luscious red lips to her breasts, smiling at her slightly smaller left tit.

"You are afraid your little love girl will see me?"

"Well...yes." Sonja's scent enveloped his brain. He pulled her close and inhaled.

She pushed him back on the bed and straddled him.

Lying beside him, Sonja was uncharacteristically sweet. "You will miss me, Leonid. We have good sex. I will miss you, too. You are good in bed. This woman will be lucky."

"You'll come down to Florida? I would love to have one last fuck with my Russian minx." Lenny stroked her cheek.

"Lenny, for you I will wear my thong bikini. We will swim in the Gulf of Mexico, where you may undo the tiny strings, and we will have the good sex in warm waters that caress our bodies."

"No, Sonja, the great sex," Lenny laughed as he squeezed her breast. "Practice makes perfect."

"You are not romantic, but not important. You are like TV bunny always ready. I am hot for sex again. We try something different now," she purred as she reached for him.

Lenny shivered with pleasure.

Sonja got up from the floor. "I will sleep now. I like you, Lenny. You are perfect fuckbuddy. You live next door. You have no wife. You give me pleasure. If not, you don't care that I pleasure myself, and then I go home to bed relaxed. This was perfect. Yes?"

"This was a sweet deal. I agree." Lenny smiled as he gazed into Sonja's deep brown eyes. He would miss her, but everything was working out. His heart ached as he thought of lying beside Lexie. He hoped from their first fuck she would be as good in bed as Sonja.

Sonja's snores echoed through the bedroom door. His footsteps were muted as he paced the carpeted hallway. The conversation with Sonja went better than he expected. He was a little disappointed he could be replaced so easily. She would be hard to give up. What he really wanted was to start a family of his own. He was ready. Now that the Andruzzi's were on board with his plan and Sal was excited about Florida, the next phase was about to begin. He woke up Sonja and sent her home. He would try and get some sleep.

CHAPTER 9

December – Queens, NY

"Lou, I'm going to the liberry, you need anything from the market while I'm out?"

"What did you say?" Louis, coming in from the kitchen, wiped his hands on the sauce-stained kitchen towel hanging from his belt. "You're going to the library?"

"Yeah, liberry, you got a problem? I'm going to find some stuff on South Florida. We should be prepared, get an idea about the terrain."

"Terrain? Who ARE you? And where did you hide my fat-fuck brother Dominic?"

"We should know what we're getting into. Maybe a guidebook, or a movie like on the *Nat Geo* channel. You know, a documentary."

Louis shifted his weight on the sofa and looked up. "We're not going to the Amazon, its freaking Florida."

"This is a big deal for us, Lou. It's sort of like a promotion. Mr. Horowitz is depending on us. We can't screw up."

"I think he knows we can be trusted after that thing in the yard."

"I told you to never mention that again." Dominic picked up his car keys.

"Bring back some chips. We can snack while we're watching your 'documentary'." Louis punctuated his words with air quotes.

Dominic winced and gave him a one-fingered response. "Fuck you. You'll see, it'll be a good thing. Open your mind a little."

CRSO

The phone rang not long after Dominic had left. Caller ID read Ferraro Salvage.

"Louis Andruzzi."

"Hello, Louis, Leonard Horowitz. I want to give you some further instructions on your upcoming assignment in Florida."

Louis bit his lip and fist pumped the air. "Sure thing, Mister Horowitz, let me grab a pencil. Hold on a second...OKAY got one."

"I made travel arrangements for you and Dominic. Because of the nature of your jobs, Mr. Ferraro and I have decided it would be best if you did not fly commercial. You both will be flying down on Mr. Ferraro's personal jet. I will not be accompanying you. You'll land at the Marco Island airport where a car will be parked beside the hangar Mr. Ferraro owns. The keys will be inside the hangar on a hook to the left of the walk-through door. Instructions will be in an envelope in the glove box marked with the initials D.L.A."

Louis scribbled down Marco Island, hangar, keys inside, Glove box DLA and PRIVATE JET! "OKAY, got it."

"This is important, you'll be traveling as Jerry and Bob Smith. I have taken care of the paperwork. The plane departs from Teterboro Airport on February second. A car will pick you up at your house at 6:15 in the morning. It would be best if you kept these arrangements to yourselves."

"Sure thing, Mr. Horowitz. You can count on us not to tell nobody."

"That's good, Louis. You need to keep a low profile. David will be leaving before you; his arrangements are different. He will not be sharing information with you. So don't ask him. Your first job will be to meet him at a specific time and place to be determined as the job gets closer. Are you understanding all of this, Louis?"

Louis scribbled more notes: Teterboro Airport, 6:15AM, Jerry and Bob Smith—2/2,

Don't tell anybody!

"Yeah, just writing this stuff down for Dominic. He's out right now, picking up some information on South Florida. You know, so we are familiar with the area."

"Did you receive the email about your accommodations near Chokoloskee?"

"Yes, we did, and it looks really nice."

"It's quiet and out of the way. You guys need to keep a low profile while you're there."

"We will and thank you, Mr. Horowitz. We saw it was a waterfront place. You know, Dom and I love to fish. We've been fishing the bay and the canals around here since we were kids. We'll fit right in. Maybe we can bring some gear with us, you know, so we look the part."

"That's good Louis, it's nice to see you're thinking ahead. You're good men. That's why we chose you and your brothers for this job. I'll be in touch after the holidays. Merry Christmas and Happy New Year to you and your family."

"Merry...er Hanukkah, Mr. Horowitz."

⚜

Dominic hadn't put the key in the door when Louis yanked it open. "Holy shit, Dominic, you're not going to believe this. Lenny Horowitz called while you were out."

"Slow down, Louis, help me get these bags in the house. I got stuff that's got to go in the freezer."

"Okay, okay." Louis went as fast as his legs could carry his three hundred twenty-four-pound frame. He sidled down the six front steps, traversed the twenty feet to the car trunk, back up the six steps, pushed open the front door and headed to the kitchen table where he dumped the seven plastic grocery bags. He collapsed in a heap on the kitchen chair unable to catch his breath.

Dominic was unloading a canvas bag imprinted with the words, Queens Borough Public Library. "I hit pay dirt. The liberrian was so nice. She found all this great shit about Florida—a Fodor's guidebook, a book on the history of Florida, and a DVD about the Everglades. I even got a liberry card. Look, it's got my name on it. I can even take out books on the computer."

Louis wheezed and stared at Dominic in disbelief. "Huhh... heh...uhh..." his breath came in massive gulps for air.

"Are you okay? Louis, signal one finger for I'm okay, and two for I need an ambulance."

Louis held up his middle finger and closed his eyes willing his heart rate to slow down. "That's better, huhh... almost back... huhh...to normal."

"You shouldn't be running like that. You're gonna have a heart attack."

Louis pushed the notes he had taken towards Dominic. "Read this."

Louis watched in disbelief as Dominic pulled out a pair of reading glasses from his shirt pocket and put them on.

"What the fuck are they?"

"Reading glasses."

"You never read anything."

"Yeah, I do."

"What, the comics?"

"Fuck you. The liberrian saw I was having trouble reading the small print. She had an old pair of glasses in her drawer, she found them last year and nobody claimed them. It was amazing. I put them on, and it was like a miracle, I could see every word perfect."

"Lenny Horowitz called. We are flying down to Florida in Sal Ferraro's private jet!"

"You're shitting me."

"No, really, we are being picked up by a car, and we are traveling incognito."

"Phony names?"

"We are Jerry and Bob Smith. This is real James Bond stuff. I told you we're in the big game now."

"Louis, can I be Jerry? You know how I love Jerry Lewis movies.'

"No, I'm going to be Jerry because I love Jerry Lewis, too, and my name is Louis so it will be easy to remember. You can be Bob, like Bob Hope. He's funny, too."

"Okay, I see your point."

"Let's break out the chips and open some beers, we can celebrate while we watch your Everglades movie. We are going to be staying right near there at a fishing resort!"

"We love fishing. You think we'll have time to drop a line?"

"I don't see why not; we won't be working twenty-four seven."

The movie started with an aerial view of the Everglades. The shot swooped down low to offer a view of the Tamiami Trail and the last outpost before entering the park, the town of Chokoloskee and the minuscule Ochopee Post office. The men settled into the sound of chirping birdcalls and buzzing insects interspersed with the popping of beer tabs.

"You did good, Dominic. We're going to get a real feel for the place."

"Thanks, bro, I appreciate that."

CHAPTER 10

Classic

Sal turned the Escalade into the security coded parking garage at the Albatross Condominiums. The flight down to Naples from Teterboro was nerve-wracking. The pilot of the G-7 spent forty minutes moving Sal and the luggage around to keep the excessive weight evenly distributed. Sal thought it might have been easier to fly commercial. On top of that, Lexie was petrified they would fall out of the sky. She popped a Xanax and drank two glasses of Pinot Grigio before take-off. He tried to get her to enjoy the first ride in their jet, but she fell asleep a half-hour after take-off. She slept through the flight and was still groggy when she got into the Escalade Lenny had waiting for them at the airport. She lowered the passenger seat back and dozed off again. He thought it was probably better she missed the strip malls, faux waterfalls, and grand gated entrances to barren fields. The ride was a contrast of Neapolitan decadence and seedy motels abutting pawn shops and tacky furniture stores.

Lexie sat upright as the metal garage gates clanged opened. Sal drove slowly, searching the walls for the designated penthouse spot. Lexie started wiggling in her seat as they rolled down the long aisle.

"Sal." She tapped him on the arm.

"Just hold it in, Lex, five more minutes."

"No, Sal, are you seeing this?"

"What, you found the spot?"

"No, Sal, the cars. Look at the cars."

Sal stopped the SUV and looked around the dimly lit interior of the parking garage. Half of the spots were filled. Some of the cars had covers, others had shrouds of dust on them but were recognizable.

"Lexie, it's like we found buried treasure. A cave full of jewels."

Lexie smiled at Sal, squeezed his massive thigh. "Sal, that's like poetry. Look at these cars. It's like a scene from that show you love, the car auction one."

"Yeah, *Barret Jackson*. Those guys would cream themselves if they saw this. It's like a dusty Jay Leno's Garage episode."

"Just stop the car a minute, Sal. I want to look around."

Lexie got out and walked further into the garage. Sal pulled into the penthouse spot and searched for her in the gloom. He found her caressing the hood of a baby blue Coupe De Ville convertible.

"Sal, this is it. This is my dream car, and it's so hot."

"Yeah, it must be a hundred degrees in here."

"No, Sal, the car." Lexie leaned over and laid her chest against the hood. The Daisy Duke shorts she had put on at the airport rode up her perfect backside revealing half-moons of soft flesh. "Sal, I love this car," she whispered as she looked over her shoulder at him with sleepy eyes.

"Wow, Lexie, you would look great driving this." Sal walked up behind her and in moments they christened their first day in Florida on the hood of the Coupe De Ville.

"Sal, I think the rivets on my pockets scratched the car." Lexie walked around the car caressing the bumpers.

"No worries, babe, a little compound, and it'll be fine."

"Lexie, look around. I see at least ten classic cars; I'm sure the ones under the covers are classics as well. I got to talk to Lenny about working a deal on this."

The two of them in relaxed post-coital moods walked out of the garage. Sal's arm was draped over Lexie's shoulder. Lexie sagged a bit from the weight, her arm partially around Sal's waist.

A covered portico with waterfalls on either side of the garage walkway led them to the Albatross entrance. Lush vegetation flanked the doors to the main building. The doors parted with an almost imperceptible swishing sound. In front of them a mahogany partition decorated with oil paintings and flanked by massive planters blocked their path. Turning right, they walked around the wall. The elevators backed the entrance way and beyond the elevators they were amazed to see the lobby had an atrium soaring fourteen floors skyward. The glass ceiling allowed the bright afternoon sun to naturally light the open space. The lobby was designed like a park with bamboo pergolas and a large, bubbling center fountain. Live greenery softened the marble floors and the surrounding balconies on each landing had cascading plants. It was a perfectly designed and manicured jungle encased in glass and stone.

The elevators opened silently behind them. Sal jumped when a petite woman in a housedress, her grey hair tousled, popped out. "Excuse me. In a hurry. Got to check. Think I left my car running. Do it all the time." She darted around the wall and was gone.

"Oh God, Sal, I hope it wasn't her car we just screwed on."

"Wow, that was weird. Lexie, I'm going to go in the office to get things straightened out. The manager is expecting us.'

"Okay, I'm going to sit for a minute near the fountain. It's peaceful here."

Heading to the glass office windows, Sal looked over to see Lexie enter a doorway across the atrium.

"Sal Ferraro. Me and the wife are going to be in the penthouse."

"Welcome, Mr. Ferraro." The attractive blond behind the counter reached out to shake his hand. "My name is Susan. I'm the property manager. Everything has already been taken care of for you. I just need the make, color, and year of your car for our records. May I ask how you found the penthouse rental? No one has occupied that unit for about four years."

"Is that important? I mean do you ask that question of all the tenants?"

"Uh, no, I mean I was curious. I've never met the present owners."

Sal stared at her for a long moment.

She shifted uncomfortably in her chair.

"My paperwork in order?"

"Yes, it's all fine."

"Good. Speaking of cars," Sal handed her the completed car registration form. "There was a lady, old, heading to the garage she said she needed to check her car. She thought she left it running. Is she okay?"

"That's Grace Benson. She runs to the garage to check on it about a dozen times a day. She has a 1968 Deville she hasn't driven in years. Really sad, no family."

"What color is her Cadillac?"

"Baby blue."

⚜

Grace Benson headed into the parking garage for the sixth time that day, though she didn't realize it was the sixth time. At age ninety-four, she didn't remember much, but she understood the importance of making sure she didn't leave the car running. She did it once to tragic results. Her beloved Shih-Tzu, Walter, was asleep in the back seat of the car as she pulled into the garage of her Cleveland home. It was winter, so she drove into the garage, closed the door, and brought in the groceries. Entering the kitchen, she was distracted by a phone call. She never realized she left the car running. She found Walter three hours later, already stiff.

That was in 1982. Grace and her 1968 baby blue Cadillac Coupe Deville Convertible now reside in the luxury Albatross Condominiums on Marco Island and have been there permanently since 1993. Grace, an independent woman, lived alone since her husband's death and refused any help from family and friends. Her frequent trips to the garage, initially a source of amusement to neighbors, had turned into Grace's perpetual *Groundhog Day*. She had not driven the Cadillac in eight years. It remained in the garage. Its only vehicular activity occurred when Preston, the condo maintenance man, serviced the car. Aware of Grace's propensity for checking the car numerous times a day, the maintenance schedule was set up to have the car tuned and running when Grace was driven to Naples for her doctors' appointments. This arrangement falls within the parameters of the HOA agreement arranged by Grace's husband before his sudden demise four years ago.

Roger Benson suffered a fatal heart attack as he reclined on his designated poolside lounge chair while reading a newspaper. The residents believe an editorial precipitated the coronary event, though that has never been determined. Mechanically the car remains mint, though a coat of dust covers its former sheen. The only evidence of Grace's visits is the clear circular patch on the driver's window where she looks in to see if the car is running.

⋘⋙

Susan placed the papers in a folder, tapped a few keys on her computer, then looked back at Sal. "We are all through here, Mr. Ferraro. If there is anything you need, I live off premises, but the caretaker is a resident. You will find his emergency number on the evacuation signage on the back of the unit's front door. My daytime number is listed on paperwork you will find in the kitchen drawer. Have a great stay at the Albatross, Mr. Ferraro."

"Got it. What's behind the door across the way?"

"That's the gym. It's small, but has brand new equipment, a sauna, showers, and it faces the pool. You should check it out," Susan blushed.

Sal headed across the atrium to the gym door, going inside he saw Lexie sitting on a Peloton bike, slowly pedaling, and staring out the window at the pool.

"Hey, babe, what's a matter?"

"Sal, "she raised her hand and pointed out the window. The pool shimmered bright blue, a rock wall glistened with cascading water flowing into a large outdoor spa. On the far side of the pool, the lounge chairs were empty, shaded by dappled sunshine through the coconut palms heavy with ripening fruit. "This place looks like heaven. What are we doing living in New York?"

"If this deal works out, this could be our home."

"It's so peaceful." Lexie was still pedaling the bike, looking pensive as she gazed out the window.

"You ain't seen anything yet. Wait till we get upstairs." Sal moved close to Lexie taking her hand and guiding her off the bike. "This place just feels right." Laughing he gave her a hug. "We sure showed that garage a sight."

"Wait, you don't think there were cameras in there?"

"Who cares, I hope they got an eyeful. We're going to bring some life to this place." Looking at the peaceful scene, Sal nodded. "This is a sweet deal. Got to hand it to Lenny, he's good at picking winners. Let's go up and see the place. Oh, funny thing, you know that lady we saw coming out of the elevator? Her name is Grace. Guess what car she's checking up on"

"Sal, you're kidding, the Caddie?"

"Yep, our baby blue sex machine."

"I hope the car is okay after..."

"Trust me. She will never notice."

CHAPTER 11

Ospreys and Blood and Bones

The ride up the glass-walled elevator offered a panoramic view of Marco Island. The green of the Everglades was a soothing contrast to the canal-laden tract developments covering the island.

"Lexie, the penthouse is comprised of two units remodeled into one huge one. It's got six bedrooms, two primaries. Susan, the manager, gave me the rundown on the floor plan. She also mentioned some mysterious foreign guy bought it from a record producer. She was snooping around about how we got to use it. So, if she asks, don't answer."

Lexie frowned and looked over. "I won't mention anything about it."

Lexie's quiet mood lifted when Sal opened the door onto a wide-open common space. He turned on the lights; the hurricane shutters were still down. The kitchen to the left had blond wood cabinets lining the interior wall, a long double-wide counter with an industrial steel sink, and a stove-top facing the dining area in front of it. The table matched the cabinets, and beyond that, a massive pale grey curved sofa faced an enormous entertainment center on the right-side wall. The view to the gulf side of the condo would be unobstructed from front door to blue water.

"Wow, Sal, this place is gorgeous. I don't care how you got it. I can't believe no one uses this."

"Crazy right? If this all goes down okay, I might try and buy it."

"Really?" She ran over to the windows. "Quick, open up these gates, I want to see the water."

"The switch should be here next to the window. Got it. There are two: one for the shutters and one for the doors. Lexie, turn around and shut your eyes. Let's pretend it's Christmas. The manager said the view is to die for."

The massive steel shutters clanged, faltered a moment, then silently slid up. Simultaneously the glass doors slowly retreated into the walls. Lexie stood hopping from foot-to- foot like a kid on Christmas morning: her back to the windows, her eyes squeezed shut as the doors parted. A final thump and Sal grabbed her hand. "Okay, Lex. One, two, three, turn…."

Lexie's scream pierced the quiet space. Sal backed up in shock. Sitting on the railing just feet from the open door was a huge bird. The osprey's wings flapped wildly as it lifted above the balcony, a bloody and shredded fish hanging from its talons. It hovered for a moment then flew off with its catch. The floor and table looked like a crime scene with the blood and bones of unlucky fish littering the tiled floor.

Lexie stumbled backward and screamed again as she bumped into a bedraggled man standing behind her, his face obscured by long, greasy hair.

Sal threw a punch that caught the guy on his shoulder and sent him flying backward onto the glass cocktail table, shattering it on impact. A million beads of glass skittered across the parquet floor.

Lenny ran through the front door, the glass pebbles under his shoes sent him into an erratic dance as he tried to stay upright. With a final flourish, his feet flew out in front of him. He landed spread eagle at Sal's feet, flat on his back and grimacing in pain.

"Welcome to Marco, Sal."

Sal reached down and grabbed Lenny by the collar. Yanking his face to within inches of his, Sal whispered, "Who the fuck is that?"

Sal grabbed Lenny's hand and pulled him upright. Pieces of table glass falling off Lenny's back tinkled as they hit the floor.

"That's Preston. He's the handyman for the building."

"Well, Preston, get your broom. This place is a mess. Lenny, what the fuck is he doing in the condo?"

"I brought him in. He's working for me. I mean us."

"Yeah, I got it. Employed by the Albatross."

A shaken Lexie mumbled, "I can't deal with this. I've got such a headache." She shuffled off, glass marbles skittering, giving Preston a wide berth.

"Sal, take a seat. I want to explain what's been going on down here."

"Just a minute." Sal pointed at Preston. "When you're done with the glass, the balcony is covered with blood and bones."

"Sal, we have to talk, now."

"Wait a second, Lenny, I got to deal with this asshole."

"Another thing, Press, can I call you Press?" Sal sneered, "Couple of carry-ons in the back of the black Escalade in the garage." Sal tossed a key fob towards Preston.

Preston smiled as the fob slid across the counter and landed in the sink. "For ten grand you can call me anything you want." Preston drifted out to the balcony as the rolling beads jingled on the tile floor. He skirted past the fish carnage and moved out of view. A moment later the smell of skunkweed wafted into the condo.

Sal jumped up.

Lenny stood firm in front of him, leaned in, and spoke, "Let me tell you about Preston."

જ

Lexie entered the master bedroom and turned on the lights, a soft glow ringed the exposed roofline twelve feet above. Steel beams gleamed in the subtle light. A raised, over-sized king bed dominated one wall, while a trio of mirrors reflected the silver palette of the carpet and linens. Across from the bed a large fireplace with a sandstone mantle and hearth was flanked by inviting armchairs, soft throws folded on the matching ottomans. Two lounging sofas faced the glass windows. Lexie found the switches and opened the shutters and doors, cringing as she prepared herself for another shock.

Preston, sitting outside, turned and smiled. "Hey, want a hit?"

Lexie hesitated for a moment then walked over, accepted the proffered joint, and sank into the lounge next to him. He seemed harmless enough dressed in a washed out Grateful Dead T-shirt and naturally ripped jeans. His long, sandy hair parted in the middle revealed a thin nose and blue eyes bright in the lowering sun. He was deeply tanned and slim, yet his well-defined arm muscles suggested he might work out.

Inhaling deeply, she muttered, "What a nightmare. Is that going to happen every time I open the doors?"

"No. Ospreys hang out on the balconies of the vacant condos. They don't like activity. They'll find another perch."

"That's good to hear."

"Hey, I'm sorry I frightened you. I don't mean to sneak up on people. I'm just a quiet guy. How about we start over? I'm Preston Thayer the Fourth, formally of Greenwich, Connecticut, and Cambridge, Massachusetts, presently residing in the Albatross."

"Wow, that's impressive. I'm Alexis Ferraro of Howard Beach, New York. Wait, I thought you were the caretaker."

"Well, that is true, and it's a sad tale. Please pass me the joint."

"Oops, sorry." Lexie took a quick hit and passed it over to Preston. Relaxed by the weed and the gentle gulf breeze, she settled in to listen.

"Tell me a story, Preston," she whispered as she exhaled.

"I come from a long line of architects and engineers. My father designed many of the buildings that hover over the Stamford waterfront. I was encouraged at a very early age to develop my creativity. Being an only child, I spent hours alone designing cities for insects living beneath the lawns and hedges on our property."

"You didn't have any friends? Neighbor kids to play with?"

"Our nearest neighbor was a half mile down the road. The kids in my neighborhood attended boarding schools. I went to a Catholic school in the area and had few friends. All I really cared about was the insects living in my yard."

"You were a weird kid. I would've avoided you."

"That was everyone's general opinion." Preston sighed. "Anyway, I ended up at MIT with all the other weird, lonely kids. That's where I developed my deep and lasting relationship with pot. Expanded my research on all thing's ant with a simultaneous major in engineering."

Lexie reached out to accept the next hit, as an easy pattern developed. "Continue."

"My parents worried I had crossed the line into insanity when I started developing ant condos in my dorm. They decided I should go on spring break for my senior year to be 'like the other kids.' I came down here to Florida, spent a drug-infused week under palm trees with half-naked drunk girls willing to have sex with me and bigger and more industrious bugs to discover. I never went back."

"How long have you been at the Albatross?"

"Probably too long. The condo is owned by my parents."

Lexie squinted as she looked over at him. "How old are you?"

"I'm probably the world's oldest slacker."

"If you're rich, why do you work here?"

"My trust fund is doled out in small bits, enough for food, not enough for my weed habit. I work here to supplement my income. I drive the old folks around for tips and sweep the floor as needed."

"A lovely place for a slow death." She extended the joint to Preston.

"That was dark. But it leads me to an interesting question." A sharp quick inhale and he passed it back to Lexie. "How does a cute girl like you end up as a mob wife?"

"*Oh, The Places You'll Go*, said Theodore Geisel."

"So, you know the classics."

Lexie blew pungent smoke at Preston's face. "Before I met Sal, I taught fourth grade in Jackson Heights. That's in Queens. I made a series of bad choices: fell in love with the father of one of my students. Nothing too sordid. He was separated when I met him. That led to all kinds of problems. He came from a devout Catholic family. I wasn't Italian, and I was a home wrecker. His mother used to cross herself whenever she saw me. Kind of funny now that I think about it."

"Not really. They blamed you. You were the slut that broke up a family."

Lexie face paled, "That was harsh. I didn't see it that way."

"You wouldn't."

"Are you always this honest?"

"Yeah, it's a problem of mine. Continue." Preston settled back in the lounge.

Lexie took a deep breath as she looked at Preston. "I haven't been this open in a long time. It feels good."

"That's the weed."

"Probably right."

"Have another hit." Preston passed her the joint. "I can tell your story is way more interesting than mine."

"We need to slow down. I'm getting as high as those birds flying around. This stuff is potent."

"It is, right? It's my own blend."

"You could market this stuff and make a fortune."

"Not interested. So, tell me how you ended up here."

"Vinnie, my first husband, was employed by Sal's company, Ferraro Salvage. I didn't know that at the time."

What's Sal's business, salvage? Plenty of that in Florida, people make a ton of money finding sunken boats filled with buried treasure."

"You're so funny, not from New York. Salvage is a broad term, covers a lot of territory, things he buried, but not treasure." Lexie laughed. "Anyway, that's what's on paper."

"So, what happened?"

"Vinnie died in an accident at the salvage yard. He didn't work at the yard. I didn't even know there was a yard. He worked in Manhattan at an accounting firm. All I know is I got a call that a Honda Civic fell off a giant metal magnet and crushed him."

"That's heavy."

"Yeah, two tons heavy."

"Did Sal do that?"

"No. It was an accident."

Preston looked around nervously. "Am I going to get whacked for splitting a smoke with you?"

"No, he's okay with pot." Lexie inhaled deeply and exhaled as she passed the joint, "Sal and I light up to relax. It makes him feel happy."

"I didn't think someone like Sal would partake."

"It's a recent development. Last spring, Lenny and Sal had been drinking a lot of beer and watching a baseball game on TV. The Mets finally won, and Lenny brought out a joint and convinced Sal, who was already drunk, to try it—a celebration of sorts. After they smoked, Sal couldn't stop laughing. He started rummaging around the kitchen and finally had me order three pizzas and a calzone. It was funny."

"You'd think it would bring out his devils."

"No, it had the opposite effect on him. After that, Lenny always made sure Sal had a joint or two in his cigar box."

"So, Sal is okay with you and me out here?"

"I don't think he sees you as a threat. He's probably more pissed about the broken table."

"When I look at him and you," Preston shook his head, "I don't see the attraction."

"Sal really does care for me. He's been taking care of me since Vinnie's accident. He literally saved my life."

"How'd that happen?"

"Vinnie and I had eloped. We hadn't told anyone accept his cousin Anthony. That was a week before the accident. At the funeral, his ex-shows up and stands right next to the coffin at the widow's spot—my spot."

"Last hit, here take it." Preston passed the roach, now in a clip he brought out of his pocket.

Lexie choked out smoke and between coughs, continued. "Anthony hated Theresa, the ex. He takes my arm and pulls me up in front of her—cause I'm the widow, right? Mama Cacciatore..."

"Mama Cacciatore? You're kidding. That's the name of a restaurant in Naples. That's funny."

"Vinnie Cacciatore was my husband's name."

"You're joking?"

Lexie gave Preston a hard look. "Yes, that was his name and would have been mine, too. Are you going to let me finish?"

"Yeah, this is great stuff."

"Mama Cacciatore is crossing herself and moaning prayers in Italian. Theresa starts cursing at me and pushes me, hard, slams me into the side of the coffin."

"Shit, I hope someone was filming this, I bet the feds have it on tape. This is nuts! Oh, the spliff is spent." He pocketed the roach and clip. "Go on."

"The coffin slides off the rails, and I fall into the open grave wrapped up in the green Astroturf blanket they put under the coffin, you know, so you don't get freaked by the hole in the ground. By now everyone is screaming. I can't see anything because I'm wrapped up in the blanket. I didn't know it, but the coffin was sliding into the hole."

Preston blew out a cloud of smoke as he giggled. "Wow, this could be a movie!"

Lexie squinted. "This was a deadly situation. A massive object landed on me. I couldn't breathe. The wind was knocked out of me. I'm thinking, I'm going to join Vinnie in the ever after. I passed out. I woke up seconds later. This huge guy is unwrapping the green carpet from around me. I felt like I was reborn. He brushed grave dirt from my face and whispered, "Don't worry, babe, I got you.""

Preston rolled his eyes "You don't see how funny this is? So, Sal landed on you?"

Lexie took a deep breath. "Yes. He jumped in the hole and stopped the coffin from crushing me." Lexie's body started shaking as giggles escaped her lips.

"Could have been just as deadly. He's a big guy."

"He saved my life." She looked over at Preston relaxed on the lounge chair smiling broadly. "This is the first time I found the humor in this. It is hilarious."

"That's an incredible story. But life is short and, hey, you got to laugh, right?"

"Finish yours, Preston. How did Lenny lure you in? I heard you mention ten thousand dollars. Is that what souls are going for these days?"

"Excuse me? Pot calling the kettle black?"

"I don't know anything about Sal's business."

"Not sure that'll hold up in court."

"I'm buried in my new life. I read my books, do yoga, meditate, go to spin class, and shop. Sal pays for everything. I got a nice nest egg set up from Vinnie's double indemnity."

"So, he gets what?"

"He gets me."

"You, all of you? Wow, you don't seem like the type to give up."

"No, you got it wrong, He really gets me, understands I loved Vinnie. I was broken; he fixed me. Well not completely fixed, but I'm getting there."

"I think you sold out cheaper than me. I did a few calculations, set up some gadgets, pointed them in the right direction and done." Preston sat up and moved to the edge of the lounge.

"That's what you expect? Do a job and get out?" Lexie shook her head and gave him a half-smile. "You must be living under a rock."

"No, I live in paradise." He pointed to the turquoise water glistening in the afternoon sun.

"You smoke too much weed. This isn't paradise. This is a death trap waiting for an innocent victim to walk in."

☙❧

"Sal, calm down." Lenny rubbed his head and grimaced. "You definitely got anger issues."

"You kidding me? The fucking bird scared the shit out of Lexie, shocked the shit out of me, too. There's blood and bones all over the goddam balcony, and that fucking hippie waltzes in like he owns the place. He breaks the coffee table and he's lying out there on my lounge chair smoking a joint.

And to top all that shit off, you tell me he's the janitor." Sal glared at Lenny from the sofa. "Why the fuck isn't he in here cleaning up this mess? I'm going out there and see what's going on." Sal jumped up and sent waves of glass skittering.

"Just sit-down, Sal. If you step on that shit and fall, you're going to break a leg. Preston is harmless."

Lenny slid his feet across the slippery glass-pebbled tiles and headed to the open kitchen. He pulled a blue ice pack from the sub-zero freezer and held it on the rapidly growing bump on the back of his head. "Sal, he didn't break the table. All of this," Lenny waved his free hand around the trashed great room, "was caused by your overreaction."

"You are blaming this on me? Lexie and I walk into a scene from a Hitchcock movie, complete with a deranged-looking freak, and you expect me to calmly introduce myself and offer him a joint and a beer?"

"He technically works for you."

"Yeah, we went over this. Janitor for the Albatross."

"No, I... we pay him for his services."

"And what does that lowlife do for us that is worth, what did he say, ten grand?"

"Sal, he's a smart guy."

"He better be Einstein, or his relativity to the planet is about to end. I'm thinking about tossing him over the balcony."

"Sal, I know I haven't gone into a lot of detail about Raul Garcia and his network. He is the real deal down in Havana. I couldn't believe when he responded to the introductory email I sent him. I guess he saw a good business opportunity opening in the States. He's been shut out of major operations for years. He was on the sidelines, witnessing Mexico and South America expand north. We, meaning Raul Garcia and I, have decided to dip our toes in slowly, you know, feel the temperature in South Florida and start with a small drop in the Everglades, a test run."

"Where does the freak play into this?" Sal said.

"The guy is a genius. He programmed an agricultural drone to fly in low from Cuba, drop our package with a state-of-the-art GPS attached into the Everglades. The drone will drop its payload and then head back to Cuba. To avoid suspicion, it will be set up with just enough pesticides to continue spraying Garcia coconut groves upon its return. Flight time for the drone is usually forty-five minutes. Preston worked on the power problem for a flight of two hours."

"He's okay with this?"

"He doesn't have the full picture. He is programming a crop-dusting drone for extended flight time. I told him we were working on an Amazon-type delivery service between Cuba and Florida concentrating on hand-rolled cigars. We chose the Everglades for testing so if it failed, no one would get hurt."

"And he believed that?"

"For ten thousand dollars and plausible deniability, he'll believe anything. It's why I haven't given you a lot of detail. I've been keeping you under the radar for a long time. You got to trust me on this, Sal."

CHAPTER 12

The Floating Ladies Greek Chorus

"Sal, which one do you think, this tropical flowered tankini? It covers up a lot. I don't want to freak out the residents. Or the red, white, and blue bikini, very patriotic, but not much hidden."

"Lexi, you are going to blow their minds no matter what you wear."

"Sal, look at me, you aren't being very helpful. First impressions are important."

"What about our first impressions? That nut job old lady, what was her name? Oh yeah, Grace Benson. Or the ospreys and bones on the balcony, and what about that hippie, Preston? Talk about first impressions. I hope they saw us fucking in the parking lot. Now, that would be an awesome first impression."

Sal walked over to the now naked Lexie and caressed a perfect breast.

"Not now, Sal, I want to look right for them."

"You always look right for me. That's all that matters. He reached down between her thighs. How about something quick to relax you? You always look fantastic after a good fuck; you have a glow about you."

"That might be your five o'clock shadow scratching my face. I'm teasing. I don't want the 'I've just been screwed look. According to Susan, the manager, most of the residents are very old."

Sal moved in closer to Lexie. "So maybe they don't remember what after sex looks like. Or even better, it gets their juices flowing and they run upstairs and drag their old men away from *Judge Judy* and into the bedroom for some afternoon delight." Sal laughed at his joke.

"I'm going with the tankini," Lexie laughed, pulling out of Sal's reach.

"I think the bikini. God and country are very important to that generation. Anyway, there are high-end hotels all along the beach, plenty of ass and tits walking by. I'm sure they get an eyeful every day."

"You can be so crude. But you do have a sweet side." Lexie blew him a kiss and slipped on the bikini.

The clock on the pump house wall read 12:55 p.m. as Lexie spread her towel down on the lounge closest to the shallow end. Dragging over a side table, she put down an Elle Magazine, a bottle of Poland Spring water, and a spray can of 15 sunblock.

"That's not going to work."

Startled, Lexie looked up into a prune face framed by long, white braids. Bright blue eyes peered out from beneath a wide straw sunhat. "Excuse me?"

"That sunblock's not going to work. You will burn to a crisp in fifteen minutes. Tropical sun here. It may be February, but the sun doesn't care. You are winter white. You'll be fire- engine red in an hour, and that will make you blue tonight when the blisters and peeling begin. Ha! Red, white, and blue, like your bikini." The old woman reached out her hand. "I'm Marge, 607."

Lexie extended her hand and felt the strength in the older woman's grip, "Lexie Ferraro, 1304."

"Hmm, That's the penthouse, hasn't been occupied for years. You the owner?"

"No, renting. A friend found it for us. Where is everyone? I thought the pool would have been crowded."

Marge pointed to the clock that now read 1:00 p.m. and then at the door leading out from the gym. A gaggle of old ladies in varying degrees of wrinkled skin waddled out into the bright sun. In unison they dropped their towels on lounges, reached into Winn Dixie bags and pulled out matching waist floats, clicked them on simultaneously, and headed down the wide steps into the pool. Childlike giggles floated above their grey heads and within seconds they had formed into a tight circle where they bobbed up and down. Contented smiles lit their faces as the cool water floated the years and their cares away. Marge smiled and snapped on her own belt and waded into the pool.

A chorus of comments commenced, and the Floating Ladies filled the air with bubbles of information: restaurants, cheating husbands, bingo winners, potluck suppers, happy hours, new great-grandchildren, divorces, and bankruptcies.

"They are quite a crew, right?" Preston spoke from the lounge chair to her left.

Lexie jumped. "When did you get here?"

"I'm a real quiet guy. Never want to startle the residents, so I try to be unobtrusive."

"Kind of creepy if you ask me." Lexie pointed at the pool. "If I was as old as one of them and you snuck up on me like that? You'd be calling 911 now."

"I don't normally sit here. Saw you alone, I, uh…just wanted to say hi. I've got to get back to work. If you need anything, I'm right over there." He nodded to the far side of the pool where the lounge chairs were surrounded by yellow warning tape.

"That a crime scene?'

"No, I'm trying to avoid it turning into one."

"How so? The ospreys haven't moved on from fish to old ladies, right?"

"You're funny. No, not ospreys. Look up in that palm tree above the lounges."

Lexie shaded her eyes. "Are those coconuts?"

"Yes, and they can do some damage if they fall on you. Statistically proven–one hundred and fifty people are killed from falling coconuts each year. From that height they could reach forty to fifty mph by impact. Those ladies don't stand a chance."

"So, just cut them down."

"That has been the usual protocol, but last year two arborists died in separate incidents removing coconuts from tall palm trees. It seems our modern-day landscapers are not adept at climbing coconut trees."

"I've seen those old South Pacific movies where kids shimmy up the sides of palm trees with machetes and cut down the coconuts."

"Hollywood. It's hard to find that talent around here. They mostly use bucket trucks, but it messes up the landscaping. Two years ago, the cement deck around the pool got cracked. Cost the association a fortune to redo. I'm trying to find a way to organically remove the coconuts. The residents love those trees, refuse to take them down, and don't want the coconuts removed. You watch. Someone will remove the tape overnight. It's a lose-lose situation."

"I forgot you're a scientist."

"Almost a scientist, but the mind never stops working."

⁍⁍⁍

"What comes next?" Sal said.

Lenny shifted uncomfortably. He was perched on a tall chair by the glass deck railing of Sal's penthouse. The brisk breeze off the gulf lowered the midday temperature. Lenny was still sweating profusely. "Well, we haven't heard from David Andruzzi. He was supposed to do the pickup three days ago."

"You checked him out good, right? We can trust him. That's what you said."

"One hundred-per-cent Sal. He's a family guy through and through. He really stepped up after he got kicked out of Boston College and came back to Queens..."

Sal cut him off mid-sentence. "What the fuck? Kicked out?"

"Gambling. He saw an opportunity—lots of money, drugs, and drinking, spoiled kids on their own. He took advantage. He set up a game, business was going great. He bought himself a Porsche, maintained his grades. He got careless, got involved with a Back-Bay bitch. When she got tired of slumming, she told her father. He was young. He fucked up. But now, he is looking for a big score. Wants to move up in the business. He's got a brain, no common sense yet, but that will come."

Sal glanced at the television hung from the balcony wall. The local station, WBNK News, was showing a long caravan of police cars surrounding a flatbed truck. A tied-down tarp covered whatever had the reporter in talking head frenzy.

"Holy shit! You see this, Len?" Sal turned up the volume.

An attractive blond spoke into the camera. "The police have not yet identified the victim of this gruesome scene. No information will be available until identification is complete and next of kin are notified."

"Kim, can you update our viewers on what we know so far about this horrific tragedy?"

"Right, Bill. A local businessman, deep in Everglades National Park south of Ochopee, discovered an unidentified man being consumed by a very large python. Estimates so far have put the python at twenty-three feet in length."

"Wow, Kim, that is a big snake. It serves as a reminder to our viewers that the Everglades is a dangerous place. The local motels and campgrounds have been filling up with people enticed by the prospect of facing this fierce predator. Do we know if the victim was an amateur python hunter?"

"No, Bill, we have no information on that. We have a clip recorded earlier from Collier County Public Information Officer Chet Conklin and Fish and Wildlife Commission expert Doctor Vanessa Treehorn. Here is what they had to say about this terrifying incident."

The screen remained focused on the reporter who was busy picking at the earpiece in her ear. Her fingers moved to her mouth where it appeared she was attempting to dislodge something from her back molar. She paled as she noticed the camera still running.

"Uh, I'm sorry we seem to have some difficulty accessing the tape." She tapped her earpiece. "Oh wait, we have it now. We are sorry for the delay. Here is Officer Conklin and Doctor Treehorn from earlier today." She turned away from the camera. "What the fuck, you guys? You couldn't focus on the truck?" The reporter gave the cameraman the finger in full view of the still-filming camera.

The screen turned to a squadron of microphones that encircled the two officials. Questions were shouted from the crowd.

"You all, just wait a minute" The officer paused as the unruly reporters settled down. "I am Sergeant Chet Conklin, Public Information Officer for Collier County Sheriff's Department. With me is Doctor Vanessa Treehorn, Florida Fish and Wildlife. Let me start by saying this event is in the early stages of the investigation. We have no substantial information to impart right now. We will know more after the autopsy and a complete investigation of the scene. We will be giving an update this afternoon." He looked over his shoulder and nodded at someone behind him who was holding up four fingers. "It looks like an official statement will be coming at around 4:00 p.m. Now, I know all of you want to know how something like this could happen and if you are, in fact, safe. For that I will turn it over to Doctor Treehorn."

"Good afternoon. I am Doctor Vanessa Treehorn, consultant with Florida Fish and Wildlife Commission."

"Could you state your name?" was the first question shouted from amid the cameras and microphones.

"Doctor Vanessa Treehorn. I want to begin by assuring the public that python attacks on humans are rare in Florida. This python was extremely large by any standard. The possibility that other equally large and aggressive pythons are lurking in the swamp is remote. Still, the public needs to be aware that the Everglades is a dangerous place. Proper precautions and vigilance when entering native areas should be undertaken. At all times, guests in the National Park should leave identification with the ranger stations, along with a detailed itinerary of their routes and expected return time. The rangers will warn park visitors of any reports of dangerous activity—python, panther, or alligator sightings. We want all our visitors to be safe while enjoying the natural beauty and pristine environment that is the Everglades."

"Doctor, can you give any more information about the attack?"

"No, I have not performed a necropsy and Doctor Lefebvre, the Collier County Medical Examiner will issue a report after he concludes his autopsy. You can see by the size of the flatbed; the snake was a large one. The victim and snake have not been separated and are being transported to the morgue in one long piece."

The camera switched back to the WBNK reporter taking a deep drag on a cigarette. "Are we live?" She blew out smoke as she spoke. "That's all the information we have right now. This is Kimberly Stamper live from the scene at the intersection of Tamiami Trail and Collier Boulevard. Back to the studio with Bill Kendall."

"Thank you for your great reporting, Kim. That is a gruesome scene—more to come on that. Now to Allison on Fifth Avenue in Naples to update us on the preparations for the Ferrari Club car show coming up later this month."

"Oh, fuck," Lenny whispered.

CHAPTER 13

February 2 - Andruzzi's, Airstreams, and Ants

Louis and Dominic Andruzzi stared at the palm trees lining the runway at Marco Island Executive Airport. The small jet taxied to the south end of the park. They deplaned into blazing sunshine. The temperature, a warm eighty-two degrees, caused both brothers to sweat profusely.

The pilot placed their suitcases outside the stairs that had been wheeled up to the cabin door. "Have a nice stay Mr. Smith and Mr. Smith." He nodded at them, gave a smart salute, and walked back up the stairs.

The closest hangar was a hundred yards across the tarmac. They could barely read the small plaque with F. S. Corporation embossed in gold print. A white, older model Honda Civic was parked in the shade next to the hangar. Dominic had a bad feeling about the car.

"This is an omen, Louis. Plus, I don't think we are going to fit."

"Grab the bags, Dom."

"Pick up your own damn bag." Louis waddled across the tarmac. "I'm getting the car keys. They're carry-ons for Christ's sake. Handle it."

"Lou, I got to get out of these warm clothes. I'm sweating bullets. Which bag has the Bahamas shit in it? I'm going in the john to change."

Louis looked around the deserted runway. "I guess there's one in the hangar."

Dominic ripped the tags off his shirt as he walked out of the empty hangar. He spotted Louis opening the Honda's trunk.

"What the hell? Why would he get us a Honda, a white one, no less?"

"This car has got nothing to do with anything, Dominic."

"It's got everything to do with it," Dominic mumbled as he dumped his carry-on into the trunk.

"You say something?" Louis glared at him. "I don't want to hear any more shit about the fucking car. The pilot mentioned there was a Wal-Mart before you head down to Chokoloskee. We can stop there for food and stuff before we find the house. Instructions said the property manager has the key at the front gate."

"Are we staying in one of those gated places? We passed over some as we were landing. They look like freaking resorts."

"See, Dom, I told you this was going to work out okay."

"We'll see."

"Lighten up."

Walmart appeared just past the intersection of Tamiami Trail and Collier Boulevard. It was a comforting sight in an unfamiliar sea of lush vegetation, trailer parks, and golf courses.

"What do you think we need?"

"Paper plates and, I don't know, whatever we eat at home— TV dinners, beer, and ice.

"Chips, and onion dip, oh, and definitely Doritos."

"You think they got good fresh bread? Olive oil, garlic and onions, tomatoes." Dominic perked up at the thought of food.

"Yeah, pasta, too."

"See brother, it's like we are on vacation," Louis smiled.

"It's not bothering you?"

"Would you stop already? No. It's not bothering me. It's like I said a million times before. We've been good soldiers. We protected the family. Now we are being rewarded for our good works."

Dominic shook his head. "I won't be able to look at her."

"So, don't."

"She's going to know it was us."

"Horowitz said she knows it was an accident. He said Sal wasn't part of it. The whole family would've have been put away for life if Cacciatore's info came out. Maybe Lexie, too. We did a good thing."

"He was her husband."

"But it turned out okay, right? She's married to Sal now. She looks happy and she's rich."

"I hate that fucking car."

"Get over it, Dominic."

Walking through Walmart, Louis picked up a box of ant traps and tossed it in the cart. "I hear there's a lot of bugs in Florida."

"I'm picking up a postcard for ma. I want to mail it at that tiny post office we saw in the movie. Ochopee, I think. It's not far past the turn-off to Chokoloskee." Dominic grabbed one showing an alligator hanging out on a log. "I hope this doesn't freak her out."

"Nah, she watches all those nature shows. She'll be happy we are seeing something besides the Coney Island freak show."

Louis stopped at the exit doors and pointed at a bulletin board displaying business cards and tear-off phone numbers. "Hey, look, this board has all kinds of local information." He pulled off a handwritten tab with a phone number on it. "This guy, Rusty Pearce, is a fishing guide in the Everglades. We should give him a call. What did I tell you? This is real adventure."

A wave of hot air hit them as they exited Walmart. The car roofs in the lot mirrored the glare. Dominic reached into the shopping bag and pulled out two pairs of sunglasses.

"Good thinking, Do ."

The ride down to Chokoloskee got more and more isolated. Dominic stared at the canal running alongside Tamiami Trail. "Holy shit, Lou, stop the car."

"What? What's the matter?" Louis pulled to the side of the road.

"Look, right there at the edge of the water. I think it's an alligator."

"Wow, we just saw one on the television. He's huge. Look at the size of his jaw."

The reptile slowly edged into the water, leaving ripples as he submerged.

"Did you see what was on his back?" Dominic opened the car door.

"Dom, what are you doing? Are you crazy? Get back in the car. Those fuckers will kill you."

"Was that blood?"

"I don't think so. It was orange and green."

"I saw something on animal planet where they tag alligators so if they show up far away, they can identify them." Louis put the car in drive. "Maybe that's it."

"I saw the show, too. They attach a collar around its neck with a transmitter on it. They don't paint its fucking back." Dominic looked out the window. He could see the round bulbs of the gator's eyes hovering at water level as Louis pulled back on to the road. "Maybe its somebody's pet," he mused out loud.

"We're almost at Ochopee, write out the postcard now so we don't waste time."

The post office was even smaller than it looked in the film. Dominic asked a man photographing his family in front of the building to take a picture of the two of them posing in front of it. He had taken a dozen photos before he politely asked them to step apart, so the building was visible.

He smiled, handed the phone back to Louis and called out as he got back in the minivan, "I hope this is okay."

"Lou, let me see." Dominic grabbed the phone. "Hey, this one came out pretty good. You can even see the name of the post office. I'm going to send it to Ma."

"I'm not sure that's a good idea. Lenny said to keep this quiet."

"Who's she going to tell? She sits in her room all day at that shithole home. Doesn't know who we are most of the time." Maybe it will make her smile and remember us when she sees it."

Dominic searched through the contacts as Louis turned the car back on US 41.

CRஐ

The entrance to the complex was about a half mile down the road into Chokoloskee. Louis made the left onto a dirt lane. Low palm fronds scraped the car as they drove up to a small shack beside a metal farm gate.

"Are you sure this is it? It looks deserted."

"Louis checked the sheet Lenny had given him. "Yeah, this is it. Lenny said it was out of the way."

"This is more than out of the way."

"We are supposed to be keeping a low profile. The business needs to be out of sight and since we are a huge part of this team, no one can know we are here."

"How is David going to find us?"

"Lenny gave him all the info. He's staying in a motel until Lenny figures out the logistics."

"Wow, logistics! Aren't you the up-and-comer."

"Shut the fuck up, Dominic. Here comes the caretaker."

A skinny man with a gray ponytail and wearing dirty camo limped up to the car. "You boys the ones from up north?"

"Yes sir. Just got in a couple hours ago. Everything set for us?"

"Well, everything's about as right as it's going to be." The old guy spit a slimy wad onto the road.

Louis frowned as drops of watery brown slop splashed up onto the car.

"Bit queasy, huh? Car's going to get a lot dirtier than that. Mr. Jones said you needed something way off the main road. Only got one place vacant way in the back, hasn't been used for a while. Sent my niece down to clean it up a bit. She put some fresh sheets and towels in and turned on the air conditioner." He emitted a deep phlegmy cough. "It might take a while to get the smell out of it. You guys are lucky. The trailer is a classic. Got offers from hunters that pass by it. Best one yet was five thousand."

"Smell? classic?" Dominic stared at him in horror.

"Yeah, a classic Airstream. All original furnishings. Looks kind of like the one in that *I Love Lucy* movie. That show made me piss myself it was so funny. By the looks of you two, I'm thinking it's going to be a bit tight. Tell you what, if something larger turns up in the next few days, I'll make sure you guys get first dibs. How's that?"

"That would be great." Louis smiled. Hey, man, what's your name?"

"Ernie, but everyone calls me Shredder."

"Why is that?"

Shredder rolled up his filthy sleeve and revealed scars crisscrossing his forearm.

Dominic leaned over to see what Louis was gawking at.

"How did that happen?' Dominic croaked.

Shredder looked at his deeply scored arm and smiled proudly. "Gator, big motherfucker, too. I drug him out of the lake, him hanging on like it was his last meal. Damn near tore my arm out of the socket. But I tugged back even harder. Yanked my arm right out from between his teeth. Pretty much shredded it to the bone. Everyone round here says they ain't ever seen anyone survive an attack like that. Once a gator got a grip on you, he doesn't let go."

"You must be a local hero," Louis nodded.

"That's some heavy shit," Dominic added.

"The glades ain't for the squeamish." Shredder continued, "There's some nasty predators out here and some of them walk on two feet, if you get my drift." He coughed out another brown wad onto the drive creating a puff of dust that disappeared into the air. He reached into his pocket and pulled out a small key hanging from a large animal tooth. He handed it to Louis. "Your trailer is that way." He nodded down the dirt trail. "Hang a left at the big mangrove. It'll be on your right."

"Oh, one more thing." Louis held out the slip of paper with the phone number. "We were wondering if you knew a good fishing guide. We found this name at Wal-Mart, Rusty Pearce, he any good?"

"Well, I don't know if he's good or not. It depends if the fish are hungry. Have a good night, fellas, don't let the bed bug's bite." Shredder cackled at his joke as Louis pulled the Civic through the gate and headed down the path.

CHAPTER 14

Two Guys, Some Beer, and a Pizza

The dirt road narrowed, and the car bumped over large dirt piles, fallen palm fronds, and broken tree limbs. The airstream appeared between the dense vegetation. Louis pulled the car alongside the rusted trailer, mowing down the overgrown sawgrass. Swatting away the sharp barbs, he heard Dominic curse as he exited the car.

"Fucking grass bit me. Nobody mentioned even the grass has teeth."

"It's sawgrass."

"Good name."

"The blades of sawgrass have sharp barbs that can cut you."

"Thanks for the timely update, Lou. Anything else I need to worry about?"

"Alligators like to hang out in the streams around sawgrass fields. Might be hard to spot them."

"Let's get our stuff in the trailer before something else gets us. I'm starving. Wait." Dominic picked up an open bag of chips from the back seat. He grabbed a fistful and offered the open bag to Louis. "We've got to remember anything open is going to get stale quick. You want some?"

Louis shoved a fistful in his mouth, crumbs falling onto his shirt. He slammed the car door. Juggling the chip bag, he reached in the trunk for the Walmart bags.

"Hey, don't hog the chips."

Louis tossed the bag towards Dominic who missed the throw. The chips spilled on the dirt path that led to the door of the trailer "You were never an athlete. Now you'll have to climb the step without fuel for your fat ass."

"Fuck you. First thing we do is open the beer and put the pizza in the oven.

"Frozen pizza, Dom? Anything ever make you lose your appetite?"

"Can't think of anything."

Louis rearranged the bags. "I got a free hand, give me the key." He eyed the tiny front step and noticed the overhang was riddled with termite holes and the small clearing around the trailer had mounds of dirt rising out of the weeds. "Hey, Dom, you'd think they would've cleaned up the yard for new tenants."

"You see that guy at the gate? You think he was coming back here with a weed whacker? The only thing he's whacking is his petrified stick."

"That was a good one. I'll be surprised if his niece showed up to clean the place." Louis slapped at a mosquito. "It didn't look this bad in the pictures. Anyways, nobody knows we are here, and the place is deserted."

"This would be a good way to get rid of loose ends. Look around, Lou." Dominic shrugged. "I'm just saying."

"Will you relax? We're in good standing now. We got respect. We're almost-made men."

"Respect from who?" Dominic wiped his face with a sweat-soaked handkerchief and placed it around his neck. "Horowitz is the only one who knows about the salvage yard. Wouldn't he be better off if we were out of the way? David doesn't know about Cacciatore."

"Lenny has it all figured out. David is doing the first pickup. Our job will be distribution. Once the first drop goes off okay, we can set up a network." Louis tested the first step tentatively with one foot.

"Really? A network? Who do we know around here we can bring in? Shredder? I don't think so, and David is so smart he got kicked out of school. None of this feels right. Open the door. It's hot out here. The frozen dinners are probably cooking."

After squeezing through the narrow trailer door, they were greeted by a blast of cool air and a faint smell of air freshener. Louis dropped the plastic grocery bags on the small counter directly across from the door. The air conditioner was humming loudly, and the place felt cooler than the oppressive heat outside. Opposite the door the small kitchenette had a sink, a half-size refrigerator with a freezer and an electric range top with two burners A new dishtowel with the tags still attached hung on the wall oven next to the front door. Dominic opened the oven and placed a frozen pizza on the baking sheet that was inside. He turned the heat up to three hundred fifty degrees.

A small sofa took up the front of the trailer. Adjacent to the sink were bench chairs and a table that dropped down to form a single bed. The chair cushions were doubled over and would roll out to become a mattress. To the left of the kitchen area were three bifold doors.

Opening the nearest door, Dominic found a very small bathroom with the showerhead located in the middle of the room. A corner sink and the toilet were almost directly beneath the shower. Clean towels were folded atop the toilet seat and soaps and shampoos from a Holiday Inn were in a basket in the sink.

Dominic laughed out loud. "This is going to save a lot of time. I'm thinking it would be easier to take a whiz outside."

"There's no fucking way I'm going out there at night." Louis pointed to the door directly in front of Dominic. "That has got to be the bedroom." He pushed past Dominic.

"Hold on, let me back-up. There isn't enough room." Dominic sucked in his gut, trying to let Louis pass.

Louis inched forward.

"What the fuck?" Dominic sucked in tighter. "Now we're stuck. You're an idiot. You got to have a little patience."

"I just wanted to get the suitcases on the bed."

"We're going to need a schedule in here." Dominic shifted his left leg towards the kitchen. "Try to move now. Suck in more and twist your shoulder."

Louis pulled himself past and opened the door opposite the bathroom. Inside was a miniscule closet with a Dust Buster and broom hanging on the door. Three bent wire hangars

hung from the twelve-inch rod. A bucket and mop, still damp, sat on the closet floor. "Looks like she mopped the floor."

"That's a good thing. See? This isn't so bad."

"Dom, you are amazing you can find a bright spot in anything. No wait, I know why you're so happy, you smell the pizza cooking. Door number three has got to be the bedroom."

Two twin beds against the outside walls were separated by a small dresser with a yellowed lace doily and an alarm clock on the top. A large window extended almost the full length of the back wall. A floral blanket and crisp white sheets already turned down covered the beds.

"Move over. Let me see." Dominic peered past Louis. "This isn't so bad."

Louis dropped his carry-on on the bed.

"I need a beer." Turning around, Dominic reached the kitchen in one step.

"Hey, Dom, toss me a bag of Doritos. I'm going to sit in here and read the paper until the pizza's done."

"Sure thing. Catch!" Dominic finished putting away the food. He made sure everything was closed and sealed. He hated bugs, was allergic to bees, and the last thing he wanted was roaches in the cabinets. The place looked clean, but the cloying smell of jasmine freshener was overpowering. He removed a semi-cold beer and downed it in three gulps. He reached for another and finished it as he stacked TV dinners in the freezer. Finishing the second beer, he grabbed a third and opened the oven. The pizza cheese was bubbling. He grabbed the dishtowel to pull out the baking sheet and slid the pie back onto the open pizza box.

"Hey, Lou! Pizzas done. I'm already two brews ahead." Looking into the bedroom, he saw Louis sound asleep on one of the beds. "Guess I'm going have to finish the six pack and pie by myself," he mumbled.

Dominic opened the door of the trailer to get rid of the flowery smell. He settled his bulk on the small sofa and turned on *The Price is Right*. Folding over a slice of pie, he smiled. *This is the life.* He looked around. *If you used your imagination, this trailer could be a beach hut in Tahiti.* With pizza cheese hanging from his bottom lip and his fingers still holding the crust of his third slice, Dominic fell asleep, oblivious to the hum of the air conditioner, the scent of Jasmine, the wildly screaming crowd on the television, and the line of fire ants marching through the open trailer door.

<h1 style="text-align:center">CHAPTER 15</h1>

February 3 – Death is part of life

"Is everything okay, Detective?" Dr. Treehorn whispered as she loosened Pete's belt.

"Uh, yes." Pete cleared his throat.

"You understand the logic for keeping the body inside the snake?"

"Uh, yes." Pete waggled his head.

"Is that a negative, Detective?"

"No, definitely not a negative."

"Let me show you exactly what happened when the victim slid into …"

Pete's early morning dream featured herpetologist, Vanessa Treehorn, practicing her reptile imitation by flicking her tongue as she slithered towards the foot of the bed. She would be in maximum pleasure territory any moment—almost there! The phone screamed and Vanessa disappeared into the morning glare.

"This better be good," Pete growled into his phone.

"Did I wake you from your beauty sleep, Princess?"

"Shut up, Charlie."

"Ooh, touchy this morning. You alone? I hope so. You're a dick when you wake up."

"Sort of…" Pete lifted the sheet and shook his head at what might have been. "I was dreaming."

"Jeez, Pete, you're too old for that. If I had to guess, I'm thinking your imaginary playmate was the snake lady, right? She called the office this morning and asked for you. I offered to help her, but she pushed me off. I think she's hot for you."

"I doubt that. She's probably got a rich boyfriend up in Naples."

"I'm sure you're right. Someone that smart and beautiful wouldn't be alone and she's

not waiting for someone like you. Though she did sound disappointed you weren't available." Charlie's deep laugh rumbled through the phone. "I probably misheard. Her heavy sigh might have been for the rich boyfriend in bed next to her."

"Go to hell, Hernandez."

"Maybe I should have mentioned you're a foul-mouthed reprobate, and you never show up for work on-time. Anyway, I gave her your cell number."

Pete checked his phone for missed calls, "She hasn't called me."

"It's only been a half hour. Also, the M.E. called. He's working on python boy's autopsy.

He wants us to go down to the morgue."

"Let me get a cup of coffee, and I'll head in."

The drive from Goodland to Naples was the usual bumper car ritual, seemingly driverless Taurus's and Chevies heading to bridge games and executive golf courses. Landscape trucks cut off moving vans heading into half-built golf club communities. Pickups and Harleys trailing over-sized American flags roared down the center lane of Tamiami Trail. Pete's headache exploded into technicolor rainbows, the aftereffects of drowning the memories of yesterday's Everglade's field trip.

His cell phone rang and went to Bluetooth, "Landry."

"Hi, It's Vanessa Treehorn."

Oh God, that's a sexy name. He looked down at his jeans, suddenly a bit too tight.

"Hey, Vanessa, good to hear from you. What's up?"

"I'm in Naples at the ... I performed..."

A loud grinding sound interrupted her words. Pete yelled. "I can't hear you, what's that noise?"

"I'll head into the hall—just a minute. Is that better? I'm at the M.E.'s office. The noise was the saw cutting into the Python victim's skull."

"Hasn't he suffered enough? Now a beautiful woman is watching his innermost secrets get ripped open."

"You're very funny, Detective Landry."

"I think it's sexy you are calling me from the morgue." He held his breath waiting for her to unleash a barrage of man-hating epithets. Instead, he heard Vanessa laugh. He doubled down. "Kind of kinky, I like that in a woman."

"This is serious business. I'd like to keep this professional."

"Sure thing, I'd do anything to please you."

"This could be considered sexual harassment."

"Only if you want it to be. Me, I'm just kidding around with a colleague. It's the pedal on the right, lady!" He shouted out the window.

"What?"

"Oh, sorry, there is an old lady doing about twenty miles per hour clogging up 41. What's going on in Castle Frankenstein?"

"Dr. Lefebvre is working on the victim. I performed a simultaneous necropsy on the python."

"Excuse me?"

"An autopsy on the python. The victim was being ingested. Separating the head didn't have the desired effect. Absorption had begun and it was impossible to remove him from the python without compromising the remains. He was partially dissolved. The integrity of the victim is important when searching for evidence and cause of death."

"That must be quite a scene."

"It was unique. It required two gurneys clamped lengthwise to the autopsy table to accommodate the python and the five-foot six-inch frame of the deceased. Even with that, there was drape over the ends. Dr. Lefebvre called in his entire staff to assist with the forensic investigation."

"Sorry I'm missing this. Hope you got pictures."

"You're a sick man."

"No, I mean for my investigation, I need photographs for when I put my case together. I'm very thorough. So, did you find anything interesting?"

"Well, Dr. Lefebvre hasn't finished his postmortem. I completed what I could get done on the python without disturbing the human remains."

"Find anything interesting?"

"I haven't written up my report yet, and I haven't completed the rest of the necropsy, but the python has offered up a few choice morsels. Dr. Lefebvre has the victim's personal property."

"I'm just pulling into the lot. I'll stop in the cutting room. I want to get a look at this. May I bring you a cup of coffee?"

"Sure, I could use one. Black, one Splenda, please. I'm working down the hall in the conference room."

Twenty minutes later, Pete opened the door to the conference room to find Vanessa Treehorn sitting cross-legged on the table. Her shoulder length auburn hair was gleaming in the sunlight streaming in through the windows. Her long legs were encased in black leggings. A black tank top hugged her tanned body.

"Wow, that's a professional pose. Do yoga?"

"Why, yes."

"I can tell."

Vanessa slid off the table and walked to a nearby chair, where a long floral shirt and a white lab coat rested. She picked up the silky tunic and slipped it over her head. Pete sighed as it dropped over her pert breasts. She buttoned the starched lab coat and donned a pair of black cat's-eye glasses. The transformation complete, Vanessa's hazel eyes fixed on Pete's slack-jawed expression.

"Wow, that was like porn in reverse," Pete whispered and took a sip of coffee.

"I heard that." Vanessa picked up a folder on the tabletop. "The harassment thing is still pending."

"Well, it could be me who brings up the case." He pushed a cup of coffee towards her.

"I needed a good stretch. The floor looked unsanitary, so I made use of the table. I've been up all night, and I'm full of kinks. I haven't found a good yoga studio yet."

"Health nut?"

"I don't eat meat, try to keep my life in balance. My transfer down here has thrown most of that out the window."

Pete's thoughts ping-ponged around his brain. Herpetologists were not supposed to look this hot. Her moist red lips accentuated her white teeth as she nibbled at her lower lip. He took a deep inhale, smiled at the scent of her perfume, and decided to try and be professional, although his brain screamed for him to play his hand and go all in. This was not the time. He shook his head, trying to stay focused on the case.

Vanessa standing beside the window flipped the pages on her clipboard. Her white lab coat glowed in the sunlight. Pete squinted at the hazy glare which surrounded her, "Doctor Treehorn, you should have waited five minutes. I could have helped you stretch. I'm good at it. I'm almost a chiropractor."

"How is that? You go to school?"

"No, but I've broken or torn most of my bones and ligaments, endured countless hours of physical therapy, and survived a hot summer with a lovely chiropractor. I have a knack for stretching and relaxing tension-filled muscles." She rolled her eyes and chuckled.

"Sounds obscene."

"Really, I'm good at it. It's a gift. I've even done Charlie. Wow, that sounded bad. Anyway, just ask him."

"I think we need to get down to business."

"It's exactly what he said this morning."

Vanessa winced. "Enough, Detective." Her tone changed abruptly to exasperation. "We can save the banter for later."

"Business, right." Pete shrugged. "Okay. What have you got for me?"

Vanessa threw him a disapproving look and said, "Let's walk down to the autopsy room, I have something to show you." She continued speaking as Pete followed her. "Did the M.E. discuss the case with you?"

"No, he was busy playing with his new autopsy saw—the MOPEC 1000. He was like a kid at Christmas. I told him he could have saved the county some money and borrowed mine. I have one just like it in my toolbox except it's black and yellow. Why don't you bring me up to speed?"

"Dr. Lefebvre has inventoried the victim's personal effects. Ted, the Medical Examiner assistant, laid it all out to dry. He knew you would want to look at the evidence."

As they passed though the opaque double doors of the anterior examination room, Pete looked over at Vanessa. Not even a nose wrinkle of disgust, he thought, as the horrendous odor of death and chemicals hung thick in the air around them. In front of them the room was alive with activity as the M.E. staff worked on a half dozen corpses stacked up like planes on a runway outside the autopsy room. Assistants took prints from stiff fingers and photographed cadavers. Phones were ringing and a radio blared classic rock. A deputy M. E. sideswiped him with a gurney, the sheet slipped off and Pete caught a glimpse of a grey face. He reached down and read the toe tag. He recognized the name; he had busted him twice for possession. The cause of death was overdose. *That sucks. I heard he was doing okay.* He looked over at Vanessa's inscrutable face. She doesn't seem to be bothered by any of this. Why would a little death and chaos upset her? She beheaded a live python. He followed her as she maneuvered around the bodies.

Vanessa turned and pointed to a plastic covered gurney at the back of the room. "It's over there."

"Did we get an ID on the body?"

"No, his prints were already dissolved." She pointed to a damp and discolored piece of oversized paper, a car key with a Dodge logo on it, and a cell phone.

"And this was found where?"

"In what remained of the pockets of John Doe's cargo pants. About a foot deep inside the python."

She picked up a bag of rags from the metal shelf beneath the table. "These are what's left of the victim's clothing. She picked up a second bag containing a still pristine pair of Sperry Topsiders. "That's everything."

"Gross, but very cool," Pete looked around at the bedlam of the exam room and back at Vanessa's composed demeanor. "None of this bothers you?"

"Death is part of life. I grew up on a farm. I have two older brothers. I've been dissecting snakes and toads since I was a kid. To answer your question, no. There's not much that bothers me."

"Doctor, I don't want to insult you, but a kid, dissecting things? That's weird. You could be best friends with Lefebvre."

"Reptiles. And I didn't kill them. When I found one, already dead, I wanted to learn what was inside of them. My dad bought me a dissection kit for my twelfth birthday."

"So, in high school I'm guessing nobody was chasing you around the biology lab with dead frogs."

"No, actually it was the other way around."

"You must have been very popular."

"I didn't really care." She turned to a cabinet behind her. Pete could have sworn he heard the words "until now." She turned back to him and held out a pair of rubber gloves. "Here, you better put these on."

Pete took out his cell phone and snapped pictures of the three items, before putting the gloves on. "Has the Crime Scene Unit shown up yet? This stuff must be dusted for prints."

"Not yet, but they won't find any prints. The acid that breaks down the python's meal would have already obliterated any fingerprints."

Dr. Lefebvre's voice drifted out of the open autopsy room door, "This saw is the best. Ted, here, try it out, this bone right here." The saw snarled in a short burst. "See? Best three grand we've ever spent."

Pete looked towards the door. "You have to admire someone who really loves his work."

"This has been an eye-opening experience." Vanessa winced as the saw started up again. "I don't spend a lot of time dealing with humans, dead or alive."

Pete took a deep breath, leaned over the table, and scanned the paper. "Have you looked at this chart?"

"Yes. It survived the initial absorption. Most of it is readable. A route is highlighted. Some handwritten notes on the edges may be legible with delicate cleaning and enhancement but not now. No names or other identifiers."

"This is interesting." Pete leaned in to get a closer look. "Navigation charts are readily available in most sporting goods store. They're usually laminated. This is a paper copy possibly pulled off a computer. It is legal document size, eight and a half by fourteen, mostly used for wills or deeds of sale."

"Is that important?"

"It could be. If someone didn't want to go into a store and purchase this or leave a trail as to its origin, they would look it up and print it out from their computer. No bill of sale. No way to search for the purchase. Most people don't use legal sized paper." Pete wrote something in a small pad he took out of his back pocket.

"Detective, you are going to love this next clue." Pete's eyes followed her deep purple nails as they disappeared into a pair of bright blue rubber gloves. She picked up the cell phone. "It's a throwaway. It can be purchased anywhere. It's brand new, no data used. Password set to 0000. Here's the amazing part."

She squeezed the phone and placed it on the plastic cloth. A small screen lit up a ghostly green; in the center, a red dot flashed. The phone emitted a pinging sound as it vibrated on the table. "It's set to a GPS app and it's still locating. It's fixing on a point in the Everglades, and the transmitter is slowly moving."

"You know, Doctor Treehorn, you would make a great detective."

"Never been my calling." She picked up her coffee, took a sip and wrinkled her nose. "Hmm, lukewarm."

"I've got to call Charlie; hope he gassed up his airboat. We're going for a ride."

"You looking for me? Good morning, Doctor Treehorn." Charlie nodded towards the autopsy room. "What's up with the ghoul-meister?"

"Charlie, my man, Lefebvre is happily sawing the shit out of python boy right now. How's that boat doing? She ready for a ride?"

"Yeah, she's running fine, why?"

"Doctor Treehorn has presented us with a clue." He pointed to the blinking GPS app and continued. "This, my friend, is a phone tracking a GPS transmitter located somewhere in the Ten Thousand Islands area. The phone was found inside John Doe's pocket." Pete pointed to the chart. "We have a treasure map."

Charlie nodded at the chart. "You get a picture of it?"

"Of course." Pete put on a hurt expression.

Charlie pretended not to notice. "Print it out, okay? Is that a Dodge Key?"

"Yep, ten bucks it fits the stolen Caravan." Pete pretended to reach for his wallet.

"Not playing any sucker bets, Pete."

Vanessa interrupted, "Detectives, we have no idea how long the battery will last. Presumably, the device has been in harsh conditions for at least two days. I think the sooner we get out there the better."

"Agreed." Charlie picked up the phone and headed towards the door.

"Wait." She offered Charlie a pen. "You both need to sign off on this evidence before we go anywhere."

"She's a stickler for protocol, Charlie. She's going to make us better detectives. How long will it take to get to the spot?"

Charlie rolled his eyes, "We need to enlarge the map on the receiver and then we can figure that out. Don't want to spend the night out there." Charlie signed the form. "I'm going to work on this."

"That's great. Vanessa and I will put together what we'll need out in the Glades. I'm thinking a nice Chardonnay. What do you think, Vanessa? Maybe you can scare up some frog legs."

"Funny, Pete. That's what you came up with?" Vanessa smiled. "I wonder if I've ever heard that joke before."

Charlie headed to the door, stopped to glare at them. "The glades are serious business, take it down a notch, Pete. Vanessa, I know you're an expert in reptiles, so I think you can handle yourself." He smirked at Pete. "It's not going to be a picnic; I'll bring the machete. Wait. Vanessa, do you have a carry permit?"

"Yes, my position requires that I be armed when doing search and rescue in the Everglades."

Pete grinned—a beautiful, gun-carrying herpetologist. It just keeps getting better. "Charlie, call me when you get the search area down and we'll meet at the dock."

CHAPTER 16

Fire Ants

The drive to Everglades City went quickly. No tourists in rented Toyotas traveled below the speed limit, no overloaded tractor-trailers, not one dead armadillo, not even an errant alligator. Pete knew this portended bad news. The alley was one screw-up of a road—two lanes and no way to escape. Swamp and canal cozied up to the blacktop, no shoulders to speak of—delays always. They were supposed to meet Charlie in Everglades City around noon. It was ten-thirty a.m., and Café de Havana's *huevos rancheros* were calling Pete's name.

"So, Doctor Treehorn, how does breakfast sound? We've got time to kill."

"Don't be so formal. Call me Doctor. Maybe Charlie will be early. He's probably going to have a smooth ride, too."

"Really? That's what you think? How long have you been down here?" Pete parked in front of the restaurant.

"Three months. I've been stationed up north of Tampa." Vanessa walked over to a quaint bistro table tucked beneath a flowering bougainvillea tree.

The menu wasn't necessary; Pete ordered breakfast for the two of them. He splashed a dot of fresh cream in his coffee and enjoyed the view of Vanessa sipping her tea.

"I can't believe you haven't been here yet. This place is gold." His words broke the silence.

"It is lovely." Vanessa looked around at the intimate dining alcoves nestled among the flowers. She scooped up freshly made green chili with a crisp tortilla and sighed contentedly. "It is a nice juxtaposition from my early morning at the morgue."

"I don't mean to pry, but speaking of the morgue, why did you transfer to the Everglades? Tampa is an exciting place."

"I requested it. My field is snakes. I offered my expertise on the python problem."

"That's been going on for years. They finally decided to send an expert." Pete smiled as he scooped fresh salsa and egg atop a wedge of tortilla. "I'm glad they did."

"Most people don't realize pythons are a real menace to the ecology of the Everglades. They're wreaking havoc on the small animal population. Her expression darkened. "Raccoons, rabbits, squirrels, bobcats, foxes—all their numbers have dropped dramatically. It is devastating."

"What's the answer?"

"Eradicate this non-native predator. It is open season on pythons from now on."

Despite the serious conversation, Vanessa seemed to savor every bite of her breakfast. She pierced a slice of mango with her fork and rolled her eyes with pleasure. "This is delicious, Pete."

"I told you, right? Stick by me, I know where all the best food is."

Pete leaned back savoring the rich flavor of his dark roast coffee. "What is the new deal on hunting pythons?"

"No more permits. They are going to pay anyone who bags a python. They'll have to register before they hunt and bring in the kill for verification."

"So now we have even less control of circus clowns in airboats with AR-15's shooting up the mangroves. They come down in their RV's loaded up with ammo, beer kegs, and moonshine. Investigating gunshot snake hunters was giving me a ton of overtime. I might be retiring at the wrong time."

"This program gives us more accurate controls on the count of pythons, and if these contractors want the money they need to sign up. People will still be able to turn in pythons that they kill on their property."

"Fat chance of that happening. A lot of these idiots don't want their names on any paperwork."

"If the contractors want the money, that is the deal. It's working, Pete."

"Excuse me, they are called contractors. How much are they getting paid?"

"Yes, the Python Removal Contractor program is looking for qualified individuals who will be paid monthly at the rate of around nine dollars an hour and will receive two hundred dollars for removal of non-native constrictor nests verified by FWC. There are extra payments, too. They will earn fifty dollars for each python under four feet and twenty-five dollars a foot for pythons over four feet."

Pete squinted his eyes. "That was well-rehearsed."

"It was my boss's idea. I helped with the details."

"Let me get this straight. If somebody bags a snake, and it is verified, they get paid, right? I'm thinking that our python is worth about five hundred bucks. Who gets that money? Can't give it to the dead guy, even though he found it. Next comes Bees. He might have a claim."

Vanessa, seeming to enjoy the game, grinned and replied, "Well, technically, I'm the one who killed it."

"But you work for FWC which disqualifies you. I think Bees should get it. Public interest in the Sasquatch has been waning. Besides, he could use the cash."

"I'll look into it."

"It must be mayhem out there. Did anybody tell them there was a dead guy in the glades who was eaten by a python, and one can assume, not registered as a contractor? Doctor, the National Park Service is basically paying an army of assholes."

"It turns out those hapless hunters have killed a lot of pythons."

Carlos, the proprietor, and chef, walked behind Pete, "Excuse me for interrupting. Detective, there is a disturbance out front that may require your attention. I already called 911. I thought you would want to be informed."

"Carlos, why so formal?"

"I didn't want to upset the lady."

"Not a lady, a doctor. Believe me, there isn't much that upsets her."

A sizable crowd had gathered out front of the café. Pete pushed his way through. The center of attention was a red-faced man, in his early forties. His filthy sweatshirt and waders suggested he was local. A voice behind him whispered, "Thank God, Pete's here."

The man staggered and swayed back and forth. A low groan escaped the masses.

"What's the problem, sir?" Pete recoiled at the smell coming off him, the man was shaking violently, and puke crumbs clung to his beard.

"I opened the door."

"Excuse me? What door? Where was this?"

"I mean the door opened by itself. Yeah. I knocked and it swung open. I was supposed to take them fishing."

"Take a deep breath sir. What door? Where? Are you okay?"

"No. I'm not okay."

"Are you injured? What is your name sir?"

"Rusty, I'm Rusty Pearce. I'm a fishing guide." This seemed to calm him down a bit.

Pete spoke with a quiet measured tone. "So, Mr. Pearce, tell me what happened."

"The room was full of them. Millions of them. The guys, I think they were guys, were huge, bloated, but covered, too, just giant shapes that seemed to be moving. But it wasn't those guys moving."

Rusty bent over and retched violently; vomit splayed across Pete's shoes. The crowd drew back, except for Vanessa, who seemed intent on staring at the shaking man.

"What did you see, Rusty?" Pete urged.

"Ants." Vanessa whispered from behind Pete. "Fire ants."

Rusty Pearce collapsed in a heap in front of them. A single ant crawled out of the collar of his shirt.

The chaos erupted immediately, screams and gagging, as patrons and residents, stared bug-eyed at the lone ant now crawling down Pearce's arm. No one noticed Vanessa Treehorn. In one swift motion, she pulled a small item from her pocketbook, her arm shot out from behind Pete knocking him aside as she stabbed Mr. Pearce waist high. The syringe remained upright as she jumped back. A platoon of ants marched single file from inside the waders, headed to the pavement and south down Smallwood Drive.

Within seconds, his eyes opened wide, an eerie wail erupted from his lips, drowning out the sirens of the approaching emergency vehicles. The crowd backed off from the scene and gathered a half-block north.

Charlie Hernandez walked up to Pete and Vanessa. "I figured you'd be at the center of this." Looking at the now shaking, vomit-covered man with an epi-pen sticking out of him and the trail of fire ants exiting the waders, Charlie chuckled, "Who's today's lucky winner?"

"His name is Rusty Pearce, and we've got to follow those ants." Pete pointed down the road.

"Gentlemen." Vanessa stepped back from Mr. Pearce and turned her attention to Pete and Charlie. "I need to remind you we've got to get moving. I can charge up the cell phone, but we don't know how long the transmitter will remain active."

"Charlie, she's right. If this is connected to Python Boy, we need to be on it from the start."

A young deputy approached them. "Excuse me, Detective Landry?"

"Do I know you?" Pete asked.

"Yes, sir, I'm Dan Barnes. We met at the sheriff's family picnic a few years ago. I was pitching for my father's softball team."

"Oh yeah, you're the high school kid who blew us off the field. First time we ever lost that game. Wow, you're on the job now? Congrats, Deputy Barnes."

Pete looked at Vanessa. "Deputy Barnes, this is Doctor Treehorn, she is a consultant with FWC."

"Pleasure to meet you, ma'am. I saw you on the news yesterday."

"Nice to meet you, too, Deputy. If you don't mind my saying, you look sharp in your brand-new uniform. You should be on a recruitment poster."

"Thank you, Doctor Treehorn." Dan blushed and turned towards Pete. "Detective Landry, I've listened to my dad's stories about your career. You've sort of been my role model for a long time."

"I think you should have higher standards." Charlie laughed. "Your dad is Deputy Superintendent now. That is something to go for."

"No sir, it's not for me. I want to be hands-on, not deskbound and doing paperwork."

"Police work is a lot of pen-pushing. You know what they say: hours of boredom, moments of terror." Pete shook his head. "You'll see."

"No disrespect to my father, but the way he has spoken about you during your career, the stories he told during dinner time had us rolling. He thinks you're pretty special."

"Ah, kid, you're going to make me cry. When did you get on the job?" Pete asked.

"Last class out of the academy." Dan Barnes smiled broadly. "Three weeks now. I did my ride along in Fort Meyers."

"That's why we haven't seen you at headquarters." Charlie stepped on an ant wandering towards them.

"My Dad says you are about ready to retire. I've been hoping for an opportunity to work with you."

"Crazy wears on you after a while." Pete's expression softened. "Tell you what. I have a stinker of a case working now. I think I could use a hand. I'll put a call in to the office. How's that sound?"

Dan's eyes lit up. "That would be an honor, sir."

"Not sure your dad would agree." Pete shook his head. "He and I have butted heads a few times about my methods."

"I have heard nothing but good about you, sir."

"Stop calling me sir. If we are going to work together, you need to call me Obi Wan. Hah, only kidding. Please call me Pete."

"Thank you, sir, umm, Pete. Everybody calls me Danny. I'll get back to calming down the crowd."

"No, wait a minute. Charlie? Danny and I will follow the ant brigade. Looks like Pearce came from Shredder's place. You need to get moving on the signal." He turned to Vanessa. "Your call on where your expertise would be most useful."

Vanessa didn't hesitate. "I think I would be of better use in the airboat. I'm not an entomologist."

"Okay. You on board with this, Charlie?"

"Yeah. Be safe, Pete. Show that kid how it's done."

"You too, Charlie. Happy hunting. And Vanessa? Next meal, I promise we'll get to finish."

CHAPTER 17

Lucy, I'm Home

"Dan, you see that line of ants?"

"Yes, sir, they're heading down towards the gate."

Pete nosed the cruiser up to the gate and got out of the car. "We need to talk to Shredder. First thing you should do is get to know the locals, especially the quiet ones. Schmooze them up a bit. You may make a friend or two. Take my friend Shredder, real character, local color. He's a nice guy. I let him beat me at pool; he keeps his eyes open for me. Makes a call when he hears something squishy. I bet you already have some connections. You went to Collier High, right? Cougars' baseball was undefeated your senior year. Your dad was proud of your pitching."

"Some guys who lived down here were on my team."

"You are still friendly with them?"

"Some, not too many left. We grab a beer at Stan's Idle Hour now and then. Most have gone north. A few went off to college, others just disappeared. Not much of a future in the Glades unless you like gators or become a cop."

"You are already ahead of the game. Let's get to work."

Shredder was bent over a disemboweled Vespa, a wrench held threateningly above the engine.

"Hey, man, what did that Italian bitch do to deserve this? You know Vespa means wasp?"

"Wasp. That makes sense. She stung me bad."

"Kind of like your ex?"

"Don't go there, Pete. Who's the kid?"

"Deputy Dan Barnes, let me introduce you to my old friend, Shredder. Shredder? This young man is Deputy Barnes. He is working on a case with me. We'd appreciate if you could give us a little help on a developing situation."

Pete shuffled his feet. "A clue is crawling down Smallwood Drive and heading our way as we speak."

Shredder gave Danny a long look. "I'm always ready to help you guys. I'd be dead if it wasn't for Pete and Charlie."

"Why's that, sir?" Dan's eyes bugged as Shredder rolled up his sleeve.

Pete laughed. "There you go with the sir, again. Shredder, how do you like to be addressed?"

"Shredder's the moniker Pete gave me a few years back and I'm damn proud of it." Shredder pulled a tin out of his pocket, a huge wad of black tobacco disappeared between yellowed teeth. "Pete and Charlie shot the gator who chewed up my arm." He rolled the sleeve down. "What's this big clue coming our way?"

"Not big, little and nasty." Pete nodded to the line of fire ants marching past the now open gate. "You see anything out of the ordinary around here lately?"

"You kidding? Weird shit happens every day." Shredder expertly spat a wad at the ants. The trail of insects detoured around the brown puddle.

"Let's start with today. See anything strange?"

"Well, yeah, about an hour ago a guy comes running down the road headed towards town. I was right here working on the bitch's carburetor. I yelled after him, but he was moaning and wailing. I figured it wasn't my problem."

"Don't you think a distressed individual running out of the property you oversee might denote a problem, sir?" Dan asked.

Shredder snorted. "You best teach your junior explorer here some manners, Pete."

"Well, he's got a point."

"Deputy, us locals like to be finessed a little before we get to the heart of things. Tell him how it works here in the glades, Pete."

"Shredder, most times we are out here looking for lost dogs, or maybe kids mucking around in their daddy's airboats or maybe a little night hunting. No big rush. But this is a little different. Fuck me if we don't have an honest-to-God mystery on our hands. Not what I was hoping for my last month on the job. But here we are, and you might be able to offer up some help."

"No shit? You're giving up all this glamour? Well, that's a damn shame. I'm sorry to hear this. You're a might young to be checking out."

"This job takes years off you."

"You got a plan, for you know, after?"

Pete shrugged. "I don't know, maybe spend a month sleeping in and fishing."

"Well, I don't know about that. But, hey, it's your life." Shredder frowned, wiped his grease-covered hands on his overalls, and extended his gnarled right hand out to Danny Barnes. "You got some big boots to fill, Deputy. Detective Landry's got the respect of everybody round here."

Shredder looked down the road towards the swamp. "The guy I mentioned before? He was wearing waders. He came running down from the back end of the trailer park. There's a small boat ramp back there. Not many folks know about it. Yesterday afternoon, two big guys from up north checked into the old airstream near the ramp. These guys didn't look like hunters or fisherman. They had one of them tear off phone numbers like you find on bulletin boards. They were asking if the guy on the paper was a good fishing guide. Think his name was Pearce.

"Dan, we need to check out the ramp. Maybe he left his boat there. Shredder, we'll be back in a few minutes."

"Wait, I just remembered. I haven't seen them big fellas go past since then. Don't think they are too comfortable in that small tin can. I was going to put them in a double wide if one opened. If you see them, let them know that a family further up their road is checking out tomorrow."

"Will do, Shredder."

Driving through the rusted gates, Pete muttered, "Gates of Hell."

"Excuse me? You say something?" Danny fidgeted as Pete drove slowly around a huge mangrove in the middle of the trail. "Did you say gates of hell?"

"Matthew 16:18: And I tell you that you are Peter, and on this rock, I will build my church, and the gates of hell shall not prevail against it." My grandmother used to read the Bible to my brother and me. She told us that only the bravest could walk through the gates into the jaws of hell and defeat evil. Since my name was Peter, I took it to heart."

"Wow, my grandmother used to make us lemonade and read us *Harry Potter.*"

"That's not that much different: brave kids and scary monsters. I see the airstream ahead. White Honda parked on the left."

Pete pulled behind a trash bin set off to the side of the dirt trail. Stepping out of the cruiser, he did a little jig as he avoided the fire ants crawling around the base of the Dumpster.

"This place is overrun with the little bastards. Ow, one of them just bit me. That burns like a son- of-a-bitch. Watch your step, Dan."

"You know I will. I hate those things. Got bit up bad on a boy scout camping trip when I was ten. Lucky I wasn't allergic. The scoutmaster ended up in the hospital. My parents took me out of scouts and signed me up for year-round baseball camps."

Walking carefully, Pete could see the boat ramp about twenty yards past the old trailer. There was an airboat boat tied up. In front of him, the airstream was covered with rust yet seemed solid; there were no obvious holes or broken windows.

Pete spoke softly as he headed towards the trailer. "When we finish inside, we'll need to check out that boat."

"Hey, Pete, the ant brigade is moving around the trailer."

"Something disturbed these ants. They're aggressive but usually the nest must be bothered for this many to be swarming."

Dan walked towards the white Honda, bent down and looked underneath. "Son-of-a bitch. Those guys parked right on top of a huge ant mound."

"Assholes." Pete shook his head in disgust. "These jokers show up thinking they're going to kill pythons, poach gators, or nab a big ole catfish, but they don't know shit about the glades and what they're getting into. Take these ants. You think they would've done a little research before they got here. They probably thought their biggest worry was mosquitos."

Dan walked slowly towards the trailer. His eyes swept the ground looking for anything unusual. He noticed ants were feasting on pieces of corn chips leading to the trailer door. There was a fresh new ant trap set out on the step. "Idiots," he muttered.

Pete smiled. "You are going to do just fine, my friend."

Dan avoided the swarm and walked closer to the trailer. "The door is open."

"Let's see what's up with our inept visitors." Getting close to the door, a faint flowery odor layered over something more ominous wafted past his nose. Pete drew his weapon and tapped on the doorframe. "Collier County Sheriff's Department. We are checking to see if everything is all right with you gentlemen. We will be entering the premises. Please come to the door, hands open and above your heads. We don't want any trouble here today."

The silence from the trailer was eerie. Pete felt a shiver up his spine as he ascended the single cracked wooden step. He kicked the empty ant trap aside speaking loudly,

"I am now entering the premises. Please announce your whereabouts. We don't want any accidents."

"Pete, maybe they went out for a walk."

"Shit on a piece of toast. I got twenty-five days left. Fuck me."

"Would you like me to go in first?"

Pete looked over at Dan's fresh face, remembering what it was like to be that eager to walk into hell. "Sure. Why not? Be my guest."

Dan tapped the frame. "Sirs. Collier County Sheriff Department. We are entering the premises now."

Dan dropped into a low stance and pushed the door open wide enough to fit through. He edged cautiously over the threshold and entered towards the right. Pete followed close behind, gun drawn, lowered towards the ground.

Pete heard a low moan escape Dan's lip, then fell backwards as Dan hurtled out of the door. Brushing himself off, he watched as Dan heaved up his breakfast.

Pete rushed inside the trailer with gun drawn, turned to the right and saw a huge undulating mound atop the sofa at the end of the trailer. A mass of fire ants squirmed over a bloated body. A pizza box on the floor beside the corpse was ground zero of ant activity. Looking down at his feet, Pete noticed the ants were splitting off in two directions. The second line was heading towards the front of the trailer. With three closed doors in front of him, the ants made the decision for him. Opening the center door, a second bloated body was lying on a twin bed. The body was distorted beyond recognition. No way to determine sex or age. *What a fucked-up way to die.* A bag of Doritos was on the bed beside the body. Ants filed in and out, enjoying their private tailgate party.

CHAPTER 18

Follow that Ping

It was two o'clock before Charlie and Vanessa reached the dock. Charlie figured they had about three hours until last light. No way they should be out there after full dark. The sky was crystal blue. Its crispness caused his hands to search for his ten-year-old Wayfarers, a gift from his wife on his fortieth birthday. A few silky cirrus clouds drifted by. Shades of green from cypress and mangrove and the muted grey beards of Spanish moss played in the light breeze. The occasional crimson of an early blooming bromeliad could be seen within the branches. He noted there was no chop on open water; conditions were perfect for a search. The local tour boat armada was quiet. Only a few of the large craft were out on a weekday in early February. They wouldn't be dodging traffic.

After looking over the boat, Charlie held out a hand to Vanessa and she stepped lightly on to the flat bottom of the vessel. Charlie unlocked a steel box under the seat and nodded for Vanessa to stow her gear inside. He pulled out a plastic chart with a route already highlighted in blue marker. He secured the map under a Plexiglass frame attached to a custom console in front of the pilot's seat.

Vanessa settled into the passenger seat on the left side. She noticed the immaculate condition of the *Miranda*. Her mooring lines were expertly coiled, her teak gleamed, the propellers shone in the afternoon light. Most airboats were a hodgepodge of mold and disrepair. This boat was loved. She pulled the recovered phone out of one of the numerous pockets in her

Safari jacket. She opened the GPS app and nodded to Charlie when it lit up and beeped.

Settling in the right-side pilot seat, Charlie pointed to the console in front of him, a laminated chart of the immediate area secured under a Plexiglass frame. "This is where I last plotted the GPS coordinates. It's located about four miles from where John Doe was found. I can see from its current hit, the transmitter traveled about a mile from the last reading I took." He traced the route with his finger. "The route seems erratic. Some of the plot points go over dry land."

Vanessa stared at the phone screen. "That's curious. Maybe somebody is searching on foot."

"It will probably take about an hour to get to that position. The last half mile will be engines off. I don't want to spook whoever has the transmitter. Vanessa, sit back and enjoy the ride. Things might get hectic soon."

Vanessa looked around the small bay. She always marveled at the verdant landscape. "Charlie, you ever get tired of this place?"

"Nah, each day brings something new."

"Like right now," Vanessa wrinkled her nose and sniffed the air. "It smells different. Like something's burning."

"It's probably a burn barrel from one of the camps hidden out in the islands. There are families that have been working out here for generations, poaching for decades longer than there have been laws against it. I feel bad when I take one of them in for being too obvious. I don't mind arresting the ones who are just in it for excitement. The old families mostly live off the land. They have some respect for the glades. They know where their livelihood comes from. The out-of-towners? Well, they are a nasty bunch. But I don't have to tell you, you've probably met your share of them out here."

"You've got that right."

Charlie handed Vanessa a high-end noise-cancelling headset with an attached microphone covered with a cowling. He switched on his own headset and nodded for her to do the same. After they were both hooked up to the frequency, he fired up the *Miranda's* engines.

Pulling away from the dock in Chokoloskee, Charlie slowly maneuvered the boat into the channel. He took care to keep the *Miranda* quiet.

"Charlie," Vanessa yelled into the mic, "Your boat is one of the quietest I've been on.

You've made a ton of modifications."

"No need to yell right now. When I open her up, even with these headsets, we'll be back to hand signals. But thanks for noticing the mufflers. I've been working on her for two years. Airboats are not known for their stealth."

They headed south with *Miranda's* blades pushing them smoothly into the swamp. The fear that the transmitter would die was becoming more real.

"So, Vanessa, how'd you get into snakes?"

"I've always been fascinated by reptiles. I grew up on a farm. We had ponds, streams, and quarries. And I had two older brothers. I tried my best to keep up with them. I was never a Barbie doll kid." She chuckled. "I should thank them. I wouldn't be in this boat if they hadn't been the ultimate pain in-the-ass older brothers. They would hide snakes and lizards in the most unlikely places. One morning I poured a baby garter snake out of a cereal box into my bowl. I named him Sammy. I kept him as a pet." The smile slipped from her face. "He lived seven years. That's a long time for a garter."

"You're an expert in snakes."

"I have a concentration in the behavior of reptiles and snakes. The Everglades is a dream come true for me. It's reptile and snake central."

"Pete is in big trouble. You sure have his number."

She smiled. "I guess you two have been partners a very long time."

"There's more to Pete than meets the eye. He's, my partner and best friend. I owe him my life."

"If you don't mind my asking, did something happen on the job?"

"Shit happens on the job all the time. Any good cop would give his life for any other. No, it wasn't what he did for me on duty. It's what he did when no one was looking."

"Please keep going, I sensed there was more to Pete. There must be something behind that glib attitude."

"I was thinking we were going to make small talk, keep it light." He scrunched up his face. "Hmm, glib? I don't have the answer to that; but he is a lot deeper than he lets on."

"So, what happened?"

Charlie hesitated, then seemed to come to a decision. "It's about Miranda, my wife. I named the boat after her. She was so full of life she blew me away with joy. I lost her five years ago. It was cancer, happened fast. We were blind-sided. Pete took charge of everything. I was like a child; I cried when I told him. She was my world, we never had children. We tried, but it never happened. We had a great life. I loved my job. She was a teacher in the Catholic school on Marco. She always said she had twenty kids. She'd laugh and say 'twenty-one' when you count me. Pete was my partner for ten years at this point. We were close, but he was single and a real hound. I went home to Miranda every night. He used to say he was jealous. I never believed him. Miranda believed him. She said he was still searching for the right one."

Charlie took a deep breath. "I never talk about this. Pete and I...well we never spoke about it, after." Charlie slowed the boat and sat back. "When she got sick, Pete contacted a top doc in Miami, made all the arrangements, came with us when she went in for surgery. Never left my side. I don't know how I would have gotten through it without him. While she was still alert, she told him to take care of me. She knew he seemed like a wild one and I had it all together, but she told him he had the strength I would need. She was my compass. Without her, I was lost. Pete stayed by my side night and day. We were there three weeks. He was at the hospital when she passed. It happened so fast. In what seemed like an instant, she was gone.

"Charlie." Vanessa reached out and touched his arm.

"I need to finish this. I walked out of the hospital that day; my gun was in my pocket. I got in my car, headed west across the Alley, back home, back to the boat, back to the *Miranda.* I stopped to get a bottle of bourbon. I sat on the bench." He pointed to the gleaming teak of the passenger bench in front of the pilot's chair. "I drank until I couldn't feel anything. Pete found me, passed out, the gun resting in my lap. I know I wouldn't have done it. He knew it, too. I could never disappoint Miranda."

"I'm so sorry, Charlie. I..."

"Nothing to say. We're well past the marina. I'm going to open her up. Hold onto your hat."

Vanessa nodded. "Ready, Captain."

Charlie opened the fan and let the *Miranda* fly. In the silence that filled their headsets, Charlie and Vanessa got lost in their own thoughts. The Everglade's eerie beauty glided past. He expertly steered *Miranda* through the sawgrass rivers, moving swiftly and following the highlighted path. Vanessa took a dry erase pen and marked fresh pings on the Plexiglass.

Forty-five minutes into the trip, she nodded to Charlie and pointed to the stationary blip on the phone. "We're getting close."

Charlie slowed the fan and steered towards a patch of cypress on a low hillock. His voice, crackling through the headset, startled Vanessa. "I'm pulling up over there." Charlie pointed to a saw grass knoll. "We'll take it on foot from here. This area is high and dry, too dangerous for the boat. Check your firearm and strap your waders tight. Eyes open, this is dangerous. What's the GPS say?"

"About a quarter mile due north. Charlie, I just wanted to say..."

"No. I want to say something first. I know Pete; he comes off brash, sounds like an ass sometimes. He's harmless, has a deep heart that he's kept close. This is the first time I've seen him this way about a woman. I don't know if you're just playing a game with him. Or if you think he is playing one with you. Either way take a good look at him. He's special. I'd like to see him have a piece of happiness like I had with Miranda."

Shutting down the engine, they bumped into drier land. Removing his headset, Charlie jumped off and secured the boat to a tall cypress knee. He opened the lockbox, placed the headsets inside and removed a shotgun with an embossed leather strap and a gleaming machete. He removed the chart, folded it, and put it in his flak vest pocket. He handed Vanessa her backpack,

"Take what you need. Travel light. There are a couple of camps back here. Not the best neighborhood, if you get my drift. Keep your sidearm ready. Some of these mutts have enjoyed Collier County hospitality, courtesy of Pete and me."

Vanessa pocketed the phone and pulled a 10-inch sheathed blade from her pack. She lifted it up to her face inspecting the heft of it, the craftsmanship of burled mahogany and its intricate carving before she strapped it to her leg.

Charlie, watching what clearly was a ritual, spoke reverently, "Wow, you and that weapon are something special."

"It was a gift."

"Like I said, Pete's in big trouble."

Vanessa smiled. "Girls got to do what she's got to do."

"You bet."

Pointing due east, Vanessa took the lead, hacking her way through the dense vegetation.

Twenty minutes in, Vanessa stopped short. "Charlie, it's moving again, the GPS blip is heading south."

"It's getting late." Charlie looked at the receiver and checked the chart. "It's too far to go on foot. We'll come back out tomorrow."

CHAPTER 19

Sal Gets Angry

Sal held the newspaper in his shaking hands and glared at Lenny.

"When were you going to tell me about this? This is one big mess, and I had to find out about it in the newspaper! It says they had to open the airstream with the Jaws of Life. The bodies were so bloated they wouldn't fit out of the door or any of the windows."

"Sal, let me explain."

"Lenny, it's in the paper. They had to rip open the trailer like it was a giant can of green beans. They opened it with a fucking can opener. What are the cops going to find in the trailer? Anything that can lead back to me?" Sal's eyes bulged, his face red, as he paced across the terrace.

"No, Sal. We are safe."

"I don't give a shit about you. I want to know if those idiots had a single scrap of paper on them that could lead back to Ferraro Salvage. I want to know if there is any link between them, me, and Garcia Enterprises."

"Sal, it was a freak accident. It wasn't a hit. You can't train ants."

"The paper says the fucking ants were eating Doritos and pizza before they ate our friends."

"Sal, calm down." Lenny cowered by the lanai railing, his hands and arms outstretched. Realizing his vulnerability, he sidestepped Sal and walked into the living room.

"Did you rent the trailer?"

"Yes, but it was a cash deal. Dominic and Louis checked in as Jerry and Bob Smith, two brothers from Jersey City."

"I've met these guys; they had a combined IQ lower than their shoe size. It would be easy for them to screw up. Who the fuck gets eaten by ants?"

"They weren't eaten, Sal, bitten, about a million times. They died from anaphylactic shock."

"What's that?"

"A severe allergic reaction. There won't be a homicide investigation. They weren't murdered."

"Well, the cops are going to wonder what the Mr. Smiths were doing in a trailer in the Everglades."

"Python hunting like everybody else down here."

"Seriously? Python hunting? They look like snake hunters to you?"

"Well, we don't have to worry that they look like Python hunters. One of the TV reporters actually puked on camera when she caught sight of them being removed from the trailer. She said they didn't even look human."

"You told me this was a good deal, Lenny. I moved Lexie from Howard Beach to the edge of the fucking world, and we aren't here for a week, and everything is turning to shit."

"Lexie loves it here; you told me that."

"We didn't move down here for the scenery. This was going to increase our cash flow and open a whole new territory for our business. Nothing else better go wrong. You are skating on thin ice."

"Come on, Sal. You and I have been working together a long time. You know you can trust me. I always come through for you. We had a setback today. I'll work out another way to move the product."

"What about Garcia? He's going to want his cut. How you going to push him off?"

"I'm on it. We will find the product before I set up a meet with him. It's got to be low-key. I think maybe it should just be me."

"No way. I want to meet this guy."

"Let me check him out first. I'll try to set something up. There's a small rundown airpark outside of Ochopee. I can see if the owner is amenable to discreet fly-ins."

"Do I own that?"

"No, but if things go well, you could."

"No more screw-ups, Lenny."

"No worries, Sal. Smooth sailing from now on."

CHAPTER 20

The Chorus is Singing

Lexie reached into the dryer for her beach towel. Sal and Lenny were arguing in the living room. She wanted no part of that. It was better to be oblivious when it came to those two. Since the day she met Sal, she never questioned him about what happened at the salvage yard the day Vinnie died. Initially, it was the shock. Later she heard bits and pieces about Sal's dealings with others. By then, she was already all in with their relationship. She had given up all semblance of independence and had sunk into a pattern of letting Sal handle everything. She quit her job, became the perfect trophy wife. If she confronted Sal about Vinnie and she was wrong, this life would be over. And she did enjoy this life. Sal was an adequate lover and provided her with everything she needed. And just like the song said, "What's love got to do with it?"

Heading to the door, she grabbed a water bottle from the fridge and tucked it in a beach bag with her sunblock, towel, and a paperback she had found in her end table drawer. "Sal, I'm going down to the pool."

"Okay, babe. Tonight, we'll have dinner in Naples. We're meeting some guys and their wives about the hangar I bought."

"Sure, Sal. I'll be ready by five."

⚜

Lexie headed to the sunny side of the pool deck and spread her towel out on a chaise. She loved the view of aqua water, green expanse of lawn, gently swaying palms. The gulf waters beyond undulated in the afternoon sun.

In front of her, the Floating Ladies were bobbing back and forth, their Styrofoam waist belts pushed their boobs up above the waterline. The daily water aerobics were fun to watch: their singsong voices gabbed as they exercised their ancient bodies. Today, the ladies had the soundtrack from *Mama Mia* playing as they swayed and danced through their aqua aerobics. Leaderless, they devised their own repertoire of moves. The only instruction: move from one side of the pool to the other without drowning themselves or their neighbor. One of them called out "noodle time!" There was a mad scramble to the pool's edge and now with the group flailing their neon swords, a new level of hilarity ensued.

Lexie lathered up with sunblock and settled in to observe the show. She waved to the group and appreciated that the noodles were raised in a salute to her. She loved these ladies, loved their giggles. There was not a pretentious bone among them. They swayed and danced. Their flaccid arms floated like delicate ribbons guiding their bodies as they journeyed from pool's edge to the stairs, twirling and reversing in a rhythmic dance.

The ladies loved gossip. They mocked the flocks of snowbirds who migrated south, down the interstates. The mass migration began after Christmas and terminated upon landing on the barstools at "Harpy Hour." Designer plumage on full display, the men and women of the I-75 and I-95 corridors hopped from scene-to-scene. They pecked at expensive, small plates which barely held crumbs. They drank dirty martinis and sweet boat drinks; their yellowing eyes squinted and searched the horizon at the end of the bar for someone to warm their winter hearts.

"Widowhores," the ladies call them. The low rumble of marital storms lingered beneath those words. Lexie felt sure that some had felt the pain of a straying husband. Now, years removed from their southern sojourns, these women had given up the auto train and divested themselves of their Versace wings. They were locals now by virtue of time served on the island. The irony was not lost on them. Twenty years gave them free range to laugh at the part-timers.

Over-heated by the midday sun, Lexie plunged into the deep end of the pool. Surfacing, she looked to the sky as water cascaded down her face. She inhaled deeply and experienced the day's first true moment of peace. Returning to the chaise, she opened her book and read a little, enjoying their banter.

"Hey, Lexie." She recognized Marge with her straw hat and long braids as the friendly lady who introduced herself on the first day. She waved her neon green noodle in the air, "Come on over and join us. We could use a dose of young blood today."

"Stop! Don't scare her away! You make us sound like aliens! She'll be checking the pool bottom for pods!"

Heavy gold jewelry laughed, "Honey, I've got an extra noodle by my lounge."

Lexie smiled warmly at the ladies. She could never get their names straight, but they didn't seem to mind. She loved how their comments flowed seamlessly across the surface of the pool. *That must be what it's like to have lifelong friends.* "Maybe later, girls."

A communal sigh ensued. "She called us 'girls.' Remember when we didn't need to hang on to these pool crutches?"

"Remember when we all had smooth asses and boobs that floated naturally like bobbers above the waterline?"

"Mine are still perky," Platinum Bob stated emphatically.

"They should be. They sure cost you enough." Marge said.

"Our guys didn't know where to put their eyes. They couldn't resist a pool full of glamour girls," Blue bathing suit giggled.

"The best was that day on the first year we all met!"

"The year the Albatross opened!"

"The men were on the chaise lounges and the whole bunch of them had put newspapers over their bulging dicks. We went hysterical at the sight of them trying not to look at anyone but their own wives."

Platinum Bob finished, "They all jumped up, dropped their newspapers, and dove into the pool. Our husbands swam to us straight-away. We got picked up and dunked: mascara running down our faces and our perfect hairdos ruined."

"We were sexy as hell. The Albatross was rocking like an earthquake hit that night," Blue suit blushed crimson and giggled.

"You girls are incredible," Lexie laughed. "Those noodles must have magical powers."

"Oh, look. There's Grace." Gold Jewelry pointed towards the now-open gym door. Grace walked over to the pool's edge and looked down at her friends bunched together below her. She was dressed in a smart, beige pantsuit with matching purse and shoes. Her hair was neatly combed, and she had put on a light swipe of lip-gloss.

"Grace, you look wonderful today." A quizzical expression washed across Grace's face.

"How did the doctor visit in Fort Meyers go, Grace? You drive in with Preston today?"

"That Preston drives too slow for my taste. I don't know why we don't take my Caddie. That car really has some pep."

"Preston gets your car serviced on your doctor days. That's why it always looks so shiny and purrs when he drives it."

"Can't remember when I drove it last." Grace's face screwed up, and she shook her head. "Did I drive it today? No, I remember. I went to the doctor in Preston's car."

"You sound chipper. Why don't you go up and get your suit on and join us for a swim? It's been a long time since you've done that. Walking around in the water is good for the old bones." Blue Suit did a little jig, lost her footing, and went under.

"Speak for yourself. My bones are just fine. I was just explaining to Roger the other day I could still walk nine holes and carry my bag at my Tuesday golf league."

"Grace, you do know that you don't golf anymore, and Roger has been gone a while now?"

Grace shook her head. Her eyes brightened for a moment. "I know it. I'm not that far gone. It makes me feel better to speak like Roger is still around."

"Shush. I bet she got some stronger meds this time. She remembered where she went today and didn't run to check her C-A-R."

"Why did you spell that out? She's not stupid; she has dementia. She can spell."

"Oh, I just remembered." The shadow crossed back over Grace's face. "I think I left the car running. I've got to go check. Maybe I'll go for a swim tomorrow."

"Well, that didn't last long. Thought we had her back for a few minutes." They sighed as they watched Grace walk out the service gate onto the driveway and enter the parking garage.

Lexie dove in and began her laps in the deep end.

CR&SO

The Floating Ladies gathered close. Their murmured words were contained within the tight circle of gray heads.

"What's the story with Lexie's husband?"

"Shush. Lenny's condo is right over there; you know, tenth floor. My condo's two floors below Lenny's. I can see and hear everything that goes on down here. Lenny and Sal hang out in the hot tub late at night, talking and smoking smelly cigars."

"Have you heard anything about what kind of business they're in?"

"Well, not exactly."

"What exactly does not exactly mean?"

"I've heard a few random words."

"Such as...?"

"Cops. I heard that one for sure. And drugs...that was clear, too. And money, I'm sure I heard money."

They all turned and looked at Lexie now doing the backstroke across the deep end. They turned back and continued their conversation.

"You think Lenny's involved with Lexis's husband in something illegal?"

⁂

"Are you discussing my Sal?" Lexie treaded water directly behind the circle.

The ladies jumped. Lexie looked at the sheepish expressions on their faces. "Lenny and Sal have been friends for a long time."

The group frowned. "How long have you and Sal been married?"

"Four years."

"You love him?"

"That's none of your business," Lexie sniffed.

"Well, that tells us everything we need to know, doesn't it?"

"You best be careful, Lexie. Just make sure you don't know too much."

"There was a renter here a few years ago. Her husband was involved in something very bad." The group's expression turned tragic. "One day she just disappeared. A week later, her husband was arrested at the airport. It was all over WBNK news. They even did a broadcast in front of the Albatross."

"No one was happy about that. We have a very respectable building with very respectable people."

Uncomfortable with the turn in the crowd, Lexie defended herself. "I don't know anything about Sal's business. He pays the bills, owns a salvage company, and a couple of hangars for corporate planes."

"Lexie, if you need to talk to someone or just want to chill out, we are always here for you. We won't judge."

"Thank you. I'm fine, really. We are just fine."

The mood shifted back, all of them now smiling broadly, reaching out their hands to touch her. Blue Suit announced, "Lexie, we are meeting in the party room tonight. It's potluck. There is going to be a reunion gala. We must get moving on the plans."

"Oh, I'm sorry," Lexie replied. "Dinner plans this evening."

"We have fliers made up to put in everyone's mailboxes and Susan is going to send out a mass email to all current and former owners. This year marks the fortieth anniversary of the opening of the Albatross."

"It's going to be a fancy dress, catered party: cocktails and passed hors d'oeuvres around the pool and entertainment."

"Renters are invited, too. We wouldn't think of leaving you and Sal out of our festivities. We're all looking forward to getting to know Sal a little better."

"Well, that is very nice of you to say." Lexie turned and headed for the ladder near her chaise.

She heard, "We would appreciate some young ideas," as she exited the pool.

Looking back at them, she forced a smile. "Maybe next meeting."

The ladies, resuming their workout, had turned up the volume on their exercise tape. Lexie smiled at the bobbing group and realized reading or napping would be impossible. She got up and headed towards the gulf, planning to walk south along the crescent towards the hotels lining the strand. She hadn't explored the beach yet, just a short walk north towards Tiger Tail Beach, to search for shells. Mostly she laid out by the pool or worked out in the gym. Sal wanted to explore with her, but he had an excuse every day since they arrived.

A half mile on, she realized she left her water bottle on the lounge by the pool. The midday heat sent her towards the M Spa Resort. A tiki bar on the sand seemed the perfect spot to get out of the sun and hydrate. She hopped onto the corner bar stool situated next to the thick beam that supported a thatched roof. Removing her hat and leaning against the worn bamboo, she was alone for the first time in what seemed like years. She closed her eyes as a deep sigh whispered through her lips.

"What can I get for you?" A deeply tanned face, white teeth gleaming in a genuine "glad to see you smile," and bright blue, twinkling eyes caused a startled Lexie to gasp for air.

"Water, please."

"Did I wake you?"

"No, no, I was just so hot from my walk. I didn't realize I could dehydrate that easily." Lexie blushed.

"Well, if libations are what you need, you have definitely come to the right place." He placed a large glass of ice water in front of her, stood back and grinned as she guzzled half the glass.

"I do have so many other delightful potions I can recommend."

"I'd go for the sparkling rum punch. Drew makes the best rum drinks on the beach."

Lexie head swiveled back and forth. "Who said that?"

A woman, deeply tanned in a white lace kaftan, seated on the other side of the beam, leaned forward. Lexie realized she was about the same age, but with her French accent and luxurious mane of raven hair, she seemed older, more sophisticated. She looked right off the cover of *Elle* magazine. Lexie straightened her t-shirt and grimaced.

"Drew, get Lexie your special spa punch."

"No, thank you. I really shouldn't. What? Wait. How did you know my name?" Lexie stammered.

"I saw you when you checked into the Albatross with your husband. We are in the condo directly beneath yours." She tilted her head. "You must have noticed the atrium offers a view of everything that goes on in the lobby. And the acoustics are incredible. I really believe they should have concerts down there."

"I'm not sure...er. Drew? I think I would like to try that spa drink."

"Perfect, you are going to enjoy it." He nodded. "Margot is already one ahead of you."

"As you just heard, my name is Margot. I'm from Montreal and I am, like you, married to a much older man." She took a long drink from her pineapple-shaped glass and pushed it towards Drew. "Again, my friend." She leaned forward and whispered, "Your husband's name is Sal, and I think you might have had sex in the garage."

Lexi's mouth dropped open. "I, I..."

"I'm not sure about that last bit, but I thought I heard some whispers about sex." She smiled knowingly. "You should be careful what you say at the Albatross. Don't assume the residents can't hear just because they're old. I learned that the hard way."

Lexi grabbed for the drink as soon as it was placed in front of her.

Drew winked at her. "Take it easy. That will hit you quick."

Lexie grunted as she took a big swallow.

Margot looked at Lexie. "I think we're not so different."

Lexie ignored her and finished her drink. "It's delicious." She pushed the empty glass towards Drew as she turned towards Margot. "You seem to know so much about me. So, tell me, how are we the same?"

"We are young, beautiful, and married to wealthy men old enough to be our fathers."

Lexie squinted. "Well, okay, but I've never seen you before. How do I know you're telling me the truth?"

"Why would I lie? I would also guess, like me, you have no close girl-friends to share your feelings with," Margot searched her face.

Lexie's eyes widened in surprise. It was true. There was no one. Hell, she sat out on the balcony smoking weed with the maintenance man, blabbing her life story. She knew she was completely alone. Realization crept in causing her to cringe. Alone—except for Sal.

Margot gave her a lazy rum-filled smile. "You see it. Now. The rum. It helps to open the mind."

Lexie struggled to put things in order. The second drink was making its way into her blood stream. She sensed her thoughts, banished into the locked abyss of her mind, had found the stream of rum, and was traveling towards the surface.

Margot held out her hand. "Let me introduce you to you," she smiled.

Drew placed a platter of nachos and two glasses of water in front of them. "It seems you two are going to be here awhile, so eat something and don't forget to drink water, or you will be hurting tomorrow."

"This is why I love Marco Island. Two women getting drunk at the bar and a handsome bartender gives them advice on how not to feel bad tomorrow. I'll be sorry to leave here." Margot picked up the water, gave Drew a nod, and took a sip.

Lexie's eyes widened in surprise, "You're leaving? I just met you?"

"Arthur, my husband, and I came here for a short holiday."

"I was hoping…" Lexie knew she sounded desperate. "We could be friends."

Margot's laugh tinkled in the gentle breeze, "We will be friends. The world is so much smaller now. And, we are rich, no?"

Lexie felt her new friend's eyes searching her face.

Margot seemed to come to a decision. "I think you have not yet managed your husband. I mean, you haven't gotten him to submit to you?"

Lexie's mind swirled in confusion, submit? Sal? "What the hell does that even mean?" she blurted.

"We are a type. No?" Margot picked up a pineapple wedge and dragged it off the red sword toothpick with her pearly teeth. "Trophy. I think that is the word."

Lexie cringed at the truth of the statement.

"So, which is the truth? Are you the trophy? Or is Sal's money the trophy? What does it matter if we all get what we desire?" Margot settled back on her tall chair.

Lexie leaned forward and saw Margot in profile. Her dark hair a curtain—everything dim in the shadow of the heavy beam. An overwhelming déjà vu appeared. *Bless me father, for I have sinned.* She shook her head, willing the image away. Yet she felt herself ready to —confess.

"I met Sal the day my husband, Vinnie, was buried." Lexie paused.

"Go on." Margot encouraged, her voice a whisper, "It is just us; you can tell me. I do not judge."

"He rescued me. I was alone. My fear was always being alone." Her words tumbled out. "My dad, he left, when I was young. My mom, she worked two jobs. I came home from school, ate whatever was in the cabinet, did my homework, and went to bed. Same every day. No friends. She wanted me to be safe. Locked inside our apartment. And I always obeyed.

She wiped a single tear from her eye. "It wasn't her fault. There was no family close by. No one to stay with me." She wiped her nose on a cocktail napkin. "I met Vinnie, and I wasn't alone." She took a sip of water. "And then I was. I didn't expect to love anyone after Vinnie…died. Sal held me close, like I was a child, whispered he would always keep me safe." She quivered at the shame of her selfishness. "I encouraged him. Gave him hope that I would love him. All I wanted was to feel safe."

"So, my friend, you gave him what he wanted, and he gave you…" She tilted her head. "What did he give you?"

"I did, do care about him. He is a generous lover." She blushed at the memory of their first time: how his big fingers fumbled with the tiny buttons on her camisole; how he tried hard not to hurt her.

"Well, you are lucky. Arthur, he only likes to pinch and bite. He has erections only from my pain. But, for me, it is a small price to pay."

Lexie felt her stomach turn. "I'm ashamed that I encourage Sal to have sex with me. I use him for that. It's always been satisfying."

"Ah, but that is what we do, yes? We allow them to have us, and we take all we need. For me, it is my lifestyle. For you? Maybe you have a kink for the big, fat men?" She giggled.

"No, I hide myself away. I pretend I have a good life. I stay safe." She cringed deep inside as saw herself for what she was.

"And do you? Have a good life?" Margot tossed her hair back and picked up a nacho.

Lexie thought for a moment. Her truth encapsulated in a tiny word. "No." She lifted her sagging shoulders. "No. I need more."

"We always need more." Margot loaded up another chip.

"I guess I never knew what I really wanted, but I'm trying to figure it out."

Margot shook her head. "What more could you want than money and sex?"

Margot's comment made the nachos and booze churn in Lexie's stomach.

"We think we are good at heart. But no, we are guilty. As guilty as the fat man you are married to. As guilty as Arthur and his tiny dick."

Lexie pushed back from the bar. "You know, I have to get going."

"Let me call you. We should be friends." Margot took out her phone.

Lexie ignored the comment. "Safe travels back home" her voice terse as she dropped a hundred-dollar bill on the bar.

Margot smiled. "Please, thank Sal for the drinks."

CHAPTER 21

Havana, Cuba – The Invitation

Raul Garcia settled down in front of the computer. While he waited for it to boot-up, he thought about his deal with Lenny Horowitz. The drone flight had gone off without a hitch. He had ignored Lenny's suggestion and sent a kilo of cocaine on the first run. The drone had already proven itself in the groves. Why wait when there was money to be made? The decision to send the drugs instead of cigars was on him. Lenny could do nothing but agree. Raul held the drugs and all the cards.

The genius Lenny hired in Florida did a great job. The flight was completed, and the drone arrived back at the grove on schedule. The mechanics at the grove had retrofitted the crop drone to the specifications, and the machine served its dual purposes perfectly. There would be hefty bonuses for them. In the future, he would have their loyalty. Spreading good will was something his father never did.

He made a mental "pro and con" list. The groves were being sprayed effectively. The first run had gone off exactly as planned. The payload had been delivered to within 30 meters of the preset coordinates. The drone had returned to the coconut grove right on time, minus its payload.

He felt confident the drugs lifted from the grove warehouse wouldn't be discovered for at least a month. His brothers' operation had been shut down temporarily while they worked a new partner in Canada. He hoped to be able to present his father with a boatload of money before the theft came to light.

Two of his friends from school were working in the warehouse. He gave them jobs after their stints in the army and supplied them with enough dope to keep them happy. They kept the shelves stocked to look like everything was in order.

The communication aspect was a problem. Horowitz was still communicating through his father's porn-laden email address. He needed to shut that down. He gave that a check on the "con" side. The drone programmer had used a secure address. Lenny said the guy was in the dark about the drone's purpose—thought it was about delivering cigars. Maybe that guy would set up a secure way to communicate with Horowitz. If his father or brothers caught sight of an email from Ferraro Salvage, he was a dead man. His brothers would have no qualms about burying him beneath a coconut tree. The land for a new grove was being stripped and fresh dirt was ready for him.

Worse than the email nightmare was the lack of response about the pickup. He could see on the app the drone had dropped its payload at the site. No word from Horowitz. That was very bad. He scratched at the rash running up his forearm. It always appeared when he was under stress. He couldn't let his father see it. He would know something was wrong.

Who did Horowitz send into the Everglades and where were the drugs? He was getting a monster headache just thinking about it. He needed to get to Marco Island.

The computer finally loaded up and surprise! A perfect view of a naked crotch appeared on the screen. Controlling the porn spam was an impossible task. Each session began with the screen opening to the last visited site. All that cyber-fucking gave rise to hundreds of porn site invitations. They were propagating like rabbits. He was a virile young man who appreciated sex as much as the next guy, but this was too much. He was beginning to recoil at the sight of fake boobs. *Shit. I hate porn.* If his venture with the Americans succeeded, he wouldn't be scrubbing computers and counting coconuts. He would be running things, telling his brothers to go fuck themselves, and gaining his father's respect.

He scratched, unsubscribed, and scrolled through the filth, hoping to find something from Leonard Horowitz or Ferraro Salvage. He worked his way through the new influx of garbage, stopping only at those appearing to be legitimate. A message from the Albatross Condominiums on Marco Island caught his attention. On the subject line was one word: "REUNION." He sat back in his seat and waited for the attachment to download. A colorful flier was adorned with a photo of the Albatross, coconut palms laden with fruit, a beautiful aquamarine pool. The words "WELCOME BACK" floated in the sky above the gulf in the background. The body of the message read:

You are cordially invited to join in a celebration
of the FORTIETH ANNIVERSARY of the opening of the
Albatross Condominium Community.
FEBRUARY 25
FOUR O' CLOCK P.M. UNTIL…
Current and former owners are invited
(as well as lessees that currently reside in the condos)
ENTERTAINMENT—FOOD—BEER—WINE
SUNSET SURPRISE!!!
Details to follow:
RSVP TO OFFICE BY FEBRUARY 15

His mind was turning. How could he use this to his advantage? Sal Ferraro and his wife were staying in his father's penthouse. Leonard Horowitz assured him they were low-key and respectable. They would not draw attention to themselves. Horowitz was renting a condo in the same building. Raul felt from the start that this was the weakest part of the plan, the only traceable connection between Garcia Enterprises and Ferraro Salvage. Horowitz was confident nothing could cause this connection to surface. He was sure the guys he was using were loyal to Sal Ferraro. Lenny's last email stated, "They would take a bullet for him."

He would have to persuade his father the condo needed to be checked. He was so absorbed in his thoughts he never heard the whir of his father's brand-new Jazzy scooter as he rolled into the room. The heavy breathing alerted him to his hovering presence.

"Papa, I'm glad you're here. I was working on the computer clean-up when I noticed an email from the Albatross Condominiums in Florida. You own a condo in that complex, correct?"

"Yes, I bought it as an investment. The American real estate agent said it was a beautiful property. I have never seen it. Maybe it is a dump."

"I think it's an invitation. Why don't you open it up?"

"Son, you are right. The Albatross is having a reunion."

"You haven't had a vacation in years. Maybe you should attend?" Raul held his breath hoping his father wouldn't agree. The old man didn't like to go out to the groves—a flight to Florida seemed unlikely.

His father squinted at him and shook his head. "If I took your mother to the states, she would run." His shoulders sagged. "Our life together is...difficult. She doesn't leave Cuba and neither do I."

He pointed at the email. "My son." He smiled warmly. "You have done such a wonderful job with the groves. The workers are happy, production is up, and the drones you've utilized are streamlining the process of pesticide application. I think you have shown you are ready for more responsibility. Go to this reunion as my representative. Hold out your hand to the Americans and offer a gift to the association to show our appreciation for the work they do. I think a box of Cuba's finest cigars would be perfect."

Raul smiled. *I couldn't have planned this better.* "Papa, thank you for this opportunity. I will make you proud. I will reach out to our American neighbors with friendship and respect. I won't let you down."

CHAPTER 22

Missing Persons

"My dear friend, Don Garcia…" Lenny deleted the greeting. No, that's not right. He frowned as he stared at the computer. Sal is going to be looking for his payday and without a product, there is no dough. Garcia is going to be looking for his cut. Lenny knew he'd have to throw Sal a bone soon to keep him happy.

Sitting back, Lenny picked up a newspaper from the pile beside the computer. The headline glared: "Unidentified Man Swallowed by Python in the Everglades." The next paper on the pile had a banner that was twice as disturbing: "Fire Ants Claim Two Victims in Chokoloskee." The only bright spot Lenny could find was the bodies had not been identified. That should buy him some time to figure things out. Since the initial reports in the paper, there had been no updates and nothing else on WBNK News about the two incidents.

Having searched everything on the web, the only mention of either incident was on an obscure blog site that chronicled Florida's more un-usual police reports. That site soaked up a good portion of his morning. Lenny shook his head. *What is going on in Florida?* It was like watching a train wreck; he couldn't turn away from the screen. Reading each post, he alternated between horror and laughter with a heavy dose of disbelief. The postings from across the state showed the level of insanity that existed here.

Lenny couldn't believe it as he read about a guy that threw an alligator through the drive-up window of a fast-food joint. Another joker used a private plane like a giant Etch-a-Sketch. His flight path showed up as a huge penis on air traffic controls radar screens. It got weirder. A 23-year-old man died after he put on his bulletproof vest, wondered aloud if it still worked, then asked his 24-year-old cousin to shoot him in the chest. *People down here are a special kind of crazy. I wish someone had warned me.*

He scrolled down to the two relevant stories:

"Everglades City: An unidentified Florida Man was found dead in Big Cypress Swamp on Tuesday. A police spokesperson gave little information except the victim had been partially swallowed by a large python. The body had been half-consumed when discovered. The victim's slacks and boat shoes were the only things visible when the body was found. More information to follow pending autopsy results."

The next day's blog:

"Two unidentified Florida men were found dead in an airstream trailer in Chokoloskee. The deaths appear to be the result of anaphylactic shock caused by numerous fire ant bites. A Collier County spokesperson described the scene as horrific. There was evidence a large insect incursion had occurred at the scene. The bodies were bloated to the size of Macy's Thanksgiving Day Parade balloons. The airstream trailer had to be cut open with construction tools to remove the bodies. The spokesperson went on to describe the pizza and Doritos found near the bodies and offered a word of caution to residents. "Please take care when leaving snacks open in your residence. Fire ants are attracted to junk food." Lenny shook his head, pizza and Doritos. It had to be Dominic and Louis; may they rest in peace.

He poured a tumbler of Johnny Walker and drank deeply. He knew he was fucked if he didn't find the shipment.

Tossing the newspapers into the trash, he noticed a small ad in the classifieds on the back page: "**You lost It? I'll find it! Contact Fernando**

Driggs at 1-888-xxx-xxxx". Wow. That can't be a coincidence." He picked up his phone and added the number to his contacts.

CHAPTER 23

February 7 – What's a rolodex?

It was time to call in the Cavalry. Pete reached for his Rolodex file, a leftover prop from a time before technology took the romance out of police work. Feeling a lot like a Dashiell Hammet character, he twirled through the yellowed cards until he came to the section marked C.I. These were his gold club members, Confidential Informants who through the years had provided information which led to the incarceration of many Naples's area lowlife's. Most C. I's were one-step removed from being thrown into the system; the smart ones managed to stay out of jail. A few found it a point of pride knowing worse scum than they were off the streets. One or two had risen to the top of the C.I. food chain and were given passes on some minor offenses. He rifled through the cards until he came to Fernando "Freddy" Driggs, the acme of C. I's.

He dialed the number figuring it was worth a shot. He hadn't used Freddy in at least three years. Three normal years were the equivalent of twenty years in the Glades. He hoped Driggs had survived.

"Hey, man, haven't heard from you in a while, what's going on?" Freddy's raspy croak swept the years away.

"How'd you know it was me?"

"C.C.S.D. showed up on the screen. I upgraded man. Got me a smart phone. Bonita and I are living the high life."

"That's good to hear. I was worried a gator got you."

"I'm smarter than those fuckers. It's going to take more than a few big teeth to bring me down."

"You and Bonita still good? That's great. You're staying out of trouble?"

"Yeah, I decided to follow in the great detective's footsteps. Don't have the bona fides to get on the force, but I'm damn good at finding things, especially people. I'm a private eye now, got business cards and everything—even pay taxes, most of the time."

"That brings me to why I'm calling. I'm looking for info on some guys found dead in the Glades. You probably heard about the python guy and the ant boys."

"Whoa, that was some heavy shit. Keeps me on my toes when I go fishing. Eyes got to be all over, even in the trees."

"Well, I can use your expertise on this one. Talk to some of your buddies and see if anyone has seen anything strange going on the last few weeks."

"Strange?" Driggs laughed. "Really? Stranger than any day in the glades?"

"Freddy, just do me this one. Why were those guys out there and was anything suspicious going on about that time?"

"That's going to go over well. I just got everybody friendly-like, even started to buy me a beer now and then. They're not happy with questions."

"I'm sure python guy and ant boys would be interesting drinking topics. Maybe see what Shredder's got to say. That guy loves to puff his feathers."

"So, what's in this for me? I got a business to run now. Got me some overhead."

"I can send some clients your way. Hell, people are always losing stuff out there. They call us up like we're the damn lost and found. Unless there's a crime involved, well, they're shit out of luck. I could offer them the services of a guy I know."

"I always liked you, Detective. Can I call you Pete now we are going to be working together and all?"

"No."

"Okay. No need to get your shorts in a bunch. I'll check around."

"Thanks, Freddy, I'll be in touch."

CHAPTER 24

Big Boy Pants

Officer Dan Barnes looked at the neatly folded stack of Tommy Bahamas clothes on the conference table in front of him. At least a dozen of the expensive shirts in size XXXL assaulted his eyes with their tropical prints and garish pastel colors. The slacks and shorts were so huge he was sure he could fit his entire body in one pant leg. It made him think of the yet unidentified python victim. He was wearing a brand-new pair of cargo pants, though in a much smaller size. The autopsy photos showed what remained of his pants still had creases after a day in the python's grips.

Looking at the store's website, he noted the items collected at the crime scene were still available. The purchases must have been recent; they had not yet been relegated to the sale section. He picked up his phone and dialed the customer service number on the bottom of the webpage. A robotic female voice with an Australian accent informed him the call wait time was forty-five minutes. He hung up and decided he'd visit the Tommy Bahamas store on Third Street South in Naples. He called the store and informed the manager he was coming. He photographed the tags on each item of clothing. He also pulled the file on the python victim and made notes on the slacks he was wearing. The victim's shirt might have been a Tommy Bahamas item as well, but it was already deep in the process of decomposition from its extended stay in the python's body. A quick call to let Pete know his plan, and he would be on his way.

"Hey, kid!" Pete walked into the conference room behind Dan and laughed as Dan Barnes jumped up and knocked the chair over.

"Hi, Pete. I was just going to call you. I've been working on identifying the victims and figured I would give the clothes we collected from the trailer a shot. I thought, how many guys that big buy expensive tropical clothes?"

"How about half of the tourists in Miami?" Pete laughed. "And don't forget the cruise ship crowd. They are big eaters. I'm sure there are some triple X's there."

"Yeah, I get that. I think these items were ordered online. I checked, and the stores don't carry a lot of stock in that size. If they were ordered together, it might show up."

"Good thinking, Dan. I knew I was right about you. You're sharp. Stick with me kid, you'll make me look good."

"I've been watching your career for a while now, Sir, umm, Pete. I'm learning a lot from you, looking outside the box, but mostly staying in the lines so to speak."

Pete winked. "Smart."

Dan continued. "I'm also thinking that maybe there is a connection between the python victim and the fire ant victims."

"Well, we think alike. I've been wondering about that myself. Strange to have two, no three unusual deaths within days of each other and none of the victims can be easily identified. The glades cough up some weird shit, but this might be the weirdest."

"The python guy still had sharp creases on his cargo pants. Tommy Bahamas sells similar slacks. What if?"

"Good catch. Python Boy and Ant Guys all wrapped up in one f'd up mess. I like your theory. So, where you are going with this?"

"I called the store on Third Street in Naples. The manger is expecting me. I copied all the tags and I'm going to let him do his magic."

"Don't get too excited, Dan. Nothing is ever that simple."

Dan shrugged. "Maybe we'll get lucky."

"Keep checking on the DNA report. Something's got to show up on those bozos. I'm heading home. If you need me, call Charlie. Otherwise, it can wait till morning. It's been days since I've seen my bed. I'm heading to a hot shower, a cold beer, and eight straight. That's my plan."

CHAPTER 25

Lenny at the Pool

The constant murmur of the Floating Ladies calmed Lenny's nerves. An errant cackle jostled him from his daydream featuring an almost nude Lexie backstroking across his closed eyelids. Her breasts pushed above the water line. With each inhale her hot pink nipples tightened from the chill of the air. She swam in and out of focus like the bright floaters that appeared after a particularly salty meal. Her sexy thong took him on a sensual journey as its slim string disappeared into soft mounds of pale flesh. His mind's eye followed it to its resting place, where her well-executed kicks pulled the thin fabric back and forth...

The unusual quiet brought him to unwanted consciousness. The old bags in the pool had ceased their incessant chatter and were gawking at him. He looked down at the bulge tenting his swim trunks and slid quickly on to his stomach. His face flushed as he grimaced in embarrassment. The babbling began again, intermingled with laughter and jokes about the recipient of the gentleman's affections. Now that the X-rated floorshow had ended, they turned their conversation to the preeminent topic of the week—the reunion.

Lenny's phone bleated its warning chime that a message from Don Garcia had landed in his inbox. Bracing for trouble, Lenny left the security of his prone position on the lounge, his shorts no longer an issue. He headed to the barbecue pit beyond the pool house. Taking a deep breath, he counted to ten and slowly exhaled his anxiety.

Opening the email, the subject read, "The Albatross Reunion Party." In the body of the email, his worst nightmare appeared.

Dear Mr. Horowitz,

My son, Raul Garcia, will be attending the upcoming reunion representing my family's interest in The Albatross. I feel it is time to have a physical representative in the United States. I look forward to the meeting between you and my son. He has shown initiative in the management of my interests in our lucrative wholesale coconut business. It has thrived under his stewardship. It is time for him to take on more responsibilities. I have apprised him of our beneficial arrangement. He will be an able agent as we move forward with this enterprise. I anticipate the fruits of this first venture will be available by the date of the Reunion. My son will be my courier in this matter.

Yours truly,
Raul Garcia
Garcia Enterprises

Shit, shit on a stick, Lenny cringed. He was completely fucked. He had no one to trust and no options left. He searched for the number he had placed in his contacts—Fernando Driggs.

CHAPTER 26

The Cheaper Detective

Fernando Driggs cursed the cell phone ring as it spooked the gator he was preparing to snag. *What the fuck? Two calls in one morning? First Pete, and now this schmuck from....* He looked down at the number on his screen, *New York.*

"Driggs. This better be f'n good, whoever you are?"

"Uh, is this Fernando Driggs?"

The gator slid under the boat and Fernando uttered a string of expletives. "What do you want? I just lost a ten-footer. If you hire me, that's going on your bill."

"Sure. No problem."

"So, what's your story? Wife cheating on you? Neighbor peeping in your window. Wife is fucking your neighbor. I've seen it all. Get great results, lots of satisfied customers. Short of making people disappear, I have a very open-minded policy that most of my clients appreciate."

"Mr. Driggs, I appreciate your honesty. You didn't mention discretion."

"Didn't think it would be necessary. Anybody who goes this route usually does it as a last resort. May I ask how you found me?"

"I saw your ad in the classifieds in the Naples News. "You lost it; I'll find it."

"Hot damn! Wait until I tell Bonita she was right," Freddy thought aloud.

"Excuse me?"

"Sorry. My wife convinced me to put the ad in just last week. She was sure we would find some suckers, oops sorry, find some people who really needed my help."

"Well, I probably fit the bill."

"Now I know you're desperate. Not a great negotiating tool, so what's your problem? If I think I can help you, we can talk money. If I can't, I don't have time to waste. Another gator is swimming towards me as we speak."

"You operate in the Glades?"

"Yeah. I like the quiet. Though lots of crazy shit goes on in the Glades for people who don't know what the deal is."

"I have some friends who went missing. They have something that belongs to me."

"And I guess you're more interested in retrieving your lost property than finding your friends?"

"Well, that is a bit harsh."

"I don't tolerate bullshit, Mr.?"

"Is my name necessary?

"I don't know. Are you Mr. Necessary?" Fernando Driggs laughed, and a deep phlegmy cough ensued.

A loud clang from the metal hull sounded as the phone slipped out of his hand when he tried to access the recording app Bonita had downloaded.

"You still there? Sorry, I dropped the phone."

"I would like to know the whereabouts of my associates and the package they were supposed to deliver to me."

"Okay, so now your friends are your associates. Which is it? I want to know what I'm getting into. Should I be looking over my shoulder, and who might be looking for the same shit I am?"

"I understand you don't want to have any liability in the event there might be some criminality involved."

"Lawyer? From up north. I'm guessing Brooklyn, maybe Queens?"

"Wow, you're good. You heard my accent."

"No, you are a pretty shitty lawyer. Your number came up with a 718-area code."

Freddy chuckled as the guy stammered, "I, uh…"

Driggs continued. "So, desperate is an understatement. The Glades is a scary place. Unless you have a guy, someone who knows the ins-and-outs of the backcountry and the locals, you won't get anywhere."

"And that, sir, is why I called you."

"Wow. My short ad revealed all that about me. You're real lucky you called the right man. Some around here ain't so honest, if you get my drift. I even got friends in high places that can maybe help me out on the police side of things as well. Why don't you tell me who are you looking for?"

"My three associates arrived in Southwest Florida about two weeks ago. They had different jobs to do when they got here. They hadn't completed their tasks when they dropped off the radar, so to speak. They were required to do some research and reconnaissance in the Everglades around Chokoloskee."

"Python hunters? That's big business around here."

"No."

"They ever go out in the Glades before?"

"No."

"They sign in at the ranger station?"

"No."

"They hunters or fisherman of any kind?"

"No."

"Did you send them out there?"

"Yes, I…"

"I hate to be the bearer of bad news, but your friends are probably dead."

Lenny sighed. "I've already come to that determination. You might have heard about the three unidentified bodies recently discovered in the Everglades?"

"Yeah. The ant guys and python boy. I might have heard a thing or two about them. You think they might be your friends?" Another spit and a splash.

"They might be— timing is right."

"They are already at the morgue, still unidentified, I think. I'm sure the police would be grateful if you helped them identify the bodies."

"That's a problem for me. The discretion thing? Well before I go any further, I want to know I can trust you."

"Wow. Mr. New York, you called me from an ad in a newspaper, reveal some sketchy story about missing friends, who may or may not have had a legit reason to be out in one of the most hostile environments on the planet earth. Then after I know you don't really give a shit about these three assholes and what you are really after is the package they were retrieving; you have the nerve to ask me if I can be trusted? How stupid are you? And yes, it's a good thing I can be trusted. But I'm not sure I can say the same thing about you." Freddy grimaced. *Shut up Freddy, your big mouth is always getting you in trouble. You might have gone too far. Bonita's going to be so pissed you didn't reel this guy in.* He held his breath waiting for the guy to hang up on him.

"Listen, I'm sorry we got off on the wrong foot. I am willing to pay your going rate and then some to retrieve my missing item and to find out what happened to my friends. I want to know where they were before they disappeared so I might be able to retrieve any valuables that might be offensive to someone who might come across their possessions."

Whew, got him. Now, be professional. "You can cut out the innuendo. You don't want anyone to know who they were, what they were doing, and if there was anything in their hidey-holes that might lead back to you."

"Yes, Mr. Driggs, that is exactly what I need. And for you to find my very important item and return it to me as soon as possible."

"Since we will be having a working relationship, call me Freddy. And you are?

"Lenny...Jones."

"Hey, man, trust goes both ways."

"You want my business?"

"Yeah. I got it, Lenny Jones from New York. I'll check around for you. If it looks like something, we can talk. My rate is a hundred an hour."

Lenny snapped back. "I see you're giving me the New York City asshole rate."

"Hey, I'm a businessman. A guy has got to make a living. I think you might know something about that. It's going to be four hundred to get the ball rolling."

"I'll get back to you, Mr. Driggs."

The phone disconnected. *Shit.* Freddy shrugged. *Guess I pushed him too hard.* He stared down into the brown murk of the swamp. The gator swimming beside the boat was of no interest to him right now. He needed to figure out how to play this. He had an ace in the hole, but what to do with it? He picked up his phone and punched in a number.

"Hey Bonita, Call me back. We got us a dilemma."

CHAPTER 27

February 9

Donna is a bitch was the only coherent thought in his brain as Pete opened his eyes, then squeezed them shut, blocking out the piercing sliver of sun that found its way through the minuscule hole in the bedroom window shade. He'd been on this train before, knew exactly when it left the station and how the destination was always a drunken, sex-crazed night. He turned over in his bed, expecting to see Donna curled up in the sweat-drenched sheets beside him. The bed was empty.

Moving at tree-snail speed, he rolled onto his side and attempted to pull himself upright. Pain seared across his forehead, and he fell back on the pillow. His feet hit the floor on the third attempt. He managed to make it to the bathroom, pee, splash water on his face and move into the kitchen, which in the small trailer was only a few steps down the hallway. Today it felt like a quarter mile—at least. He was hoping to find either a bottle of tequila or coffee dregs remaining in the pot from three days ago. That was the last time he remembered being home. The smell of fresh brew surprised him and the sight of Donna placing a Bloody Mary and a steaming cup of Joe on the newly cleaned kitchen table sent an electric shock through his body.

"What are you doing?"

"Is that any way to greet the person who dragged your butt out of the bar last night?"

Pete squinted. "Wait, aren't you are the one that got me drunk? You know bartenders are libel for over-serving their customers. I'm a cop; I know the law."

"Well, I might have been behind the bar, but last night most of Goodland made its way in after hearing you were making an appearance. Word spread about you being on the case of the guys that got themselves dead in the glades. That was way more interesting than talking football and hockey. Everyone and their brother were buying you drinks. They had you tucked away in the corner. I guess they figured you get drunk enough you would spill the gruesome details."

"So, you and I didn't?"

"No, we didn't, but not for my lack of trying."

"Oh, okay. I just thought that was, you know...our pattern. I get drunk. We fuck like rabbits. You leave, and then we wait until the next time. So, why are you still here?" His cheeks flamed. "I'm sorry, Donna, I guess that sounded insensitive."

She stared at him. "No, you were completely wasted last night. I'm not sure a threesome of *Sports Illustrated* models could have gotten a rise out of you. But you used to give it a try no matter how drunk you got. Last night was different. You weren't interested...in me." Her mouth curled into a tight smile. "I thought you might appreciate the domestic side of me for a change— breakfast, a spotless kitchen, perfect Bloody Mary complete with olives and shrimp. I even put on a pretty sundress and lipstick."

"So, where are your pearls, Donna Reed?" Pete rubbed his forehead trying to ease the monster headache encircling his brain. "I'm sorry. I'm being an ass again. I appreciate all this, really. I'm not sure we should... "

He watched as recognition dawned on Donna's face. "Maybe if we had ever gotten to this part of a relationship, I don't know. We never did get to this." Sadness clouded his eyes. "We've had five years of great sex and after-hours confessions. I was selfish. You deserved so much more than I could give." Pete shook his head. "This doesn't seem like enough now."

"Because now there is Vanessa." A series of emotions ranged across her face. "I bet she's great in bed and you're sober when you two make love." Donna's eyes glistened with pooled tears.

"How do you?" He squinted. "We haven't gotten to that yet; haven't even had a date yet."

"You were drunk last night. You might have mentioned her name a few times." Resignation tinged her words. "We're done, aren't we?"

He nodded. "Well, yeah, the sex part. But you still are one of my best friends."

"Me and Charlie. At least I'm in good company. I bet he doesn't give as good a blowjob as me."

Pete sniffed "There you go ruining this quiet moment."

"Hey, I'm fitting into the buddy role pretty nicely." She placed her hand on his and smiled reassuringly. "I can't say I didn't see this coming. I've known for a while this run was ending."

"I'm really sorry, Donna."

"I know. I've been preparing myself for this. Hey, you're not the only fish in the sea. But you may be the best damn lover I ever had."

"Come here, babe. Give me a hug. You'll find someone better than me for sure. You're smart, beautiful, and deserve way more than a part-time lover and burnt-out cop. You might even get to like Vanessa. You don't have any girlfriends to, you know, hang around with."

"No. I don't see that happening." She took a deep breath. "Okay. Can you dish on the assholes in the glades?"

"I'm not drunk anymore but let me tell you it was a shit show."

"Here," Donna pushed the Bloody Mary in front of him, "hair of the dog. I got all morning."

CHAPTER 28

Everglades City – The Pinging Stopped

"Charlie, shit! We've got a problem." Vanessa passed the phone over to Charlie. The green dot that had been their guide was gone—the signal lost. It was inevitable. They could charge the phone, but the transmitter had been living on borrowed time.

"We knew this was going to happen. It should never have lasted as long as it did. The battery manufacturer would be pleased to use this as a selling point, but damn, it sucks for us. A real tease, almost there and, poof! Gone." Charlie shut down Miranda's fan.

"What are we going to do? Everything looks the same out here. We've been searching this area for days. I still can't figure why the location was moving." Vanessa chewed on her lower lip.

"I'll tell you my theory. Either a poacher picked up the GPS or a gator has it. I'm going with the gator. Poachers wouldn't want a tracking device anywhere near them. We found some string near the crime scene, right? What if it got tangled up on a gator's leg? The GPS was high-end, waterproof, shock proof. It would have survived a freaking tsunami."

"Well, if you're right about the gator, they are territorial. It makes sense that it wouldn't have traveled too far from the crime scene." Vanessa put the phone into her backpack and pulled out two water bottles, handing one to Charlie. She drank deeply and continued, "A GPS transmitter is tiny, impossible to find out here. If it was attached to a larger item, maybe we have a shot at seeing it. But by now it's mucked up and wet, whatever it is."

Charlie started up the fan. "No sense staying out here. We'll head in and figure out our next move."

CHAPTER 29

Gator High

Freddy Driggs sat in his pole boat, tucked in a mangrove thicket hidden from even the most observant tracker. He had been following the gator for over an hour. The movement of bright color in the olive drab green of the swamp caught his eye. Its back was painted a putrid shade of orange with what appeared to be a lime green gang tag swirled down its tail. *What the fuck is that about?* His binoculars verified what he saw: graffiti.

The gator, a big one going on twelve feet, appeared to be struggling through the swamp. A closer look showed he was wrapped up in some sort of rope and was dragging something behind him. Freddy Driggs wished he were still a gambling man. What were the odds he would spot this sum bitch? It was at least a mile and a half from python boy's final resting place. An hour ago, he had seen Charlie Hernandez skim by in his airboat with some chick next to him. They were heading in the opposite direction from the gator. "Freddy, looks like they lost it and you sure as shit found it." He cackled loudly, spooking a heron that took off and floated gracefully above him, its large wings swooping in slow motion. "Yep, today is a beautiful day." He picked up the pole and headed down the small stream.

He watched as the gator slid out of the murky water and crawled up to the base of a large mangrove. "Well, lookee here. You are one fancy mama." Turning to stare at the intruder, the alligator's piercing yellow eyes revealed dilated pupils, unusual in the bright light of day. A pod of excited, squealing baby alligators squirmed between the mangrove roots. Their excessive movements caused Freddy some concern. Hatchlings are usually active, but the bizarre gyration of these little guys was beyond anything he had ever seen before.

He pushed his hat back and rubbed his forehead. "What's going on with you little fuckers?" He looked at the mother gator, her crazy eyes and garish graffiti-covered back made the entire picture seem like a drug-induced dream. Freddy closed his eyes and counted to ten just like Bonita told him to do when he got stressed. When he opened them, the scene hadn't changed. He shook his head in disbelief. *This shit is messed up.* He gripped the worn seat of his boat. *Oh, my God, maybe I'm having flashbacks.* He shivered as he stared at the Fellini nightmare in front of him. He tried another piece of Bonita's Zen bullshit. *Breathe through your nose, Freddy boy, just another day in the glades.*

He pushed the boat clear of the nest and watched from a distance. Through his field binoculars he again noticed the string attached to the rear leg of the large gator and what appeared to be a small section of cardboard dangling from the string. Dingy white foam bobbed on the surface of the water around the tree roots and clung to the backs of the babies. Grabbing a long pole with a razor-sharp machete he had attached to the end, he pushed closer to the reptile. With an expert flick of the pole, he separated the string from the mama's leg. Flipping it into the boat, he noticed a small electronic device duct-taped to the cardboard. Next, he looked at the scum, decided it might be important, and rigged up a makeshift scoop and brought a large sample into the boat. Satisfied he had everything important, he took a few quick photos with his iPhone.

He started the small engine and pulled away from the nightmare, stopping only to remove a small notebook adding the date of the sighting, location, approximate number of babies, and the strange behavior of the entire pod, including the graffiti. Shaking his head, he looked down at the scum-soaked debris he had grabbed and wondered if this was a piece of the item the schmuck wanted him to find.

CHAPTER 30

Marco Polo

Sal sat over in the smoker's jail beyond the pool deck. Lexie had convinced him he needed to get out of the condo and get some sun, but relaxing wasn't in his DNA. He would much rather be checking his email and blasting his guys on the phone for slacking off on their jobs. The truth of it was slackers weren't the problem. The whole organization was in the shitter. Protection wasn't necessary. Graft out the window. He wondered when things had gotten so screwy. Being a mob boss wasn't what it used to be.

He chewed on his lip as he contemplated the changing world. Young people today don't have respect for authority. Just watch the news. The kids in expensive colleges were hiding out in safe zones. He could show them a safe zone. If he and Lexie had a kid, which could never happen, they would know the truth about the real world. You need a tough skin and a big pair of balls to get ahead today. Feelings didn't come into it at all.

Lexie sure doesn't feel the same way. She is so sensitive about everything. She is the ultimate snowflake. Sal shook his head. She won't even step on an ant. Look where it got those Andruzzi assholes. Killed by fucking ants. The world has gone nuts. The status quo is gone, and here I am smoking a mediocre cigar in a safe place fifty feet from the edge of the pool so as not to cause anyone to hyperventilate from a little smoke. Maybe if this works out, which I doubt, just maybe I could get a box of fucking Cuban cigars. After all, I am a man of simple pleasures. Picking up the tattered Elmore Leonard book Lexie found in the condo library, he smiled as he began to read about crime the way it used to be.

Lexie looked up from her book and watched Sal sitting alone. He was sulking and looked like a little kid in the time-out corner in school. At least he had a paperback in his hand. She had gone into the well-stocked condo library and picked out a crime novel published in the early nineties, hoping that would hold his interest. Her past life as a teacher came in handy with Sal. He responded well to positive reinforcement. If they ever had kids, she would have two to manage, and at least a baby was easily distracted. Sal, on the other hand, was demanding and wanted her attention constantly. Lexie laughed out loud knowing Sal was a lot like an infant, always reaching for her boobs and craving her affection. It was his hard side that scared her. They seldom fought, but she had heard him screaming on the phone to his men, and he and Lenny had been having a difficult time lately.

Lexie cringed just thinking of Lenny. He was a pervert. She felt violated every time he looked at her. She knew he sat up on his balcony and watched her when she was down at the pool. She didn't think Sal knew Lenny was infatuated with her. If he ever found out, Lenny would be a dead man. Lexie shivered. She never allowed herself to think of Sal as a killer. She always pushed the thought away as soon as it entered her mind.

She watched the children splashing in the pool. Their parents were chatting away on the other side and were not inclined to get up and reprimand them for jumping and screaming too loudly. She saw it all as innocent fun; they were obviously grandchildren or great-grandchildren of some of the residents. She glanced over at Sal, who was looking up from his paperback and scowling at the children in the pool. Hopes of him sitting beside her were now dashed. He would never put up with the commotion and would yell at the kids to keep quiet and then end up in a fight with their parents. She could see the whole scenario unfolding in her mind.

Sal would not be open to her way of raising children. He would be inclined to be heavy-handed with discipline. Well, another month had gone by, and no sign of it happening. She had stopped taking the pill six months before, never told Sal, hated to deceive him. She knew he wanted nothing to do with children. He told her that before he married her. Lexie watched as a young mother cuddled her toddler in a fluffy beach towel. If Sal could just hold his own child in his arms, he would feel differently. Like every woman, she thought she could change the man she married into the man of her dreams. Sal would never agree to fertility testing. She had contemplated collecting a sperm sample after one of their romps in the sack but being that devious wasn't in her nature. She was trying hard to keep her moral compass intact, remaining distant from Sal's businesses and his loose interpretation of right and wrong. Flushing the pill every night was difficult enough, but she had convinced herself it was for a higher purpose.

❧

Preston picked up his toolbox, exited the pool house. Another sunny day had lured about twenty of the residents poolside. The brisk east-southeast wind rippled the surface of the water. The children in the shallow end were engrossed in a game of Marco Polo. The smoking section had one visitor—Sal Ferraro. He sat reading a paperback with a large lit cigar between his fingers. The wind had shifted and carried the stench of smoke away from the pool and out to the Gulf. He had been deflecting complaints about the "disgusting cigar smell from that fat slob." There would be no complaints about that today. He spotted Lexie on a lounge chair by the shallow end of the pool. Looking like a swimsuit model, sleek and tan, she was smiling at the children playing in front of her.

He was heading to the far side of the pool deck where a large coconut tree heavily laden with fruit was shading the lounge chairs near the hot tub. Still two months away from the coconuts being ripe, the heavy winds of the last few days had shaken one or two loose, and he knew it was almost time to call in the harvesters. He would need to rope off the large tree with caution tape, always a source of contention with the residents. The yellow tape was unsightly and gave the beautiful pool area the look of an inner-city war zone. The taped-off lounges reminded them of a crime scene; all that was needed was a chalk outline. They fought him about it every year.

Last year he acquiesced. To assuage them, he removed the lounges from beneath the tree and did not put up the warning tape. The next morning, he found the chairs had been dragged back over and one of the residents just missed getting beaned. The coconut went right through the chair next to the old guy. Still, they didn't care. "No tape!" was their cry. He thought either they didn't remember the coconut trees, or they never looked up. Yet a few months later when the arborist arrived, it was like a holiday for the residents. They clapped as the nimble climber left the security of the ladder with nothing but a strap around the tree trunk and a chain saw and machete hanging from his belt. The browned, wrinkled residents lined up early to be one of the lucky ones to get a ripe coconut. Caution tape forgotten, peace once again prevailed poolside. Today was the day for the battle to begin again. The condo board agreed on the need for safety, so the tape was going to be put up.

Preston thought it was ironic how coconuts had taken over his life. For the last two months he had been working on a computer program involving coconut groves in Cuba. Lenny Horowitz had offered him a substantial amount of cash to program a drone to spray coconut groves in Cuba and travel long distances to deliver a payload of merchandise. The weight specifications were questionable, and the range of the drone was excessive. He had learned enough about Lenny Horowitz and his pal Sal Ferraro to know not to question the actual purpose of the project. It was a lot of cash. Plausible deniability, the watchword in politics and business, was okay with him. His passion for engineering and pot overwhelmed any trepidation lurking in the back of his mind. He had completed the drone plans and its accompanying Global Positioning System specs four weeks ago. It was a thing of beauty. It would have guaranteed him a position at a major agroculture conglomerate. Preston had seen what ambition had done to his parents. That wasn't his bag.

The cash Lenny had given him was up in his condo. A small portion had been initially slated for a visit to a friend, another MIT dropout, who had started a small but profitable farming enterprise in the back woods of the middle Keys. That plan was off the table. He was pursuing a more important dream.

Looking over at the sunny side of the pool, he smiled at a relaxed Lexie reading a book while a group of small children splashed and played in the pool directly in front of her. Preston sighed as he saw her smile as the spray from their splashing drizzled around her. He opened his tool bag and brought out the caution tape. Time for battle.

CHAPTER 31

Truth Be Told

Lenny sat alone, tucked away on the shaded dining tier of the pool deck. His table, located behind low palms, hid him from view of Lexie reclining on a poolside lounge, and Sal, puffing away in the smoker's area. His concealed vantage point gave him the opportunity to watch Lexie while he planned how he was going to engineer his escape. He hoped she would come along. His heart melted as he watched her smile at the children. He knew she would be a great mother, if only he could pry her away from Sal.

Screams from the children in the pool caught his attention as they pointed at a small boy that had bobbed unattended into the deep end. Lexie popped up from her chaise, dove in, corralled the child, and delivered the giggling tot to the shallow end and his apologetic mother. Lexie gave them both a beaming smile and walked up the wide staircase at the end of the pool. Lenny could barely breathe as water cascaded down her sleek body. Her fingers combed through her long hair. Beads of water shimmered on her skin in the bright sunlight as she walked along the pool deck and back to her lounge.

Lenny had never given fatherhood much thought. Money and power were his sole purpose until he met Lexie. Sal had told him Lexie wanted kids, and he didn't. She deserved better than that. Everything Sal had, the life he lived, the cars, the clothes, the money, all of it, was because of him. He had spent the last fifteen years manipulating Sal, gaining control of his businesses one signature at a time. This last deal was almost perfect. He was hoping this big score and the new connections in Cuba he had forged would finally give him the clout to break off from Sal. That was not going to happen now. He needed to find a way to square this with Garcia and somehow make Sal take the fall.

Lexie rolled over onto her stomach and undid the strap on her bikini top. Lenny shuddered from four years of pent-up frustration. His first step would be to give up Sal's secret, the one thing which might break the unholy bond that existed between Sal and Lexie. She was enthralled by his money and power. Sal had scooped her up from death, but she did not realize she was still buried alive. Lenny would set her free.

Watching her struggle to spread suntan lotion on her back, Lenny left the security of his chair and without a second thought walked over to Lexie, took the tube of lotion out of her hand and in a whispered croak offered, "Lexie, let me help you. You missed a spot. I wouldn't want to see your lovely back burn."

Knowing that Lexie, in her current state of undress would not be storming off, Lenny decided to take this opportunity to tell Lexie Sal's secret. Time was getting short. The authorities might be discovering the Andruzzi connection any moment. He decided to go for it.

"Lexie, you know I would never hurt you. I see the way you've been looking at the children in the pool, the longing in your eyes for a baby. I know you will make a wonderful mother. Sal doesn't know what a treasure he has in you...."

"Lenny, stop right there. I don't want to hear anymore." Lexie sneered.

"I can't stop. I must tell you now, this minute. No more time to waste. I love you. More than you will ever know. I can give you the children that Sal won't. No, that Sal can't."

"Shut up, Lenny. Sal will come around. He loves me."

"No, he won't. I've been holding this in for a while. There is something Sal told me back home, right before we came down here."

Lexie hissed, "Shut up, Lenny. Get away from me." She squirmed as she twisted her arm behind her to trying to reach the open strap.

"You need to listen to me. Sal had a vasectomy right before you guys got married."

"You're a liar."

"I'm not lying. I will never lie to you, Lexie. I love you." Lenny leaned over and placed a gentle kiss on Lexie's back.

A scream erupted from Lexie's lips. Lenny jumped back as she scrambled up from the lounge. She reared back, her face contorted in rage and slapped him full handed across his face. The children playing in the pool howled and pointed at Lexie's bare chest as she dashed into the building. Lenny turned to see Sal jump up and drop his paperback. Lenny donned a calm expression and casually sauntered back to his table.

Sal stubbed out his cigar butt and walked up behind him. "Hey, Len, what the fuck happened? Where did Lexie go?"

"Uh...Lexie's bathing suit strap broke. Everybody got a good view of her tits. I think she's embarrassed. You should leave her alone for a bit."

"Yeah, you're probably right. Just between you and me she's on the rag right now and not too happy about it."

⁓⁂⁓

Preston had just finished up taping off the area of the pool deck beneath the coconut palms when he saw Lenny place a kiss on Lexie's back and her horrified reaction. *That guy is seriously messed up.* He looked at a frantic Lexie racing bare-chested into the building. *It's probably time to move on. Lexie needs to make a break for it, too. Man, she does have great tits. Hey, I'm only human.* He smiled as he picked up his tools and walked into the pool house.

CHAPTER 32

The whistle

Freddy was happy Bonita talked him out of keeping the phone call from New York to himself. It was tempting to go on the hunt for Mr. Jones's treasure, but Detective Landry had helped Freddy out of a lot of jams. She convinced him going straight meant going straight all the way. No dilemma in her mind.

Freddy placed the call. He was relieved to be sent to voice mail, certain his shaking hands would be heard in his voice. "Hey, Detective Landry, it's me, Freddy Driggs. I have some info on the subject we discussed. Might be something, maybe not. A little bit after I spoke to you, I got a call from a dude says he's from New York. From the accent, that part's true. Anyways, he's looking for his three friends. They were supposed to deliver a package to him, and they never showed. Oh, he said his name was Lenny Jones. He's a lawyer. Thinking they might be your dead guys. You know where to reach me."

ℭℜℨ𝔒

Pete's callback went to Freddy's voicemail. "Freddy got your call. I am on my way into headquarters. Thinking we could meet up for a cup of Joe. I'm buying. Head to the usual spot." Pete looked at his watch. "I can be there in about 45 minutes. I'll stick until my coffee gets cold. Guessing you still take it inky, super sweet."

The Judge S.S. Jolley Bridge crosses over the Marco River giving Marco Island residents a quicker trip to Naples. That was the plan when it opened in 1969. An additional span added two lanes and hadn't shortened travel time. The trade parade wound south towards the bridge every weekday morning and back north each evening. It caused miles-long delays in the sun-drenched macadam of Collier Boulevard. Weekends saw the bridge crawling with kayak and bicycle-topped SUV's hauling trailered boats. Older model minivans were filled with beachgoers. Rental cars crawled forward inch-by-inch, loaded with fishing gear. Convertibles with their tops down, Harleys, and pickups were all headed to fishing charters, sunset cruises, and the pristine white crescent beaches that lined Marco's shores. Jet-skis screamed between bridge pilings, ospreys circled, and dolphins danced in the wakes of passing boats.

This was one of Pete's favorite coffee spots. A steaming cup from 7-11, a short drive to the turnoff before the bridge on the Marco side and he was out of harm's way for twenty minutes. The view was spectacular, the riverfront on the mainland side was still undeveloped, nothing but green, open land and calm water.

He'd been meeting Freddy here for years; they both shared an appreciation for the beauty of the place. Despite coming from different worlds, Pete understood everything was relative. Freddy never steered him wrong. Anyway, how could you not like a guy who loved to fish?

Pete saw a late model Subaru Forester drive down the sand track leading to the small beach. It pulled alongside his crappy department-issued vehicle. Freddy, wearing a straw fedora and carrying a saddle-brown leather briefcase, got out and opened Pete's passenger door.

"Freddy, looking good my man. Nice ride, nice hat, nice case. PI business must be booming."

"You know it is, brother. That car?" Freddy nodded to the Subaru as he entered Pete's unmarked car. "Man, I bought it. Not a rental. I got through the credit shit with flying colors."

Pete handed the hot cup of coffee to Freddy. "So, I shouldn't be wondering how you came up with the cash for that?"

"Thanks for the coffee." Freddy pulled open the tab and blew into the hole that was leaking steam. A short whistle sounded from the cup as he blew. "No way, Detective. It's all legit. Bonita has been cleaning condos on Marco. She's a neat freak so her clients love her. I told her she should charge more money; she's worth way more than the going rate. She's not greedy."

"She still working nights at that store in Golden Gate?"

"Yeah. She feels guilty about leaving. Nobody wants that job. They were stuck up twice last month. Anyway, she and I pooled our resources, got us a nice bank account, pay our bills on time."

"I'm glad to hear that. Your name hasn't come up in a while. I was hoping that was good news and you weren't lying dead in a canal along Forty-one."

"It's nice to know you've been thinking of me."

"Hey, Freddy, I mean it, man. I'm happy you and Bonita are doing okay. This is kind of like old times, but better."

"Yeah, you're not threatening me with jail."

"Let's keep it that way. I've got to head in soon, so what have you got for me?"

Freddy opened his case and pulled out a leather-bound notebook.

"Wow, Mr. Driggs, you go to law school since the last time I saw you?"

"Shit no, man. It's Bonita. She gave the lot to me after I solved my first case. She says I need to exude professionalism and authority. Carrying around my shit in a plastic Walgreen's bag says, 'this guy's a dirt-bag and hold on to your wallet'."

"The woman's got a point. So, what's in your fancy notebook?"

"A little bit after you called me, I get a call from a guy who wanted some info about his missing friends." Freddy flipped the page. "The guy, Lenny Jones, I'm thinking alias, a real asshole, finds my name in the *Naples News*. He calls me thinking that some joker with a fifty-dollar ad is desperate for money and doesn't pose a risk."

"You got all that from the guy's phone call?"

"I've been dealing with scum my whole life. I got a handle on it. So, yeah, I got it from this one call. You going to let me finish?"

Pete pulled out his iPhone. "I'm going to record this. That all right with you?"

"No problem. I'm good."

"Continue. Lenny Jones from New York calls you…"

"He's looking for his missing friends. He'd be the one who sent them out onto the glades. When I mentioned the ant guys and python boy, he didn't deny they might be his associates. What he is really looking for is a package they were supposed to collect and deliver to him. It sounded like he was worried if they were found with said package his ass would be done for."

"Send me the contact info on this guy."

"Doing it right now." Freddy pulled out his iPhone.

"Anything else that might be of value to my case?"

Freddy sighed, looked down at the phone, pressed an icon and scrolled down through his recent photographs. "I was out fishing the other day, past Ochopee, not far from your crime scene. I spotted this weird-ass alligator. Its back looked like it was covered with paint. When I got closer, I saw that it was a gang tag. Orange and lime green swirls."

"Fucking weird."

"That's what I thought. Even though I was just out there fishing, I thought I should get a closer look, you know, in case it was injured?"

"Sure. Right thing to do, Freddy."

"Yeah. I follow it, and I see it's dragging something behind it. There was a string wrapped around its leg. It looked like a flat piece of board or plastic was connected to the string. I get a bit closer and underneath a mangrove, I see a pod of maybe twenty little gators scurrying around real frantic-like. The momma, with the graffiti on her, turns to look at me; her eyes are all fucked up, pupils dilated. The whole group of them are swimming around in this mucked-up water with what looks like soap scum floating on the top. I got pictures. Look."

"That's some crazy shit. Wait. I don't see the string."

"I snipped it off. Thought it might be what the asshole was looking for. I couldn't leave it there. Might not find it again. I also picked up some of the scummy water. I duct-taped my thermos cup to this pole I carry. Scooped up about a half cup of the shit. Smells weird, but kind of familiar. When I got back home, I poured it into a plastic wonton soup container from Su's Garden."

"Send me all the photos you took. Did you contact Jones? Tell anyone about what you found?"

"No, well um, I told Bonita. We knew you would want this. It might be evidence."

"You're right about that. Did you bring it with you?"

Freddy opened his briefcase again, pulled out a plastic Walgreen's bag and handed it over.

Pete looked into the bag. Four items were visible – a soggy string, a piece of corrugated plastic, an opaque quart container and a small electronic device the size of a deck of cards. Taking his coffee stirrer, he poked at the device, flipped it over in the bag, and laughed. "Freddy my man, you did good. Bonita has reason to be proud."

"Thanks, Detective. I can see why you love your job. This feels good. Anytime you need something, give me a call. Hey, like my slogan: 'You lost it, I find it.'"

"Will do, Freddy. Send my best to Bonita. She's doing good keeping you in line."

"You bet, Pete."

Pete reached out his hand. "That sounds fine with me, Freddy." Watching Freddy Driggs pull out of the lot, Pete Landry sat in his car, sipped his coffee, and thought about his next move.

Searching the glove box, he pulled out a USB cable, located the lighter adapter, carefully removed the GPS transmitter from the Walgreen's bag and plugged it in. After a few minutes, he located the power switch and turned it on. He slapped the dashboard, as the small unit sent out a vibration and its small screen gave off a faint green glow. "Damn," he laughed aloud, "you got to love technology." He smiled and pulled out his iPhone. "Hey, Charlie."

"Hey Pete, what's up? You are heading into the office?"

"No. I had a stop to make. Charlie, please tell me you didn't sign the burner phone back into evidence?"

"No. It's not going to do any good, the transmitter died yesterday afternoon."

"Is the phone in the car with you now?"

"Yeah, on the seat beside me."

"Turn it on."

"Wait, I've got to pull over. Okay, you want to tell me what's going on?"

"Hold on a minute and all will be revealed."

"Holy shit, Pete. I got a signal, what the f?"

"Calm down and follow it. Call me when you get close."

Twenty minutes later, Pete's phone screamed loudly in the confines of the car. He turned to see Charlie's PD enter the turnoff by the bridge.

"Son of a bitch, Pete. How did you get a hold of that?" Charlie pointed at the transmitter on the dashboard of Pete's car.

"I got some friends in low places."

CHAPTER 33

You are Cordially Invited

The Reunion invitation was prominently displayed in the glass-fronted case on the podium in the condo lobby. It was also posted in all elevators, at every outside entrance, in the mailroom, in the gym, the restrooms, and locker rooms. It was cardboard-backed and standing upright on every table in the social room, adorned the door to the library. It was on the walls in the garage at every fifth parking stall. It was also laminated and stapled to a driftwood log planted in the sand close to the beachside gate. Every resident, renter, and guest who had ever graced the condominium with their presence received a save the date, followed by a second notice to "Be there or be square." The third and more formal invitation featured the original pen and ink drawings of the Albatross on its grand opening announcement and welcome party invitation.

The Reunion Committee was leaving nothing to chance. Attendance by current residents was perceived as mandatory. With only ninety-eight condos on the property, it was such a small and exclusive contingent anyone not attending would surely be ostracized. The Floating Ladies had wholeheartedly accepted the reunion challenge, had draped their wrinkled bodies with the beach towels of destiny. They had morphed into their natural roles – the arbiters of all Albatrossly values. As original owners, their authority was never in dispute. They acted as one cohesive unit. They were a free-floating island directing events from their private Sargasso Sea, a refuge for endangered octogenarians whose loose skin, enhanced by a lifetime of sun exposure, had bred new growths which dangled and crusted their bodies. Each year their numbers dwindled through an inevitable natural attrition despite a generous, though not eternal, Florida lifespan. The ladies drifted unencumbered in the turquoise pool water. They were not to be ignored; the reunion was a life-giving event to their aging souls.

CRSO

Sal and Lexie stopped in the mailroom to check for their non-existent mail. No one knew where they were staying; all mail was delivered via Lenny. Habits are hard to break and checking the mail was on the top of the to-do list, something Sal and Lexie often joked about. Though they hailed from different generations and upbringings, a small stability they shared was the daily ritual their parents had required of them. As children they were always sent to check the mail.

Today's mail run offered a surprise. Three notices graced the usually empty box. The first was a reminder about the reunion and its requisite meetings - menu tastings, talent auditions, table linen choices, and decorations.

The second flyer, also about the reunion, offered a new bit of information causing Sal's heart to flutter. All those beautiful dusty cars, relics from the past, were to be detailed and lined up outside the pool gates. The service gate to the pool area was to be opened during the cocktail hour so attendees might enjoy the car show without swiping in and out of the building. Sal appreciated the configuration of the property; its excellent layout afforded the most privacy found anywhere on the beach. The Albatross driveway curled around the parking garage, leaving the front entrance free of prying eyes and traffic. One-way in and one-way out. Safety first for the residents. The pool gate sat to the south of the main portico and was always locked. The attendees would have unfettered access to the cars just yards from the festivities. Sal needed to thank the committee for such a wonderful addition to the party. The flyer stated two security guards would be manning the entrance and the beach gate to prevent party crashers from entering the premises.

An addendum at the bottom of the memo revealed a local island car wash and temperature-controlled car storage facility was giving a special discount to Albatross residents. A full detail with hand-rubbed wax and tire rotation was being steeply discounted in honor of the Albatross and its venerable position as the first luxury condominium on Marco Island.

Through conversations Sal had with the few smokers in the building, he learned about the history of the Albatross and Marco Island. The prosperity on the island could be attributed to the shrewd developers that recognized the value in Marco Island's lush vegetation and white sand beaches. The venture was widely mocked in Florida development circles: too far from railroads, too close to the Everglades, too far from Palm Beach and Miami. Surely an Albatross that would bring any company down. The developer considered this a point of pride and chose to name his first project the Albatross. A current tenant, George Neuwirth, was part of that original project. The complex sold out immediately. The Eagle and the Osprey followed on the Albatross's soaring wings. Much later, major hotel chains and higher, more densely populated condominiums appeared on the strand. A suburban sprawl of stucco and stone littered the island. Wetlands were filled in, canals were dug and bulk-headed, and lawns manicured. The rest was Marco monetary history.

The third notice left Sal speechless. It was the proverbial answer to his prayers. Lexie had been cold and distant the last few days. Nothing he could say or do could make her smile. He thought she might be homesick. Her thirty-fifth birthday was the day after the Reunion party. Maybe she was upset about that milestone. He had been struggling with gift ideas. She had everything she wanted and visited the Waterside Shoppes in Naples at least twice a week. She would meet women from her spin class for lunch and they would spend the afternoon shopping for something unique or pretty to wear. She always had on something new. He realized he had never seen her wear the same outfit twice. In the mailbox was the answer to the gift dilemma. This Saturday, February 18th, Fifth Avenue in Naples would be closed to traffic for the Annual Ferrari Club of America Car Show and Charity Benefit. Sal knew exactly what to get Lexie for her birthday. He would buy her a vintage Ferrari. And, the best part, she would be able to show it off at the Albatross Reunion Car show. He was a proud man, and the Ferrari and Lexie would both be showstoppers. How perfect is this! Sal smiled, leaned over, and gave Lexie a gentle kiss.

CHAPTER 34

Shave and a Haircut Two Bits

Preston couldn't believe what he was seeing. The old ladies were rolling up the caution tape he had put around the coconut tree. One of them noticed him watching by the pool house. They put their heads together as they mumbled. They turned in unison, as precise as a chorus line dance move. They took one step towards him, grabbed each other's hands, and gave him their most menacing glares.

Their designated spokesperson mustered an angry tone. "Preston, leave it alone. You can put it back up after the Reunion. We will make certain no one sits underneath it. Anyway, we are going to have an entertainer placed near the hot tub. Everyone will be on the other side of the pool enjoying the show."

"What kind of entertainment?" Preston laughed to himself envisioning the old ladies performing the dance of the seven veils.

"You'll see. It's going to be a surprise."

"Just make sure you inform Susan YOU took down the tape. This isn't going to land at my feet."

The ladies smiled, their bodies deflating as the bravado dissipated. "You are such a nice young man, Preston. Are you bringing a date to the Reunion?"

Preston shook his head, gave them a wave and headed inside the building. *What the fuck am I doing here? I don't need the money or the aggravation. I'm thirty-four years old and spend my days mopping up after a bunch of old crows and incontinent geezers.* His next thought was of Lexi. *She is caught here, too. She's too smart to spend her life with that ape.*

Preston straightened up, tucked his shabby Hawaiian shirt into his work khakis and decided to head upstairs and pay a visit to George Neuwirth, the oldest resident at the Albatross. Infirm and on oxygen, Mr. Neuwirth had been asking Preston to drive him to Miami Beach to visit his newly widowed son, Michael. Preston had been putting it off for a few months; he was either too busy keeping the Albatross running smoothly or too stoned to drive. It seemed now would be a good time for a road trip. He felt terrific, had started working out, and hadn't been high in...he smiled...since the day he met Lexie.

Preston rang the doorbell of Unit 402, waited for a few minutes, then took his master key and let himself in to Mr. Neuwirth's apartment. Though situated Gulf front, the room was dimly lit, the drapes were open barely a foot. The television was on, but the volume was muted. "George, it's me, Preston. I'm coming into the apartment."

Preston listened intently until he heard faint squeaking sounds coming from the master bedroom. Old Mr. Neuwirth, looking disheveled, was slowly wheeling his walker across the tile floor from the bathroom. "George, are you okay?"

"Ain't dead yet, young Preston. Your shirt's tucked in. What's the occasion?"

"Can't slip anything by you George. Still sharp as a tack."

"That's about all I got going for me. You'll let me know when I start slipping. I trust you. Can't say the same for the rest of this crowd. What brings you up here? Thought the old bags would have you going nuts preparing for their big soirée."

"Well, they gave me a list a mile long. But I got to thinking, you've been asking me to take you to Miami to see your son, Mike. How would you like to go next week? Get you out of this apartment, see some sights?"

"That sounds just fine except for one thing. I already sent in my response to the Reunion invite. I am planning on going. Might be some people coming in from the old days. People I might actually like to see. Anyway, how are you going to get away that week?"

"I've been ahead of schedule on the party preparations. I'll tell you what, if you have everything together and all packed, I'll have the car gassed up and ready to go, and we can leave right after the reunion."

"I saw the notice about the car detailing. It would be nice to see the Rolls all cleaned up. I know you've been running her, but the old gal could really use a little polish. Here, take the keys and drive her down to the car wash. Do her up right. She might be the talk of the car show. A lot of people don't know what's been hiding under that tarp all these years. A 1985 Rolls Royce Corniche, that will get their tongues wagging." George let out a cackle that turned into a deep, wet cough.

"Take it easy, George. This is a good plan. You need to stay healthy. I'll get your suitcase and put it in the spare room. Start packing. I'll pick up your meds this week and an extra oxygen tank for the road."

"You know, kiddo, I'm up here every day watching the pool and listening to what the old ladies have to say. Lately, there's been a real pretty girl hanging around. I know you've seen her. It seems you have a hard time keeping focused on your job when she's lying around in those teeny bikinis." George giggled. "I noticed she's been looking at a lot more than that big book she carries around. She seems to have taken a shine to a certain young man." He winked. "If you catch my drift." His eyes squinted and his expression hardened. "You better watch your back. That husband of hers—he's no good. I've spent my life dealing with pricks like him. The construction business is loaded with those particular kinds of rats." George seemed to shake off a bad memory as he continued, "Why don't you get a haircut while you're at it? Spend the two bits. We are going in style."

CHAPTER 35

That's Huge

Dan Barnes opened his emails one last time before heading home for the day. It was frustrating. A week had gone by with no response from the Tommy Bahamas offices. He had explained the rudiments of the situation to the manager of the Naples store and had been given a verbal promise Collier S.D.'s request would be forwarded to the administrative offices to be expedited. He was sure it was just a matter of hitting a few keys on their computer. He couldn't believe his eyes when an email suddenly appeared at the top of the inbox. It was quitting time here. In Seattle, where they were based, it would be three o'clock in the afternoon. Opening the email, he read through the company's policies on client privacy. The bottom paragraph hit pay dirt. *In consideration of the extenuating circumstances concerning this purchase, our legal team has advised us we would incur no liability in forwarding the requested information. We hope this will be of help to you as you resolve this situation. Enclosed please find an attachment containing the pertinent invoices.*

Danny looked over the invoices attached to the email. The items were purchased by Dominic Andruzzi of Ozone Park, Queens, New York, and delivered to that same address. All the tagged items recovered at the crime scene were in that on-line order as well as numerous items in size small. It was very interesting the pants worn by the python victim were identical to the ones in the Andruzzi order. It seems all the deceased have been tentatively identified. Dan picked up the phone. He knew Pete didn't want to be disturbed, but it looked like this case was about to break open.

CRSO

The next morning Danny walked into headquarters and noticed the big smiles on the usually dour early morning faces of his fellow deputies. He continued into the squad room and headed to his temporary desk: a cleared-off section of the coffee table set up in the back of the room. He had a computer, a pen, an official department notepad, a phone, a file folder, and a chair. He was in heaven. This assignment was a great opportunity; most rookies never saw the inside of the squad room. Right place, right time worked out for him. Detective Landry needed a puppy to fetch, and Dan Barnes was a willing golden retriever, a service dog through-and- through.

Looking down at the MacBook, instead of the department authorized screensaver, a CCSD shield superimposed on the blue water of the gulf, Dan spotted a bloated, suppurated body reclining on an ant and Dorito-covered sofa filling the screen. A scroll across the bottom read "Congratulations Deputy Sheriff Daniel Barnes! Dominic and Louis Andruzzi thank you for your great detective work in identifying their remains. Job well done!"

Turning to see who might have been responsible, he was greeted by the entire squad standing and applauding, with Pete Landry front and center.

CHAPTER 36

February 16 – Blue Plate Special

"Collier County Sheriff."

"Detective Landry, please."

"This is Landry. Whoever this is, make it quick. I'm real busy."

"Good morning, Detective. I'm Detective Carl Schreiber, N.Y.P.D., 106 Squad. I'm calling about your investigation concerning Dominic and Louis Andruzzi."

"That was fast. Figured it would take a week to hear back from you guys. I know how busy you are up there."

"We are, but when I saw a call came in from Florida, I felt like I needed a vacation even if it is only via the phone. Tell me, how warm is it right now?"

Pete laughed, "I don't want to torture you. I hardly know you."

"That's okay. Hit me with a number."

Pete checked his weather app. "It's 74 now. Forecast says 85 by this afternoon, light chop on the gulf, no advisories. That painful enough for you?"

"That felt good."

"You northerners are masochists. I never tell my friends up there what the weather is doing, though they love to throw shit at me when it's hurricane season. What have you got for me?"

The address you asked about is a private residence in South Ozone Park, Queens. It is owned by Matilda Andruzzi, age ninety-four. She no longer lives in the residence. She's in a nursing home in Valley Stream, out in Nassau County. Her husband, Anthony, deceased, worked as a mason. He died in a freak accident almost thirty years ago. A cement truck dropped its load on him. He worked for Ferraro Associates now DBA Ferraro Salvage.

"The death was mob related?"

"No proof of that. Ferraro gave a generous payout to the widow Andruzzi. Paid off her mortgage and gave her a monthly stipend. Matilda never remarried. They had three sons, Dominic, now thirty-eight, and Louis, thirty-six, reside in the house. They've got no priors. The youngest, David, age thirty-two has that address listed by DMV. Matilda's brother, Alberto Spano, eighty-six, lives across the street."

"Did anyone report these guys missing?"

"I went down there, talked to some neighbors. The house is closed up. No lights on at night. Trash cans empty. David hasn't lived there for years; no one has seen him. The two brothers, Dominic and Louis, left the house the end of January. Old lady next door remembered. She's a nosy broad, full of information. Every block in Queens has got one. Anyway, a black Escalade picks up the two big guys. She remembered because it was the day before the big snowstorm, and she was on her way back from the bodega down the street with milk, eggs, bread, and an Entenmann's crumb cake. Oh, I forgot! You boys in Florida don't know about snowstorm supplies."

"Down here it's hurricane supplies. Besides plywood, we stock up on a fair amount of beer, chips, and yes, Entenmann's. What else you got? Did you talk to the uncle?"

"No, not yet. I wasn't sure how you wanted this to go. What's this case looking like?"

"We found two bodies in a trailer in Chokoloskee, down near the Everglades."

"Are these the ant guys? They're all over the news. They even got a mention in turnout the other day. The Sergeant made a point of how lucky we are we don't deal with messed-up shit like that. It was bad right?"

"Yeah, you could say that."

"What makes them the Andruzzi's?"

"The address we gave you came from an invoice for a shit-ton of Tommy Bahama resort clothes. Most in sizes XXXL. Picked up the clothes at the scene. There was other clothing purchased in size small. Those haven't turned up yet." Pete shuffled through his notes.

"The third brother?" Carl questioned.

"The day before the ant guys were found, a small guy turns up dead. He was wearing brand new clothes. It might be David."

"How did he bite it?"

"Bite it. That's funny. He was out in the glades, a poacher found him half swallowed by a monster python."

"I read about that guy, too. That's fucked up. No identification on any of them?"

"All preliminary as far as ID."

"You want NYPD to do the notification? Those Italian widows dressed in black for twenty-five years? They don't take bad news well. You should come up here and do it. I'll be there to offer moral support, but I'll be standing ten steps behind you. Be prepared to duck."

"Let's not get ahead of ourselves here. My gut says it's them, but no one is visiting mama without proof in hand. Would you reach out to the uncle, um, Alberto, and see if you can get into the house? Maybe get a hairbrush or toothbrush for DNA. Link them up that way. No criminal history for any of them, you say?"

"You are looking at something criminal?"

"If stupid is a crime. There might be something, drugs, smuggling. We're waiting on the lab. You get anything else on our guys?"

"A Lexus-Nexus check revealed that Dominic and Louis Andruzzi are employed by Ferraro Salvage. They run the forklifts and strip down cars. The junkyard is on Linden Boulevard, Howard Beach. Salvatore Ferraro, Jr. owns the business. It seems he is out of town also. The yard is still open. I put in a call. Voicemails are sent to an associate, Leonard Horowitz. He is listed as the CFO of the company. I didn't leave a message."

"The name Lenny has come up before." Pete wrote down Ferraro Salvage and Lenny Jones/Leonard Horowitz on a Post-It.

Pete could hear phones ringing, radios squawking, and muted laughter through the phone. "I appreciate you taking the time to check this out for us, Detective."

"Please, call me Carl. Interesting note—there was a case at the salvage yard before I was assigned here. One Vincent Cacciatore, thirty-three, an accountant that worked for a firm hired by Ferraro Salvage, was killed in a freak accident while hand delivering some tax papers. He wandered around looking for the office; it's like a rat's maze out there. He turned a corner and found himself beneath a giant claw that was holding an old Honda Civic about twenty feet above him. Don't think he even knew what hit him when it dropped."

"Wait, a fucking car fell on him? This case gets more bizarre at every turn."

"There was an investigation. Dominic Andruzzi had picked the car up with the claw. It was left hanging there unattended while he went to take a shit. When he got back, the Honda had dropped off and the only thing left of Mr. Vincent Cacciatore was a large splat seeping from beneath the car. It seems cars slip out of the claw all the time. The case was closed out as an accident. Still, a lot of questions linger, but nothing solid to implicate Sal Ferraro or Dominic Andruzzi."

"Sounds like a hit to me."

"It gets weirder. The deceased was the first husband of Alexis Ferraro. Four months after the accident, Lexie Simons Cacciatore becomes Mrs. Salvatore Simons Cacciatore Ferraro of Howard Beach, Queens. She collects a big payout from the insurance company: double indemnity. Met Life took a big hit, investigated the shit out of the case. No connection between Sal Ferraro and Lexie Cacciatore before the accident. She didn't know that Vinnie's firm did work for them. They were only married a few weeks when the accident happened."

"She's Sal Ferraro's present wife? Ferraro and the Andruzzi's, they're mob guys?"

"No proof of that. The attorney, Horowitz, keeps a tight lid on everything, taxes and permits all by the book and up to date. Our OCCB–Organized Crime Control Bureau–has had them on their radar for a while. I'm looking at surveillance photos of the Andruzzi's from the Cacciatore investigation." Carl laughed. "They don't look like adventurous types. No kayaking in the Everglades for these slobs."

"Well, it seems they ended up the as the blue plate special in the Everglades."

"Ha. Blue plate special–oversized portions."

"Carl, I need to know what those assholes were doing down here, and who sent them."

"I'll get on the uncle, see what I can pick up in the house."

"Thanks, man. With any luck we can get a positive ID within the week." Pete hung-up the phone, pulled out his notebook, and started writing.

CHAPTER 37

Don't Forget the Cigars

Raul dropped the empty suitcase on the tufted divan in his bedroom's conversation area. The large room contained a king-sized bed, an elaborately carved armoire, a sitting area with a leather sofa, a sixty-five-inch television, and a cocktail table inlaid with imported Moroccan tiles and hand carved lion claw legs. Raul thought it was ghastly. The divan faced the massive French doors opening onto the stone veranda with magnificent city views. His mother, Cecilia, as she preferred he call her, had whore's taste and a millionaire's wallet. Afraid her young son would not be shown the same deference as his older stepbrothers, she had insisted he have the largest bedroom, which she decorated with expensive custom furniture. Raul hated it. He preferred the clean look of modern Danish design. If this trip goes according to plan, he will arrive back home with cash and finally be able to move out.

Cecilia's efforts to have him respected in the family were in vain. His brothers hated her, and they hated Raul even more. This trip to Florida was a thorn in their sides. Their wives had been complaining since the day his father announced that Raul would be going to the Albatross Reunion and would also be taking on a larger role in the business. His brothers were upset at the cost of the flight and the passport. They had never been out of Cuba. Raul couldn't wait to see their faces when they discovered he had worked a deal with an American attorney and was on his way to creating a new path for wealth in the family business.

Raul heard his father's heavy footfalls stop outside his room, then a rap with his cane, something his father did not usually do. Raul smiled. Things were already looking up.

"Come in."

The old man stood erect on the threshold. He looked almost youthful in a beige sports coat topping a salmon polo shirt. His stone-washed jeans, a new development in his wardrobe at Cecelia's insistence, were perfectly creased; sockless feet were nestled in soft, handcrafted brown leather loafers, and the ubiquitous cane was at his side.

"You are looking well, Papa."

"I have brought you cigars to take with you on your visit to Florida. Manuel rolled these this morning. You will offer these as a... what do they say? Icebreaker? The Americans are unfamiliar with our culture. They see only what is in the newspaper. Show them we are a warm, generous people."

"That is a very nice gesture. I will certainly offer them with your respects."

"*Mi Hijo*, I have been to the altar, petitioned and donated to the Babalawo. He assured me all would be as it should."

Raul cringed knowing his sex-addicted father was also an ardent follower of Santeria. He played along. "Thank you, Papi. I will take that as a sign I am on the right path."

"There is only one path, Raul—the family. Your half-brothers need to see you not as a usurper but as their equal in all ways. Cecelia makes that hard for them. Their mother, Nadia, was not of that kind. She was gentle and deeply religious. She ignored my machismo ways and tended to the boys. Your mother is concerned only with herself and by extension, you. I know even you find her... difficult. But I feel alive when I am with her."

Overwhelmed the old man had shared this with him, the derision from his brothers, the endless porn was briefly forgotten. Planting kisses on his father's cheeks, he escorted him to the door. "I will make you proud."

Raul placed the brown, wrapped bag atop his suitcase and walked through the French doors to the balcony. The evening winds had lessened the humidity, and the temperature was a comfortable 26 degrees Celsius.

Looking over the city, Raul breathed in the scent of Havana: car fumes—burning oil and exhaust layered with the occasional fragrance of flowers, and when the breeze quickened, the clean smell of the sea. He could hear the faint strains of guitar drifting upward in the darkening sky. Watching a jet flying north above the city, he smiled. His destiny awaited him in Florida.

CHAPTER 38

The Perfect Gift

Downtown Naples had turned into heaven. Exotic cars as far as the eye could see were diagonally parked on both sides of the street. Fifth Avenue from Tamiami Trail to Third Street South, the shopping mecca for the elite, had become an exotic car aficionado's paradise. Sal was reliving the exact feeling that happened every Christmas morning in his family's Bronx apartment when he was a child.

His anticipation began as he headed north on Tamiami, and built up crossing the bridge near the Tin City Shoppes. Just like his childhood, the delay—waiting for his parents to wake up—was the twin feeling to finding a valet to park the Escalade and the slow walk from the parking structure to the turn on Eighth Street. Entering the hallowed ground of the car show, his expectation turned into a full-blown brain orgasm. Arrayed in front of him as far as his eye could see were Ferraris: all colors, all models. The noontime glare on the perfectly detailed vehicles created a glow that burned his eyes as if he was looking directly at the sun. Turning to Lexie, his mouth opened, but no words came out.

He watched her mouth form words; they were lost in the loud music from a live band a half block up the street. Journey's "Don't Stop Believing" filled his head. That was his song, had been since he was a teenager. The finale of his favorite show, *The Sopranos,* ended with a haunting scene in a diner. That song was playing when the screen went black. The unforeseen ending left him dumbfounded.

Memories roiled him, year to year, moment to moment, all coalescing in this perfect place, on this perfect day with Lexie beside him. He felt destiny calling him. Smiling, he grabbed her hand and led her down the street.

Regaining his composure, he remembered what his goal was this day—finding the perfect gift for Lexie. Walking past car after car, he noticed she wasn't drawn to a particular color, though most vehicles lining the avenue were red. Worried that his enthusiasm didn't extend to Lexie, he wondered if this gift might not be what she desired. Maybe she didn't share his love for Ferraris. His passion was borne a half century ago when he associated his surname with these amazing machines. That connection sent him on his journey to attain the success which would afford him the ability to procure one of these legendary vehicles.

That dream had been realized many times over. The path was slippery at times, created a need to skirt his morals. But in the end, he felt he had earned his wealth, his stature, and his young attractive wife.

"Hey, Lexie, if you could have any one of these cars, which one would you choose?"

"Sal, they all look the same to me, exactly like the ones in the garage back home. How can you even tell the difference?"

"To the casual observer, I guess they do seem similar, but there are major differences from year to year. The engines, they speak for themselves. Listen, you can hear when one starts up. You hear it? Down the street? That is the Ferrari sound. I would know it anywhere."

Sal knew he was getting nowhere. He would have to give up on the Ferrari idea. Turning to Lexie, he noticed she wasn't beside him. She was walking down a side street that had only a few cars on display. He watched as she passed by the newer models, each with a for sale sign. She stopped abruptly near the end of the short line of cars. She was staring at an older model Ferrari and was in an animated conversation with the man standing beside the vehicle. Sal watched as her hand gently caressed the gleaming fender. *Wow, I know that feeling.*

"Sal, this is Robert. Robert, this is my husband, Sal Ferraro. He is a Ferrari fanatic."

Robert held out his hand. "That so? You ever drive one of these?"

"I've never driven this model before. This is what, an '85?"

"That's right. A Mondial QV Cabriolet, only 629 built between 1983 and 1985. I snagged this one new, when I was riding high. My wife, gone now ten years, really loved this car." Lexie opened the door and slid inside while they were speaking. "I think the young lady is interested in this one. You in the market?"

"I was thinking of a newer model." Sal shook his head.

Lexie gasped. "Seriously? You were planning on getting another Ferrari?"

"I was seriously planning on getting **you** a Ferrari for your birthday."

"You asked me, 'If I could have any one of the cars which would I pick'? Sal, I love this one. It's even got those great flip up headlights. This car is amazing."

Sal turned to see that Robert had moved out of hearing range.

"No, Lexie. This car is a piece of crap."

"Sal, how can you even utter those words? You love Ferraris."

"Yeah, well, even Ferrari makes mistakes now and then. This was Ferrari's attempt to enter the affordable car market – middle class buyers who wanted to own a 'legendary' vehicle. Shit, Lexie, a tricked-out Corolla could overtake this car. It's a poor man's Ferrari, and if you haven't noticed, I'm not a poor man."

"This is the one."

"You're sure?"

"Yes." She nodded, her eyes locking on his. "This is the one."

"You do realize that your excitement about this car has sunk my ability to make a good deal. I have no bargaining chip. I'm going to pay top dollar for this. I just hope it runs."

Sal waved Robert over. "Robert, can I start her up?"

"Keys in the ignition."

Sal opened the car door.

"No, Sal, let me. I want to hear her purr." Lexie slid into the driver's seat.

"No purring from this cat, my dear. This one roars." Robert gave her a broad grin.

"Robert," Lexie giggled, "You are the best."

As Lexie started the car, the growl of the engine brought a satisfied smile to Sal's face. Though he never liked this model of Ferrari, the day was still a success. He found the perfect gift, something she really wanted. He consoled himself with the fact he had four beauties in his garage back home.

"Robert, let's talk money." Sal now looked at Robert as an adversary. He knew how to make a smart deal. Looking at the scuffmarks on Robert's loafers, the tear in the fabric seat of the fold-up sports chair that sat on the curb and the fact he was willing to part with his dead wife's car, Sal knew he held all the cards. Robert's grim expression said he knew it, too.

Sal noticed a frown appear on Lexie's face. She must know that Robert was desperate. He was shrinking before their eyes. His fate rested in his hands. It was time to go in for the kill.

Lexie moved in between Sal and Robert and placed her hand on Robert's arm. "How much do you need to get for the car? "Sal stepped back stunned. He watched as confusion caused Robert's head to swivel back and forth between Sal and Lexie. Lexie continued. "Robert, look at me. No negotiating. How much for this car?" Sal tried to intervene, "Lexie, Babe, that's not the way I make a deal."

"Is this my birthday present, Sal?" Her eyes sparked as she stared at him.

"Yes, but..."

She stepped closer to Sal, planted her feet, and raised her chin high. "No. Part of my gift is going to be me making this deal."

"What?" Sal gaped at her.

"Sal, you heard me." Turning back towards Robert her voice softened. "I understand this is more than a piece of metal to you."

Robert's words came out in a whisper, "Thirty-five-thousand dollars."

"What the fuck?" Sal's face turned red. "Lexie, you don't know anything about this car."

"I know it was loved, Sal. I also know that I can help someone by buying it. Everything happens for a reason. I've told you that since the day we met. It may not seem obvious now, but somewhere down the road buying this car will mean something."

"Okay." Sal raised his hands in surrender. "If you want it, you feel it's the right thing to do, then it's a deal."

Lexie extended her hand to Robert. "Is this alright with you?"

Robert clasped her hand and smiled. "You are quite a lady. My wife would have loved you."

Sal took out his iPhone. "Robert, you got a PayPal account?"

"Yes, sir, I do."

"If I secure the deal with a ten-thousand-dollar transfer to you, can Lexie drive it home today? We can figure the rest on Monday. I will give you cash, or a wire transfer of funds."

"That seems fair." Robert smiled at a beaming Lexie. "I don't think your wife would let you steal my car."

Sal looked over at Lexie, a satisfied smile illuminating her face. "No, she has the upper hand. Knows just how to play me every time."

"You're a lucky man, Mr. Ferraro."

❧

Lexie decided not to mention to Sal that she wasn't comfortable driving a stick. The gated shifter on Sal's Ferraris had always given her trouble. She usually ran around town in a Chevy Equinox Sal leased for his business. She managed to get the car in first gear, with only a slight bucking noticeable. Lucky that Sal had gone to pick up the Escalade from the garage. The low profile of the vehicle made her nervous.

She turned the corner out of view of Robert and headed down Tamiami Trail. Feeling exhilaration and power, Lexie gave it some gas and realized too late that the car was too much for her. She missed a shift. The car slid out of control, hitting the curb hard with the right front tire. The sound and thump made her cringe. She got it back in gear and proceeded slowly south. She needed to get the car into the condo garage before Sal noticed the damage. Tires can be replaced, she thought, as she downshifted and settled into a more reasonable pace.

CHAPTER 39

The Lone Ranger Rides Again

"Ladies, you are going to have to exit the pool for a few minutes. I'm trying out a new vacuum. It's a robot."

"But it's our exercise time," they collectively whined.

"I know. But the Aqua Bot rep let me have it for the afternoon. I need to see if its suction is strong enough for a pool this size."

The giggles began immediately, and Preston braced for the onslaught of risqué comments from the old ladies.

"We can show you some strong suction."

"Size has got nothing to do with it."

"Speak for yourself. I like a big, clean pool."

"How long will it be sucking?"

"You ladies never disappoint." He smiled as the group slowly walked up the stairs, their bodies shaking with laughter.

"Oh shit. My ring slipped off."

"Girls look around. Do you see it on the stairs?"

"We told you not to wear your jewelry in the pool. You lost a lot of weight. You didn't get your rings resized, did you?"

"What do you think? I hate driving during the season."

"Preston would have driven you. Did you hear that? Preston, you would have taken her to the jeweler, right?"

"Could you look for that huge rock before you send that sucking machine into the pool?"

Preston laughed. "Sure, no problem." He pulled his oversized sweatshirt over his head.

The collective gasp from the ladies surprised him. He immediately jumped in and began a grid search in the shallow end of the pool. The ladies lined the edge and watched with mouths open as Preston, his muscles rippling, swam back and forth in front of them.

"Girls, did you see that?"

"Is that really our Preston?"

"I should have been dropping things in the pool all along."

"I'm really thinking about sucking right now."

"You are disgusting."

"Tell me you aren't thinking about that?"

"Well, yes, I am. But I didn't say it out loud."

"You just did."

"He's like Adonis."

"No, Tab Hunter. You remember him in the beach movies?"

"He was so hot."

"A real lollipop. I would have liked to suck on him."

They noticed that Lexie had arrived poolside and was laying out her towel behind them.

"You know who should get together with him?"

"Lexie!" in unison.

"Shush. Lower your voices."

"They would make some beautiful babies."

"Yes. Children of the gods."

"She's married."

"Yeah, to that fat slob, Sal."

"She must love him."

"Why do you say that?"

"She's still with him."

"She doesn't love him. She's just afraid to go off alone."

Preston's head popped up out of the water, his right arm extended upward in victory. The diamond glinted in the sunshine.

The ladies parted, giving Lexie an unobstructed view of Preston climbing the pool ladder directly in front of her chaise.

Lexie's eyes opened wide as Preston's dripping wet body appeared in front of her.

"Hey, Lexie," he smiled. "What's up?"

She appeared frozen and uttered no sound.

"Okay then, see you later."

Turning back to the ladies, "Here's that boulder you were looking for."

Silence.

"You're welcome. Ladies. Stay out of the pool. The vacuum is going in."

Preston shook out his long shaggy hair and let it drop like a curtain, his face once again obscured.

"Wow. Who was that masked man?"

"Why does he hide all that under baggy clothes?"

"And behind that greasy mop of hair?"

"He should be in the movies."

"No. Now that we've got a peek, we want to keep him right here."

They turned to look at Lexie, who was staring at the wet footprints that led away from the pool deck.

✿

The gaggle headed into the condo, and except for a slight hum from the robot in the pool, Lexie savored the silence. She had forgotten how restorative a quiet moment could be. She used to be introspective. Sal's constant badgering about sex and his controlling nature had closed off that part of herself. He desired her so badly. He appeared confident, but he was desperately afraid of losing her. His weakness was exposed. Armed with that knowledge, she grew stronger. She needed to be if she was ever going to escape.

Florida had changed her. She saw Sal and their marriage for what it really was. She had to face reality. He had lied about the most fundamental part of any marriage. Her future was slipping away. It was time to climb out of the grave she had dug for herself. Life was filled with possibilities; she needed to find them before she completely disappeared within Sal's suffocating grasp.

The rhythmic wake in the pool created by the vacuum's laps lulled Lexie into a dream-like state. She brought her meditative skills to bear, took deep slow breaths, and tried to clear her mind. What replaced her purposeful practice was the vision behind her closed lids of Preston with glistening water dripping off his chiseled body. She had caught a mere glimpse of a bright smile that appeared behind his sodden blond locks. Her meditation gone, she relaxed into her daydream. She longed to push those strands back and fully see the face of this enigmatic genius.

"Hey, sleeping beauty."

Lexie startled from her reverie, stared up at her dream come to life. But, instead of the bare-chested vision, the real Preston appeared covered in his usual oversized clothes, his face hidden by uncombed soggy curls. "Hi, I didn't hear you." Embarrassed by her thoughts, her face flushed.

"You should put on sunblock. You look a bit red."

"I have some in here somewhere." She pulled the beach bag onto her lap. "I was just napping. It's so quiet here with the ladies gone."

"How are things going with you? We haven't spoken much since that first day you got here. Not alone anyway. That was quite a conversation."

"It must have been the pot," she sniffed.

"It could have helped, but there were some honest words being tossed around. I was wondering if you have any further thoughts about, you know, Sal and Lenny."

"That's personal. You get right into it, don't you? No small talk."

"I saw what happened at the pool last week. That freak Lenny shouldn't be allowed anywhere near you."

"He's harmless." Lexie stiffened. "I had the situation under control."

"That's not what I saw. Say the word, he's history."

"That's disappointing. You sound like Sal. Violence isn't the way to solve your problems."

"I didn't say anything about violence."

"Oh, sorry. I just assumed. You know the men in my life tend to go that way."

"The men in your life? Sounds like you included me in that description."

Lexis face reddened even more. *Damn!* *What the hell is going on here?*

"Your face really needs some block. If you can't find yours, I have some in the pool house. It's no problem."

"No. I found it." She pulled the tube out of her bag.

"Besides the Lenny scene, things seem a little tense with you and Sal as well."

"Are you spying on me?"

His next words were spoken softly. "No. I just noticed that the lovey stuff that was going on when you guys arrived doesn't seem to be happening lately."

"My love life is none of your business." With those words spoken, Lexie noticed Preston's demeanor had changed. His slouch disappeared. He seemed to come to an internal decision.

"Well, then you need to be a bit more discreet. You do know that there are cameras in the garage, right?" His voice was now deeper, stronger.

Her eyes widened. "You shit. You were watching?" She spat out, "Are you some kind of a freak?"

"The day you arrived I saw you land on Mrs. Benson's Cadillac. I turned away. I'm not a pervert. Later, I checked that there were no scratches on the hood. That's part of my job. I take care of the cars. I didn't know who you were."

"We drove up in an Escalade. We look like car thieves?"

"Who knows what anyone is capable of these days? You could have been terrorists."

"Sal is a lot of things, but he's not a terrorist. He loves me." She folded her arms across her chest. "He bought me a classic Ferrari for my birthday."

"I saw it in the garage. It's going to need a tire. Your devoted husband should have spotted that. Don't take it out until it gets fixed. It's dangerous to drive. Anyway, what does his buying you a Ferrari prove?"

Preston sat down on the edge of the adjacent lounge and leaned towards Lexie. "You're a smart woman. You know the term "terrorist" covers a lot of territory. La Cosa Nostra is basically a terrorist group. They use intimidation to keep people under control. They fund their operations with gambling, drug money, and illicit sex rings. They murder people who get in their way. Sounds like terrorism to me."

"I don't have anything to do with that. Besides, Sal's told me he's not doing any of that shit."

"You sure of that? Sounds a lot like denial."

"He might have some issues." Lexie looked away from Preston's penetrating gaze.

"Well, at least you're admitting there's a problem. That's the first step in recovery."

"What do you know about recovery? You've been doing a bang-up job keeping your weed habit afloat. Oh, wait! Didn't you do some work for my terrorist husband?"

"I programmed a drone and a global positioning device. I was not involved in anything illegal. I was paid for a contract. Engineers do that type of work all the time." He tucked a sweep of hair behind his ear, revealing smiling eyes. "I am writing a dissertation about the project. I was in touch with MIT. They awarded me my BS. They were open to my completing my master's coursework remotely and are anxious for me to publish my work on drone technology. My doctorate will follow."

Her head tilted. "How are you doing that while high?" Her eyes narrowed as she sniped, "Does pot make you smarter?"

"About that. I quit. I haven't smoked since ..."

"That's great, Preston, I'm so glad to hear it. Was there a particular incident or did you just grow up?"

"That's harsh. I guess I realized that I needed to gain control of myself. I wasn't doing myself or anyone else any good hiding out, stoned in my condo. I can attribute some of my change to Lenny. When I worked on that project, I was happy. I didn't need to get high. When I was finished, I didn't go back to... my old ways. After I saw the way Lenny treated you, I was angry. I needed to be stronger." His clear blue eyes drew her in. "It was going to take courage to get what I wanted."

"What do you want?"

The buzzing from the vacuum's motor turned into a squeal. "Saved by the bell. I'll be right back."

"Preston, you are not off the hook."

Lexie watched as he walked away. Her thoughts, swirling in different directions, finally settled on Preston, an unlikely hero, and her role as the long-suffering victim. She realized how pathetic she had been. An involuntary shiver passed through her. Looking up at the building she noticed Lenny perched on the balcony ten floors above, peering down at her. She blinked and he was gone.

CHAPTER 40

Did I mention Jack Kerouac lived down the street?

"Carl, first off, I got to thank you for getting this done so quick. I only have ten days left until I retire. I'll be glad to get this case closed before I go. You saved a lot of time and aggravation."

"I didn't do much, found some samples, bagged them, tagged them, and sent them FedEx to you. Found the dentist quick, everyone in the neighborhood uses the same guy. That wasn't a big a deal."

"Well, the dental records on Dominic and David Andruzzi gave us the ID we needed. DNA is going to take a bit longer."

"It's going to be harder finding something on David. He didn't go to that dentist, at least not since he lost his baby teeth. He hasn't lived there for years. The visit to the mother is going to be a bitch. Notifications are rough, but two sons...hope she's a tough lady."

"I'm sorry you've got to do that."

"It's my job."

"Tell me how this went down. Start from the interview with the uncle." Pete paused. "How did that go?"

"Alberto Spano was a gusher of information. You want the background?"

"An abbreviated version would be okay. You write a report on it?"

"Of course. Nothing goes anywhere without documentation. I'll send it to your office."

"Spano. How did you start?"

"I told him I was looking for information on Dominic, Louis, and David Andruzzi. Did they live across the street? What was his relationship to them? When was the last time he had contact with them?"

"Was he forthcoming? Or evasive?"

"He couldn't wait to throw up all the bile he'd been carrying around. There was bad blood between him and his sister, Matilda Andruzzi. Benedetto Andruzzi, Matilda's husband, died in a mob turf war when the boys were young. After his death, Sal Ferraro senior took care of the family, paying for Catholic school. He gave David, the smart one, room and board to Boston College. The kid got a full tuition ride on his grades."

"No shit. That was a home run."

"You would think so. You can take the kid out of Howard Beach, but you can't take the beach out of the kid. Sophomore year, David gets bounced for running a card game. No charges filed. I'm thinking Ferraro money greased some palms."

Dominic and Louis, no brains to speak of, got odd jobs at the salvage yard. Uncle Al wanted the boys to get out of that life. 'Tilly' was a goombah wife all the way, said she owed the Ferraro's too much.

Uncle Al cried when I told him they might be dead in Florida. He started yelling and shaking his fists to the sky. It was in Italian, so I'm not sure exactly what he said. He let me into the house when he knew I needed something personal from his nephews to positively identify the bodies."

"He had a key?"

"Yes. He said he's been taking care of the house since Tilly went into the home. Does all the odd jobs, fixes things that break. He laughed when he said those boys couldn't fit under a sink if a pipe let go. Then he started crying again."

"That must have been difficult. You got the DNA samples from that visit?"

"There was a large portrait of the older boys, Dominic and Louis. They were babies. Taped to the back were two locks of hair. Each labeled with their names and dates of their first haircuts. As a bonus, Crime Scene also picked up some used dental floss stuck to the bottoms of the bathroom waste baskets. Still had bits of food and blood on them. Bingo."

"No baby picture of David?"

"You got kids?"

"No, never get around to that."

"Well, I have five. By the time the third one shows up, either the camera's batteries are dead or everybody is too busy to take pictures."

Pete shook his head. "Matilda is not going to take this well at all. Is Uncle Al joining you for the notification, you know, for support?"

"No. He hasn't spoken to his sister in years. He watched out for the boys from across the street. He kept his distance, fixed things around their house. She never thanked him. He said on occasion the boys would come over to ask advice about girls and stuff. He liked to think he was a substitute father. Their deaths hit him hard. I'm going to head over to the nursing home now. I arranged to have the staff doc meet me there."

"That's protocol down here, Carl. Plenty of nursing home notifications in South Florida. Some of the frail ones drop when they hear bad news."

"I'll give you a call if anything interesting turns up."

❧

Pete was knee deep in his notes when NYPD called back.

"Pete, you got the file I sent?"

"Yeah. Very thorough. Thanks. Still wondering, how come no dental records on David?"

"Not sure. We checked every dental office in the area. Had Boston look into offices near the BU campus. Nothing."

"I've heard about people with phobias about dentists. Maybe he just never went."

"Did the M.E. say he had bad choppers?"

"No. He mentioned how fastidious the guy was—perfect teeth, all organs in tip top shape, not an ounce of fat on him. He seemed impressed at the victim's well-developed, partially exposed muscles.

"Sounds like your M.E. had a bit of a man-crush on the corpse."

"He loves his work, wouldn't want to go that far. I like the guy. That would creep me out big-time."

"Just saying. Odd way of discussing dry autopsy details."

"Carl, how did the meeting with Mrs. Andruzzi go? She still breathing?"

"Yeah. This was a gut punch for the old girl—two sons. She went off after I told her. The doc gave her a mild sedative. Once they sank in, the news and the shot, she offered up some interesting information. For one thing, she never did ask about David."

"Bad blood, you think? Could be another reason no baby picture."

"Who knows? Italians are notorious for holding grudges. She also seemed to think they died happy. They were following their calling."

"What the fuck does that mean?"

"Not sure, but I have an idea. I let her go on a bit, reminiscing about the neighborhood, how it's changing. When she and Benny, her husband, moved in, it was all Italian families moved out from Brooklyn. They bought the place cause of an advertisement. Ozone meant fresh air. That's what brought them all out from the city, fresh ocean breezes—that and the race-tracks, fresh air. Funny, I never knew that."

"So, the calling, what's with that?"

"She's been in the mob culture her entire life. My guess, it went back generations."

"Like in the *Sopranos*?"

"Well, that was fiction. But Italians, they have long histories. Some families push for their sons to become priests, other families, cops. And more common in these parts, they push for them to become soldiers in the "family.""

"Carl, you got to be kidding."

"Pete, I'm not joking. Around here, to these old school Italians, family is everything. You should have seen Mama Andruzzi. She was showing off a photo album of her boys at her husband's funeral standing next to Sal Ferraro, Senior. The way she spoke, you'd think he was the pope."

"Okay. She was happy her boys followed their calling and became mob flunkies. How did these assholes end up in the Everglades?"

"Matilda was proud to tell me they had gotten a big promotion."

"All three of them?"

"Yeah. She said her novenas were finally being answered. She showed me her altar, complete with a statue of Mary dressed in silk robes. I stopped her when she wanted to show me the scapular pinned to her bra."

"What's a scapular?"

"It's a religious symbol, two pieces of felt attached by strings, worn under your clothes. She wanted to know if her boys were wearing theirs when they were found. If they were, she said 'they would be forgiven and welcomed into heaven on the first Saturday after their deaths.'"

"Wait. Back-up. A promotion?"

"She said Sal Ferraro, Jr. had spoken to them in person and asked them to go to Florida to head up his new business there. Her exact words. It's all in the report."

Pete exhaled loudly, "This just got very interesting."

"The report also has an attachment. It's a photo of Dominic and Louis standing in front of what looks like a small outhouse. There is a sign next to it says, "United States Post Office, Ochopee, Florida." Is that a real place?"

"It sure is. Not far from where their bodies were found. Any date on it?" Pete walked over to the squad whiteboard and made a note on it.

"The nursing home attendant who covers Matilda's floor said her son had sent it to the office email. I had him forward it to me. The email was dated February second. He printed it up and framed it for her."

"The timing is right. The bodies were found the next day."

"Pete, were there scapulars on the evidence list?"

"I don't remember. Why?"

"Just wondering if they made it into heaven on Saturday."

"Carl, I'll check, if it makes you feel better."

"Oh, Pete, one more thing. Matilda mentioned something that was out of character for her. Got nothing to do with the case, but it was weird. She was talking about her street, with all the Italians living on it. She mentioned that one of her neighbors was a famous writer. He lived there when he was young – a good catholic boy, name of Jack Kerouac."

CHAPTER 41

Tengo un Chico

First class was a waste of money. The flight to Fort Lauderdale had landed before Raul had finished his rum and coke. *It takes one hour to travel from hell to heaven.* Not willing to let good Cuban rum go to waste, he downed the last of his drink, picked up his carry-on outside the jet-way door, and headed to customs. Sure this would be the most difficult part of the journey, he was pleasantly surprised to find that the concierge package he had purchased expedited his way through U.S Customs. His next worry was that his name would trigger an alert. He held his breath as the agent examined his documents, typed on his computer, and frowned. He had two questions for him.

"Mr. Garcia, English or Espanol?"

"English, please."

"I notice you have booked your return flight for two weeks from today. Are you entering the United States for business or pleasure?"

"Pleasure, sir. A reunion of old acquaintances."

"They can't be too old. It says here you are only thirty-two."

Raul shrugged and gave him a half-smile.

"Enjoy your stay in the United States, Mr. Garcia."

"Thank you."

Retrieving his bag, he was relieved to see the contents had not been rifled. The box containing the cigars was intact and unopened. America is a wonderful place. Raul smiled as he walked out into the bustle of the concourse and turned on his phone.

His cousin Diego answered on the first ring. "Diego, I am exiting the International Arrivals building."

"Can't wait to see you *primito*. I am in a white Ford Explorer with a Cuban flag flying from the roof rack."

"Very subtle. I said not to draw attention."

"You're kidding." His laughter through the phone eased Raul's tension. "Cuban flags are all over south Florida. I took down the fringe and scraped off the decals. You can't hear the stereo I have the music down so low. Cousin, I wasn't giving up the flag. Our heritage flies loud and proud. Pulling up now. I see you, the good-looking kid with the big attitude. Man, you are a Garcia alright."

A car slid to a stop in front of Raul. An older man jumped out, ran around to the curb, and threw his arms around him.

"*Mi familia por fin.* Welcome to America, Raul Garcia." Diego, his eyes damp, kissed him on both cheeks.

"Cousin, it is an honor to finally meet you." Raul said as he placed his bag in Diego's outstretched hand. Raul looked him over, noticing his graying hair and trim build. Diego's muscles bulged beneath the t-shirt that hugged his body. The resemblance to his father and uncle was uncanny.

"You look good, Diego. I have seen only one photograph of you. A picture placed on your mother's altar. You were very young."

Diego stowed the bag in the back of the SUV and headed into the snarl of traffic outside the terminal. "A lot has changed, Raul. *Dios es grande.* Your email arrived just in time."

"What has happened?"

"I was low, cousin, rock bottom. Had nothing to live for. *Familia,* the last thing I thought, would come to my rescue." Diego exited the airport and expertly maneuvered through the heavy traffic heading south down I-95.

"Tia Rosa told me things were sad for you."

"Sad? Yes, very sad." Diego nodded.

"I didn't know. I just thought you might be interested in helping me, er, the family out." Raul looked at Diego's stoic expression.

"What did *mi Madre* tell you about my departure?"

"Not much, but she is heartbroken. Her altar to Elegua is littered with offerings for your safety, mostly popcorn and smoked fish. It stinks."

"That is disrespecting her faith, Raul. Santeria has kept her sane all these years."

"*Lo siento.*" Raul bowed his head. "I did not realize you were a follower."

"I'm not. I attend Saint John Bosch," Diego bowed his head. "The Catholic church near my apartment."

"I did not think you would be religious."

"Why? Because I am gay?"

"I, I...did not mean to suggest..."

"It's okay, I took the rainbow flag off the car. Not sure how you felt about that."

Raul turned towards Diego. "I always thought that might be the reason you left."

"I didn't leave voluntarily. I was banished. It was nineteen-eighty." His knuckles whitened as he gripped the steering wheel. "Gay men were ostracized. At my father's request, your father had me expelled. I ended up on a raft in the Florida Straits."

"The Mariel Boat lift? That must have been hell."

"It was. The only people who hated homosexuals more than my father were the lunatics and criminals on those rafts. I put on my best macho attitude, told them I was a murderer and drug dealer, and they left me alone. Almost to the Keys, and someone whispered the words 'Don Garcia.' They threw me in the water, cursing me as '*hombre rico.*' I struggled for hours to stay alive." Diego's face lit up as he looked over at Raul. "Jeffrey Stiles found me half-dead, hanging on to a mangrove root near Key West. He saved my life. He was, like me, separated from his family. Not as dramatically, but they couldn't accept him for who he was." Diego shuddered and exhaled deeply. "It was a miracle. I found Jeff and my faith on that day."

"Tia Rosa told me of your loss. I am so sorry."

"After Jeff died last year, I closed the house in Key West, left everything exactly as it was the day he died—hired a house watcher to keep things running and never looked back. I moved into an apartment in Little Havana. I started drinking heavily, doing coke, hanging out in the worst parts of the city." His body slumped as his confession twisted his handsome face. "I had lost the only thing that mattered to me. I was killing myself." He sucked in a breath and shivered. "And if I couldn't do it, I wanted some fucked up bastard to do it for me." Diego shook his head and rubbed a hand through his hair. He looked over at Raul. "I am sorry to open my heart up like this. I should not have said this to you. I haven't had anyone to confide in for so long. I don't want you to think I am a crazy old man."

Raul searched his face. "I don't think that at all. I can't imagine all that you have gone through. I feel honored that you would share this with me."

"Then I received a letter from a cousin, *mi familia,* but brand new to me, another miracle! I climbed out of the hell I was in and prepared to start over. It is a lucky man who is reborn twice." He relaxed and smiled. "My mother should be popping corn and smoking fish in thanks. I am finally welcomed back in the family. I guess Cuba's awakening has softened their hearts. Working as a Garcia in the family business has given me a new life. I have many connections. More than just the cars, I have been supplying."

Raul shifted in his seat. "You are not exactly working for the family. Your mother gave me your address. She knows nothing about this. The work you have been doing is for me."

"Don't you run the groves?"

"Yes."

"The family still running two games?"

"Yes, but I have started a side business that I hope to merge into Garcia Enterprises. My father and brothers are not aware of this venture. When the money starts rolling in, I will tell them."

"You've got Garcia-sized balls, Raul. I like that. You have come to America, the land of opportunity."

Raul's jaw tightened. "If only my brothers would see it that way."

"In time they will appreciate the doors you are opening."

Raul looked out at the passing landscape of large construction projects, luxury communities, golf courses, and suburban tract homes. He saw first-hand that America was still growing and ripe with possibilities. Beside him, Diego's pleasant voice sang along with the radio. He inhaled deeply and felt the tension from his travels exit his body.

"The cars I sent over to the west coast, they were satisfactory?" Diego asked as they exited the interstate.

"Yes, they were fine. I do need one more vehicle, for myself, to drive to Marco Island. Something that will show the wealth and taste of the Garcia Empire."

Diego laughed. "I have the perfect car, and it is legal. It is sitting in a warehouse near my place. I had it detailed when I knew you would be coming."

"Legal?"

"It was Jeffrey's car, the car he owned when we met. I will never part with it. I haven't driven it since he passed." Diego crossed himself. "I think he would be happy that my family has need of it. He was very generous."

"I will take good care of it. You may trust my word, *Primo*."

"When will you leave for Marco Island? Will you join me for dinner? Little Havana has the best food in Miami."

"Ciertamente."

"I want to hear everything about *mi madre and la familia*. I want to know how you, Raul Garcia, came to be."

"There is much to tell. And more opportunity awaits both of us, Diego."

"Raul, it seems you have secrets. Tonight, we talk and celebrate!"

☙❧

The next morning, a gold 1975 Porsche 911 Turbo gleamed in the sunlight streaming through the high factory windows. Raul was stunned at the beauty of the car. Cuba's roads were crowded with older model American cars, but this German vision would never be seen on a Sunday cruise along the harbor.

"Diego, this car is magnificent! I can't wait for us to hit the road."

"Jeff treated this car like it was his child. He said it was the only thing he loved nearly as much as me. Thank you for inviting me to come along." He put two gym bags in the front boot of the car and Raul's carry-on behind the driver's seat. He turned towards Raul and patted his now dark brown hair. "You don't think the hair color is too much?"

"No. The gray was distinguished, but with this change you look ten years younger at least."

"You have given me new life, my young friend." He handed the keys to Raul.

"You drive, Diego. I think Jeff would like to see you moving on. I am sure he is watching you." Raul looked skyward.

"*Si,* it is time to head west."

CHAPTER 42

Cougars on the Prowl

Driving across Alligator Alley, Diego let the car have its way. The engine growled at each shift, passing cars that seemed to be standing still. Raul felt unsettled as the car lost grip on tight turns.

"This is a dangerous car, Raul," Diego said looking over at his nervous passenger. "I will pull over and let you drive. You need to experience this before you set off alone. You can drive a stick, *si?*"

"Most of the cars in Cuba are standard transmissions. I grew up in the groves driving trucks."

"This is no truck, my friend. Go slowly at first. Get used to it. Do not hit the gas too hard. It is difficult to adjust to the turbo lag. It will seem as if nothing has happened and then, *'Dios Mio!'* A rocket takes off. So much fun when you get used to it."

Raul reveled in the joy this journey was giving him. In a short time, Diego had become his friend, and he hoped, soon to be partner. A bonus was this magnificent car, and a payday at the reunion this coming weekend. *La vida es buena.*

Raul drove the Porsche through the gates of the M Resort and Spa. The stunning landscaping and cascading waterfalls had the desired effect of jaw-dropping opulence.

"I have made the right decision to join you for the weekend." Diego smiled.

The valet approached, but Diego refused to valet the car. The young attendant seemed relieved.

Diego laughed. "You don't want to drive the beast, boy."

"No, thank you, sir. It looks like it's speeding just sitting there. Besides, management has orders to keep top-end vehicles out front."

"It is a good to respect powerful things."

"Have a great day, sirs. I'll watch over the car."

"*Gracias.*" Diego smiled as he put his arm around Raul's shoulder.

Smiling broadly, they walked through the gilded doors of the M Spa and into the opulence of the grand foyer. A scent of jasmine hung thick in the air. "What is that smell?" Diego looked around.

"I think they are infusing the air with a tropical fragrance. I read about it in the description of the hotel." Raul looked around trying to detect the source of the odor.

"Well, it stinks. The tropics do not smell like this. The rooms better not be infused. I will be sleeping on the beach." Diego looked at Raul's horrified expression. "I apologize. It was rude of me. Your generosity has been too much. I have no right to complain."

"I agree. It does stink. I'm sure it will lessen as we enter the lobby."

The cavernous space in front of them was refreshingly free of odor. The glass atrium roof was crisscrossed with exotic wood beams. Sunshine dappled the planked floors as it blinked through slowly revolving bamboo fans. Massive palm trees filtered the tropical sun offering the guests an ambience of cool, green serenity. A small, pebbled stream bubbled up though a floor-level fountain and meandered through the open space. A subtle tinkling sound could be heard as the crystal-clear water tumbled over delicate pebbles and sea glass and then flowed into a boulder-strewn pond on the glass-fronted balcony.

Raul walked to the front desk and was greeted with generous smiles from the waiting staff. "I am checking in. Raul Garcia. I have a reservation for a king Gulf-front room."

"Yes, sir. Your room is ready."

"I have request. Would I be able to upgrade to a two-bedroom suite?"

"Mr. Garcia, this is our busiest season. Our suites are completely booked. I would be able to offer you a second king room if that will fit your needs."

"*Si*. That would be fine." Raul picked up the key cards and hotel information and turned to see Diego standing at the balcony railing.

Diego had followed the brook to its terminus, a waterfall created by the infinity edge of the pond. Below the balcony, the pool and bar were crowded.

Raul walked up beside Diego. "Look down, young Raul. Witness the native wildlife of southern Florida! They have expanded their territory west from South Beach. It is the seasonal migrating cougar! You are in luck. You will get laid tonight, my friend!"

Ranged below them was a rippling throng of tanned flesh. Sleek limbs were burnished bronze and glowed with natural oils. Luxurious manes, in shades of auburn, gold, and black shone brightly in the early happy-hour sun. The pride flowed en masse between the bar and the dance floor with an occasional rogue creature escaping the troop to move in on unsuspecting prey.

"You must be choosy, Raul. You are fresh meat and good-looking. You may get torn apart if you head to the bar. Stay by my side. You will look like my young lover until we find a safe place to drink and observe."

"I have never thought about taking an older lover."

"Then you have been missing out on one of the finer things in life. With age comes experience. Inhibitions are gone and for those lovely creatures below us, the search for pleasure is paramount. One of them," Diego nodded towards the dance floor, "will give you a night you will never forget."

Raul smiled broadly. "Let's go."

Diego placed his arm around Raul's waist, and they headed into the jungle.

Beneath the balcony, a small bar shaded by palms offered a view of the pool area and the dancing crowd. Two rum runners were placed in front of them. The bartender smiled warmly at Diego and poured a large rum floater atop each of their drinks.

"You have caught someone's eye, *Primo*."

"Not interested, Raul. The same holds true for men. Stay away from the young ones."

"Weren't you young when you met Jeff?"

"Yes, but I was new to all of it. I wasn't sitting in a bar waiting for a rich old man to keep me. I have seen a lot in my time in Key West. I have seen even more since Jeff died. Tonight I might want passion, but I will get in a plane and leave for home. Someday, I will look for love."

Raul looked over at the crowd. "Tell me where we begin."

"Right there." Diego pointed to voluptuous brunette sipping a white wine and tapping her foot in time with the pulsing beat.

"What makes her special? She's pretty, but how do you know," Raul hesitated, "she is willing?"

"She is not wearing a ring, but she has a band of pale skin where her wedding ring should be. She is married. Not desperate for company, she just wants sex. Something exciting. She has money. Look at her jewelry, real. Her breasts? I am guessing real, too. She's waiting for you. See? She just looked over." Diego pushed him towards her. "Buy her a drink, maybe show her your car, take her for a spin, buy her another quick drink at a beach bar, give her a little nuzzling. Then head back here. Make her feel wanted, hot, sexy."

"What about you?"

"I already see where my night is headed." Diego nodded at a trim, older gentleman sitting alone at the end of the bar. He was wearing a ring. "That is my night's entertainment."

"He's married."

"I know. His wife doesn't sleep with him anymore—probably a relief since he's been pretending for years."

Raul looked over at the man and then back at Diego. "How do you know that?"

"I know who he is. He is Jeffrey, before I met him. He wants exactly what I want. See you in the morning, cousin."

⊱❧⊰

"May I buy you a drink?" Raul settled into the open seat next to the woman and nodded to the bartender.

"Uh, sure. Pinot Grigio." She shifted nervously in her seat.

"A Pinot Grigio for the lady and a Cuba Libre, *por favor*." Raul placed his black card on the bar. He turned back toward the woman. "I am Raul. And your name, lovely lady?"

"I'm Jeannette. Mc... McDonald."

"Like the hamburger? That's interesting." Raul chuckled.

"Speaking of happy meals, aren't you a little young for this place?" Jeanette smiled at her clever joke.

"Age is a state of mind. I have just arrived for business here on Marco. I noticed your quiet beauty as I entered the pool area." Raul observed her demeanor tighten. "You have a serenity about you," he waved his arm towards the dance floor, "that seems to be lacking in most of these creatures."

"I, I...I came here with friends for the weekend. I'm from Ohio. We thought it would be a nice getaway." Jeanette shifted nervously on the barstool.

"I do not see your friends around you." Raul noted the absence of extra glasses on the bar. "Did they abandon you?"

"They went to dance. I'm sure they'll be back soon." Jeanette looked over at the crowd, turning back to him, she spoke softly. "May I ask how old you are?'

Raul laughed. "Would you like me to ask your age, sweet lady?"

Jeanette's glossed lips curled up in a slight smile. "No, I get it."

"There is nothing to get, Jeanette."

The bartender placed their drinks in front of them. "Enjoy." He winked at Raul.

Raul handed her the generously poured glass and picked up his own. "We should toast to the chance meeting of strangers in a strange land." Their glasses met. Raul leaned in close to Jeanette and spoke softly, "*Salud por que la belleza sobra* - to your health, since you are already so beautiful."

Raul studied her face. He saw the frown that creased her brow had softened, as she appeared to come to a decision.

She leaned in close. "You're very good-looking and sophisticated. I didn't know what to expect. I've never sat alone at a bar before."

Raul nodded, knowing he had surmised the truth. "Ah, I see, but now, you are not alone. We are the same. In Cuba, I do not go out to the clubs. I find the patrons to be, I think the word is 'shallow.'" He paused, took a sip of his drink, and continued with small talk. "Those trees hovering above us is my business." He pointed up at the coconut palms laden with heavy fruit shading the bar. "*Mi familia,* my family, runs large coconut groves. I came here with my cousin this evening to relax. He has abandoned me, as your friends did you. It is fortunate, for now we have met."

The bartender kept their glasses filled and the lubricating alcohol seemed to release their inhibitions. Raul marveled at how much he enjoyed her easy conversation and elegant style. He hadn't noticed how much the bar crowd had grown until they were jostled by partiers ordering drinks. He considered Jeanette's relaxed posture. She gazed into his eyes as she took a sip of wine and licked her lips. Raul moved in closer and whispered into her ear, "Maybe it is time to leave. We have found what we were looking for."

She nodded.

Raul signaled to the bartender. He left a generous tip between the empty glasses that glistened with condensation in the warm evening air. Raul took Jeanette's hand and led her away from the bar. They walked slowly through the lobby. "We can take a ride in my car. I thought we might head towards the Everglades and stop at the Café de Havana for a taste of my home. It was recommended by the bartender. He says he goes there often. After, I will bring you back here and then..."

Jeanette leaned over and kissed his lips softly. "And then we shall see."

⚜

Diego sat at the bar and watched as the older man he had noticed drank alone. He appeared to be in his mid-seventies. He was neatly dressed in a linen blazer, a polo shirt beneath was tucked into neatly pressed jeans, a gold watch and his wedding ring the only noticeable jewelry. His arms and face were deeply tanned. His left hand, less brown, signaled he was a golfer. His white hair was freshly cut, and the drape of the tailored jacket suggested he was trim and well-muscled. He reminded him of Jeffrey.

A seat opened beside the man. Diego picked up his drink, caught the bartender's eye, and pointed to the empty chair. The bartender picked up the fifty Diego had placed on the bar and smiled. "If that doesn't go well, I'll be here until closing."

"I noticed you over here drinking alone. That is no fun. Want some company?"

"Sure, join me."

"Diego Garcia."

"Garret Tomlinson. Friends call me Gary.

The hand extended before Diego had perfectly buffed nails. On his tan wrist a Patek Philippe watch peeked out from beneath the white linen blazer. His firm grip held Diego's hand a moment longer than customary.

"A pleasure to meet you, Gary."

"I'm sure the pleasure will be all mine, Diego."

A wink sealed the deal for Diego. It was time to join the world again.

CHAPTER 43

February – and the results are in...

The inter-office mail sat unopened on Pete Landry's desk as he stared off into space flipping rubber bands at the small, circular trash bin across the aisle. An assemblage of crushed Post-Its, paper clips, and rubber bands surrounded the can. His fellow detectives sat silently working at their desks, giving him a wide berth.

Charlie walked in and disrupted the peace. "What are you doing Pete?"

"What do you mean? I'm sitting here at my desk."

"You're supposed to be working."

"I am working."

"Really?" Charlie pointed at the can and its surrounding refuse. "This is working. What is your problem? You haven't left the building yet, but it looks like you shut off the lights. You still got to put in some time here before you sail off into the sunset."

"Do you think I should ask her out on a date?"

Charlie stared at his friend. "Have you lost your mind? No, I think you should invite her to the prom."

"That's a good idea," Pete mumbled.

"Get a grip. I got a call from the lab. They said they sent over the results from Freddie's scum sample two hours ago. What did it say?"

Charlie looked over the mess on Pete's desk. "Shit, it's right here. You haven't opened it? You need to get your head back in the game."

"Christ, Charlie, I got it bad. I can't stop thinking about Vanessa."

"Women don't like dumb assholes that drool over them. You need to wipe that shit off your chin. I'm still your partner. You're going to make me look bad. I'm not going to let that happen. I can't believe I'm even saying this, but you keep this up, I'm out of here."

Pete picked up the manila envelope. "I've never met anyone like her before."

"There is a whole world out there that you've been missing. You think you have this sweet life hiding in the shade of the mangroves. Look around you, brother." Charlie waved his arm, the gesture encompassing the squad room and the Wizened Dicks, huddled around a computer screen that featured an infomercial about testosterone supplements. "You have no life."

"I know it. You're exactly right. The last couple of days we've been working so hard. I go home. No, I go to the Buoy and get blasted. Donna, she's no help. It's 'blah, blah, blah, Vanessa, blah, blah blah,' then I think, why not go back to Donna since I probably got no shot with Vanessa? But truth is, I can't get it up for Donna anymore."

Charlie swiveled Pete's chair around until it directly faced him. "Leave Donna out of this. You hurt her bad, but she's tough. She's finally ready to move on. Let her do it." Charlie smacked Pete on the shoulder. "So, you think this is just the last few days? How about the last ten years? Same story. You work, get drunk, jump on Donna, and go back to work. You never noticed life passing you by?"

"How come you never gave me this talk before, Dad?"

"Because you wouldn't have listened. Something or someone has changed the equation. It could be the impermanence of life. With all the weird shit going down lately, it's like the state of Florida has turned into a fucking serial killer. You know you can't catch that sum bitch. My second guess? Vanessa."

"I don't even know what to say to her. I've never been speechless before."

"I don't see that. Your running sexual banter is epic."

"I mean speak to her like a grownup."

"Well, son." Charlie placed a hand on his shoulder, "I think when you see her, it's like you are looking in a mirror. She gives as good as she gets."

"Damn straight. It's so exciting. Sometimes I feel like I'm being stalked."

"Like every girl you've had in your sights?"

"Ouch. I never realized what a prick I am."

"Just ask Donna. She'll tell you what a prick you are."

"As far as Donna goes, she knows we're done."

"Okay. That's a first step. Next thing, admit what you are feeling, grow a pair, and don't run away from this one. You won't find another woman as tough. When you two finally consummate this dance, it should be on *Nat Geo* or *Pay per View*. I'm not big on porn or on watching my friends in the sack, but that will be quite a show."

"Yeah. That will be..." Pete shook his head. "I can't go there, yet."

"That's my man. Cut the pity party. Vanessa is completely into hard-ass, funny, successful Detective Pete Landry. This guy sitting here? He doesn't have a shot. As far as Donna goes, she knows she wasted ten years waiting for you. She was trying to hang on anyway she could. She deserves the chance to have a life. Man, seeing the fucked-up way the two of you chose to live was like watching two people clinging to a life raft and never noticing that the tide had brought them close to shore. Neither of you could see past the fog of sex and booze."

"Wow. Don't hold back, Charlie."

"I'm not. I wish I could've gotten through to you sooner. My last word on this. Take your hands off the booze and Donna's ass. Let's solve this shit-show of a case and then you and Vanessa can screw happily ever after."

Pete poured himself a cup of black coffee, pulled out the lab results and started reading. The cloud that had permeated his brain dissipated. "Bingo! Charlie, we got a winner! Cocaine. The Andruzzi brothers were into some bad shit. It's time to find Mr. Ferraro's rat hole and flush him out."

"Welcome back, Pete."

"Let's get everything on flights in and out of RSW, Naples, and Marco Island Airpark. Manifests for the privates and passenger lists for commercial flights." Pete held out his hand to Charlie. "It's good to be back. Thanks, Charlie. I'm steering clear of the booze."

"I'm here for you, brother." Charlie reached for his phone. "I'm thinking business transactions, too. Contracts, property transfers. Crank up those databases. Dan Barnes has done great work so far. Let's put him on the paper trail."

CHAPTER 44

"Hi, Vanessa. You look terrific! I was just thinking about you when you called." Pete sat down across from Vanessa in the restaurant's screened in back porch. The large space sat on pilings above the water and offered a view of the swamp and the busy waterway. "Surprised you picked this place."

"I found it the first week I was assigned down here. I figured you'd like it. You live in Goodland, right? Close to home for you..." she pointed at the thick Everglades vegetation across the canal, "...and close to my office."

Pete smiled, thinking maybe he had a shot with her. He didn't remember mentioning Goodland.

"Charlie mentioned you live in Goodland, up the alley a bit. In case you thought I was checking up on you." Vanessa said.

"Wow. She's good," he thought as he looked around. "It's perfect. I love this place. Although, I seem to remember you saying you were a vegetarian."

"I don't eat animal flesh. I'm a pescatarian; I do eat seafood."

"I prefer you call it meat, not animal flesh." Pete grimaced. "That sounds too ghoulish."

"You cover homicides." Vanessa smiled and patted his hand. "How does animal flesh gross out a man who deals with death, daily? It's just words."

"I work with broken flesh. I don't eat it. I eat meat, burgers, and steaks. Doctor, I've seen you in action. You handled that python well. It was a clean cut with that monster blade you had strapped to your thigh. What's your aversion to meat?"

"I grew up on a farm, seen too much. The best days of my childhood were spent fishing on the river with my dad. We would eat what we caught. Nothing tastes better than fish right out of the water. That's one of the reasons I love this place. The boats bring in their catch, and they cook it up and put it on your plate."

Pete looked over his shoulder just as Krissy the hostess/shuck girl snapped a photo of the two of them. He noticed her tight-lipped smile and her fingers typing away as she appeared to send a text.

She held up one finger. "I haven't forgot about you two. Be right over, Sugar, an emergency just arose, and I needed to get on it right away." She slipped her cell phone into her apron and answered the phone by the hostess stand.

"Poseidon Seafood, Krissy speaking. Donna? You got it?" Pete watched as she turned her back to him. He strained to hear her whispered words. "Yep, he's here. Wait, let me move out front."

"I guess you know everyone around here. It would be hard for a girl to surprise or impress you," Vanessa said.

"Oh... yeah. It's my beat. I've cracked a few crabs here. You like crab?"

"Yes, but I'm more of a grilled fish of the day girl."

"Please tell me you are not one of the diet-obsessed, doesn't seem your style."

"No diets for me, just love the sweetness of fresh fish. I get plenty of exercise traipsing around the swamps, climbing trees."

"And decapitating pythons. Hey, we should toast to that. You imbibe?"

"Are you kidding? I was beer pong champ my freshman year."

He put on a serious expression. "That's illegal."

"Statute of limitations has run out. I think I'm safe. You'll have to think of a different way to get me in handcuffs," she giggled. "I would love a cold beer."

"Thank God. I thought you were going to ask for a nice California rosé." Pete flushed. "Not that there is anything wrong with that."

"I enjoy a nice glass of wine. Sitting here on a wood bench facing the swamp calls for a cold brew and a plate of oysters."

"You read my mind." Pete said. "Let's do this."

"My plan exactly." Vanessa leaned in, her voice now a sultry whisper, "How about we knock back a few, slurp some oysters, and you know what they say, '*Carpe diem*'." She gave him a wink and a half-smile.

"Wow. I...sure...beer, oysters..." Pete felt himself losing control of the evening.

"Sorry for the wait, kids. Emergency came up...at home." Krissy's too sweet tone jolted Pete back to reality. "What can I get you all?"

"Two Coronas with fruit." *That's better. You got this.*

"And for the lady? We just got in a new Chardonnay."

Pete cut her off. "We will be sharing the beer, a dozen oysters, and a half dozen large stone crab claws to start."

"Wow. You cutting back on the booze? Oops, sorry. I guess I shouldn't have mentioned that. Waitress-client confidentiality and all. But hey, she should know what she's getting into, right? Pete, you going to introduce me to your girl?"

"She is a work colleague of mine. Krissy, this is Doctor Vanessa Tree-horn."

"I've seen you in here a couple of times, you're usually alone, though. You're the new Fish and Wildlife doctor. Story going around that you like to work with snakes." Krissy gave a slight nod in Pete's direction.

"Well, yes, I love snakes. I'm a herpetologist. That makes me a snake expert," Vanessa snarked.

"Uh, okay then, Doctor Treehorn."

"Please call me Vanessa."

"Sure, Vanessa. Beers will be right out, and I'll put in your order right away."

Pete smiled at the exchange but knew his next visit to the Buoy was going to be a rough one. Even though Donna and he were done, they were still friends—he hoped. If Krissy sent a photo to her, it would hit her hard.

It looked like he was on a date, and the split with Donna only happened a week ago. Looking over at Vanessa happily pushing a lime wedge into the neck of the Corona bottle, he wondered, were they on a date?

"Charlie told me you put in your retirement papers." Vanessa slurped down an oyster. "That true?"

"Yes, end of the month." Pete cracked a crab claw and grimaced.

"You, okay?"

"I'm fine, I…just thinking about leaving the job."

"You must be excited about starting a new chapter. You know, having free time?"

Pete shook his head. "I don't know what free time is."

"Me, neither." Vanessa reached into her bag and pulled out a bright orange Koozie decorated with a snake, a fish, a lizard, and a reptile that encircled the letters "J M I H." She expertly slid the cold, glistening bottle in and zipped it up in one swift motion.

Pete gulped as he took a huge swig of his Corona. He pointed at the beer jacket. "What's the significance of that?"

" 'J M I H' stands for Joint Meeting of the American Society of Ichthyologists and Herpetologists." She smiled sweetly. "They are my people." She picked up the bottle and took a sip. "I got this at the last annual meeting in New Orleans—awesome town. Have you ever been?"

"No, but it's on my list."

Her face glowed with excitement as she continued. "There was a great presentation on the determinate growth and reproductive lifespan in the American alligator. It was a real showstopper for the crowd."

"I can see why—with a title like that." He laughed.

"Don't be fooled by the big words. They're a rowdy bunch—they like their beer cold. This was the most popular swag item at the convention. They spent hours and consumed multiple six-packs coming up with the perfect technical name for this —High Grade Functional Liquid Refreshment Temperature Preservation Device." She raised the beer bottle in a salute. "We are a special group of nerds."

Pete leaned back and laughed. "You continue to surprise me. You always keep one of those in your bag?"

"Yes, I do. This and an epi-pen. I'm prepared for any emergency."

"I'm impressed. I've seen you handle both. You're a good person to have around."

Vanessa put her hand up and shook her head. "I'm sorry we got side-tracked. Your retirement. Are you having second thoughts?"

"I live on second thoughts. I eat them for breakfast, lunch, and dinner."

"You know, Pete, you don't seem like the wavering kind."

"I'm not. When it comes to the big stuff, I get hung up on the details, the 'what ifs?' You know what I mean?"

"Not really. Explain."

"Well, take my retirement. I've been doing this job so long that nothing surprises me anymore. Wait, I take that back, until recently."

"What happened recently? Oh, you mean all the gruesome deaths?"

He rolled his eyes. "No. This is Florida; bizarre deaths are a fact of life here." He inhaled deeply and blew out a long breath. "You happened."

"I didn't happen. I'm just doing my job. I love my job."

"That's just what I'm talking about. I think I'm ready to walk away. I didn't love my job anymore. No surprises, dirt bags all around me. Drinking at night to forget how bored I was. Getting wasted and waking up some mornings with a woman I can't commit to. I told her that last week. Hurt her bad. I should have done that a long time ago."

"What's wrong with straightening out your life?"

"I didn't know it wasn't straight until…"

"Pete, how long have you been on the job?"

"I've been a cop for thirty years. Five in Orlando, not as happy a place as you would think. Twenty-five here in Collier County. I used to believe it was the best damn job in the world. Then the crazies got crazier. And the job got… I don't know, sad. I decided to get out. I'm trying to think of a life after. Then one day my phone screams."

"Excuse me?"

"When Charlie calls, his ring is a death scream."

"Why a death scream?"

"Usually signals a local tragedy."

"Nice. Go on." Vanessa took a long pull of her beer.

"You know the story from here on in. A dead guy in the glades, a beautiful, strong woman who can handle a blade and a bottle." He nods at the beer. "It's not such a sad job anymore. It's downright interesting. More dead bodies show up. More contact with the beautiful woman. My domestic arrangements start to look like shit. I decide to stop drinking so much."

"None of that sounds like a problem to me, especially the part about the contact with the beautiful woman. I like that part of your story. Let's go there."

"Hold on a minute. Put the brakes on, Vanessa. I'm not exactly sure where this thing between you and me is going or if there is even a thing going on. But you need to know, I have a terrible record when it comes to relationships. I have had exactly zero serious ones. I'm trying to clear out my brain, get things on track, and make good, lasting decisions. No more flying by the seat of my pants." He placed his palms on the table. "I'm fifty-two years old. I know nothing but police work. Never married, never had kids, I live in a trailer in a small fishing town alongside too many folks just like me. You're crazy if you want to get involved with that."

"Pete don't sell yourself short. You've got way more going for you than you think. Charlie told me..."

He abruptly sat back. "What did Charlie tell you?"

"He told me what you did for him, how you saved him. You're a good man. You know how many marriages end in divorce? Maybe, you haven't found the right woman. Maybe, you needed to be here in the Everglades working with Charlie, helping the yahoos who look up to you. You're a local legend around here. I've heard some stories."

"Charlie can never keep his mouth shut. So now you know Pete Landry and his tale of woe. It's your turn to spill. I don't see a ring on your finger. I can't figure that out at all."

"It could be I haven't found the right one either. Not a lot of men can handle a woman who can slice the head off a twenty-three-foot python. I guess I'm kind of intimidating."

"I thought that was amazing. Handy to have a woman like that by your side, especially in this part of the world."

"I was always too competitive, tried to keep up with my brothers. I needed to do anything they did, but better. That started when I was young, never really got over it. I never got invited to the prom. Never had a lot of dates. Decided to go into the only field I knew anything about, where I thought I could make a contribution, herpetology. That is something that my brothers instilled in me—not to be afraid of the unknown. If they found a snake, guaranteed that night it would end up in my bed. Instead of running away screaming, I began to learn all I could about what makes them so unique."

"I guess I should call and thank them for contributing to the formation of this amazing woman." Pete raised his glass and locked eyes with Vanessa.

A deep flush crept up Vanessa's throat. "Wow. I don't know what to say to that."

"You don't need to say anything. It is a pleasure and an honor to be sharing this meal with you." He took a breath, exhaled deeply, and continued, "Don't take this the wrong way, but I don't want to see you like this anymore." He couldn't believe he had just uttered those words. What he really wanted was to spend every waking minute with her and then find her beside him each morning.

Vanessa's eyes widened as she stammered. "Wha…What are you talking about? We…I'm having a lovely time. Aren't you?"

"Yes. The best evening I've had in a long time." His eyes searched her face. "I do want to see you, just not until this case is done. I think it will be too much of a distraction… while we are working together."

"Oh, okay. I get it. Let's keep it professional. We can do that. No need to back off on— whatever this might be."

"Not possible." Pete took Vanessa's hand, brought it to his lips, and gently kissed it. His breath faltered as a deep heaviness gripped his core.

Vanessa inhaled and exhaled slowly. "Pete, we can put this on hold, but I believe this thing we have going. It will only get stronger. The urges to follow this through will still be there. You sure we can work under these conditions?"

"Yes, I can. We can. I've never been surer of anything. I need to change up the patterns in my life. I am thinking long term here. You on board with that?" He realized that was the closest he had ever come to a proposal.

"I see. If we jump in the sack and then try to work together, it could mess up our chances for a...future?"

His face blanched as he blew out quickly. "Whoo. I wish you hadn't said that. You are making this hard for me. I'm serious. We'll have time to get to know each other after this case is closed, and I'm retired. Okay? It's only a couple more weeks." He prayed she would agree.

Her shoulders sagged as she offered him a resigned nod. "Okay, Pete."

"Vanessa." His eyes burned with desire. "When we get there, it will be..."

She signaled a full stop with her hand. "Don't. This is hard enough. Not what I had planned for this evening."

"I'm planning for more than one night. I've had too many of those. I know it's ridiculous to think someone like you would be interested in an old burn-out."

"I was interested from the moment you asked to have the picture taken at the scene. I had been thinking the exact same thing."

He slapped the table and smiled broadly. "I knew it. I felt it that moment, too. Your smile, the blood dripping from the blade, you a vision in camo and netting–you were a dream come true." Pete pulled out his phone. "You got to look at this photo. Bees sent it a little while ago." He handed over the phone. His bright smile evident in the photo was repeated in the face in front of her. "It needs to be kept low key— at least until the case is closed." He turned the screen around. "You are such a badass! You have that 'don't fuck with me and my knife look.'" He put the phone away. You understand why I'm asking you to hold on a bit, to be patient?"

"I do."

Pete felt his heart skip as the look on her face turned serious. "What's wrong?"

"Red flags."

Here it comes. "About me, right?"

"Well, yes." She took a sip of beer. "I'm not normally impulsive, you know, my job being dangerous. And my co-workers, they aren't always supportive of me as a woman." She took another swallow and pulled another bottle out of the bucket. "I would be remiss in not asking why you've never been married." She put her hand up. "I know you just gave me the whole spiel about being this cop in a fishing town."

"That's a thing." Pete nodded his face serious. "It's like being on spring break, for like, thirty years."

"That's it?" She blinked rapidly. Her face reflected disbelief. "That's what you're going with? A fifty-year-old on perpetual spring break."

Pete's shoulders slumped. *This was not good.* He shook his head. "My life, here in Florida, I'm not going to apologize for it. I have great friends, an interesting, no, important job. I fucking save people. I never did find the 'one' and it wasn't frowned upon by anyone I knew. A lot of people here feel the same way I do...I did."

"Okay." She looked around at the tables, locals all living at the edge civilization, lots of booze. "Got it." She looked back at him. "I had to ask."

He decided to turn it around on her. "So, you. No ring on the finger. What's the story? You are going with 'men are intimidated'?"

"Yes, actually, that would be it." She sighed deeply, nodded, then smiled at him. "But it seems, not you."

Pete waited out her silence "We good to go?"

"Oh, I'm good to go. But wait, are we going somewhere?" She giggled. "Are we backing off the backing off thing?"

Pete blew out a deep breath. "You are killing me." He looked at her lovely face, wanting more than anything to move-in and get this thing started. "No. All on hold for now. But trust me not for long."

"Detective Landry, I've never had a work-related slash deeply romantic discussion before. Should we shake hands?"

"No. Doctor Treehorn." He leaned across the table, took Vanessa's face in his hands, and kissed her soft, moist lips.

They groaned. Then in unison they leaned back, reached for the oysters, sprinkled on some hot sauce and locked eyes as they slurped them down.

Pete stood up and twisted side-to-side. He removed a folded sheet of paper from his pants pocket and returned to his seat. "Back to the case. I was planning to call you, but you beat me to it. We got our lab reports back today. But ladies first, if I'm allowed to say that now."

Vanessa squinted. "How did you do that? You're good at switching gears."

"It's a guy thing. We compartmentalize."

"I can keep up with that." She pulled a notepad from her pocketbook. "I got some lab results back, too. Remember those alligator babies that Freddy Driggs photographed? Some kayakers brought in a half dozen of them, dead. It was heartbreaking. I did necropsies on them. Sent some samples out for testing."

"Let me guess. The samples came back positive for cocaine."

"How did you know?"

"The labs we got back showed high-grade cocaine from the site where those babies came from. Freddie Driggs remarked the mama's eyes looked like she was stoned."

"Well, her babies died from drug overdoses."

"The puzzle pieces are beginning to fill in. We got the three dead guys who had no business being in the Everglades. We got high-grade cocaine killing gators in the swamp. We got a connection to a New York Crime boss."

"It sounds like you got your case."

"No, not quite there yet. Some big questions remain to be answered. Where did the drugs come from? Where is Sal Ferraro?" Pete looked over at Vanessa. *She is spectacular. And the most important question, "Will you marry me?"* popped into his brain.

Krissy walked up behind them, startling Pete. "You lovebirds ready to order dinner?"

Pete blushed and croaked, "What is the fish of the day?"

CHAPTER 45

Come out, come out, wherever you are

Danny Barnes took a mental inventory of the case; nothing led him to the Florida address of Sal Ferraro. He knew about the Ferrari Mondial Sal purchased in Naples for cash and registered to his address in Howard Beach. He knew about the hangar Sal owned at Marco Island Airpark and the Gulfstream that was inside. But where did Sal lay his head down and by extension, Mrs. Ferraro? Her pretty blond locks must be sleeping in luxury somewhere near Marco Island. Lenny Horowitz would be holed up nearby. He checked all the hotels, all the luxury condos, all the waterfront McMansions that were multiplying along the canals and gulf-front lots from Isles of Capris to Goodland.

He remembered something important he learned in the academy: chart out the problem, the suspects, the leads. Visual learners are often helped by concrete methods. *Damn. I'll chart them all out.* He grabbed a fresh pack of Post-Its, a Sharpie, and he began scribbling.

"What ya got, kid?" Charlie walked up behind Dan.

Dan jumped as his notes scattered across the table.

"You're a bit jumpy this morning. Too much caffeine?"

Dan sputtered, "Hey, no, I don't drink coffee."

"You're young, that'll change. What's going on with the Post-it piles? You got a lot of errands today?"

"I thought I'd make a chart, you know, to place everybody. I mean the suspects to identify: the who's, what's, when's, and where's. This case is like a puzzle, a lot of pieces." Dan pointed at the squad room whiteboard. "Four columns, suspects, evidence, crime, location."

"I see five columns."

"That last one is the addendum—for stuff that doesn't fit the other columns: explanations, open questions. You know that kind of stuff."

"Yeah, everything about this case should fit nicely in that last column."

Dan shuffled the Post-its. "We've got three dead Andruzzi brothers, accidental deaths. At least two of them worked for a reputed mob boss." Dan placed three Post-its on the board. "Mob boss, Sal Ferraro is in the neighborhood with his trophy wife, Lexie." Two more Post-its were slapped on. "Leonard Horowitz, Consigliere Jewish lawyer." Another Post-it applied. "We got a swamp guy, Freddie Driggs, in contact with weasel lawyer." Dan was about to place Driggs on the board when Charlie grabbed a green Post-it, scribbled Driggs name on it, and handed it to Dan.

"He's on our team."

"Yeah, I get it, but Horowitz reached out to him."

"But he's not a yellow, he's a green. Yellow and blue make green. Blue is always the good guys, us. He's working both sides, but mostly our side. So therefore, not yellow, green. He has helped us a lot over the years. You need to respect him. Some C. I's are assholes. Some just want a get out-of-jail free card. Some, like Freddie, are trying hard to do the right thing. If Pete sees Freddy up there as a yellow, he just might pull you off the case."

Dan crumpled up the yellow "Freddy" and placed a green one on the addendum side.

"That's better."

"Crime—red Post-its. It's not technically a felony murder case. I mean, you can't train pythons and ants." Dan smiled.

"You're right, but who put the brothers there? Who put them in a dangerous situation? Maybe some criminality on that point."

"Put it on the addendum. I will add all the charges that might be applicable."

"Not a lot of names on the chart." Charlie frowned. "I see a lot of white spaces."

"This is a fill-in-the-blank exercise. I'm working down a list from all the work I...uh, you, and Pete put together."

Charlie squinted, then gave Dan a half-smile. "I like it. You're ambitious.

"I didn't mean to..."

"That's okay, Dan. You've put in a lot of hours on this. You deserve credit for getting us to this point. Toot your horn. Nobody else around here will do it for you. Back to this chart."

"It's got a spot for everybody affiliated with the Andruzzi's and Ferraro salvage. But not everybody is going to make it on the chart. Someone down here must be involved, accomplices. This isn't their home turf. Of course, we get to fill in the over-arching blank."

Charlie smiled "And that would be?"

"What was going on in the Everglades?"

"All together now, Dan, my man."

"Drugs!" Dan slapped a red Post-it in the crime column.

"What is your focus now?" Charlie said as he pointed at the chart.

"Mrs. Lexie Ferraro, almost thirty-five, her birthday is this weekend. She is probably out all the time. She sure isn't holed up inside in Southwest Florida in the winter. Looking at her, I'm thinking yoga classes, spin classes, shopping, lunches out. I printed up this photo of her, I'm going to canvas Marco Island first."

"She's hot."

Dan shuffled through a folder. "Check out this picture of her husband."

Dan handed Charlie the picture of Sal Ferraro. "This was taken at the funeral for Mrs. Ferraro's first husband, Vincent Cacciatore. Sal Ferraro is the one taking up the middle of the frame. He is so big he's completely blocking out the two people behind him."

Charlie's eyebrows rose. "Big guy, he could easily crush her. Missionary out of the question for them."

Dan put the photo back in the folder. "If Mrs. Sal Ferraro is out and about on Marco, I'm going to find her and follow her back to her love nest."

"Why Marco? Why not Naples? What are your thoughts on that, Dan?"

"There is a lot more going on up there. It's the place for people to see and be seen. It's turning into Miami west and that's exactly why they might be on Marco. I don't think they want to be seen. Also, because of the Airpark and the Everglades thing, Marco Island would be a better location for...whatever they are running."

"Good thinking. You are going to make a fine detective. Start there. Give me a heads up when you fill in more blanks. I'm thinking if you are doing any canvasing, you should wear plain clothes tomorrow."

Smiling broadly, Dan took out a black and white notebook and diagonally folded a fresh page. He wrote the words "Alexis Ferraro" in Sharpie on the triangle.

CHAPTER 46

Sal Dreams of Paradise

Lexie cleared her search history, checked to see if her new email address was activated, and closed the laptop. She leaned back on the leather divan and stared out at the turquoise water of the gulf. The last few mornings she had been researching teaching positions on the east coast. Her best options seemed to be Miami-Dade, Broward, and Palm Beach Counties. She knew with the money she had invested from Vinnie's insurance payout she could live comfortably without working another day in her life. She also knew it would be impossible for her. She had been in denial for years—thinking being kept by Sal would be enough. No feelings involved. That was not living. She missed teaching, missed working with kids, missed the faculty lounge, and Friday night drinks with co-workers complaining about parents. She had sent out a dozen inquiries and as many actual applications to both private and public schools. Her resume was solid except for the gap in employment. The sudden death of her husband and the upheaval in her life would best be explained in an interview. She prayed she would have that opportunity. She headed into the shower and got dressed, hoping to head out before Sal got back from wherever he had been off to these past few mornings. She squinted at the thought he was always hiding things from her.

"Where are you going?"

Lexie jumped as Sal placed his hands on her butt. "Shopping, I want to find something nice for the reunion party."

"You got a walk-in filled with clothes; most still have tags on them. It's like you are stockpiling for the end of the world. Shopping can wait." Sal moved in closer and tickled the back of Lexie's neck with his tongue. "I got something I want to try out on you. You will be climbing the walls. Good thing we got no neighbors up here. It's going to blow your mind. I read about it in a men's magazine that was in the gym."

"You went to the gym?"

"Yeah, I started a couple a days ago." Sal tightened his gut and turned sideways. "I think it's starting to work."

"It's good you are taking care of yourself. Don't give up on it this time."

"I got plans, Lexie. I need to be in shape."

"You going to run a marathon?" Lexie smirked.

"Well, I got to be able to keep up with our kid, teach him how to throw a perfect spiral."

Lexie stiffened. *He doesn't know Lenny told me about the vasectomy.* She forced a smile, "What are you talking about? You said, 'No kids.'"

"I know what I said. A guy can change his mind, right? I want you to toss those pills. What do you think? Will that make you happy?"

Lexie shook her head in disbelief. "A woman can change her mind, too, right? I'm not ready for a kid right now."

"I thought that was what you wanted. We haven't had sex in days. I thought it was because you were mad about a baby, or...not having a baby."

Lexie stared at him in horror. "You are willing to get me pregnant because you haven't fucked me in a while? That's your logic?" *I should tell him I know about the vasectomy. That I haven't been on the pill for over a year. I thought it was his sperm or maybe me. Never knew he was such a bastard. I got to thank Lenny for this anyway.* She sighed and moved out of reach. "You are such an asshole."

Sal grabbed her hand. Lexie cringed as he pulled her close. His whispered words chilled her to the bone. "You know you want it, babe. Let's put it all behind us. Let's fuck like it's our last time. If you don't want a kid, hell, that's fine with me. I thought trying would make up for a lot that's happened."

"I don't want to fuck you, Sal. I'm tired of that." Lexie thought about all the lies, thought about poor Vinnie who wanted kids more than anything in the world. She thought about hiding under Sal's roof, in Sal's bed, while the world passed by. She wanted out of this life. It wasn't all Sal's fault. She knew she'd be dead if were not for him. In her mind, she was still buried and now she was a liar, too.

Lexie, her decision made, took his hand, and led him to the bed. "Let's start this moment over. I can tell you've been working out Sal. You look great."

His eyes widened in surprise. "You really think so?"

"Yes, I think so." She kissed him softly on the mouth. "I want you to make love to me, like you just said, like it's the last time." She slipped off her sundress and lay down on the bed. There were tears in her eyes as he pulled her on top of him.

Forty-five minutes later, Sal collapsed next to Lexie covered in sweat and wheezing heavily.

"You okay, Sal?"

"Okay?" he wheezed. "Wow! Babe, that was the best sex I've ever had in my entire life! And you and I have had some amazing sex. You really put your heart into this one. If I croaked right now, I'd die a happy man. I think I've just been fucked by an angel."

Lexie smiled. "It was stellar, the best. I won't forget this day, I promise you." She rolled over and sat up on the edge of the bed.

"Hey." Sal reached out his hand. "Where are you going? I thought, you know, we could just lie here awhile, bask in the moment. You always complain we don't cuddle enough."

Lexie shook her head. "I'm going shopping. I'll be back by dinnertime. I'll pick up some steaks you can throw on the grill, a nice bottle of wine, and a salad."

"No need. I made a reservation at the M Spa Hotel, that fancy place upstairs. I know you've wanted to go there. Since the reunion is on your birthday, I thought we should celebrate early. What do you think?"

"That would be nice, Sal. What time did you make it for?"

"Seven-thirty. We can have cocktails on the patio before dinner. Go on, you shower first. I'm going to rest here a few minutes."

Lexie dried off from her shower and put the sundress back on. "Sal, you alright?"

"Yeah, I'm great. Just thinking about how much I love you."

"Everything cool with work?"

"Yeah, it's all good. Lenny has it under control."

Lexie cringed at the sound of Lenny's name. She was making plans on what that slimy bastard told her. What if it was all a lie? She wouldn't put it past him. The lecherous creep had been drooling over her for years. Sal said he wanted to have kids now. She knew in her heart it didn't matter. This was not a good spot to be in. Lenny and Sal were bad people. She couldn't remain insulated from that any longer. She looked over at Sal breathing heavily from exertion, a contented look plastered on his sweaty face. She knew he loved her; even bad people can fall in love—bad people like Lenny. She shivered with a sudden chill.

"What are you thinking about, babe?"

"Nothing. I'm going to walk down to the shops."

"I would suggest you take the Ferrari, but it is getting detailed today. All the classics in the garage are getting a day of beauty. You know, for the reunion car show."

"Right, I forgot." Lucky, she thought, he hasn't seen the tire. "A walk it is."

"I could drive you in the Escalade."

"No, thanks. You just relax. Take a day to yourself. You look tired. Maybe you are working out too hard in the gym."

Lexie walked into the closet for her bag. By the time she walked back into to the bedroom, Sal was asleep.

CHAPTER 47

Shot down by a widow maker

The Porsche shimmered in the Florida sun as it sat in the prized location twenty paces from the M Spa Hotel's front portico and entrance. Across the way, a bubbling stream cascaded over strategically placed boulders, rambled past exotic plants, and fell exuberantly into a koi-filled pond beyond the cobblestone drive. A cooling mist from the fountain chilled the air.

Walking through the lobby, Raul hopped like a kid waiting for a lollipop. Realizing he looked over-anxious, he stopped in his tracks, turned to Jeanette, and put on a mature expression. "You are going to love the ride I will take you on." Jeannette stopped abruptly beside him and looked at him quizzically. "Maybe I didn't say that in good English."

"Well taking someone for a ride here in the states has more than one meaning."

"I didn't mean any offense, *mi amor*." He watched as her expression softened.

"I haven't been...romanced in a very long time, Raul. I'm enjoying your excitement. I look forward to our—ride. Go slow. Show me affection. I crave that more than anything. Make me feel wanted for this one night and I will make you feel that way as well."

Raul stared at the lovely woman beside him and watched the years roll off her. She had taken command of her situation and was now leading him away into the night. *Fate is a funny thing.* He had heard papa say that on more than one occasion.

"So, show me your dream car."

Together, they walked out of the doors, skirted past a livery Town Car discharging a guest and nuzzled as they walked out into the sun beyond the portico. Raul steered her to the right, where in a display of pride he swept his arm out to reveal the Porsche. It shimmered golden in the sunshine. The mist from the nearby fountain created a perfect rainbow above the car. Raul couldn't believe his good fortune.

A scream pierced the serenity of the moment.

"This...car...I...can't." She gulped for air looking up towards heaven. "You are watching me, aren't you? I thought it was time. I'm so lonely," she moaned. She looked over at Raul his mouth agape. "I'm so sorry, this car k...k...killed my husband. He loved it, maybe more than me. I can't." Jeannette turned and ran; her tortured sobs followed her into the hotel.

Raul, stunned, stood staring at the car. "What the fuck just happened?" he said aloud, unaware that anyone was in earshot.

The valet walked up, "Sorry, man, what are the odds? The widow-maker shot you down."

"Widow-maker?"

"Yeah. That's the name this model's got—not by the manufacturer, but because of all the people who got killed driving her. She's a beauty, but she's deadly. How did you pull in driving this car and not know she was such a bitch?"

"It's not mine, it's my cousin's. He told me about her quirks."

"Well, you're lucky it was this kind of crash and burn. You learned the widow-maker's lesson the easy way."

⚗

Sonja exited the Town Car and picked up her Aeroflot-issued carry-on. She walked under the portico in time to witness an attractive young man and an older woman, obviously ob-sexed with each other, exit the lobby. The woman howled and ran off sobbing into the hotel. She heard the man's words, "What the fuck just happened?" Sonja watched the valet commiserating with him as they discussed the magnificent Porsche 911 on the drive. The man, visibly shaken, tossed the keys to the valet and headed into the lobby. *Interesting.*

CHAPTER 48

What was he thinking?

The vibration in Lenny's pants was relentless. He reached deep into his pocket and turned the phone off. He didn't want to know that Sonja had arrived or that she was "so wet thinking about her little lion." He had a major screw-up going on, and Sonja in the picture would only make things worse.

Lenny knew Sal realized something was messed up with the Garcia deal. Raul Garcia's son had arrived and was staying at the M Spa— so was Sonja. If he went to see her, he might run into young Garcia. That could be good or bad. He wanted any news getting back to Señor Garcia to be positive. The conversation Lenny wanted heading to Cuba: "Papa, Leonard Horowitz is a business whiz, everything running smoothly." Not this:"Horowitz is a frog's ass. He lost the drugs. There is no money. He got his men killed. Say the word, and I will kill Horowitz."

Worst of all, it looked like Lexie was getting ready to run away from Sal. She had been shopping like crazy and he noticed numerous boxes and new Luis Vuitton bags had been stored in the owner's community closet. Lenny fretted she would leave before he had a chance to give her the birthday gift he purchased. He had spent a fortune on it. He needed to convince her that he was her best option for escape.

He walked into the convenience store craving a taquito and a Cherry-Coke slurpy, his version of comfort food. Waiting online at the counter he continued his brooding. If he showed up at the hotel, and Sonja wanted to go for a drink, or walk the beach, or worse yet soak in the hot tub with him, how would he get out of it? They were all reasonable requests when you invite a woman to a high-end hotel. If any of those things happened, he might find himself hiding behind potted palm trees or hopping in and out of rooms like he was in a Marx Brother's movie—all to avoid Raul, Junior.

Sonja would only stay in the suite long enough to get laid. How could he prolong sex? He was so nervous; he wasn't sure he could get it up for her. When he suggested Sonja come down to Marco, everything was going fine. He had been thinking with the wrong head.

He whined inside, not realizing he had moaned out loud. The 7-11 clerk gave him a weird look and stepped back after he handed him his change and the hot taquito. Lenny impulsively asked for a lotto ticket. Looking at the quick pick in his hand, he wondered if luck runs both ways.

CHAPTER 49

Forget Cougars, Kittens Have Claws, Too

A shot of tequila was in Sonja's hand before she stepped across the hotel bar's threshold. The time was 6:35 P.M., and the music was blasting. The smell of a hard day's work permeated the air. It could not be disguised by the expensive perfume that clawed its way past the unwashed scent. Vaping, prohibited in public spaces, was evident in every corner. Wafting in through open beachside doors, an underlying reek of skunk weed copulated with the pungent fumes above the dance floor. The frenetic mob inhaled the vapors as if it were an aphrodisiac. The gyrating, grinding, throng danced with fevered sexuality beneath pulsating waves of light. Enthralled and aroused, Sonja tilted her head back, drained the tequila, and dove in.

☙

Raul shifted his attention from Diego's smiling face to the crowd that was three-deep at the bar. This trip was turning into a nightmare. Diego had a lot to smile about. He had found love and cashed in on the cars he sold to Mister Horowitz. Raul had nothing to smile about. He hadn't heard from Horowitz since he arrived on Marco. The last email, addressed to his father, hit his inbox two days before he left Cuba. It suggested that they would finish up the business of the drop after the reunion and that he was looking forward to meeting his son. This would have to be addressed. He needed to find a way to remove his father from the deal. A handwritten letter might work.

Raul pulled an embroidered handkerchief from his jacket pocket, looked at the initials R.G. intricately swirled in delicate cream-colored thread. His *tía*, Diego's mother, had made one for Diego as well, but he refused to use the gift, not wanting to damage the delicate work of love. *Familia* was still important to his cousin even after their rejection of him. Raul mopped his brow, blew his nose, then stuffed the soiled fabric into his back pocket. He noticed a look of disapproval cross his cousin's face as his eyes followed the path of the handkerchief.

"Are you alright?" Raul asked.

"*Sí.*" Diego shrugged. "I am worried about you. You are nervous, jumpy. What is going on with you?"

Raul reached for his drink, the glass shaking as he brought it to his lips. "I have had a lot of disappointment these past few days."

Diego tilted his head. "You want to tell me? We can head outside where we can talk."

"No, no, it's not that important." Raul steered the conversation away from his business problems. "Your car fucked up my plans last night."

"How did my car stop you from getting laid? Women love that car, men, too. You don't know how many propositions I turn down when I drive it. It had to be something you did or said. That woman was into you."

"No." Raul shook his head. "It was the car."

"You must have seemed too aggressive, or maybe your inexperience was obvious? Cougars love strong, confident men."

"I did nothing to chase her away. It was your widow-maker."

"Who told you it is called that?"

"She did. Right before she took off sobbing into the hotel."

"You must have done something…"

"Excuse me, gentlemen. May I squeeze in between you to order a drink?" The raven-haired dream pushed in between them, causing her voluptuous breasts, barely contained in a spandex tube top, to press against Raul's arm.

Diego smiled warmly. "You may squeeze us all you want, but I would never allow a lady to buy her own beverage." His smile beamed at Raul.

"My cousin and I would be honored if you would allow us to buy you many drinks."

"I think you," she poked Diego's chest with her finger, "would like to get me drunk, so this one," she reached out and placed her hand on Raul's chest, "can have his way with me. I am of mind," the woman looked closely at Diego, "that you are not interested in sex with me." She pouted her shiny, plump lips. "So handsome, a shame. But him?" She nodded towards Raul and breathed deeply. "That is different tale. He has not moved his arm from the press of my breasts. Maybe he looks for companion."

Raul turned to her, pressed his arm more firmly into her chest. "Are you a *puta*?" He chuckled. "My mother was—no—is a whore. She fucks my very old, rich father and gets everything her heart desires."

A deep laugh erupted from Sonja. "I like you. You are honest. I think you are handsome when I watched the pretty woman leave you outside this hotel. I felt bad for you. I am not a prostitute. I work for Aeroflot as a first-class flight attendant. My name is Sonja." She offered her delicate hand, her nails blood-red in the throbbing lights.

Raul ignored her.

Diego reached over, gently lifted and kissed her hand. "Please forgive my companion." He bowed. "I am Diego Garcia-Stiles, and this brooding man is my cousin Raul, recently arrived from Cuba." He winked at Sonja. "Tell me, *senorita*, does Aeroflot still follow the old ways: you must keep the customer satisfied?"

"Times change. We are not seen as servants or ... gold diggers." Her disapproving look was pointed at Raul. "You should learn from your cousin. He has good manners." She turned her attention back to Diego. "I am an independent woman. I know what I want. I do not need to be cared for. If our desires match, then I will stay and allow you to purchase my drinks. If not, I will find a willing partner among this drunken crowd." She studied Raul's impassive face. I prefer someone serious who will not slobber over me. If you are that man, then..."

Diego leaned in and spoke into Raul's ear. "Cousin, I don't think you can scare this one. A fast car is no match for her. I think she's just who you need right now. If I were straight, you'd have to fight me for her."

Diego waved at someone across the room. "I see my new friend, Gary, has arrived. I'll leave you to her. Tomorrow, you will tell what is truly bothering you."

Raul embraced Diego, "*Gracias*, cousin."

"Remember, *la familia es muy importante*, young Raul."

Sonja smiled warmly at Diego. "Enjoy your evening, *señor*. I hope we will meet again."

"It is my hope, Sonja. I'm certain your time with Raul will be most pleasurable."

She slid onto the vacant barstool beside Raul.

"*Mañana*, Raul." Diego clapped him on the back and headed towards the patio.

Sonja signaled the bartender. "Two glasses Russian Standard, neat, please, and Zakuski." She looked at Raul. "You will continue to brood, and I will walk away, or we shall drink and see what this night brings?"

The vodka materialized in front of them followed by a platter filled with pickles, mushrooms, and artichokes fermenting in pungent oil. "*Spasibo*! Thank you," she nodded to the bartender.

Handing Raul a glass and lifting her own, she looked into his eyes. "To lovers, old and new." Her voice, now softer, held a hint of expectancy.

They drank and banged their glasses on the bar top. "Maybe you keep up with me." She laughed and signaled for two more. Clinking glasses, they drank again, the smooth liquid going down easy. Picking up a gherkin she put it in Raul's mouth, leaned over, and kissed him deeply.

Raul's heavy mood lifted, and he reached over and pulled her close. "Is it true Russian women have a fire inside that keep their lovers hot all night?"

"Maybe so. You may tell in the morning. Is it true Latin men are best lovers?"

"See for yourself."

Two more glasses appeared. The liquid within, clear and pure, summoned them. In unison they drank and dropped the glasses. The bottle almost drained, Raul dropped three hundred-dollar bills on the bar. Arm-in-arm, they walked out onto the beach.

"I will teach you my favorite Russian pastime." Sonja giggled, kicked off her sandals, and spun in circles, arms outstretched. "Shush, it is secret game." She approached Raul. Her eyes gleamed in the light from the hotel. "You will be wild Siberian wolf." She slid her hands up his chest. "I am lost in woods. You catch me, but I tame you; I climb on top and ride you up and down the mountains."

Raul interrupted, "Or on the beach?"

"Da. You are smart one. I like that. We take nap and play again. This game, everyone wins. See? Is fun, yes? I am very good at this. You think I am crazy Russian bitch?"

Raul smiled at her accent that had become more pronounced with each glass of vodka. "No, not crazy, I think you are—"

A beach cabana appeared in front of them. Sonja raced ahead stopping only to peel her jumpsuit off and toss it at him. Her nakedness glowed in the moonlight. They ducked inside and landed on the double lounge hidden behind sheer curtains.

He whispered, "*gracias*" and melted into the night.

CHAPTER 50

Move Over, Sonny Crockett

Dan Barnes walked in the squad room well before 7 am. He removed an old ratty sweater, two baseball caps, and a broken umbrella from the coat tree. He placed his pristine, beige, linen jacket on a Men's Wearhouse hanger and hung it on the empty stand. Admiring it amid the squalor of the institutional drab office, he walked over and pulled the tree a few steps further from the coffee machine. Satisfied the jacket was out of harm's way, he walked carefully in the new skinny-fit jeans he purchased. Though the tag said "stonewashed," they were rubbing against his nuts. He worried he would have a bad burn by the end of the day. Screw it all! He looked damned good. He puffed out his chest, his snug black t-shirt hugged tight to his well-formed physique. Brand new leather loafers, no socks, completed his look. South Beach would have welcomed him with dropped, velvet ropes.

Grabbing a cup of black coffee, he sipped the dark syrup slowly, grimacing at the taste. He was going to get used to it. The old guys drank it down by the bucket. He powered up the MacBook on the makeshift desk they assigned him and opened the file labeled "Mrs. Alexis Ferraro." Her date of birth was on the first line: February 26, 1982. He tapped a Bic pen against his newly whitened teeth and thought about his plans for the day. Alexis Ferraro's smiling face filled up the screen. Her date of birth was three days from now. Well, well, happy thirty-fifth birthday, Alexis! What did you wish for this year? Was it the Ferrari Mondial, or were you hoping for something more personal? Three days from now, you'll be blowing out candles and maybe opening a little white box with an expensive piece of jewelry inside. You might be placing exotic flowers in a crystal vase. How about a new dress for the occasion? He pulled up the tags on the Ferrari and emailed it to the desk officer. The day shift could keep an eye out for it. It would be hard to miss.

Next, he made a list of all the high-end boutiques on the island and some of the funky designer shops his sisters liked to frequent. He added the names of jewelry stores, florists, and lunch spots near the shops. The last entries he added were hotel spas and nail salons.

He took out the black and white notebook, opened the cover, and looked at the first page folded with "Alexis Ferraro" printed on it. He turned to the next fresh page. Feeling like it was his first day at St. Ann's Elementary in Naples, he brought a freshly sharpened pencil to his nose and inhaled the scent of the rubber eraser. His new clothes, his fresh notebook, his sharpened pencil gave way to a euphoria of all the firsts in his life. Today was a great day; his career path stretched out in front of him. He placed the tip of the pencil on the pristine page and wrote the first thing that came to mind.

"Sniffing erasers, kid? Wow, that was a flashback. You look nice! You even got a new marble notebook. Looking for brownie points with the teacher getting into class early?" Pete laughed.

"No, I just had some ideas about finding Alex, one of the suspects."

"Don't worry about what I said, Dan. We've all been there. The day when everything seems golden, you got the world by the balls, and you are going to make a difference."

"That's pretty observant."

"Hey, I'm a fucking detective. Nothing gets by me." Pete snorted. "At least nothing did when I actually gave a damn."

"You had an awesome career. You deserve to spend your days fishing or whatever it is you want to do." Dan watched Pete's expression take a turn, his eyes squint, and his fists ball up. "What? I'm sorry. I didn't mean anything by that. You know when it's time, right?"

"Yeah, that's what they say." Pete shook his head. "I'm still in my prime. Fifty is the new forty and all that bullshit. A guy can have a damn good time if he doesn't have to get up for work every day chasing assholes all over the county."

"Damn straight! Lots of stuff to do, places to go, people to see."

"Shut the fuck up, Danny, and get back to work. I see by your list you got a lot of places to go yourself. Oh, you look so pretty I think you should take the Mustang convertible on your tour of Marco Island's girly spots."

"Wow! Thanks, Pete!" Danny grinned from ear to ear.

Pete snapped back at him, "Don't ever answer that way again. You sound like Andy of Mayberry, if you even know who that is— Golly, Pete'? Really?" Pete growled, "Don't be an ass-kisser. The correct response is 'Fuck yeah, baby, that's what I'm talking about' or something along those lines. Free advice, Dan."

The old-timers began arriving. The first one through the door, Bruce, absentmindedly dropped his windbreaker on the floor next to the coffee maker. The second one in, Craig, backed into the coat tree, avoiding the jacket on the floor.

The third detective, Jerry, the oldest at sixty-three and squad wise ass, offered his commentary. "What the fuck is going on here? Who's moving shit around, and where is my wool sweater? It's freezing in here. My wife knitted that sweater for me."

Pete laughed and bowed toward Dan. "First day undercover for our youngest team member."

"Wow, you look like a male escort," Craig, the second oldest detective in the squad, laughed.

"You would know, Craig. Those are your kind of guys," Bruce replied.

"It was a case; I wasn't soliciting anybody." Craig whined. "Cut this shit out. You guys never miss a chance to ride my back about that."

"That's what he said," Jerry quipped.

"Yeah, you keep saying that. It wasn't funny the first time, and it's not funny now."

"I disagree. It's fucking hilarious. Am I right guys?" Jerry spread his hands out waiting for a response.

Craig advanced. "I'm sick of your shit, Jerry."

"What's a matter? It rubs you the wrong way. Oh wait, I forgot! For you, there is no wrong way."

Dan's face flushed as he offered an apology. "I'm sorry, guys. I shouldn't have moved the coat rack."

Craig turned and scowled at Dan. "What should we do with the little pecker who messed with our shit? How about we spill coffee on that nice new jacket hanging up on our misplaced tree?"

"No, I got a better idea." Bruce smiled. "Back in the day, the new guys had to be initiated. We should return to the old ways. No smart asses in the office after we got through with them."

"That is a bit harsh, Bruce. We could get in serious trouble. I only got a few days left. I don't need any problems. Let's think about this." Pete put his hands up palms out.

Dan gave Pete a weak smile. "What are you guys talking about?" He looked over at the door and noticed the rest of the squad had arrived. "I just moved a coat tree."

Jerry moved next to Pete. "No, I'm thinking we make it look like an accident."

"What if the twerp spills his guts?" Craig squinted at Dan.

"He won't. Look at the new get up he has. He wants in the squad bad. Pete, you got the most to lose. What should we do with him, you know, to bring him into our brotherhood?"

"You're joking, right?" Dan noticed the grim faces around him. His balls shriveled in his pants at the thought that these old bastards might be planning something serious.

"Don't take this personally, Dan. It's about history and trusting the guys who have your back." Pete patted Dan's shoulder.

"Pete, what are they going to do to me? This is like hazing, right?" *They couldn't be planning anything dangerous. These guys were the police. His dad never mentioned that the detective squad was filled with psychos.*

"Shut up, Dan," Pete said, quietly. "Just let this play-out. We have all been in your shoes." Pete looked solemn. "Boys, I think we should shoot him, not dead, just wing him. Dan, we've all had our initiation. I got the scar to prove it. It's twenty years old, and you can still see it." Pete rolled up his left sleeve where a round, white scar stood out against the tanned skin of his forearm.

Dan's face turned pale. "I'm sorry, but you can't... maybe, you know, years ago. But today," he shook his head back and forth. "You can't..." Dan searched the room for a friendly face. The entire day shift, stone-faced old men with their arms crossed, encircled his desk.

Pete, standing directly in front of him, leaned forward and in his deepest voice said, "Take this like a man, Dan. Suck it up. It only hurts until you pass out. It'll only graze you. I'll make sure of that. In fact, I'll be the one to pull the trigger since I brought you into the squad. I'll use my twenty-two instead of the nine-millimeter—less damage. You'll be patched up and out of the ER in ten minutes."

Pete looked over his shoulder. "Charlie here yet?"

"Yeah, Pete, I'm with you." Charlie, holding his cellphone, muscled through the crowd pressing in on Dan.

"Call the ER. Let them know we got a wounded baby bird on the way in." Jerry chuckled.

"It's been a while." Charlie nodded; his expression grim. "They are going to be excited. They love the young ones."

Dan jumped up. These guys were serious. His eyes bulged as he realized, they didn't care if he brought up charges. "You guys are fucking crazy. I'm not going to sit still for your shit. I may want to be a detective, but not if I've got to work with a bunch of loony bastards. I'm out of here."

"Dan," Pete pushed him back in the chair "you tell anyone what went down here today, you best keep a lookout over your shoulder. It will give new meaning to watching your back."

The day-shift detectives pushed in close. The stench of coffee, cigarettes, and Old Spice fouled the air. Surrounded by menacing faces, Dan pushed himself deeper into the chair.

Pete pointed to his scar again. "Want to know who gave me that scar? It was Charlie. Best fucking day of my life." He looked over at Charlie and smiled. "Charlie, remember that day?"

"Yeah, Bro. It was Dry Tortugas, off Fort Jefferson."

Pete, his hot breath infused with the odor of stale coffee and a hint of toothpaste, drew closer to Dan. He placed his lips up to Dan's ear. Dan's stomach turned; he held his breath praying he wouldn't puke. "So, young Dan, the day was going just fine. Just like today." Pete's breath felt hot against his ear. "Until Charlie got a bit overexcited trying to hook the line with the gaff."

Dan scrunched his face up trying to comprehend what Pete was saying.

Charlie smiled. "You looked like you were getting tired. I just wanted to help."

"Instead of hooking the line," Pete's voice was now a whisper, "the tuna lurched hard to the left and the gaff whipped around and impaled my forearm." Pete shoved his arm under Dan's nose. "So much blood, I swear I can smell it even now. Can you smell the blood, Dan?"

Dan shook his head side to side, then up and down, not knowing what response would end this nightmare.

"You paying attention, Dan? I don't think you are. You still look...scared."

A voice from the back of the crowd yelled, "Finish the story, Pete."

"Okay, boys." Pete stood upright smiling at his rapt audience. "So, what happened next was, big sissy Charlie panics and cuts the line and the biggest catch of my life swims away. No tuna steaks for me." He winked at Dan. "Just this scar and an opportunity to scare the shit out of you."

The room burst into laughter and applause.

"Way to go, Pete. Best one yet!" echoed through the squad.

"You fucker." Dan jumped up and swung at Pete, who ducked and laughed, catching Dan's arm as it whizzed past his head.

"Dan, welcome to the Order of the Wizened Dicks."

Pete held out his hand. In it was a set of keys. "Mustangs gassed up, cleaned, and the rag top's down. She's waiting out front. Happy hunting, Dan."

Dan smiled and shook his head as the old guard cleared a path. He picked up his marble notebook and walked past grinning faces and pats on the back. At the coat rack, Jerry, wearing his tattered sweater, held out the linen jacket and helped Dan slip it on.

CHAPTER 51

The Floating Ladies get down to business

"Did you see Preston?"

A collective "no" followed by a deep sigh emanating from the gaggle of ladies bobbing in the blue pool water.

"Why isn't he out here directing the landscapers?"

"I haven't seen him all week."

"See over there on the beach walkway? There are anthills rising from between the bricks. Totally unacceptable."

"At least he didn't put the yellow tape back."

"He should be taking care of the list we gave him."

"Well, the car wash people have been here all week. He took care of that."

"And the front entrance flower beds have been replanted. I noticed two new flowerpots by the pool gate."

"I think he is doing a great job. You are just upset because you haven't seen him by the pool in his cut off shorts."

"Oh, you be quiet."

"We may be old, but we're not dead yet. He's got a great body to look at."

"Remember when we went to Chippendale night at the bar in Naples?"

"You remember that? It must have been thirty years ago."

"Of course, I remember it."

"Me, too!"

"That was a great night. We should do that again."

"I don't know. My doctor says I shouldn't get over excited."

"Your doctor thinks you're dead already. He's just collecting your Medicare payments and hoping you'll hang on until his boat is paid off."

"You might be right."

"My doctor told me to lay off the booze. Really? Can you imagine what a bitch I'd be if I didn't have my wine? I've been drinking every day since I was sixteen. I never had a drinking problem. Always just enough to get through sex with my first husband, then my second."

"You're a widow six years. What are you drinking for now?"

"Now? I don't need a reason."

"I know the reason, it's because…"

"Because what?"

"That's the reason because — of everything, anything — it's so freeing not needing a reason."

"I drink at night when Gary goes down to the hotel."

"That is so sad."

"No, it's not. I'd rather he bangs anyone else but me."

"You two always seem so happy."

"We have an agreement. I don't ask questions, and he doesn't give me any diseases."

"That's gross. I was really surprised when he turned gay."

"He didn't turn gay. He was always gay."

"You have kids."

"So what? He got it up for me in the beginning. Tried to hide his tendencies. It didn't work for too long. His first affair was a young sales rep who came into his office."

"Why didn't you leave him?"

"Why would I? I had everything I needed: my kids, a nice house, a condo on the beach."

"What about love?"

"Overrated."

"Really?"

"I had an affair when the kids left for college. Gary was fine with it, offered to divorce me and let me have a new life. The thing of it was, I really liked my life. I like Gary. We even sleep in the same bed at night. We are comfortable."

"That is not a marriage."

"I don't think you can say that. I don't have it as nice as that, and Cliff and I have been married for fifty-six years."

"I can't remember the last time Bill and I had sex."

"I bought a vibrator when Joe had his prostate surgery. Sometimes he watches when I use it. He almost gets a hard-on."

"When I see Preston sashaying around here in his trunks, he reminds me of those dancers."

Deep breaths bubbled the surface of the water.

"And with his long hair hiding his face, he's anonymous like those guys. I often wonder if the waiters or the cable guys are dancers by night."

"You have too much time on your hands if you're thinking those things."

"You're thinking those things, too."

"Well, at least we have Preston to keep us young and smiling."

"I think he's been distracted by Lexie. Have you seen the way he looks at her?"

"How can you see how he looks at her with his hair hanging down?"

"The day she screamed at Lenny, boy, did he seem upset. He was trimming the hedges by the gate, and he attacked the bush like he wished it was Lenny's head."

"Well, I don't know if Lexie has caught a glimpse of him recently, but I saw him dropping off George Neuwirth at the front door. The Rolls had been detailed for the car show. It looked amazing, but it paled to the shiny new Preston driving it. Wow. I need to say that again, WOW!"

"Wow, what? What happened to him?'

"I'm not going to say a word. I wouldn't want to spoil the surprise."

"You already did spoil the surprise. 'Wow' says a lot."

"No, not in this instance. Just wait till you see."

"Did he finish the car show parking diagram?"

"Yes, I found it in my mailbox yesterday. I didn't talk to him about it, but when I drove to my hair appointment this morning, I noticed some of the cars in the garage had numbered placards on the windshields."

"I saw that. The parking spaces are all screwed up, too. My car was all the way in the back corner."

"Your car isn't in the car show. Nobody wants to see an old, dented Ford Taurus."

"Yes, it is in the show. Preston said if I wanted it in, it would be in. Anyway, your car is dented, too."

"I know. You dented it. Your space is across from mine. All the dents are on the rear bumper, and there is green paint on it. Your car is green. You don't have to be a detective to figure that mystery out."

"I never..."

"Oh yes, you did. The only reason I never mentioned it was because my car is a piece of shit, too. Neither of us are going to spend the money getting them fixed. Anyway, the worst drivers in Florida live on this island. Forget going to bingo or mass. I'm glad we live close enough to walk to church. It's bumper cars in the parking lot.

"How many cars are in the show?"

"We've got twenty-six."

"How are the spots assigned? Age? Value?"

"All I know is Grace's caddie is going to be right outside the pool gate because Preston doesn't want her wandering in the garage and freaking out when its's not there. He wants her to be able to see it from the pool deck."

"God, I love that man. He is so considerate."

"I left a message for the sunset fire dancer. Did you all get the diagram of the pool deck layout?"

"The fire dancer is going to be on the far side of the pool next to the hot tub. I think we should have torches lining the rocks around the hot tub for effect."

"Where is the steel drum guy going to play?"

"He's going to be over in front of the pool house."

"I think we should have Preston pick up a bamboo screen to hide the pool house. That is the only bland spot on the entire pool deck."

"How come you never mentioned the pool house was unattractive at any of the HOA meetings?"

"Yeah, you bitch about everything else."

Don't make Preston do that. He has too much to do already. Order something online, maybe a bamboo screen, and have it sent overnight."

"You really should have mentioned this at the decoration meeting."

"I'm putting the lounges back under the palm trees next to the hot tub. Nobody is going to sit there. The smoke from the torches will be annoying."

"Preston isn't going to like it."

"We should do it the afternoon of the party, so he doesn't notice."

"Look who just walked out the gym door."

They all followed Sal Ferraro's progress as he headed towards them.

"I saw him in the gym twice this week. See? He's wearing sneakers."

"That's a new look for him."

"Maybe he's worried about Lexie, you know, finding someone younger and more attractive. Ssh. He's walking over."

The ladies performed a perfectly choreographed synchronized turn and waved to Sal.

Sal waved back. "Hey, you ladies are like professional swimmers. You know, like Esther Williams or the Weekee Wachee Mermaids."

"We've been swimming together every winter for forty years."

"Well, keep it up, ladies. You look amazing. Maybe Lexie should join you. I want her to be that fit when she gets up there. Uhm. Sorry I didn't mean to imply..."

"That's okay, Mr. Ferraro."

"Call me Sal, please. I'm going to be an owner soon."

Sal looked up at the building and let out a whistle that pierced the quiet of the pool area. He pointed at Lenny sitting on his balcony and signaled him to come down. Lenny disappeared inside. "See you at the reunion, ladies."

They watched him head to the walkway and sit on the smoker's bench. The deep puffs of smoke from his freshly lit cigar floated over the water. Lennie rushed by, barefoot and disheveled.

"I think Sal is going to figure out that Lenny has a thing for Lexie."

"You think he doesn't know?"

"No, I don't think he think he sees Lenny as a threat—too schlubby."

"Well, I would watch my ass where Mr. Horowitz is concerned."

"Who are you, Miss Marple?"

CHAPTER 52

Ouch

Lenny exited the condo wearing his bathing suit and his favorite Jimmy Buffet concert tee shirt. The thin fabric and faded smiling face of the beach troubadour was the last physical reminder of his college days of drinking beer and hanging at the Jersey shore. He looked down at his shoeless feet and chuckled. *Just like Buffet when he perform.* Lenny knew he was going to have to give an academy award winning performance when he talked to Sal.

Pushing the elevator button, he noticed a tightening in his throat. Breathing deeply, he tried to ease the pain that now had a grip on his heart. *This is the way it ends.* He grimaced as he rubbed his chest—a fucking heart attack in an elevator.

Lenny clasped his hands together. "God, if you are listening, I know I haven't been in touch for a while. But I figured, what do I have to lose? I've done some bad things. I admit it. I am not, what you would call, a nice guy. But I see where I took the wrong path. If I survive the next few days, I'm going to take Lexie as far away from this as I can. Start over. Maybe Nicaragua, or someplace with no extradition and where the Garcia's won't find me." He sniffled. "And, Lord," Lenny crossed himself, figuring it couldn't hurt to cover all the bases. "If you throw a small miracle my way, I know I can do some good. I could start a law practice and take on a few pro-bono cases. Not too many, because you know, I'll have Lexie, and she likes nice things. And before too long there may be a couple of rug rats running around. We are going to get busy on that real fast, after we get married, cause I know you are big on ceremony. So, as a new husband and dad, I'm going to need to make some serious money for the family. But definitely a few indigent clients for sure. You will see. I'm a resilient guy. I can change. Just give me a chance. Uhm, yeah. That's all I got. Oh, I almost forgot—please. Amen. This is Lenny Horowitz if I didn't mention that."

Lenny rubbed his damp eyes as the doors opened. He breathed deeply and sighed as he realized the pain in his chest had subsided. His eyes were drawn to the soaring glass-domed atrium and the blue sky and scuttling clouds rushing past. He gave the thumbs up sign. Smiling, he headed out to meet Sal with a believable story already forming in his mind.

"Hey, Lenny, I got a couple of cigars, hand-rolled Cubans. Garcia sent them to the office for the reunion. Susan gave me a couple to try out. Have a seat. We got some things to discuss."

Lenny squinted, confused at the happy Sal on display. He looked up and gave a moment of silent thanks. "Sounds good, Sal. You are in a happy mood. What's up?"

"Yeah. Sex in the afternoon will do that to you."

Damn! I shouldn't have asked. The tightening in his chest had returned. He took a deep breath as he watched Sal cut off the end of a cigar. Passing it to Lenny, he continued, "You know, Len, if this all works out, you should find yourself a nice girl. Someone like Lexie. You're young. You could start a family. I think I finally got it, you know, about the family thing. I told Lexie today I'm on board with it."

"I don't understand. You planning to adopt?"

Lenny leaned in as Sal lit a match to light his cigar.

"No way. I want my kids to have Lexie's genes for sure. I been seeing a urologist. With this new robotic surgery, he said I could probably reverse the big V. Great, huh?"

Lenny inhaled deeply and exploded in a coughing fit. Sal patted his back. "Take it easy Len. You aren't ready for a wife and kids. That's fine. Maybe if you don't fuck this up, you can be my kid's godfather."

"That would be quite an honor, Sal. But you do remember I'm Jewish."

"We can figure that out. Anyway, I'm jumping the gun a bit. A lot of pieces got to fit together, not the least of which is my ball connector." Sal laughed at his joke. "Funny, Len, you get it? Ball connector?"

"Yeah, Sal. You're a real Don Rickles."

"Man. Don Rickles, I loved that guy. Did I tell you I met him once when I was a kid? He was with that actor, you know the one, he was married to a Kennedy."

"Peter Lawford?"

"Yeah. That guy. He was friends with Sinatra and Marilyn Monroe. My dad took me to a fancy hotel in the city. Everybody was dressed up. It was kind a like an audience with the Pope. Rickles tweaked my ear. I remember Lawford was staring at my mom's chest until Rickles elbowed him and told him to say hello to me. My dad met Sinatra in the dressing room before the show. They sent me home early with my dad's guy, Carmine Calamari. Funny the things you remember."

"Great memory, Sal."

"Yeah. I got a lot to share with my kid. So, back to business. What is going on with the Andruzzi's and when is my pay day coming?" Sal sucked in his cigar and blew the pungent smoke directly into Lenny's face.

Lenny paused, knowing his response would need to be carefully framed. He opened his mouth, his lips already forming the words that might diffuse the danger he faced. Instead, an ear-piercing scream erupted from his lips.

Sal jumped up, reaching for Lenny as he shouted for help.

Lenny twisted out of his grasp, ran towards the pool, and jumped in, scattering the old ladies who screamed, "FIRE ANTS!" They flailed their arms and knocked each other out of the way as they scuttled towards the stairs.

CHAPTER 53

If I fall

"Detective Dan Barnes." He liked the way that sounded as the words rolled comfortably off his lips. Driving down Collier Boulevard in the super-charged pursuit Mustang, Dan allowed himself to dream. It was a perfect rag top day as his sandy hair was tousled by the breeze. The powerful pony's deep rumble turned heads as he crawled by. A month ago, he was wearing a day-glow vest directing traffic outside the elementary school he once attended. Today, he was investigating serious crimes, wearing a week's salary of designer clothes, and checking out the babes in skintight jogging pants running down the sidewalks. He let his mind wander, thinking if it all went well, maybe he'd get his tin.

A slim brunette trotting past his car, turned, smiled, and gave him a little wave. The traffic sped up. Dan looked in his mirror as he passed by her. He slowed the car down thinking maybe he'd make a U-turn and talk to her. She was hot and would probably be getting a lot of unwanted attention from the construction crews working on the new hotel going up beachside. He could let her know he was on the job and watching out for her safety. Dan reconsidered, knowing any appearance of impropriety would be reported. Who knows the next time he would be driving this car and looking this good? The internal battle continued. On the other hand, Internal Affairs would put an end to his detective dream if she filed a complaint. In the rear view he watched the beautiful jogger turn into a condo complex parking lot. Dan's logical side won the day. The old guys weren't joking; he was no Sonny Crockett. Anyway, he considered, in today's p.c. climate, that dude would be drummed off the force. Dan continued down the road, pulled into the Marco Shoppes lot, and parked in front of the jewelry store.

He opened his Tumi briefcase, pulled out his department issued pad and a Bic pen. His marble notebook remained snapped securely in the upper pocket out of sight. He would fill in the day's events in that personal diary when he got home. He radioed into headquarters he was entering Sundown Jewels Design Studio.

He pulled open the flower-etched glass door; the sound of delicate chimes tinkled above him. The smell of fresh brewed coffee layered with a vague hint of incense, caressed his nose. A sheer gauze curtain draped across the ceiling muted the overhead lights. The counter was devoid of circular display towers. Instead, there were only a few trays containing gemstones and shells. The glass cases beneath were backlit where a few individual pieces of jewelry adorned a black velvet swirl of fabric. It was an unusual jewelry store. Dan wondered how they paid the rent with so few items for sale. This shop was very different from the two others he had already checked out.

"Be right out," a voice called.

A curtain behind the counter area parted and a slight-framed girl with long red hair backed out, a wooden tray held in her hands.

"I thought I heard someone enter," her voice low and melodic as she turned and placed the tray on the counter.

"Welcome to Sundown." She offered her hand as she looked up from the countertop.

"Kelly." They spoke in unison.

"Wow. Dan Barnes. You are the last person I expected to walk in here."

Dan stared as his thoughts raced thinking of the last time they were together. She was even more beautiful than he remembered. His heart pounded as he gazed into her dark brown eyes. He had been such an idiot, but they were kids. She couldn't still be angry. Could she?

"I didn't know you were back in town." Dan murmured.

"I came back after graduation. My dad needed my help after my mom, you know."

"I heard. I'm so sorry, Kelly. I would've come to the service, but after the way things went down, I didn't think you'd want me there."

"Don't worry about it, Dan. It's fine. Probably better you weren't there. My dad had enough to deal with, me too, honestly. I had some open wounds. It would not have gone well."

"I should have come. Your mom was a wonderful person."

"No worries. Thank you for saying that, though. But hey, you're looking mighty fine, Dan. Things must be going well for you. You need something special for your girl?" Kelly looked directly in Dan's eyes.

Uh oh, she thinks I'm rich. "No, no, nothing like that. I'm not," he gestured to his clothes. "This isn't me. I mean, it's me, but not how I am normally. I don't have a girl." Blushing, he continued, "I'm here on a case. I'm with the Sheriff's Department."

"You're a detective? I wouldn't have figured you'd go that route. I know your dad was a big shot, but I remember you wanted to get out of here so bad."

"I'm not a detective, yet. I'm a deputy, temporarily assigned to a case. I'm usually in uniform. I'm supposed to fit in, not draw any attention to myself."

"I don't think you achieved that goal. The ladies on this island will be all over that after a few happy hour drinks." Kelly smiled.

He couldn't believe she just said that, maybe... stop it, Dan. You're working here. "You've changed, Kelly, a lot more direct. Anyway, the baseball thing didn't work out. Not many options, so I took the test, and here I am. How long have you been working in this place?"

"I don't work here. This is my shop. I make all the jewelry myself. Everything is one of a kind. I design with the client's personality and desires in mind."

"You'd have to make a lot of earrings to keep this place afloat."

"My clients are looking for unique pieces. They are willing to spend whatever it takes to have their heart and soul on display. It can take weeks to come up with a design. Several consultations take place before I even begin the design process. In some cases where a surprise is involved, I suggest the client bring in a list of the recipient's likes and dislikes."

"Sounds more like you're a shrink. Weren't you an art major?"

"Yes, but I learned metal working from my dad."

He remembered watching her father in his shop. He was a master craftsman. He was also very intimidating when he had his blowtorch in his hands. "I remember your garage was full of strange contraptions."

"He loved to tinker. He started doing art pieces after mom passed. She had a book of drawings - jewelry ideas. He regretted he didn't make them for her when she was alive. When I came home, he taught me how to work with metals. I had a knack. He gave me the start-up money. It took off."

"Sundown Jewels. You always wanted to be near the water at sundown."

Kelly sighed. "Yes, the jewels on the gulf. I remember when you would dip your hand in the water and drip jewels into my palm. I thought that was so romantic. Hey, we were teenagers, right? Everything seemed like it would go on forever. So, Deputy Dan, what brings you to Sundown Jewels?"

"I'm trying to locate someone. There is a possibility this man is staying on the island. Any credit card activity has been going to a New York address. His wife is having a birthday next weekend. He's wealthy. He would spend a lot on a gift. So, I figured I would check jewelry stores, florists, you know, to find if he bought something and had it sent to her.

"My clients require discretion. The purchases often go to... special friends."

"I get it. If I give you a name, could you at least let me know if I'm on the right path?"

"I don't know. What is the name?"

"Sal Ferraro. His wife's name is Alexis. She also goes by Lexie."

Kelly's eyes opened wide in surprise. "This might be your lucky day, Danny Barnes. I can't supply you with an address. I don't have one and the name Ferraro is not familiar to me. But a guy came in a few weeks ago looking for a necklace. When he realized I designed jewelry, he got very excited. He asked me to design something special for a dear friend's birthday. Time was short he needed it by..."

Dan interrupted, "next weekend."

She smiled at him. "Yes. I got the idea she was more than a friend. He offered to pay in cash and described exactly what he wanted."

"You get a name, phone number? Delivery address?"

"No. I told him it would take a few days to design the piece, and at least a week to fabricate it. He agreed to come in and view the design. He showed up with a wad of cash. The pendant was made of platinum and rhodium with a woman's name spelled out in diamonds. It was a unique piece and the most intricate thing I've ever done."

"And the name?"

"Lexie."

"Is it here? Can I see it?"

"No. He picked it up yesterday."

"How much did he pay for it?"

"Twelve thousand."

"Whew. Did it seem like he was purchasing it for someone else?"

"What do you mean?"

"You know like, maybe someone sent him in to make the buy?"

"You know you sound very cop-like right now. I got the feeling it was for someone he truly loved. He caressed the necklace when I showed it to him. He was smiling, very happy with how it turned out. I have a picture of it. I photograph everything I design for my portfolio."

"Kelly, I think I love you. Oh, I'm sorry. I didn't mean…"

She gave him a long searching look then laughed. "Dan, I think I've heard you say those words before."

Dan laughed with her. "I guess you have."

The album was filled with Kelly's designs. Dan realized he shouldn't have worried she wasn't making enough to pay the rent. She was probably making way more than he did as a rookie cop. As he paged through the album, he could see she was talented in a way that was out of his league. At least he had some great memories.

"Here it is." She pointed to an intricately designed bird. "See the twisting metals on the wings? I studied ornithology books to get it exactly right. The name is engraved in diamonds on the ribbon the bird is trailing."

"That bird, it's not a heron or an egret. What is it? It looks familiar."

"It's an albatross."

"Doesn't that bird have negative connotations? I remember reading "The Rhyme of the Ancient Mariner" in tenth grade."

"It is supposed to portend bad luck. The buyer seemed oblivious to that fact. He was very pleased. I never mentioned the omen thing."

"An albatross. I've got to think on that for a while."

Dan's phone buzzed. Looking down, he saw Detective Landry's name come up on the screen. "Kelly, I've got to go. Thank you for your help. Is it okay if I call you, you know, about the case?"

"Sure, Dan, I would love to hear from you. Maybe we can meet up for coffee some evening after work. I close at six most nights."

"I'll definitely call." He smiled as he revved the Mustang and dropped the top down. He grinned as he pulled out of the lot. *Damn, this was a good day.*

CHAPTER 54

Just doing my job

Freddy Driggs pulled into the deserted Wawa parking lot. He was fifteen minutes late to pick up Bonita from her swing shift behind the counter. The neighborhood in East Naples where the store was located could be rough, especially after dark. At this hour, desperation was the only customer that entered the last remaining store in this part of town. Bonita knew to stay inside, but in or out made no difference around here. The neon sign over the entrance was blinking erratically. The second W in WAWA was missing. What flashed in the dark sky was an infant's cry: WA_A...WA_A...WA_A. Freddy knew there would be no comforting arms to soothe the despair curdling the heart of this place. Tomorrow, Bonita would make the call. She wouldn't be coming back here.

As if on cue, two tricked-out sedans, a lime green Honda with an Incredible Hulk likeness painted across the hood and a dung brown Toyota with orange rims on its low-profile tires crawled into the lot. They met up next to the dumpster in the corner, driver's windows adjacent. Hands reached out, one white, one black, an exchange was made. They were gone in less than two minutes. Freddy took out his notebook, copied what he had made out on the mud crusted tags, and the makes and models of the cars.

Bonita hopped in the car; her expression murderous. "Freddy, I think you want me to get killed the way you are never on time." Bonita slammed the door extra hard as she glared at him. "You know, Andre gets in early so I can get out of here before the dealers show up. That boy cares about me."

"If that's what you think, Nita, why don't you get with him? He's young and has a great future in the gas and food service industry. I'm just an old fucker that has officially gained respect from the community."

"What are you talking about old man?"

"I just came from the Collier County Board Meeting. I was invited by the Business Commissioner."

"Why haven't I heard about this before now?'

"You know all those phone calls you hang up on cause caller id says Collier County?"

"Yeah, those are bill collectors 'bout our property taxes."

"No, not about our taxes. I've been paying down our bills. We are almost completely out of debt." Freddy smiled proudly.

"Wait a minute, I gave you the bills to do cause I'm tired after working twelve hours a day, and I'm done being aggravated. I figured it'd set a fire under your ass." Bonita leaned back and wagged her finger at him. "I finally got us right; first time in years, so with those calls coming in, I'm thinking maybe you dropped us back down that hole." She side-eyed him. "You are bullshitting me?"

"Nita, I'm responsible. You working two jobs is going to stop."

"Never happen."

"It will. You're not coming back here."

She rolled her eyes and raised her hands up to the roof. "Heaven help me. You told me you were off the drugs."

"Stop being so dramatic, Nita. You know I'm sober. I get it. You're mad. I'm sorry I'm late. Let me tell you why. Pete Landry…"

"You mean Detective Landry."

"No, Pete. He told me to call him Pete."

"How come he is giving you that privilege?"

"You know the PI stuff has been working out really good; I've been out every day for the last few months working on cases."

"Yeah, but except for this car, I've never seen a dime come in from your business. You go out every day with that new briefcase I got you when you started this whole thing, and I don't know what you're up to."

"I'm getting us right, honey. I am being fiscally responsible."

"Where did you hear that word from?"

"I bought a book on accounting for small businesses. There is an entire chapter on how to be fiscally responsible."

"So, things are getting better you say? And I can quit this job?"

"I am a licensed business owner and a credit to our community. That's what I was trying to tell you. I was invited tonight to accept an award."

"Really? How come you didn't tell me about this?" She huffed as she pulled off her green Wawa vest.

"I asked you to come, remember? Two days ago, I mentioned there was a big meeting at town hall." He leaned over and tucked an errant wisp of hair behind her ear.

"I didn't know you were getting an honor. I would have liked to have been there. No way I can take any time off, there isn't anyone to cover my shift."

"Aww, honey, I wish you were there." Freddy reached across the console pulling her closer and kissed her hard on the mouth. "I owe everything to you. I said that tonight, too. In front of a roomful of people, I swear. I said I owe my life and my future to my wife, Bonita Esperanza Mendez Driggs."

"You're going to make me cry."

"They tape every meeting so when we get home, we can look on-line and watch it."

"Let me see this award."

Freddy reached into the back seat and pulled out a bubble wrapped package. Carefully peeling the tape back, he picked up the plaque and handed it to Bonita. A polished wooden frame held an official-looking document that featured the name of the corporation along with the principal officers and date of inception. A brief message of thanks for hard work and outstanding dedication to the community was written in delicate calligraphy. It was signed by all the members of the County Board of Supervisors and the official Collier County seal was embossed on the bottom of the award.

"You changed the name of the business."

"Of course. I wasn't going to leave you out of this." Freddy's eyes filled with tears. "I am nothing without you, Nita. You know that ad you made me buy for the paper? Well, I got a client from it. And I met up with Pete, and he really liked the briefcase."

Bonita wiped her eyes and held up the plaque. The name B and F Driggs Investigation Services in ornate gold letters glowed in the blinking red neon light of the crying Wawa sign. "I love you, Freddy."

"There is more to tell. Remember I told you about Doctor Treehorn, the snake expert who was working on the case with Pete?"

"I remember. You said she was beautiful, like a movie star playing the part of a doctor."

"Yeah, she is still that good looking. Well, she was there tonight. She offered me a consulting job. She wants me to go back in the glades with Bees Smithens and Shredder Cochran, if I can drag him away from the trailer park."

"Don't go getting a fat head." Her eyes twinkled. "Why does she want you back in there?"

Freddy puffed his chest and stuck out his chin. "She called me after I found the stoned gator. She thinks there might be more to learn from the area where Bees found the dead guy.

They pay pretty good, and it would be great we are Florida Fish and Wildlife contractors. That's going on our new website."

Her eyes squinted as she answered, "What website?"

"The one you are going to design as soon as you quit your job at Wawa."

"I never thought this could happen. I hoped, prayed we could overcome all the bad shit surrounding us." Her words tumbled out in a rush. "Is this real Freddy? Are we on our way?"

"We worked hard for this. It's going to be okay." He hesitated. "I'm even thinking we could move out of our shack... if you want." He searched her face for a reaction. "I know it was your family home and all, but we can afford something a bit nicer now."

"Let me think on that." She gave him an awkward smile. "I know I've been telling you the reason I don't want to move is because my mama left us the place when she passed. But the truth is, I knew we couldn't afford anything better." She sniffled and looked out the window. Turning to face him, she continued, "I'm thinking you and me pulling ourselves up might be an inspiration, an incentive for people to try something else. We are getting old. A young person dreaming big, this might show them it can happen. You were on the wrong side for so many years. It got us nothing. Now...we have so much to be thankful for. Maybe the people round here need to see more than we escaped. We are building something."

Freddy laughed, "Who would have guessed we could be role models?"

"You know that kid lives next door?"

"The girl going to computer school at night?"

"Well, she's trying to stay straight. Maybe we should give her a leg up. Bet she would know how to put together a website. I'm going to pay her a visit and see if she'd like to work for B and F Driggs Investigation Services." Her eyes locked onto his. "You okay with that, boss?"

"Partner, anything you want to do is fine with me." He smiled warmly as his calloused hands caressed her cheek.

"Let's go home, Freddy. This truck may be fancy, but I miss the bench seat in the old piece of junk we had. You are going to have to wait until we get home to unwrap your other special award."

He started up the Subaru. "This is why I love you, Bonita girl."

CHAPTER 55

Birds of Prey

Pete sipped his Starbuck's Café Americano, no sugar and read over the notes Dan had left on his desk. Charlie sat across from him, his expression worried. "What makes the kid think he can go off and surveil someone without running it past us? These guys are dangerous. Where is he perched?"

"He's on Marco Island, not the Bronx. The only trouble he might get into is if some old guy backs into the car."

"What did his report say?" Charlie reached out to grab the folder.

Pete swatted his hand away. "Hold on, I'm not finished. He mentions a piece of jewelry she..." He shuffled the pages and removed an invoice. "Wait, here it is. Kelly Fitzpatrick, proprietor of Sundown Jewels, a piece designed for a wealthy client. He was a walk-in. It was inscribed *LEXIE*. Paid for in cash – twelve thousand dollars total." Pete whistled, "That's a shit-ton of money." He rubbed his head, brushing his hair with his fingers, and leaned back in his chair. "Who carries that much dough around?"

"Mob guys who don't want a paper trail. A legit guy would want all those points on his credit card," Charlie said.

"Still, that much cash is noticeable."

"Let's give Dan some credit here," Charlie said. "If he hadn't canvassed that shop, we wouldn't have known about it. Miss er... Fitzpatrick didn't make a call about a large cash purchase."

Pete frowned, "Why would she? I bet a lot of her business is cash, men or women who don't want anyone looking at their credit card statements.

Anyway, it was picked up yesterday morning. Dan's file has a Post-it attached, says Lexie Ferraro's birthday is February twenty-six."

"No coincidence," Charlie shook his head. "The kid is good. Maybe I'll make him my partner after you go fishing next week."

"Hey, I'm not dead yet." Pete turned to the next page. "He wrote here there's no video footage. No cameras in the shop on Collier and the eyes on the lot have been down since the last storm."

"What did the jewelry look like? Maybe he thinks he can spot it on one of the ladies strutting up and down Collier."

"It's a pin on a platinum necklace. Here, look, he has a photo of it." Pete held up the page to Charlie. "What kind of bird is that?"

"A frigate. No, wait." Charlie reached over and entered the term Albatross into the search engine on Pete's laptop. "I think it's an Albatross. Check this out. The piece looks exactly like the picture in the Audubon Society site. This designer is top notch. Hey, Pete, if you ever need an engagement ring, you should hit her up. She's talented."

"Not likely to happen."

"Well, I'm on standby to be your best man. Vanessa would be perfect for you. She wouldn't put up with your shit."

"Let's focus here, Charlie. It is an Albatross, a weird choice for a birthday gift. Lot of bad news attached to that bird."

"It must have a personal meaning." Charlie shrugged.

"Why does that remind me of something? It's playing around in my head, but I can't grab it." Pete pushed Charlie out of the way and typed in Albatross, Marco Island.

"Pete, that's why it sounds familiar. The Albatross is the name of one of those high-end buildings, gulf-front on South Collier."

"Where did Dan say he was parked?" Pete reached for his phone.

"At last check, he was parked in the Resident's Beach Lot."

"Next door to the Albatross." Charlie grinned. "Told you that kid is smart. Definitely partner material."

"That didn't take a scientist to figure out."

"Just saying," Charlie grumbled, "He's out there, following leads, and we're in here, drinking coffee."

"He's young and has something to prove."

"You know, partner, you really have checked out. I'm disappointed."

"Call his cell. Tell him to hang in the car." Pete stopped and looked at Charlie. "What unit is he driving?"

"He's still got the Mustang. I wouldn't be in a hurry to switch that out if I was him."

"Well, it's loud and sexy as hell. Not flying under the radar. We've got to get a different crew in there. The young girls doing yoga on their lunch hour are going to see Dan wearing his Miami vice get-up in a hot car, and he's done." Pete continued. "He's not going to fool anyone."

"Well, maybe they'll think he's a talent scout or a pimp." Charlie chuckled.

"You're sick. No, I don't think he could pass for a pimp, maybe a pervert sitting in his car waiting to expose himself. I'm surprised the crazy parking lot monitors haven't told him to move yet. They hate anyone clogging up their prime parking spots." Pete said. "They have some issues."

"Should we pay a visit to the condo?"

"Not yet. We need to keep an eye on it. See if we spot any of the..." Pete's phone began playing "Take me out to the ballgame." "That's Dan."

"You're kidding, that's his ringtone? How come he gets a classic, and I get screams?"

"Charlie, yours is my favorite." Pete laughed, pretending to strangle himself.

"What's Vanessa's sound like?"

"Donna Summer, 'Love to Love You, Baby.'"

"You're an ass. I'm going to tell her that."

Pete gave Charlie the finger and answered the call. "Hey Dan, what's going on? We were just discussing how you broke protocol and started a one-man surveillance on the Albatross. Got something you want to say about that? I'll put you on speaker because Charlie has been clucking like a mother hen all morning. Wants to know his little chick is alright."

"I'm sorry. I know I should have called you. I did tell the main office where I was heading. I guess I got carried away. I wanted to help wrap this up."

"You mean you want to take my spot next week," Pete growled.

"No, no, that's not..." Dan stammered.

"I'm just messing with you kid. So, what you got?"

"Dan," Charlie interrupted, "you are keeping your head down, right? Not drawing any attention to yourself?"

"Hold on a minute..." Dan said.

Charlie and Pete heard a muffled conversation and could just make out Dan identifying himself. The phone dropped as he must have reached for his shield.

"Just looking at the cars. No, I don't have a warrant." Dan picked up the phone as another voice, too muffled to decipher, came through. A minute of silence, then the phone went dead.

"Damn it, he got out of the car." Pete slammed the desk.

"Sounds like something you would do, Pete."

"He should know better. You got a lot of work to do with that kid, Charlie."

Two minutes later, the phone sang out again. "What the hell are you doing, Dan? Get your ass back in the car and head in."

"Will do, Pete, but I found it..."

"Found what?" Charlie yelled.

"I can hear you, no need to shout. I found the red Ferrari Mondial. The one Sal Ferraro bought for Lexie. It is in the Albatross garage. It's far up the row. I couldn't see the tags. But it is the right make and model."

"You had eyes on a car that might be the one we are looking for? How many of those cars are in the county? What was the number you came up with? Eight?" Pete barked at the phone. "You remember, Naples is the Ferrari capital of the East Coast."

"And how many did the uniforms find?" Charlie sneered. "I'll tell you, son, they found two. Do the math, it might or might not be the car. You get it?"

Pete finished. "We will check this out, it's a solid lead. But remember, you are assigned to this squad TEMPORARILY. Don't blow it by being a hotshot," he scolded. "Get in here and write this all up."

CHAPTER 56

Always Something Interesting on the Beach

Diego waved the olive and shrimp festooned Bloody Mary in front of Gary's sleeping face. The strong, pungent aroma had the desired effect, and his eyes opened.

Handing the drink to Gary, he smiled. "I brought breakfast." Diego gestured towards the welcoming scene. "I see you're set up for the day."

Two surf-casting rods already secured in PVC sand-spike holders were placed beside a tackle box, a large white bucket half-filled with water, and a cooler. A bottle of 30 SPF Sun Bum spray, the *New York Times* opened to the day's crossword with a pen at the ready, and the new Carl Hiaasen paperback, it's spine unbroken, all lay enticingly on a fluffy beach towel on the vacant lounge.

Dropping on the edge of the chaise, he pointed at the rods. "I see you remembered I love to fish."

"I remember every word you've said to me," Gary smiled warmly. "Cheers."

Diego's expression darkened. "On my walk here from the hotel…"

"Diego, wait, I need to say something before I…. Well, I hope I don't scare you off, but I am not going to hold this in. That's how I've always lived my life. Holding things back. Burying how I feel." He took a deep breath, "So here goes nothing."

"Diego, I started thinking about life and how short it is. We sail through rough seas always trying to find calm. I think about all we give up keeping things on an even keel. I decided, I don't want to live that way anymore. I don't know if you feel the same way I do. I hope you do. I am not giving up on life."

Diego squinted. "What was this decision? What is it that changed your life?"

"You, my friend, changed everything. I hope to have many years left. I don't mean to spend my last days sitting beside the pool reading the *New York Post*, going inside at four o'clock to watch *Judge Judy* in the social room with the rest of the old men. My friend dropped dead last year." Gary turned towards Diego, planting his feet in the sand so their knees were touching. "One minute he's sitting by the side of the pool. He got excited about something he read, and the next minute, BAM, dead as a fucking doornail. They carried him out on a stretcher. He had been sitting in the same damned chair every day since he retired twelve years ago. He was seventy-eight. The doctor had given him a clean bill of health the week before. I want more."

"Well, that was quite a soliloquy. Do you feel better saying that?"

"I'm not just saying it. I mean it. It's time for me to go. I want—no need—an adventure."

"What about your wife?"

Gary looked at him and smiled. "I believe she would be relieved. We haven't had sex in years. She has her pool friends and her mahjong friends and her Zumba and book club friends. And she knows I am gay."

"Why did she stay with you?"

"Because it was easy. I am easy. I sit and wait to die, and she has no worries." Gary shifted on the lounge, his knees no longer touching Diego's. "Wait, maybe I spoke too soon. What did you want to tell me?"

Diego looked out at the blue water of the gulf just as a pair of dolphins broke the surface. Looking over at Gary, he sighed deeply. Pointing to the mammals breaching in unison, he smiled. "So, maybe we swim away together into the sunset." His reached over and squeezed Gary's hand.

"Nothing would make me happier, Diego. I know this is fast, but this, what we found, maybe it won't come again."

"I agree. It isn't easy finding a partner…I never thought I would after Jeff died."

"When were you planning on leaving Marco Island?"

"Raul is going to the condo reunion on Saturday. We were to leave for Miami on Monday."

"You said you have a Porsche, a two-seater. I have a Range Rover that could hold the things I want to bring."

"Or you could leave everything behind. Start fresh with nothing to hold you back."

"Drink up, Diego, and look!" Gary pointed at the fishing rod now bobbing up and down. I think you've hooked something big."

Diego winked. "I have, haven't I?" Grabbing the pole, he started expertly reeling in the catch. Whatever he had caught was large. He let it run out a bit then reeled in some more line. The ray's wings were visible about twenty feet from the shore.

"That's a big mother," a beach walker commented as he paused to watch. A crowd started to gather as Gary grabbed the needle-nose pliers and donned a pair of work gloves that were in the tackle box.

Diego struggled for a full twenty minutes until he pulled the ray on to the sand. Turning towards Gary he was surprised to find the Marco Island Beach Patrol ATV had arrived on the scene.

Gary pointed towards the whomping sound of the WBNK News helicopter. "Looks like the cat's out of the bag now, my friend."

The ray flapped violently on the sand. "I don't think those pliers are going to do the job," the officer yelled over the sound of the hovering news copter. He began pushing back the crowd. The two-way radio attached to his shirt squawked announcing a second unit would be on scene in five minutes. The officer yelled into the mic, "False alarm, no shark! Copy that? No shark! It's a big ray. Get out to the street and divert traffic away. It's a mob scene here."

"Copy."

Diego held down the ray's wildly flapping wings while Gary extricated the hook from its mouth.

"There," Gary grimaced as he pulled the hook free. "Not too much damage. Let's get him back into the water."

Diego and Gary were joined by two burly bystanders as they dragged the huge manta back into the gulf water.

Diego looked over at the throng of spectators and the helicopter. "Is this common around here?"

"Is what common? Oh, you mean the crowd, the police, and the helicopter?"

"Yes, a bit of an overreaction I'd say."

"Marco Island is billed as the safest city in Florida. Nothing much happens here. The locals and the tourists get their grins where they can. If this was a shark, you would be interviewed on the spot and appear tomorrow on *Good Morning Naples*. As it is," Gary pointed to all the phones recording the catch. "We will be a YouTube hit in about ten minutes."

"Shit."

The sand was swirling, and hats flew as the news crew tried to get closer and the pilot seemed to be attempting to land.

"What the hell is that asshole doing?" The officer began frantically waving his arms and directing the chopper towards the road, while yelling at the crowd. "Show's over. Nothing to see here. Move along." He spoke into his mic, "Somebody tell the I-missed-it news chopper it's over. They're causing a sandstorm on the beach."

The Albatross gulf-front balconies were filled with residents; even the Penthouse's new occupants were watching the spectacle. Among the faces in the crowd was Gary's wife standing stone still, looking intently at Diego. Her friends encircled her, all of them dripping pool water. When they saw Gary looking in their direction, they turned as one and headed up the path to the condo.

"Diego," nodding towards the troop of women walking up the path, he continued, "I am done hiding. Anyway, it's all out in the open now. I'm sure my double life has been a source of pool gossip for years. How about you come to the party as my guest? I think it would be a hoot. The old biddies will piss themselves watching you and I, hand in hand. We might even throw in a random kiss."

"I'm not sure that's a good idea. Even if you've had a platonic marriage for years, she deserves some respect. I'm surprised you suggested this."

Gary took a rag hanging on the side of the bucket and wiped blood off the pliers. "I am feeling free for the first time in a lifetime. I guess I got carried away. But I am serious about this. When the party is over tomorrow night, I am walking away from all of this—with you.

Diego toweled off the fishing rod and dropped it in the sand spike holder. He stared at Gary. "You think you can walk away that easily?"

"You won't find any doubt, no matter how hard you search my face. I have only felt this way once before. I never thought I would feel this way again." Gary breathed deeply, pushed his shoulders back, and stared directly into Diego's eyes. "I am not going to let you go, not going to give up on living my life. We are neither of us young. What the fuck do we have to lose?" He dropped the pliers into the tackle box and snapped the locks.

"I will be at the party. I'll come with Raul. He is representing his father at the reunion. You remember, I mentioned he owns the penthouse apartment? I will be packed and ready to leave. My gold 911 will be parked out front of the hotel."

Gary smiled. "No room for my luggage, I guess. I'll travel light."

"No worries, love. If you don't care, my home in the Keys is filled with designer clothes in just your size."

CHAPTER 57

Bird's Eye View

"Lexie, come out here. Something's happening on the beach."

Sal sat in the high-top chair and looked through the telescope set up on the balcony. The Sky-Watcher Pro-ED refractor telescope was a gift from Lexie along with a *National Geographic Field Guide to the Birds of North America* and an astronomy book: - *Night Watch: A Practical Guide.* He knew Lexie was aware he was gazing at celestial bodies, just not up in the night sky.

The helicopter arrived just as Lexie walked out. Her hair whipped around her face from the rotor's powerful wash. Two of the chairs flew over, and Sal cursed as sand flew up into his eyes.

"What the fuck? That pilot should know better than to get that close." He reached for his phone.

"Hold on, Sal. He is being waved off by the cop on the beach. What is going on down there?"

"Some guy hooked something big. I can't tell what it is yet. If the copter would freaking move…"

"Maybe it's a shark. That would be exciting—and terrible. I swim in there every morning." The helicopter banked away from the Albatross and headed out over the gulf. "Thank God, he's gone. Can you see what it is?" Lexie squinted at the large crowd gathered fourteen stories below.

Sal fiddled with the telescope. "Come look. It's a manta ray, must have a span of about ten feet."

"They don't bite, do they?" She adjusted the dial. "I see it. It's huge!"

Sal nibbled Lexie's neck. "No babe, they don't bite, unlike me. You know how I like to take a little nibble now and then."

"I'm serious, Sal. Are they dangerous?"

"Well, yes, they can be. They have a long-barbed tail that can cut you badly. The barbs have a poisonous venom that can be fatal. You remember the adventure guy, Steve Irwin? He died from a stingray barb hitting him in the chest."

"Oh my God, Sal. I didn't realize I was swimming with stingrays. I've been looking around for shark fins all this time." She stepped out of Sal's reach.

"You wouldn't see one unless it was jumping out of the water. They hang out on the bottom. I read about them in an old *National Geographic* that was left on the treadmill in the gym. You are supposed to shuffle your feet when you walk into the water. They'll swim away when they get disturbed."

"Thanks for telling me. It would have been good to know a little bit sooner."

"I only read about it last week when I started going to the gym."

"A week?" she snapped at him. "You know I swim every morning. I could have been dead by now." Lexie pointed to the beach. "Look at the size of that thing." She shook with anger as she shouted, "IT'S IN THE WATER—RIGHT THERE!"

"I'm sorry, Babe, I should have told you. It's very rare someone gets stung." He moved in close to her, his hands open in front of him. "You haven't heard of it happening since we've been here, right?"

"Sal, look! It's taking four big men to drag it back to the water." She shook her head. "Honestly, do you ever think of me at all? And I don't mean because you want to get laid."

Sal watched her storm off into the bedroom. He cringed as she slammed the door and pulled down the shades. He wondered what he was doing wrong. She never seemed happy anymore.

Looking back towards the gulf, he noticed the ray floating on the water. Shaking his head, he felt a deep pang of sadness tighten his heart. Tears erupted as he watched the inert form drift away from the beach. He wiped them away with the back of his hand and looked down at his damp fingers in disbelief. *I must be getting soft.* He looked around to see if anyone had witnessed his breakdown, then walked inside and slid the glass doors shut.

The crowd on the beach erupted in applause and squeals of joy as the ray came out of its stupor, leapt dramatically into the air, submerged, and swam off into the sunset. Sal blew his nose, poured a can of Diet Coke, and turned on "Let's Make a Deal."

CHAPTER 58

A Falcon and a Snowman

Dead. Rest in peace. My beautiful plan buried along with any chance of surviving Sal or Don Garcia or the feds or any other fucking jerk-off who will get a piece of me. It succumbed at the hands of second-rate wannabes. Sal is going to put this on me; it's not going to stick. Lenny started to gag, took a swig of scotch, and spiraled into his thoughts again. He needed to salvage something. Lexie. He needed to come out of this with Lexie. *She'll leave Sal and come with me.*

Lenny took another snort of the powder on the glass coffee table. His hands were shaking as he brought them to his burning nostrils. He hadn't left the condo for two days—not answering the door, the phone, texts, or emails. Hiding out on the terrace, he brooded, got high, drank Johnny Walker out of the bottle and watched those bitchy women in the pool ten floors below plan their big celebration.

He tried to remember where he got the coke. Two plans merged into one in his brain. Raul Garcia, right? Was this the missing shipment? No, wait. The window-cleaner guys floating outside his terrace. They were talking about some great blow. He remembered the conversation. They were receptive, overcharged him for the dope. He left it, suggesting he might be interested in picking up more and they should pass that information on. He took another gulp of scotch.

He bought an ounce as an investment, thinking he could get an in with them, maybe find out who was their supplier. If he could purchase a kilo, maybe he could pass it off as the missing dope, then he could sell it and give Raul the money. If he could pull that off, he might come out unscathed or maybe just a bit dented. The other side of the coin— if he replaced the money for the dope with his own cash, maybe sixteen thousand would keep Garcia satisfied. Then he could set up the old plan with new players.

He tried to follow the mental string floating just out of reach. He looked over the railing and spotted Preston walking out to the driveway. He did a great job on the drone. That was the only part of the plan that went right, and he hasn't been coming around looking for more money. Never asked any questions. Did the job and moved on. Lenny shook his head, grasping at something. Wait! Preston seems to have a hard-on for Lexie. Lenny started trembling. No. Lexie wouldn't go for a dirt bag, pothead, handyman…or would she? And Sal, he's on a health kick trying to win back Lexie.

He grabbed his chest, felt the solidness of his body. *Fuck, yeah, I'm still alive. She must not have told him. If he knew that she knew about the vasectomy, I'd be dead already.* He pinched himself, still not dead. He bent over and did a half line. *Sal is on a mission to salvage his marriage; he's not looking at me. Okay, that might buy some time.* A flash of brilliance penetrated the fog. *Freddy Driggs!* He reached for his phone, spotting a bunch of texts from Sonja. He sobbed. *Get a grip. Call that Driggs guy.* Lenny remembered something Driggs said, he knew the Everglades "like a baby knows his mama's tits, can find the juice with his eyes closed."

He felt his thoughts falling apart, could see them floating in front of his face like feathers in the wind. Soft, downy feathers like the ones in his overpriced pillow that was waiting on his bed in Howard Beach. That reminded him he hadn't slept in days. *Too much to figure out, no time to sleep.* The feathers drifted in and out of focus until one landed on his open hand. He reached a tentative finger out to caress the silky bits of feather. Shredded plumes joined the fluff. Blood spots dotted his open palm, on the table the white powder was now tinged pink. He turned his face skyward and was met with the macabre vision of a falcon ripping apart the lifeless body of a morning dove. The bird's head, now separated, fell from the railing above and landed on the remains of the line of coke. His eyes glazed over, he tried to remove the floating visage of Luca Brasi that wavered in front of him.

He tried to create an order to the events that brought him here—not possible through the blizzard enveloping his brain. *I should get out NOW...Wait, Lexie.* He moaned. *She's got to leave Sal. Maybe I should kill him. No. I can't do that. If I fucked it up, I'm dead. What the hell, I'm dead anyway.* His brain went back to Lexie. He wasn't going to leave without her.

He looked at the small, wrapped box on the coffee table, the present to Lexie in its pristine white wrapping was now dotted with pinpoints of red and spots of powder—blood and blow. He tried to wipe the evidence away, succeeded in sending a snow squall scuttling into the air. *She can't see these spots.* Lenny tore open the present, ripping the paper to shreds. The box slipped out of his hands and skittered across the terrace's ceramic tiles, landing at the edge of the balcony. He crawled over and rescued the gift just as a strong wind gripped the box and sent it falling towards the pool. The precious pendant, with its gleaming platinum chain, dangled on a prayer between his fingers. The Albatross spun in the wind. Its diamonds glistening in the falling snow.

His phone vibrated on the coffee table. He crawled over, the necklace still held tightly in his fist. An Ozone Park exchange showed up on the screen. He watched the phone as it stopped buzzing. *Get a grip.* He scraped a matchbook across the tabletop, hoping to gather enough blow for one more hit. *Maybe this last one will kill me, or it'll give me the courage to jump off the fucking balcony.* The ping of a voicemail sent him into a panic.

"Mr. Horowitz, this is Ozone Park Acres Assisted Living Facility. You are listed on Mrs. Matilda Andruzzi's intake form as the employer of Dominic and Louis Andruzzi. A few days ago, the New York City Police Department notified us that Dominic and Louis Andruzzi were deceased. As their employer, I am sure you are already aware of that sad news. Mrs. Andruzzi mentioned on numerous occasions that her sons received a promotion and had relocated to Florida. I am sorry to inform you that Mrs. Andruzzi died this morning. Her death occurred as a New York City Detective was delivering the news that her third son, David, was identified as a victim of a tragic accident. She suffered a massive heart attack. Mrs. Andruzzi was very old and had many other health issues that were diligently addressed at our facility. Her demise may have been exacerbated by this terrible news. I am truly sorry to burden you with this information but other than her deceased sons, we have no other next-of-kin listed. Please call us at your earliest convenience. We are hoping to have this terrible situation resolved quickly. We have a long waiting list. I think you can appreciate that those on the waitlist have serious time constraints. Thank you, Mr. Horowitz. All of us here at Ozone Acres are very sorry for your loss."

Lenny grabbed his head and sat back on the blood-stained tiles. Hugging his knees to his chest, he mumbled as he rocked back and forth.

CHAPTER 59

"I Am the Walrus"

Freddy's phone vibrated on the kitchen table. He had been going over his closed cases, six in the last month, checks already in the bank. With the extra cash he had purchased a mini recorder and camera for surveillance. Bonita didn't bitch about the purchases. She was onboard and even told him, "You have to spend money to make money." God, he loved that woman.

The caller ID displayed Lenny Jones. This must be my lucky day. That jack-off must be desperate. Freddy smiled as reached for his new recorder and answered the call.

"B and F Driggs Investigations."

"Is this Freddy Driggs?"

"Yes sir. Whom am I speaking to?" Freddy placed the recorder next to the phone and turned on the speaker.

"Mr. Driggs, I, uh, err, have a job for you. Are you interested in doing some work in the Everglades?"

"Could you please identify yourself, sir."?

"Oh, right. I err. Forgot, my name…"

"Did you say you forgot your name?" Freddy picked up a pen and started taking notes: Jones —high as a kite.

"Oh, sorry, we spoke before. I mean, I contacted you before about finding a package that went missing in the Everglades." Jones exhaled deeply into the phone.

"I'm going to ask you one more time, what is your name?"

"Right, right, Lenny..."

Freddy heard Lenny sniffling. "Lenny what?"

"About finding..."

"No, your name. What is your name?"

"Leonard Jones...no, Smith. No. Jones."

"I remember you, Mister Jones. Did you ever find your missing package?"

"Shit. Fuck me, no."

"Mr. Jones, what can I do for you? You seem...out of sorts."

Lenny giggled. "Did you know it snows in Southern Florida? And Luca Brasi came here. He must have been hiding on the balcony upstairs, sent me a message. Whoa, I got that message, loud and clear, not a fucking horse head. A head though, a bird head, landed smack on the line and then blew it all away. It was fucking snowing."

Freddy could hear Lenny snorting and the phone drop. In the distance he heard him mumbling. "No horse heads. I am the horse's ass... no wait! I am the walrus." Lenny picked up the phone. Freddy cringed as Lenny cackled, "That was Paul, right? No walruses here, big sea cows, floating in the pool. I can see them. I fucking hate Florida."

Lenny must have turned away as he shouted, "Fuck you, Ka Choo."

"Mr. Jones, would you like me to call for help? Where are you right now?

I can send an ambulance. You seem to be in distress."

"No. No, I'm fine. Just need to get things on track, back in the game. I need a few good men. Are you a good man, Mister Driggs?"

"I'd like to think I am. Why did you call me, Mr. Jones?" Freddy listened intently as Lenny loudly blew his nose and gulped down something. Freddy hoped it was water.

"I need help..."

"I can tell."

"No, I need a crew to do some work for me."

Freddy sensed that Lenny was pulling himself together. "A crew? I do private investigations. Do you need something investigated?"

"I need someone discreet. You told me you were discreet. I remember that is exactly the word you used."

"What type of work are we talking about?"

"I, uh have started a business... a start-up company, on my own, delivering stuff, by air via the Everglades."

"Why would you need someone discreet in the Everglades?"

"I might have been mistaken. I thought you would be open to making a shit load of money, tax-free. Are you someone who might be interested in a business proposition like that? And if so, do you have some other trustworthy quiet guys who might want to get in on the ground floor?"

"You have a procurement procedure in place?" Freddy smiled, so happy Bonita gave him a thesaurus. It made him sound smarter. He read it every night before he shut off the light.

Lenny snorted and laughed. "I got a delivery from the sky just yesterday. Rolled on by me, perfect handoff, ten stories up and there it was. Added bonus, my windows are...were super clean, except for the snow and blood." Lenny sneezed into the phone. "But when those guys roll by again, maybe they can do my windows."

"I might be interested, but it sounds to me like you are under the influence of the products you might be discussing. I wouldn't want to do business with someone who is... shall we say, fucked up."

"I am doing my due diligence, quality control, product reliability. I am an attorney. I can't afford to make mistakes," Lenny huffed into the phone.

"I see. Well, Mr. Jones, would you call me back, say tomorrow morning, when you might be a bit more clear-headed? I'm interested in your proposition. But you must understand, I can only deal with a serious sober individual. My reputation is at stake."

"So is mine, Mister Driggs, so is mine."

Freddy heard the phone click. He shut off the recorder, chuckled, picked up his pen and took more notes on the call.

CHAPTER 60

More Cool Stuff on the Beach

Pete opened his laptop and pulled up the file on the Albatross. He began a new page to create a surveillance schedule. Six patrol guys were assigned to the squad to supplement the original team—four from Collier Sheriff's and two from Marco Island PD. They were a group of motivated guys, happy to get out of watching school crosswalks and pulling over speeders on Collier Boulevard. Advancement was slow in Southwest Florida, Marco Island in particular. With only two bridges in and out, the serious criminals chose to ply their trades elsewhere. DWI was the most serious crime, occurring at alarming rates between the hours of five and seven p.m. Most street cops loved "Happy Hour." It generated the most overtime.

That kid is something else. Pete typed Dan's name as the lead on the team. He was going to make damn sure he got a leg up on a promotion. *Going to raise some eyebrows, probably piss-off a few people— nepotism: he's too young, not enough experience. The kid has done more in two months on the job than half of Collier's finest with ten years all doing squat.* Pete knew he was not going to retire without getting that him a shot at the squad.

The phone rang, and Danny's name popped up. "Hey, Scooter, just setting up a stakeout schedule. You'll be first with eyes on the beachside."

"Well, I just got eyes on the Ferraros!"

"Hell, my man, I was just thinking you are going places. Lay it on me boy, make this papa bear proud."

"About an hour ago there was all kinds of commotion on the beach in front of the Albatross. Crowd gathering, the WBNK copter even swooped in for a peak. Two guys fishing landed a monster ray. I was standing at the back of the crowd checking if any of our 'friends' were around. I looked back to the Albatross. Out on the penthouse terrace, I see a guy looking through a telescope at the commotion on the beach. I moved away from the crowd, went under those tiki umbrellas. You know, the ones the city installed gulf side?"

"Yeah, I got the picture, keep going."

"Okay. I didn't want him to pick me up with the scope, so I'm under the umbrella, eyes on the balcony. I see him turn and look at the sliders. He says something and he's pointing to the beach. A woman comes out, a very hot woman. It's Lexie Ferraro. I check out the guy again—big guy, bare chested, lot of gold around his neck. Sal Ferraro. Larger than life, right there, shit."

"Fucking A. Kid! You are something else."

"What's next, Pete? You want me to go in and talk to him?"

"Slow down. Take a breath. No. Don't go anywhere near that building. We still don't know the whereabouts of Leonard Horowitz. I never thought this would fall into place this quick."

"I'm sorry, Pete. I got so excited. This is a major break."

"Damn straight it is. Just don't get ahead of yourself. Right now, we need to find the best way to approach the Ferraros without spooking them. Get back in your vehicle. Stay out of sight. Watch the driveways. I'll have someone else go beachside in case they take a walk. From your description, sounds like they are relaxed."

"Will do, Pete."

"Check back in about an hour, unless something else breaks."

Pete called out to Charlie, who was furiously scribbling notes, his cellphone tucked between chin and shoulder.

Charlie held up one finger and returned to his note taking. Hanging up, he turned to Pete.

"We just got a major break, Pete."

"Yeah, we did. How did you know? I just got off the phone with Dan."

"I just got off the phone with the lab, wait we are talking about two different things, aren't we?"

"Guess so. You go first."

"DNA results came back, all three of our dead Glade guys are related. Closely related. We already knew about the two Andruzzi's in the trailer. The third body is a DNA match. A third brother, David Andruzzi, hasn't been seen or heard from in weeks. It's confirmed. He is our Python boy. NYPD just got back from the nursing home. Matilda Andruzzi went into cardiac arrest. Dropped like a rock when she heard the last of her three sons was dead. "Pete, your turn. What have you got?" Charlie sat back in his chair his hands laced behind his head.

Pete took a sip of coffee. "Dan has eyes on the Ferraro's—" Pete's phone played the theme song from the Pink Panther. "Hold on a minute, I got to take this. It's Freddy Driggs."

CHAPTER 61

Cars

The Caddie roared to life, then settled back into a contented growl. It always impressed Preston how well the old ones withstood time and the elements. This classic spent years in extremes— frigid northern climes, oppressive southern heat, steel-rusting humidity. Yet here she sits purring contentedly in her Florida retirement home. He moved the car into place in front of the exterior pool gates, her distinctive grill grinning at the ladies floating serenely in the pool in front of her. There was no question Grace's car would be front and center and visible from the pool deck. He didn't want her freaking out if she went into the garage during the reunion and the Caddie was gone. This way she could see it and be reassured she hadn't left it running.

The detail guys had done an amazing job on the cars. All of them gleamed in the bright Marco sun. Preston looked around and realized you couldn't put a price on the assemblage in front of him. Hidden for years under slowly disintegrating tarps was a veritable gold mine. Lost treasures the residents were unable to part with, even after they had surrendered their keys to children who flew down bi-annually to check mom and pop were still breathing and the assets they coveted were still intact.

He checked the diagram and pulled the keys to a mint 1969 Shelby Cobra from the valet board he built for the occasion. The keys on the board were located to reflect each car's position in the driveway. It was a fascinating puzzle. He spent an entire evening reflecting on the possibilities: make, versus year, versus condition. In the end he decided to mix them all up, new models beside old, pristine next to well-loved—just like the residents they belonged to.

The Cobra slithered gracefully into place beside the Caddie, top up for now. But tomorrow the tuck and rolled white leather interior would be open to the tropical sky. A rare, limited edition, Preston knew this was probably the most valuable vehicle in the Albatross car show. He walked around it and respectfully touched the distinctive snake coiled on the corner of the grill. Like the car, it appeared ready to strike with lightning speed. From the pile of spec sheets he had created, he pulled the Shelby's stats and placed it on the passenger seat along with the hard label he designed. A burgundy snake on a white background was an exact match of the car's original color. Its coils spelled out GT500 Super Cobra Jet. Tomorrow, the plaque would rest on the windshield. He thought about the owner, a grey-haired widow who cherished her late husband's prized possession and vowed never to sell it. She would be inundated with offers after the reunion, but like most of the residents, she didn't need the money. What she needed was the memory of her husband, seated behind the wheel, driving down I-75 top down— his once luxurious mane blowing in the breeze.

He opened the one-subject spiral notebook he had purchased at CVS the day after he had spoken to George Neuwirth about his Rolls Corniche and the trip to Palm Beach. The story he heard that afternoon affected him deeply.

George began with his arrival in Florida forty-seven years ago. He was flat broke with a wife and a two-year-old son. He worked as a deck hand on a fishing boat out of Everglades City—making barely enough to get by. They lived in a trailer in Chokoloskee. "I got lucky." He shrugged, shook his head, and gave a sad chuckle. "Went in on a real estate deal, beachfront land, Marco Island. The wife, well, she was pissed." His sad eyes looked over at Preston. "Can't blame her. Me spending what little we had on what was probably a scam."

George Neuwirth told Preston the Rolls was not his most valuable car in the garage. That would be a 1970 Ford Falcon station wagon, faded blue with a dent on the left front fender from the time he hit a bridge rail avoiding an alligator. Through the wheeze of his oxygen tank, he continued, "The seats were shredded and probably still smelled of baby puke." He laughed. "We had fun in that car. At night we would drive down one of the dirt tracks to the gulf, our boy asleep in the way back while the wife and me fooled around in the front seat. Come to think of it, I'm pretty sure that car is where my son, Michael, was conceived. That's the one in Palm Beach. Humble beginnings couldn't keep that kid down.

Well, the Falcon's been sitting in the corner of the garage since the Albatross opened. I bought the Rolls after my wife left with the kids. I put the wagon where I can see it every day." The old man seemed to shrink. "I used to think I was somebody important. That fucking Rolls. I keep the Ford around, you know, so I remember everything I lost: the wife, the kids, my self-respect. I turned into a ruthless piece of shit, would sell anything for a buck, helped destroy the back roads of old Southwest Florida during the building boom of the seventies." He paused and took a sip from the water bottle Preston opened for him. "All those stone and terra cotta condos looked gorgeous. People bought them up. Most got suckered in, then found out they couldn't afford them. They overpaid for sprayed-on stucco and cheap plywood—kind of like the whole Disney World thing, smoke and mirrors. That would be my sin." He patted Preston's knee. "I think, if you put my cars in the show, you need to put the Falcon in the place of honor. I'd trade a dozen Rolls Royces for one afternoon playing I-Spy with my kids in that old station wagon."

Preston reached over and hugged George Neuwirth. The trip to Palm Beach was even more important now.

It turned out that most of the cars had stories and their owners were happy to tell them. Some were sad, some happy, all deeply personal and important. Preston decided he would detail all the cars and pay for it himself. He would photograph the cars and the owners if they would let him and see if they had pictures of them and their cars when they were young and new. On the spec sheets, he would print the photos and write their stories.

He had been up half the night for a week straight writing these pieces of Albatross history. The money Lenny paid him for the drone plans covered the cost with a bit left over to get him to Palm Beach.

He went over the driveway diagram again and decided Lexie's Ferrari and the Rolls would be on either end. He would be driving the Corniche heading to Palm Beach to take Mr. Neuwirth to see his son. He was finished taking care of the Albatross. He knew he would not be returning. If Lexie wanted to join them, he would have her bags in the Roll's trunk. He was determined to get her away from Sal. He cared for her, no, it was much more than that. She didn't know and he would never tell her. Besides, he thought, he had nothing to offer. It would take a while to see any income from his drone design. And what good was a degree if you didn't have a job? He wanted to thank her for helping him—get straight, get out of the rut, pushing him to begin his life.

He looked at the next car stat in the pile. A 2001 Toyota Camry, gold with a tan leather interior. That one had a story too...

When he finished, he had thirty-two cars ready to go.

"Preston, I was looking for you. The tent guys will be here in forty-five minutes." Susan looked at the cars lined up on the driveway. "Wait, I thought you were doing all those expensive cars under the tarps."

"They are still in but take a look at this." He handed her the sheets. She flipped through them one by one.

Her voice quivered. "I didn't know. How did I miss this? I've been working here for fifteen years." She looked up at him. "This was all you?" She waved her hand towards the cars. Old ones, new ones, bruised fenders, and pristine chrome all lined up revealing a forgotten history of the residents. Her face returned to him presenting a new emotion, one Preston hadn't seen in years— respect.

"I want them to know what you've done here."

"Susan, no. Please, don't say a word. I wanted to give them this."

She looked at him, nodding. "Alright, I...You're an amazing man, Preston, a lot deeper than any of us imagined." She seemed to consider something then continued, "With that new haircut, well, you have turned into quite a catch. Wondering if you have anyone in mind?" Susan pulled the Ferrari specs out of the pile and handed it to him. She hugged him tightly and kissed him on the cheek. "This, I didn't miss." She took a few steps towards the garage entrance, stopped, and turned towards him. "And Preston? Be careful."

CHAPTER 62

Joining Forces

I am never going back to Cuba. Raul reached over and tweaked Sonja's nipple.

"Ouch, you are ready again. You and I are perfect match." She reached over and grabbed his semi-hard shaft. "I am hot for you right now. My lover, he used to be like you. Lately, he thinks only about his future wife. I keep fake dick in his nightstand. I am thinking I do not need it anymore." Sonja ducked her head under the sheets.

Raul, now exhausted, looked at the woman beside him. He needed to thank the widow-maker for sending Sonja his way. He made a decision and turned to her.

"Again? I think I am in love. Young lovers are best."

"No." He laughed and gently pushed her away. "That's not ... I want to ask you something. You mentioned you were waiting for someone."

"He is nobody. That is done."

"I have a party to go to tomorrow evening, down the beach at the Albatross. I must attend. I'm meeting someone about a business venture. The invitation says I may bring a guest. Would you go with me?" He watched as her brow wrinkled in thought. "He, my new partner, isn't answering my calls. I think if he has a problem, you're with me, too bad."

"Your business, young stud." She reached over and stroked his leg. "What you do? Are good relations with America helping? I hear on my flights, so much opportunity now. I am sorry if I pry too much."

Raul looked at her as she stretched out and yawned. Her left breast, smaller than the right, was a minor flaw in an otherwise stunning body. Her sex rouged nipples, pointing towards the ceiling, seemed to beg for his mouth. He couldn't believe he was getting hard again. *I am more like my father than I thought.* He smiled.

"What is reason for your sly smile? You are very sexy when you look at me with hungry eyes."

"I was just thinking how lucky I am." *Lucky I'm getting off on a real woman and not a computer screen.*

"So, tell me?" She circled her nipples with her fingertips. "What is this business?"

Raul looked away from her tits and tried to focus. "Import /export. I...we, my business partner and I are importing...cigars. The twist is we are using drones, very big drones."

"So smart of you...and your American partner."

"It might be if he was answering my calls."

"Is this person you were trying to contact on phone? You are having same trouble as me. My friend is avoiding me." Sonja grinned sweetly, her voice a low purr. "I would love to go to party with you. I need to shop for something nice to wear. I brought mostly bathing suits and lingerie. But now I have met you, I think I will be doing the town."

"And me?"

"Oh yes, I...we will do each other day and night. She kissed him gently on the lips. I think we were meant to meet. You know they say, there are no coincidence." Sonja giggled, rolled over, and sent one last text to Lenny— I will see you soon.

Raul picked his linen slacks off the floor. His found his shirt rolled inside the sheets and his sandals in the living room by the door of Sonja's suite. Her boyfriend must have money to put her up in this place. He smiled. *When I finally take control of Garcia Enterprises I will be staying in the penthouse,* he looked at the bedroom door, *making love to Sonja.* He buckled the leather straps of his sandals. No word from Horowitz. That was a problem. He had a moment of concern about Sonja's lover. She seemed to kick him aside quickly. *What man wouldn't be wild to spend a week in bed with this woman?* Just thinking of her, dripping wet, walking out of the gulf, caused him to breathe deeply. Raul shook his head, trying to clear the sex fog. He had no proof things were going wrong, except for one: Mr. Horowitz not answering his phone. Well, all would be revealed tomorrow at the reunion.

CHAPTER 63

Shell Game

The Uber dropped Lexie off in the heart of Naples. Fifth Avenue traffic was crawling. She had plenty of things to wear for the reunion, but she had given Sal the excuse she needed something new, something that would blow his mind. She was sure he got off on watching other men drool over her. The old-fashioned brute he is, always fell for the lady- in-need tale. He denied her nothing. She felt bad she misled him so many times. He never really knew who she was. He beat his chest about how he stopped the coffin from killing her, how he would be her protector. In the beginning she was willing to fall into the role. She had woken up from the deep fugue she resided in for years. It was time to make her own way. If a man was by her side that would be fine, but she would never again give up her power.

Since they arrived in Florida, her life had changed. Sal didn't notice she no longer needed him. He was oblivious, only seeing what he wanted to see. She didn't need his money. Vinnie's insurance policy made that possible. The police found no evidence a crime was committed. The insurance company, after years of testy correspondence and threats of legal proceedings, finally acquiesced and she was awarded a hefty seven-figure payout. She invested it on her own. The stock market, against all predictions, turned skyward. Neither Sal's nor Lenny's fingerprints were on her money. She gave Sal credit for stepping aside when it came to her windfall. She chose to think he trusted her judgment. The other more worrisome thought was that Sal felt some guilt about Vinny's death. He was hands-off her money. *Why, when he couldn't keep his hands off anything else?* She had suppressed the idea Sal was culpable in some way. She chose to remain blithely ignorant in her fancy house and Prada shoes.

She checked her debit card at the ATM kiosk then entered the bank and withdrew fifteen hundred dollars in cash. All the items hidden in the condo were paid from her own account. She made significant purchases with their joint credit card; those were on obvious display in the walk-in closet and dangling from her ears.

She tried on the form-fitting, royal blue silk dress. Its halter top plunged deeply, offering a view of delicate mounds of tan flesh, courtesy of nude sunbathing on the terrace. The dress gently hugged her tight Peloton-trained butt and showed off her flat stomach. The soft fabric gently flared just above her knees. It would be perfect for the party and the price tag of eight hundred dollars would give Sal a moment's pause before he would look her up and down and decide she was worth every penny—and then he would want to fuck her.

A last-minute decision sent her into the lingerie shop. She made her purchase quickly and once outside texted for a nearby Uber. One was trolling down Fifth and was only two stores down.

Returning to Marco, Lexie considered her options. She had researched vasectomies; they could be reversed. It wasn't a hundred per-cent effective, but a high rate of success. Maybe Sal is being truthful. She thought about how considerate he was lately. He was very gentle this morning; he usually attacked her like a rutting bull. She never had a problem with that before, but it never felt like lovemaking. This morning was different; he made sure she was totally satisfied. It was as if he sensed she was losing interest. She had to admit it was the best sex they had ever had. Thinking of Sal's soft caresses, instead of his usual heavy-handed kneading, she felt her nipples harden beneath her t-shirt. She willed her body to stop. She couldn't keep making excuses for him. He was a liar and probably much worse.

Lexie stopped at the storage closet before heading into the condo. She looked down the hall to the penthouse door making sure Sal wasn't watching. She checked her watch, noticed it was time for his afternoon television break. Once inside the small room, she removed a small package from the shopping bag. She pulled back the tissue paper and held up the delicate lace nightie. It was lovely. The impulse to buy this last item surprised her. She had already bought new bras and panties. She had purchased comfy pajama pants and a matching tank top. She had even bought a black sheer teddy that revealed every curve and secret. This was not the same. This was a statement. Thinking of Preston, his brooding blue eyes hidden behind a forest of sandy hair, the suggestion of well-defined muscles under baggie old t-shirts, what did she see in...what did Sal call him? That burned out hippie. She needed to get it together, jumping from one freak show to another. She rolled up the garment and walked towards the trash bin. One more impulse turned her around, and she unfurled the pale lace, folded it carefully and wrapped it back between the sheets of tissue. She placed it in her carry-on. Shutting the light in the closet, she closed the door and walked down the hall. Maybe this time she would get it right.

The condo door opened just as she placed the key in the lock. Lexie jumped. "Oh, God, you scared me." Lexie placed her hand on her racing heart. *Did he see me come out of the closet?* "I thought you were still asleep. Isn't *Judge Judy* on now?"

"No, I mean, yeah, she's on. But I wasn't interested in watching TV."

Lexie squinted at him, confused.

"I woke up not long after you left and went for a walk down the beach. I made it all the way to Tiger Tail. I stopped there and took a break. This exercise thing is still new for me." His broad grin surprised her. "Anyways, all the sirens and ambulances running up and down Collier Boulevard, I don't want them to be coming for me. I got a lot to live for."

Sal followed Lexie into the bedroom where she took the dress out of the shopping bag. Sal continued talking, not even looking at the expensive item she held in her hands. "I went to the snack bar and had grilled chicken over salad and a Diet Coke, not bad for concession stand food, and headed back. Oh, I almost forgot, I got something for you." Sal walked past her into the kitchen.

Lexie walked in behind him thinking, *it's probably another piece of jewelry or a new sex toy.* She prepared to look thrilled. She studied his beaming face as he held something behind his back. *What is going on? He is fidgeting like a fourth grader.*

"Close your eyes, Lexie." Sal commanded.

She heard something clink along the side of the sink.

"Okay, open them." Sal held out a perfect conch shell. It was large, almost ten inches. He turned it over in his hands. "Look, babe, I've never seen a more perfect shell. I walked into the water, about up to my knees, the tide was just starting to go out. I felt something bump up against my ankles. When I reached down, I pulled this out of the water." He offered his gift to Lexie.

This is a new side of him. Lexie hesitated, then reached out and took the shell. "Sal, this might be the sweetest gift you've ever given me."

"Really? Better than jewelry? Even better than the Ferrari?"

"This is a heart gift. I used to tell my students the best gifts come from the heart. When you see something special and you think of someone who would really like it, and you give it to them, for no reason, not a birthday or Christmas, just because you think of them? That is a heart gift."

Sal tilted his head like a puppy, and as if a light went on inside of him. He smiled. "A heart gift, yeah, that's what this is. I'm glad you like it. You know, I'm trying Lexie. I haven't been the best husband, but I can change. I lost ten pounds, and I'm not going to drag you into bed whenever I get horny. That's a really hard thing for me, since I get horny every time I look at you. I know how lucky I am. When we have a kid—"

Lexie stiffened and cut him off mid-sentence. "Thank you for the shell. It's very special. I will always treasure it."

She turned abruptly and walked away.

CHAPTER 64

Let's Get this Party Started

"Vanessa, this is Charlie Hernandez. I'm heading into Goodland to plan Pete's party. If you're around, I'm going to be at the Buoy around four-thirty. It would be great to have your input. No worries about Donna, she's over it. I think it would be best if you guys meet before the party. You got my number. Call me if you can't show."

Vanessa listened to the voicemail as soon as she got back to the dock. She had been out in the field all morning with Rosa Martinez, following leads on weirdly marked alligators. She was ready to call bullshit on it, except Freddy Driggs had spotted one, and she didn't think he would make it up.

The last thing she wanted to do this afternoon was have tea and biscuits with Pete's ex. She recalled the "what might have been" dinner with Pete when the waitress, who turned out to be Donna's best friend, took photos of her and Pete. That was creepy. She was sure it contributed to the celibate relationship she was in now. What do they call that? Cockblocking? She might have heard the expression on some sick late-night reality show. Vanessa couldn't get into the heads of some women. Like pack animals, they stuck together. She had never been part of a herd, a cheerleading squad, a sorority or even a book club.

After she tied off the boat, grabbed her gear and thanked Rosa, she tried to find a reason not to meet Charlie and Donna. If she begged off, she might avoid today's awkwardness. If she waited for the big "meet" until Pete's retirement party, it might put Pete, Donna, and herself in an uncomfortable spot. It wouldn't be fair. Donna worked at the Buoy; it was Pete's party. The third alternative was to not go to the party. She wasn't a longtime friend or co-worker. She only met Pete a month ago. After hearing the message, she sent Charlie a text. "See you at four. Hope you're right. Maybe I should come armed. LOL."

Charlie responded, "Leave the blade at home. A glass of wine and you'll both be fine. Trust me."

ↀↁ

Charlie watched in amazement as these two strong women circled each other like sleek predators. They sparred a bit, and then after a bottle of wine, sat laughing and talking about Pete as if they had been friends since junior high.

They had gotten through the party plans without incident. Vanessa, wisely, let Donna take the lead. The details were a concrete exercise that gave them a safe place to begin—food, drinks, band, and invites. Toasts and roasts and an appropriate Pete-centric gift were left for Charlie to figure out. He knew he would be turning away people to share their stories, so many had already stepped up. Everyone wanted to share their love of Pete and burn him at the same time, albeit in a funny way. The gift was taken care of, but if it would be ready in time, was the bigger question. Pete moving his retirement date had put a strain on Charlie's plan.

The party was set for the following Tuesday, Pete's last day at work. Charlie frowned. *God damn, Pete's retiring. I'm not sure he's ready.* He shook his head. *I know I'm not.*

Donna reached over and patted Charlie's hand. "You alright?"

He looked over at her, noticed her eyes were gray and she had cut her hair. *How did I not see those eyes before?*

"Yeah, sure, Donna, I'm fine. Just thinking about working with a new partner."

"Believe me, I get it. Things change. But you know they say change is good." She smiled at him. "Give me a hug, no need to be sad."

Charlie wrapped his big bear arms around Donna. *This is the first time I've held a woman since…*He wiped the thought away and let himself fall into the hug. He pushed back and looked at Donna. "You got a haircut, I like it. It shows off your eyes."

"Why, thank you. You're the first person who's noticed." She blushed. "I made a fresh pot of chili for tonight's starter. You want to share a bowl before the happy-hour crowd shows up?" She stepped back out of Charlie's embrace and turned to Vanessa who wore a fascinated expression.

"Vanessa, my chili's the best on the island. Everybody says so. Have a bowl."

"Thanks, but I want to go home and shower the swamp off me. You two enjoy your meal. I'll be in touch over the weekend about the party. Donna, I really enjoyed meeting you. I hope we can be friends." Vanessa extended her hand, and Donna was quick to take it in both of hers.

"Yeah. I think we can. I've heard some crazy stories about how you can slice the head off a python. I could use a friend like you. We got a lot of snakes hanging around this place." Donna lowered her voice. "No need to worry, about, you know, my feelings. This all has been coming a long time. I'm just glad it was someone like you."

"Charlie, thanks for getting me over here today. You're a good friend to all of us. Make sure you get our boy to his party on time." She gave him a quick peck on the cheek and headed out to her car.

Charlie smiled. *Like Donna said, "Change is good." Maybe everything was going to be all right.*

CHAPTER 65

Floating Ladies Swan Song

"Can you girls believe it? Tomorrow's the big day!"

"I think we're ready. Can't think of anything we missed."

"I hope the tent isn't going to block the sunset view from the pool. Did anyone tell Preston where we want it set up?" The singsong talk followed the ladies as they bounced from one side of the pool to the other.

"Yes, and the folks in the front condos by the lawn had a hissy fit until Preston said the tent was coming down the next morning. Since they were going to the party, they were gracious about giving up their front row seat to sunset for one night."

"Wow, that was really special of them."

"Now, now. Be nice. A lot of people are down here for a limited time, the renters especially. Many of them are still working."

"Anyway, Preston smoothed it all over. He is over on the lawn, making sure the tent is put up in the right spot."

"The fire dancer was here this morning. He said the waterfall will look awesome with the torches burning at sunset."

"Did he blow the conch when he was here?"

"No. And I think that should be a secret. Don't tell anyone he is going to do that."

"How about the DJ? Did you give him the playlist?"

"I did, but I changed it a bit."

"What did you do?"

"I just replaced some of the older songs with more up-to-date ones."

"Like what?"

"Well, the Macarena, for example. Who does that anymore?"

"We do and some of the guys do, too. Sometimes it's the only song they dance to, except for that one slow one. Wait, what was that one? You know, by that guy, the one who swiveled his hips a lot?"

"Elvis, you mean Elvis Presley. Wow, he is so sexy! We should go see him if he comes to the arena in Naples."

"Oh my. Did you take your Aricept this morning?"

"What did you say?"

"Elvis is dead."

"Well, I know that. But he sure can sing."

"No, he can't sing. He is d-e-a-d."

"What is that romantic song he sings? The one that gets the guys off their butts without too much prompting?"

"Can't Help Falling in Love"

"That's the one. That song got everybody horny. It was best if they played it last, then everyone went home and had sex. I used to think about Elvis when we were doing it."

"You know, that's a sign of old age. You lose your filters.

"We don't want to know you were thinking about Elvis during sex."

"Well, I bet I wasn't the only one."

"Did anyone check on the caterer?"

"They're using the kitchen in the social room for set-up. They have their own vans with ovens and stove tops. They're going to use our grills for the ribs."

"What about the bar?"

"I called the bartender this morning, He is going to the liquor store this afternoon. I made an executive decision—booze."

"I thought we decided beer and wine."

"You can't have BYOB at a formal party. We are having a cocktail hour not a beer and wine hour."

"How are we going to pay for this?"

"It's going to be a cash bar for liquor."

"The party is tomorrow; the guests don't know about the cash bar."

"I took care of it. Susan sent an email to everybody attending about the change."

"That's tacky. You should have consulted the committee."

"You all would have said no, and I, for one, am planning to enjoy a nice martini."

"I think it's a good idea. I love cosmos."

"How does the bartender feel about dealing with cash?"

"He's happy. It will increase his tips. You do know if people don't have to pay for drinks, they never tip."

"He is setting the cocktail hour up on the upper pool deck. A second bartender will arrive for dinner. The pool bar will remain open the whole night and a bar will be at the back of the tent. Cocktail bar opens at five o'clock, dinner served at seven."

"Did someone decide on a cocktail buffet or passed hors d'oeuvres?"

"The lounge chairs on the building side of the pool will be removed to make room for buffet tables. The caterer has arranged for high tops, and the lounge chairs will stay on the far side of the pool."

"Looks like we thought of everything."

"Fingers crossed all goes well."

"Preston has done an amazing job."

"We should give him a bonus. Next board meeting, I'm going to bring that up."

<h1 style="text-align:center">CHAPTER 66</h1>

Seeing the Light

Lexie had been watching the time since about five-thirty in the morning. When it read seven a.m., she slipped out of bed. Sal rolled over and reached for her. Finding empty space, he opened his eyes. "Where are you going, Babe?"

"The gym." She walked into the closet, put on her Lulu Lemons, and went into the bathroom. She washed her face, brushed her teeth, and ran a comb through her hair, tying it up with a scrungy.

"You want me to get up and come with you?"

"No, Sal, go back to sleep. You have a routine that's working for you. You shouldn't break it for anyone. That's something I learned from years of classes. It's all on you, so be good to yourself and follow your program." She picked up her gym bag. "You've been looking great; keep it up. We can have a healthy breakfast when I get back."

"That's good," Sal grunted. He fell asleep before Lexie closed the bedroom door.

Lexie looked back at the condo door before she opened the storage closet. No Sal in sight. She went in and picked up the small duffle and carry-on she filled with necessities. She took a final look around the area to make sure she hadn't left any receipts or tags that might give Sal an idea this was planned.

She headed to the driveway and her Ferrari, parked at the end, out of view of the pool and main entrance. She admired the gleaming red beauty and chuckled at Sal's comment it was a piece of crap. The tire's damage from the curb hit was on the inside sidewall. Sal never mentioned it, and it must have escaped the notice of the detail guys. She hoped it would get her to Palm Beach in one piece.

Opening the passenger door, she placed the carry-on on the seat. Her other bag would fit nicely on the floor in front of it. Turning to grab the duffle, she jumped at the sight of a clean-shaven man in slim fitted chinos and a snug tee shirt standing beside her. She gasped as he reached down and picked up her bag.

Preston's face filled her field of view as he stood up. A bright smile, aqua eyes, and a chiseled dimpled chin were now visible. The curtain of tangled hair was gone. A soft masculine hairstyle completed the transformation. *How did I not recognize him?* She patted her hair nervously, regretting her decision not to shower or put on make-up. "I didn't expect to see you here."

He smiled warmly at Lexie. "I hope I didn't frighten you. I told you. I tend to startle people." He put down the duffle, reached in and pulled the carry-on out of the Ferrari and placed it on the ground.

"Preston, put those back in the car."

"No. You can't drive this."

"You bet I can. I learned to drive on a stick."

"No, that's not what I mean. There's a problem with the tire. I told you when you first got the car. You never got it fixed. It isn't safe."

"Will it get me to Palm Beach?"

"You can't take that chance. I won't let you. The sidewall could blow out at any time. I'm surprised it hasn't happened already."

"What does that mean? You won't let me. I don't care how great you look, shit..." Lexie's face turned red. *Did I just say that out loud?* "Anyway, it's not that bad. I took it to a gas station and the guy said it would be fine for a while."

"You knew about this, and you were planning to drive it?"

"Well, I haven't since it happened. I figure the less I drove it, maybe the tire would last longer."

"It's not going to get any better."

"Well, now what am I supposed to do?"

"I am driving Mr. Neuwirth to Palm Beach right after the party. Drive over to the East Coast with us."

"He won't mind?"

"Are you kidding? You haven't seen him up in his condo staring at you? If you haven't seen him, maybe you've heard him. He wheezes loud when he's not using his oxygen tank. I guess you can say," Preston paused for a beat, "you take his breath away."

"That was so corny."

Preston took a step closer. "You take my breath away, too."

Lexie stiffened. "Preston, I don't think..."

Preston's lips covered her objections.

Pulling back, she shook her head as she placed her hand firmly on his chest.

"I can't do this now, Preston. I've losing a piece of myself with every rash decision I make. Lexie stood up on her toes and kissed him gently on the lips. "I would be lying if I said I didn't want to...want this to happen between us."

Preston paled. "Lexie, I don't think—"

"Wait, let me finish. I'm not saying that someday we won't, er ...that this won't be something." She saw his crestfallen expression. "I have to find my way...alone for once." She steeled her spine as her voice grew stronger. "I will head over to Palm Beach with you. But you and I —that is not going to happen anytime soon."

"Lexie..."

She reached out and put her fingers to his lips. "We've been dancing around this since we met. I'm not living in a bubble anymore. I see you. I see Sal. I recognize the truth of what I thought was a life."

Preston seemed to pull himself together. "I'm not going to break up a marriage. I just want you to get away from him. There is something very dark going on here."

"I agree. Something dark and I am not going to play any part in it." She stood back and stared at him. "And what about you? You never thought you might get out of this place?"

"I always hoped. When you arrived, something changed for me. I stopped hiding. I didn't want to be invisible anymore."

"I was hiding out too. It feels good to be free, doesn't it?"

He moved in closer and tucked a wisp of hair behind her ear. "I think that as much as I dislike Sal and what he stands for, I am grateful. Because of him I finally see a way out. I guess I should thank him for that. And for you."

She looked past Preston at Collier Boulevard; the pavement shimmered in the morning sunshine. She could swear she saw Vinnie walk past the Albatross Driveway. The vision stopped, gave a wave, and disappeared into the glare.

"Lexie, are you okay with this? I'll put the bags back. You don't have to leave with us...if you don't want to."

"Preston, It's okay. I'm okay. I'm ready to do this." She smiled; her eyes bright. "You need to know something. I don't want anyone taking care of me. I can take care of myself."

"I never thought anything else." He squeezed her hand, picked up her bags, and headed to the other side of the driveway. "These will be in the boot of the Rolls. We can leave during the cocktail hour. The fire dancer starts his show at just before sundown he'll be distracting everyone. Are you alright with that?"

Without hesitation, she nodded her head. "Sure, that'll be fine. I've got to get back upstairs. I'll see you this afternoon." She looked at her shaking hands as she pressed the penthouse button on the elevator.

CHAPTER 67

The Albatross-Ready For her Close-up

By noon, the pool deck was already a beehive of activity. The caterers were setting up the buffet tables and the party rental company was shuffling back and forth through the open gate wrestling with high tops for the cocktail hour and banquet tables for dinner under the tent. The Floating Ladies were nowhere to be seen. The smokers had vacated the jail and were heading inside. Thirteen floors of gulf view windows sparkled in the sun. The pool water shone deep turquoise with gentle ripples from the cooling breeze. The Albatross was almost ready for her big night.

❧

Preston walked past the cars, a chamois in his hand checking for missed smudges. The placards were placed, the stories with accompanying photos were laminated as keepsakes for the owners and the baby blue caddy was front and center, a visible reassurance to Grace.

❧

Sal, back from the gym, showered and shaved. He picked out a subtle Hawaiian shirt and splashed on the after-shave Lexie had bought him. He hadn't bothered her with sex for a couple of days, so he was hoping to get lucky. He looked at his watch. *The Price is Right* was on; he had time for a snooze and a little TV.

ॐ

Raul shifted off Sonja; he was gasping for breath. He had never met anyone like her. He always thought Cuban woman were the sexiest. But this Russian, she was a whole different level of sexy. Must be how they stay warm through those cold Moscow nights, that, and the vodka. He gathered his thoughts and wrote down the things he needed to go over with Lenny Horowitz. He had to leave the reunion with the money.

ॐ

Sonja picked her bathing suit off the floor and headed into the shower. She wanted to look extra hot tonight. The blue dress she picked out was by the same designer that dressed all those crazy entertainers at the award ceremonies. She was glad she purchased special tape to keep her boobs in place. She hoped to drive Lenny insane. No way his little love girl could look as sexy as her. She wanted to see him squirm when she rubbed her breasts against her Latin lover, nibbled his ear and slid her tongue into his mouth. She giggled at the thought of how great it was going to be. Thinking of that made her horny. The shower would have to wait. She headed back into the bedroom.

ॐ

The Floating Ladies had reserved their favorite salon for the morning. A dozen heads were in various stages of beautification. Grace had been assigned a designated watcher; all the ladies would take turns for the duration of the reunion. Right now, she was busy getting her hair done. She wondered aloud if she left the car running. Eleven voices answered in unison, "No, you didn't!"

ॐ

Lexie sat on the terrace, not even the brilliant blue gulf waters could distract her. She was lost in her thoughts. Everything was ready to go. If she could only assuage the guilt that kept bubbling up. Lying about a vasectomy was bad, very bad. But running away from a marriage? That seemed just as wrong. Sal didn't have a clue. Maybe that made it worse. If they had an awful marriage, fought all the time, never had sex—a runaway wife might make sense. Lexie shut her eyes, took a couple of deep cleansing breaths trying to erase her treachery.

ॐ

Gary and Diego planned to meet after the reunion. They would not spend too much time together during the party out of respect for his wife. Gary would inform her of his plans when the event was over. After the scene on the beach, it wouldn't be a surprise. She never complained about his dalliances, even if he stayed away for a few days. But this time was different, and he was sure she wouldn't take it well. The reunion was all she talked about these past few weeks. It was a perfect distraction, and her friends would flock around her to comfort her. There had been many breakups at the Albatross before. Most were messy affairs, with sobs and obscenities carried on the wind. Those heartbreaking cries flew out from the terraces bounced off the neighboring condos and hovered miserably over the pool. Young mothers with their children, hoping to enjoy a peaceful day grabbed the kiddies and ran inside. The drama was accompanied by the slamming of terrace sliders...boom, boom, boom. All closed to muffle the drama.

This would not be like that. They were civil and understanding—best friends.

ॐ

Pete, Charlie, and Dan decided six o'clock would be the ideal time to visit Sal Ferraro. The residents would all have their eyes peeled to the west to see the sunset. They would have the best chance of arriving unobserved.

Dan suggested they synchronize their watches.

Pete mocked him. "I don't know, Nordberg. My phone tells perfect time and has this amazing feature—an alarm."

"You guys do realize I don't get most of those old movie references."

Charlie ignored him and reported the surveillance detail had been called off except for a local officer that kept an eye on the driveway and the beach patrol cruising by once an hour. The Ferraro's had shown no sign they knew they were being watched.

The Albatross reunion would be a perfect distraction. The Ferraro's would never expect the police to show up on a Saturday during a party. "Keep them guessing" was Pete's motto. He would get a lot of grief from headquarters, overtime and bad optics being the main concerns. What did he care? Three more days and it wouldn't be his problem.

CHAPTER 68

Lenny comes down

Lenny couldn't breathe. His heart was doing flips. He placed his shaking hand on his chest. It felt like an alien was ready to rip through his rib cage and bite off his face. Sobs racked his body. *I've lost everything: Lexie, the shipment. I sent three men to their deaths. I am a monster. Mrs. Andruzzi, that poor old lady. I killed her, too. She died of a broken heart. That's what's going to happen to me. I'm going to die up here— alone.* A black depression clouded his sight. He walked out on to the terrace. *I should jump.* He grabbed the railing, intending to climb over and end it all. He opened his eyes and saw the pool deck looked different. *Wait, what is going on down there? Where are the pool bitches?* He watched the swirl of activity. A man in a grass skirt was placing Tiki torches on the rocks around the hot tub. A full bar was visible on the pool deck and the smoking area was empty. Caterers were setting up a buffet, a raw bar was arranged over gallons of ice. Shrimp, oysters, and stone crab seemed to be squirming in the haze of late afternoon sunshine. His stomach roiled and he ran inside to void himself of the poison he had ingested the past two days. His watch said four-thirty. *Everyone must be getting dressed for the party. I need to get dressed.* He rubbed his eyes, trying to remove the squiggly lines that had suddenly appeared.

He wiped the sweat from his face, reached into the hamper for a golf shirt, sniffed, and thought...*it smelled fine.* He ran his fingers through his hair and rubbed at the itchy spot beneath his nose, getting a tiny buzz in the process.

Lexie will be there. Tomorrow is her birthday. Where did I put the necklace? Staggering back out onto the terrace, he dropped to his knees and searched the terrace floor. Pulling himself up by the low cocktail table he saw the necklace was laying there surrounded by feathers and white powder. He picked up the Albatross, kissed it for good luck, and shoved it into his pants pocket. He crab-crawled over to the railing and noticed the bottle of Johnny Walker that was laying on the floor. He paused to finish off the bottle. He remembered his dad always said, "A little scotch gives a man courage."

Looking through the railing's metal bars, he saw some residents had started arriving for the party. The pool deck was filling up. He recognized the bitches even with their hair all puffy and their saggy boobs hidden behind fancy dresses. He pulled himself upright and held on to the railing as a wave of vertigo hit him. He turned and lurched towards the doors where he crashed face first into the glass slider, missing the open door by mere inches. He felt another tickle beneath his nose. He started rubbing vigorously, hoping to lift himself up out of the hell hole he was in. The smell of blood caused another moan to escape his lips.

He slipped his feet into the only shoes he could find, a worn-out pair of crocs. He took a deep breath, walked out of the unit, entered the elevator, and prepared himself to win the girl of his dreams.

CHAPTER 69

Lexie Puts on a Party Dress

Lexie put on the blue silk designer dress and decided she shouldn't wear any underwear—every line and bump would show. She reached for the skin tape and applied two small pieces to each side of her breasts. The plunge was deep, and her breasts were still perky. Amazing they held up, the way Sal squeezed and kneaded them like they were Playdough. She pressed the dress to her skin, hoping it would be enough to keep an errant nipple from slipping out of the silky fabric. She wondered if this dress was a bad idea. When she bought it, she thought she wanted to break Sal's heart, to show him she was worth so much more than he could ever give her and that lying to her was the last straw. But now—now—she felt sorry for him. This dress would rub it in his face.

She looked at herself in the mirror and didn't like what she saw. She thought of Preston, so innocent. Or was he? He was ready to walk away with another man's wife. She thought of Vinnie. He was innocent, but he left his wife, Teresa, for her. Oh, fuck it. I'm wearing this dress! I'm leaving Sal. I'm walking away. I'm ready to start a new life.

CHAPTER 70

High Times

The elevator opened into the lobby; the swoosh of the doors caused Lenny to back-up against the glass wall of the elevator. The sun was pouring in through the glass ceiling above. Without his sunglasses, he squinted and commanded his lurching stomach to heel and behave. He walked out and prayed he could make it to the pool deck without pissing himself. He shook his head violently, causing a sharp pain to strike above his brow and travel back across his skull. He grabbed his head and felt the sweat flatten his usually well-coifed hair. He gave his appearance a passing thought then decided he had to find Lexie and win her away from Sal. That need was much more pressing than his appearance. Shit, he's seen Lexie all sweaty after a workout in the gym. He giggled. She never knew he was watching. Her hair wet and her crotch damp from the exercise bike always got him hard. He looked down at his shorts, no sign of the little lion. Wait, that's what Sonja always called his dick. Sonja, where was she? She must be down here. He vaguely remembered deleting numerous texts from her. He stumbled out onto the pool deck and tripped over the first step. He thought he made a quick and graceful recovery, sure no one noticed.

⚮

Everyone watched as Lenny fell through the door and landed on his face on the pool deck. They all winced as the disheveled, wretched man crawled over to the railing and heaved himself upright.

CRSO

Leaning against the wall, Lenny tried to smooth his stained shirt and soiled pants. He rubbed beneath his nose, sniffled deeply, and walked slowly towards a group of people eyeing him with revulsion. *S'gonna be okay. Where's Lexie?*

An attractive woman backed away as he drew near. "Oh my God, what is that smell?"

The gentleman beside her pushed Lenny away. "Listen, buddy, you need to take a shower and get dressed. This is a nice party. You look like hell."

Lenny stood tall. "What do you mean? I don't look ...." Lenny lifted up his arms and took a deep sniff at his armpits. He remembered he hadn't showered since...he couldn't remember. He needed to take a shower. He was relieved he had a short-term goal to concentrate on—one step at a time. Lexie would not have sex with him if he smelled bad. Looking around, he spotted the shower head on the outside of the pool house. He stumbled over to it and removed his shirt. "This is perfect," he smiled as he put his hands together in a prayer pose and silently thanked God for this favor. He sniffled. He must have heard his request the other day. Another saying crossed his mind "ask and you shall receive." He didn't die, and now a shower appeared in front of him. He laughed with glee as the tepid water washed over him. He considered what his next request to his new friend should be. Maybe to get Lexie to leave with him.

Lenny, put the shirt back on, though now it was inside out. Dripping wet, he lurched towards the pool. Realizing how wet he was, he grabbed what he thought was a towel from a lounge chair and tried to dry himself off.

"Put my shawl down, asshole," an angry face glared at him.

He dropped it and walked past the whispering Floating Ladies who parted to let him pass.

Searching the crowd for some sign of Lexie, he glanced towards the gate and noticed the cars lined up. *The car show.* He remembered Sal had mentioned Lexie's Ferrari was getting detailed. *We could get away in style. Lexie and me, flying down the road carefree, her long blond hair blowing in the breeze. Maybe she'll give me a high-speed blow job. Wait! I think that car is a stick! I haven't driven a stick since college. Fuck. She's going to have to drive, Ha, Ha, guess I can't kidnap her and ask her to drive.*

Preston tapped him on the shoulder. "Are you okay? You're not looking too good. You've got some bloody drool…" Preston pointed to his own chin, "right here."

Lenny reached over and touched Preston's chin.

"No, dickhead, your chin."

"Hey, you can't talk to me that way. Who the hell are you?" He squinted. "Don't you work here? Wait, you work for me. You're Preston."

"Yeah, Preston. But I don't work here or for you anymore. Stay away from Lexie. I mean it." Preston scowled and walked into the building.

What the hell was that about? Lexie, why can't I see Lexie? He searched the pool deck and saw her walk in alone. *Oh my God, look at her, she's she's… not wearing anything under that dress. It's open in front, I can see her bellybutton. I really want to lick that.* Sal walked up behind Lexie and placed his hand on her ass. *Nooo.* Lenny averted his face, unable to watch Sal abuse her so carelessly. *I would be so much more respectful. She's got to know that about me. I respect the shit out of her.* He turned towards the beach, hoping to slow down his breath, only to see a trim, young Hispanic man walking in from the beach path. An older gentleman was talking animatedly in his ear. *The Garcia kid was staying at the M Spa. He would walk here. Hmm, maybe that guy's his bodyguard. Señor Garcia would want to protect his son and his investment. Oh no, the money.* Lenny patted his pants and his shirt where a breast pocket should have been. *I don't have the money.* He moaned out loud. He watched as Garcia settled on a lounge under a palm tree next to the hot tub. A woman. *No, wait. Lexie. No, Lexie doesn't have dark hair. But now she's over there in that same sexy dress. She must have dyed her hair. And she still forgot her underwear. What is Lexie doing with that guy? She just licked his ear.* Lenny gagged.

Lenny watched as the older guy walked over to one of the residents. *How does that Cuban know? What's that guy's name? He's always fishing. Wait, I got it. His name is Gary. How does he know Gary? He's married to one of the pool bitches. Is Gary moving in on my deal? How does Garcia know I don't have the money? Are the pool bitches dealing at the farmer's market?*

The steel drums began. Lenny's head was spinning. He squirmed as everyone started gyrating. Tiki torches blazed atop the rocks that lined the hot tub waterfall. He rubbed his burning eyes. Next to the hot tub, a heavy shirtless man, his gut flopping over his grass skirt, was throwing flaming sticks into the air. Lenny grabbed the sides of his head willing the pain to stop. Garcia was laughing loudly across the pool and smoking a fat cigar. *He can't smoke there. He's got to smoke in the jail. That woman. No Lexie. NOOO. That's Sonja. What is she doing with Garcia?*

℮℠

Sonja spotted Lenny across the pool deck. There seemed to be something wrong with him; his body was twitching. She squinted into the glare of the sun and tried to figure it out. Unshaven, hair greasy, clothes soaking wet, he was rubbing under his nose vigorously and smelling his fingers. *Ugh. Little dick man is high.* She smiled. *Maybe business trip is not working out so well.*

She followed his progress and watched as he walked towards …*That bitch is wearing my dress. This is supposed to make Leonid the prick squirm. She looks very hot, but he will see I look better. That must be his little love girl.*

She caught his eye and gave him a very subtle finger. His face contorted in horror. Sonja smiled sweetly and reached down to Raul reclining on the lounge and danced her fingers lightly up his leg to his crotch.

℮℠

Lenny had turned away, hoping that Sonja/Lexie didn't see him. Too late. *She is smiling at me. She just gave me the finger. She is rubbing Garcia's crotch.* Another moan as he envisioned Sonja and Lexie meeting. In that cat fight, Sonja has the upper hand. She is a tough bitch. Lexie is so sweet and delicate. Lenny paused and smiled at a random bit of sunshine. *Those two will be tearing those dresses off each other, seeing who would win …me. Lenny, get your head together.* He turned back to the buffet table and watched real Lexie pick up a seafood fork and daintily dip a large chunk of stone crab into mustard sauce. She looked up at Sal. *Is that a smile? Is she smiling at that fat fuck?*

Lenny muscled his way past the Floating Ladies who had gathered around Gary's wife and were moving toward the Cuban and Gary. *Wait. Those guys are holding hands. What the fuck is going on here?* He paused to let crazy old Grace pass; he could hear her muttering something.

He staggered slowly towards Sal and Lexie. He reached into his pocket, checking to see if the albatross was still there. He adjusted his shorts, spit in his hand, slicked back his hair, and decided a confident swagger would be the perfect attitude to win the girl. He puffed out his chest and put his hand possessively on Lexie's butt.

"Get your hand off of me, Lenny." Lexie hissed.

Sal, whose head was turned, didn't notice. "Hey, babe, do you see that chick over there by the hot tub? She's wearing the same dress as you." Sal smiled at Lexie, "I mean you look a million times hotter than she does."

Lenny blurted out the first thing that popped into his head. "She's hot, maybe a close second. But you got her beat."

Sal's mouth dropped open. "What?"

Lenny looked confused. "Wait, I…I forgot." He stammered, "I got you a birthday present." He reached into his pocket and pulled out the necklace. He moved closer to Lexie. "I had it made for you. It was wrapped nice, but Luca Brasi showed up, and the head was all bloody and it was snowing. It was kind of pretty in a way. All that snow. I used to eat snow when I was a kid…"

Sal pushed Lenny away from Lexie. "What the fuck is wrong with you? You smell like shit, and you look like a bum."

"Lexie," Lenny took her hand and placed the necklace in it, "it's an albatross, for luck."

"Lenny," Sal growled, "get the fuck away from her. That bird is bad luck, and I think yours just ran out." Sal grabbed Lenny's shirt and pushed him away.

"Lexie, you got to come away with me. You can't stay with him." Lenny's eyes flew open wide as he croaked, "Vinnie was murdered!"

Sal slapped Lenny hard across the face. Lenny staggered backwards. Sal's nostrils flared as he whispered, "Shut your fucking mouth. You're delusional."

☙❧

She stared at Lenny. "What? What did you say?"

"Lexie, you got to believe me. Vinnie found out Sal was moving into hard drugs."

"Lenny," she whispered through clenched teeth. "Is this just something you're saying to get me away from Sal? I know you've been watching me; you creep."

Sal's hands turned into giant ham fists. "What the fuck? You been after Lexie? I'm going to kill you, you piece of shit."

"You've got to know the truth, Lexie. In the end, you'll thank me." Lenny's expression hardened. He stood taller as he spoke. "The Andruzzi's were pawns. They walked away from the claw. That day at the yard, Sal told me to get them out of the way. I put a big dose of ex-lax in sandwiches I had picked up from the deli down the street. Those guys ate every crumb."

Eyes bulging, Sal pulled in his gut and took a menacing step forward.

Lenny's words tumbled out. "When they rushed to get to the john, Sal was in the crane waiting for Vinnie. Vinnie was a good guy, Lexie. He told Sal he didn't want any part of the drug deal. He was going to tell the feds."

Lexie's heart pounded in her chest. Her face paled as anguish overtook her. She shook her head violently back and forth. Squeezing her eyes shut, she trembled as the venomous thought echoed in her mind. *Sal killed Vinnie.* The rapid-fire words ricocheted around Lexie's brain.

"You're a liar." Sal roared.

Lenny pointed at Sal and sneered. "You dropped the fucking Honda on his head."

"If I didn't, we'd both be in jail." Sal's face turned white as he looked at Lexie.

Lenny smiled.

Lexie's tortured scream pierced the air as she lunged at Sal. Using the only weapon available, she stabbed him in the neck with her seafood fork. Sal staggered backwards; his expression confused. Completely off-balance, he fell face-up into the pool.

The chunk of stone crab flew off the fork, its trajectory sending it flying towards the ladies moving in on Gary.

The conch horn blew as the sun set. The roar of the Cadillac joined the conch's howl. The massive blue car careened through the open gate, with Grace's gray, well-coifed head barely visible above the steering wheel. An earsplitting screech echoed between the buildings as the undercarriage scraped along the jagged rocks bordering the pool area. One oversized piece of pointed granite tore a huge gash in the Cadillac's full gas tank. The out-of-control car, now gushing a trail of fuel, rocketed up the handicap ramp. The astonished crowd watched as the car went airborne and landed in the pool.

The shockwave generated a tsunami that splashed up on the hot tub and sent the Tiki torches tumbling. The smell of gasoline and torch fuel filled the air. A large, hand-rolled Monte Christo twirled end-over-end landing on the Tiki fuel. Flames erupted with a loud whoosh as a volcano of burning fluid cascaded over the hot tub and flowed into the pool. The residents ran screaming, running pell-mell around the pool deck. Several ran down the beach path, others into the Albatross.

Preston, pushing through the mob, found a catatonic Lexie staring at the blue Cadillac while chaos erupted around her. He grabbed her hand and led her towards the building. Opening the door, he pulled Lexie back as three men ran out towards the escalating pandemonium.

CRSD

Lenny shook uncontrollably. He had watched the seafood fork pierce Sal's throat, saw the blood as it trickled between the tiny prongs, saw his huge body fall backwards into the pool, heard the powerful engine and the screech of metal on rock. He witnessed the moment when the big blue missile went airborne and landed on top of Sal. He cringed as he played it back in his mind. *Sal's eyes were open. He had seen what was coming. As much as I hate the bastard, no one should have to watch death coming at you. I don't know what killed him: the fork, the car, the water—me? I killed him.*

No one noticed as a sobbing Lenny slipped out of the pool gate.

CHAPTER 71

Five minutes earlier - What a Way to Go

The two detectives and one overexcited deputy entered the Albatross, at exactly six o'clock p.m. —much to the delight of Dan Barnes who had everything timed out. Prior to going through the automatic doors, Dan had kept announcing the time at five-minute intervals until Pete demanded he hand over his watch and told him it would be returned at the end of their conversation with Sal Ferraro.

Susan was manning the desk, checking in latecomers to the reunion. When the line finally dwindled, Pete showed his badge and stated, "Police business."

She shook her head. "Forget it, Pete. You're not getting in without a warrant. I'm not going to let the residents be harassed, especially during such an important event."

"I'm not into harassment, sweetheart. You should know that by now."

"Yeah, but you are still not going..."

A loud crash and then screams erupted from the direction of the pool. Well-dressed partygoers flooded into the lobby, staggering like zombies around the large atrium, not knowing whether to go up to their condos or out into the street.

One of the residents ran up to the desk. "Susan! oh my God! Grace drove her car into the pool!"

Pete turned to Susan. "Lucky you got us cops here. Call 911 and have them send all available ambulances. Tell them Landry is requesting Emergency Services as well.

Pete, Charlie, and Dan pushed against the tide of partygoers fleeing into the lobby as sobs and screams echoed off the walls and glass.

"What the fuck, Charlie, our plan is shot to hell." Pete shouted over the screaming throng.

"Wait a minute, Pete," Charlie looked concerned. "You don't think it's a mob hit?"

"No." Pete replied without a lot of confidence.

Dan was bouncing up and down as he avoided the old people with walkers. "Should I have my gun out?"

"Calm down, sonny," Pete snarled. "Last thing we need is for one of these geezers to freak out when they see a gun. As it is, it looks like quite a few are going to croak from the stress of whatever the fuck is going on out there."

Making their way out the door, Pete took a moment to take in the scene.

Before him was a tableau straight from Dante's Inferno. The hot tub and deep end of the pool were ablaze. It was spreading slowly toward the shallow end where an old Cadillac, partially submerged, was rapidly filling with water. *Holy shit! Three days left on the job, and I walk into this cluster fuck.*

He could make out the top of a grey head in the driver's seat. "Jesus. She's still in the car." He handed his gun, phone, and wallet to Charlie and jumped in. He struggled against the weight of the water and finally opened the car door, pulling out a fragile old woman, while keeping an eye on the rainbow slick of gasoline leaking from the car. He carried her up the staircase to a chair away from the pool, grabbed a dry tablecloth from the overturned buffet and wrapped it around her.

⚘

Dan ran around to the opposite side of the pool near the hot tub. A beautiful woman, her bare breasts freed from the flimsy cocktail dress she wore, screamed while pointing at a lounge chair covered by palm fronds.

Dan looked at the flaming water, the hot tub bubbling lava into the pool and the sexy woman with the great tits and felt a rush of adrenaline hit him. *God, I love this job.*

He reached the shrieking woman, who immediately threw her arms around him and pressed her shaking body against his. "Oh please," she sobbed, "You've got to help him."

Dan slowly extricated himself from her embrace and pulling the greenery away, found a man reclining on the lounge chair with his head split open. Surrounding him were ripe coconuts. One of them was covered in blood.

⚬⚬⚬

Charlie ran over to a woman lying on the ground writhing in agony. The gentleman next to her was repeating, "I'm so sorry," over and over. Her hip and leg were turned at a strange angle. "Are you her husband?" he asked as he knelt to examine her leg. He winced at the compound fracture and probable broken hip. He noticed a large piece of seafood stuck on the bottom of her high heel sandal. "Ambulances are on their way. Keep her still if you can." *This is a real shit show.* He headed to an old guy who had dropped to his knees while grabbing his chest. *If we don't get some medics in here soon, the body count is going to rise.* He looked over the area and noticed the oldest partygoers were no longer fleeing. Most likely in shock, they stood motionless their mouths agape as they stared at the flames in the pool.

A group of women, in a chorus of hysteria, pointed at the Cadillac, "There is someone under that car."

⚬⚬⚬

Pete handed the shaking, water-logged old woman over to the care of a hyperventilating bald gentleman. "Stay by her," he commanded and jumped back into the pool, the flames spreading rapidly towards the Caddie. A man's legs were protruding from beneath the car. The rest of the body was certainly crushed. A swirl of blood drifted towards the surface. Pete took a deep breath and dropped under the water hanging on to the car door. He gave a tug on one of the feet. The guy was wedged solid. *Oh fuck, this is going to be ugly.* He knew that a tow truck or a salvage crew was needed to remove the car from the pool to recover the body. He climbed out just as the torch fuel copulated with the gasoline and the entire pool erupted in flames.

Standing beside a sobbing, chattering mob of old ladies, the word "Ferraro" caught his attention. He tried to block out the noise of chaos and listened carefully to the conversation going on around him.

"She was upset about something."

"Did you see Lenny? I think he was on drugs."

"They were arguing."

"I think Lenny pushed Sal in the pool."

"Grace is never going to get over this. First, she kills her dog, and now she kills a man."

"She's not going to remember any of this."

"She's sitting over there. Look, she's shaking. We should be with her."

"Who was supposed to be watching her?"

Two of them pointed to the woman writhing in pain on the pool deck. "You saw what happened. Gary walked in with that, that...man. How could we know Grace would find the car? She always goes into the garage."

Pete stopped to catch his breath as he tried to process what had just happened. Looking over at the bar, he wished he could have a drink. This was going to be a long night. He signaled to Charlie, who was reassuring the remaining poolside residents help was coming.

"Charlie, we've got to shut this place down. Nobody goes in or out except for emergency services. Call this into the squad and get everybody down here. The old guys are going to earn their fat paychecks today." He pointed at the burning car, "There is a guy under there. Pretty sure it's Sal Ferraro."

CHAPTER 72

Time to Go

Diego headed towards Sonja, hoping her screams were just a reaction to the mayhem. As he got closer, he saw a young cop, the giveaway—a badge on his belt—approach her. She was half-naked and hysterical, pointing at the lounge chair that a few minutes before held a smiling Raul. He veered towards the beach path, keeping an eye on the scene and saw Raul's bloody, lifeless head appear from beneath the coconut palm frond. He picked up his pace, determined to be on Tamiami in his Porsche before the circus arrived. *Too bad about Raul. He was a good kid.* Growing up gay in Cuba, Diego had gotten used to tragedy and loss. *Time to move on.* He looked back to the other side of the pool and saw Gary, tending to his hurt wife. He gave him a subtle nod. Gary made the "I'll call you" hand signal. Diego headed swiftly down the path towards the gulf. He melted into the crowd that had gathered on the beach to watch the unfolding disaster.

◯��◯

Mr. Neuwirth was on his balcony staring down at the bedlam when Preston and Lexie arrived.

"Time to go, Mr. Neuwirth." Preston went into the closet and pulled out an extra oxygen tank. "I put your bags in the car yesterday. You got your wallet, keys, and phone?"

"Yep, my boy. I'd say it's about time to get the hell out of Dodge. It ain't going to be pretty when the dust settles." He spoke with surprising strength as he shuffled into the room, his tank wheezing alongside him, his eyes gawking at Lexie. "Preston, I don't think I've met this lovely lady. I've been watching her down at the pool." He pointed at the terrace. "I can see everything that goes on down there—fourth floor and a bird's eye view. I might be old, but I still got all my marbles. She's got the place drooling. Water rises an inch when she wears that patriotic bikini."

He walked closer to Lexie, smiling in a dirty old man way. "That dress, doesn't hide much more than that bathing suit." He seemed to remember something and spoke softly, "I'm sorry for the loss of your husband. But you know, I hear a lot of what goes on down at the pool, and that fat SOB was no good. You're better off without him. This young buck right here?" He winked at Lexie. "He's the one for you." Mr. Neuwirth giggled and broke into a coughing spasm.

Lexie, still shaking, looked blankly at Mr. Neuwirth and then at the Albatross pin in her hand. She dropped it in the tiny cross-body bag she had worn to hold her lipstick and pen-size hand sanitizer.

Preston gently shooed the two of them out the door. "We've got to hustle. We're taking Tamiami. If we don't encounter a Winnebago caravan, we should be okay. The big road is going to have eyes all over it. Let's go. This place will be swarming with emergency vehicles in minutes. We've got to get out before they block the driveway."

"So, young lady," Mister Neuwirth spoke as they headed into the hallway, "how do you like our new, squeaky-clean Preston? He's a looker, right?"

Preston locked the door behind them and picked up the wheeled tank, pushing them to hurry.

"And a bit bossy, too," the old guy chortled.

Lexie stared at him, looking confused. "I think...."

Mr. Neuwirth cut her off. "You two will make some mighty pretty babies."

A blushing Preston spat out, "Let's go, now!"

Mr. Neuwirth straightened his bent over frame and thrust out his chest as he pressed the elevator button. Turning to look at his young friends, a twinkle of joy appeared in his gauzy blue eyes. "Hey kids, let's get this show on the road." His lips curled up in a contented smile as the elevator doors swished closed.

CHAPTER 73

Alligator Alley

Lenny jammed the Ferrari's gearshift into second but let up the clutch too fast. The car lurched and stalled. He hadn't traveled more than six hundred feet from the Albatross— all the distance covered in first gear, with the car's engine whining in pain. *Okay, Lenny, you got this.* He took a deep breath, coughed as he exhaled and gagged at the foul smell coming from his mouth. He squinted at the worn-out diagram on the gearshift head. He started the engine, remembering at the last second to put the clutch down and to shift into neutral. *Okay, it's not so different from my VW beetle back in college. It'll come back.* He moaned out loud as a fire truck and two cop cars screamed past him and headed towards the Albatross.

He made another attempt. *VW, VW, VW.* Within minutes, he had traveled down San Marco and was rolling smoothly in third gear.

He downshifted and put the transmission in neutral as he rolled to a stop at the flashing light at the T-intersection of San Marco and Route 41. Feeling exhilarated he had the Mondial's powerful transmission tamed, he made a snap decision to take old Tamiami Trail east, thinking I-75 would be crowded on a Saturday in season. He turned right and roared into the Everglades.

Lenny let the Ferrari have its way, no longer thinking VW. This car was a thoroughbred. His mind wandered as he thought how grateful Lexie would be when he showed up with her stolen Ferrari, lovingly polished. The car whipped along Tamiami Trail. Ochopee was a blink and gone. With no traffic, Lenny let the car loose. He felt he had escaped for a reason;

he would take control of Ferraro Enterprises and win the biggest prize of all—Lexie.

He looked down at his phone and noticed his battery had died. *Shit. Wait, maybe it's better this way. They can't track me if my phone is dead. But why would they be tracking me? I did kill Sal. Oh no, I didn't, Lexie did. He moaned. I wish I had some coke.* He looked down and noticed his hands were shaking.

His eyes returned to the road in time to avoid a large tortoise straddling the double yellow line. He jerked the wheel, and the car's rear end reacted by spinning out. He pressed the brakes and overcorrected. The car now lurched towards the shoulder. The right front wheel hit the pavement edge, and the tire blew with a loud BOOM. Lenny gripped the steering wheel tighter, hoping to keep the car from landing in the mangroves. He braked hard, slammed the clutch, hoping to downshift. Too late. The Mondial skidded completely off the road. It came to rest at the edge of the water, its right side buried up to the rocker panels in mud. *That was close.* Lenny ran his hands over his body looking for evidence of injury. He opened the door and crawled out of the tilting car. He looked down the road in either direction, hoping for someone to stop and help.

❧

Diego followed the strict Marco Island speed limit as he threaded the Porsche through weekend traffic on Collier. He drove by the Albatross just as the first responders arrived. He headed down San Marco and turned right onto 41, heading south, then east towards Miami and home. He checked his phone to see if Gary had called, knowing that was unlikely. He would be involved with taking care of his wife for weeks, if not months. Diego was certain they had something worth waiting for.

He picked up speed past the traffic light for Everglades City. Traveling at a decent seventy miles per hour, he saw the road ahead was empty. Beyond Ochopee, an older model Ferrari was listing oddly off the side of the road. He slowed up a bit to see if he could help. The guy standing beside the car looked a lot like the asshole that was at the Albatross. He was pretty sure

Raul had pointed him out as the American that had fucked him over. He hit the gas and shifted into third. The widow-maker's rear spun out, kicking up road dirt. Diego expertly got the car under control and flipped the guy the bird as he flew off towards Miami.

⁂

The Corniche grumbled to life, as if it needed to shake out its old, cramped muscles. Mr. Neuwirth requested to sit in the backseat, preferring the experience of a chauffeured limo. Lexie, staring blankly and shivering, sat beside Preston in the passenger seat pressing herself deep into the soft kid leather.

Heading towards Tamiami, Mr. Neuwirth called out from the rear, "Preston, put the top down. I think Lexie would enjoy feeling the fresh air."

"I will, when we get out into the glades. We are conspicuous enough in this car. With Lexie's blond hair blowing in the breeze, we will garner even more attention."

Lexie bit her lip. "Do you think I'm in trouble? I… I stabbed him with a fork."

Mr. Neuwirth snorted. "I saw the whole thing. I don't think that teeny piece of metal hit anything important. That guy had a thick bull neck. A two-ton piece of metal landed on him. That's what killed him. In all my years I've never seen anything like that. Anyways, he probably deserved it."

Preston drove over the Goodland Bridge and noticed barriers were being off-loaded from a pick-up truck on the side of the road. In the rear-view mirror, he saw a Marco Patrol car with lights flashing stop in the middle of the south-bound lane. He breathed a bit easier knowing that they had gotten out in the nick of time.

He stopped at the Big Cypress Visitor Center to let the top down. The sky above them glowed red and purple in the gathering darkness. The Everglades right after sunset was glorious. Preston smiled at Lexie as she removed her hair clips and shook her hair loose.

Mr. Neuwirth giggled from the back seat. "This is the life, kids? Wind in your hair, the open road ahead. Two young runaways and an old geezer. They could make a movie about this, right?"

"It isn't a joke. We aren't out of the woods yet." Preston shook his head at the old man.

"Well, we are heading off into the sunset."

Lexie reached back and patted Mr. Neuwirth's hand that was gently stroking her hair.

Preston turned the car onto the road and headed towards Ochopee, surprised the only other vehicle on the road was a WBNK News van heading west.

Lexie reached into her purse to pull out a tissue and felt the cold metal of the necklace Lenny had given her at the party. She pulled it out of the bag and dangled it in front of her.

"What's that?" Preston reached over and spun it around.

"Lenny gave it to me at the party. It's an Albatross."

"Albatross? Albatross? I know something about that fucking bird. Life was better before that fucking condo came into my life. Get rid of it, bad luck." Mr. Neuwirth started coughing and turned up the oxygen.

Lexie gasped. "Preston, you see the car on the side of the road up ahead. I think that's my Ferrari. There's someone crouching by the car. Oh, my God! It's Lenny."

Preston slowed down. "The tire must have blown."

"Well, that's my fault, too." Lexie hugged herself tightly and leaned forward, rocking back and forth.

"He's an asshole. He stole your car." Preston growled, "He deserves whatever he gets."

"I don't like that fucker. I say run him over." A cackle that turned into violent coughing spasms erupted from the backseat.

"Turn up the oxygen, Mr. Neuwirth. This air is loaded with mold."

The Rolls crawled alongside the Ferrari and Lenny stood up. "Lexie, wait, help me." He started to cry.

Lexie took another look at the Albatross and flung it at Lenny. "I hate you," she screamed as Preston hit the gas and sped away.

Diamonds glittered in the last light of the day as the Albatross took flight. Lenny reached up and caught it. The car sped away as Lenny sunk to the ground, the Albatross gripped in his hand.

CHAPTER 74

Getting the Story

Sirens filled the Marco Island air. Every available emergency vehicle from the surrounding area had been dispatched. The inbound lanes on the S.S. Jolly Bridge into Marco Island were at a standstill. A decision was made to close the bridges entirely. Emergency vehicles were using the exit lanes to get on the island. Collier County Emergency Management, unsure what had transpired, decided an extra modicum of caution should be exercised. The facts were sketchy, and terrorism could not be ruled out. The bridge to Goodland was blocked by old A-frame wood barricades borrowed from a popular local watering hole. Hundreds of people descended on Goodland on Sunday afternoons, and the barricades were employed to control the overflowing crowds.

Marco Island was now effectively closed off from the mainland. Three cars, heading east and traveling at high speed, were the last to leave the island. No one paid attention to the Ferrari, the Porsche, and the Rolls Royce, each about five minutes apart, heading into the Everglades. The barricades went up as the last car, a Rolls Corniche, exited the east end of the bridge and headed towards Ochopee.

The WBNK news team was deep into a fifth take of a live report of a skunk ape sighting south of Chokoloskee just off Tamiami Trail. The elusive creature, the south Florida version of Bigfoot, hadn't been seen since November 2014. "The Skunk Ape Saga" was featured in an *Unsolved Mysteries* episode in 1998. This recent sighting was reported in an anonymous call to the Florida Fish and Wildlife Commission. According to Doctor Vanessa

Treehorn, a consultant with FWC, the sighting was never corroborated. No additional sightings were reported. On the recording of the call, several voices could be heard giggling in the background.

It was just the kind of story WBNK news loved to cover. The personal mission of the lead field reporter, Bill Kendall, was to find a story no one else would touch and prove them all wrong.

Kim Stamper, the junior news reporter, and part time cocktail waitress, walked over to Bill and suggested they shut down the shoot. "Come on, Bill, the light is fading. Let's head back to town. We could stop at Everglades City. I'll treat you to a brew."

"None of that IPA shit. I want a Corona, no fruit."

"You got it. Chris?" She turned to the new kid. "You heard the boss. Let's pack it up."

Chris, the intern on the second day of his job, grabbed the gear and within minutes had it stowed in the van.

Kim looked over at the fresh young face sitting in the jump seat in the back. "Anxious to get out of the swamp?" She had read his application, a Park Shore boy, private schools and clean hands. He wrote that his goal was a network position in management.

Bill turned on the police scanner. He had shut it down to keep the area free of noise while waiting for the Skunk Ape to make an appearance. The radio screamed in the deep quiet of Big Cypress National Preserve. The intense chatter gave glimpses of a horrific scene unfolding on Marco Island. Bill hit the gas, determined not to be the last to arrive.

The team was still stinging from the last debacle. They had broadcast the scene of a two-day-old accident, focusing the camera on a dent in a palm tree. On the actual day of the accident, the General Manager thought it would be more appropriate to follow around a local nature buff protesting new building permits on land environmentalists deemed ideal nesting sites for gopher tortoises. The flaw in the story was the tortoises did not have nests in those sites and appeared to have no interest in relocating.

The team, and Bill Kendall in particular, was endlessly mocked because they had filmed an empty lot and broadcast it that evening instead of the horrific crash. The accident they didn't cover had killed a local veteran beloved throughout the area for his kindness and generosity in helping wayward teens. A cartoon lampooning WBNK appeared in the Naples News the next weekend. This time they would get the story.

Flying west down Tamiami Trail just before the miniature Ochopee Post Office, they passed a red Ferrari that looked to have spun out and landed in muck on the edge of a canal. A disheveled man was standing beside the car looking at the tire.

"Bill, maybe we should stop and help him. It's getting late." Kim looked at the tilted Ferrari at the swamp edge.

"He looks fine. No time, Kim. Screw him. He's driving a Ferrari. He's got money. Let him call Triple A."

The radio squawked the bridges in and out of Marco Island were closed to all traffic accept emergency vehicles.

"Shit." Bill swerved onto Collier Road, and headed into Everglades City, stopping the van in front of the first airboat rental place he came across. He grabbed the equipment bag and shoved it in Chris's hands, then picked up the camera. "We've got to get on that island. I rented an airboat in Everglades City with my family last year. We need to commandeer one of them. This could be a national emergency." He puffed out his chest and looked over at Chris who wore a puzzled expression. "Look tough, kid. This is how you get in the game. Always remember—we are the press."

"You're not serious. You can't take an airboat into Marco Island." Kim glared at Bill. "You're nuts."

He grabbed his credentials and held them up, as if to convince his wavering crew of his importance. "Let's go. We are going to be first on this."

The sound of a helicopter turned their eyes skyward. The logo of their archenemy news organization was displayed on the side.

Chris squinted up at the impressive Jet Ranger flying overhead. "Why don't we call our chopper to pick us up?"

Kim sneered. "The chopper is up in Tampa, ferrying the company CEO and his family to a Red Sox/Yankee game. Spring Training is big news, especially to the station owner. You'll be covering a lot of Grapefruit League events. Hope you like citrus."

They arrived at the dock to find an angry crowd demanding to rent airboats. Bill looked over to his crew and put on his best swagger. "I got this."

Pushing his way through the crowd with his press pass held aloft, he worked his way to the front. Face-to-face with the owner of the tour company, he demanded to have access to their largest airboat and their best driver.

"WBNK News. We need to rent one of your watercraft immediately."

"What the fuck, asshole?" someone shouted from within the menacing crowd. "You ain't getting shit."

"Yeah, I been here for twenty minutes. Get to the back of the line."

Bill 's eyes squinted, and his nostrils flared. "We have to get out to the scene on Marco Island."

"Well," the man shrugged as he sized up the crowd and the WBNK news guy that had taken out a credit card. "It seems to me there is high demand for my boats. Now, I do have one still left out behind the shed. Price is going to be a bit steep. You realize it is Saturday and weekend rates are significantly higher."

Bill leaned in menacingly "I don't give a shit about the price. WBNK news will pay for it."

"Okay. Calm down. We've got procedures in place here. I will need valid identification of all passengers."

Bill looked back and saw his crew being bumped and roughed up by the crowd. "Can we hurry this up?"

"Well, I can start the credit card process and the waivers for personal injury that need to be signed. And there are insurance forms, as well. You should be on your way in about forty-minutes."

"Here's the corporate card. I don't care how much it costs."

"Well, all right then. I might be able to speed this up a bit. Let me run this card and you can be on your way. You can complete all the paperwork when you get back."

"Fine. Just hurry up." Bill looked back at Kim's ashen face. She seemed frozen in terror as the crowd had her cornered. "Kim!" Bill shouted, "You and Chris take the equipment and meet me at the dock behind the shed."

"Just so you know, Mister News Man." The owner coughed up a huge phlegm ball and spit. "I am a veteran, and I noticed how you ignored my good friend's accident the other day. He used to bring poor kids down here and pay for them to have a day out on the water. Mighty nice guy." He laughed as he swiped the credit card. "Guess you blinked and missed it. Oh, lookee here." He handed the credit card back. "Declined. What a surprise. Have a nice day, asshole. Sorry we couldn't do business."

"Psst. Hey, Mister over here."

Bill looked over at a grimy man standing next to an old wooden boat with a rusted fan.

"You got cash, boy?"

Bill looked at the slime-covered hull and two short wood benches. The pilot's seat was a white plastic deck chair duct taped on top of milk crates. "I don't know."

"She might look a bit rough, but she'll get you where you need to go."

"I need to get to Marco." Bill barked.

"Well, that I can sure do. I even got some plastic tarp to keep your camera dry. Not a lot of chop. Should be fine."

"How much?"

"Well, how much you got?"

Chris and Kim walked up, lugging the equipment. "You guys got any cash?"

They had two hundred sixteen dollars between the three of them and handed it over.

"Thank you kindly." The cash disappeared in the man's shirt pocket. "I'm thinking just you and the camera." A gnarled, scab-covered hand gestured towards Bill. He shook his head at Kim and Chris. "There ain't room for all y'all and that stuff. You're gonna have to stay here."

"Fine. Kim, put the shit back in the van and head to the bridge. When they open it up, meet me at the scene." Bill gave the guy a tough look. "Some extra in it for you if you speed this up. I'll make sure you get it tomorrow."

"You sure about this, Bill?"

"I'm getting this story, Kim. You'll see. Top of the broadcast stuff." He saluted as the small outboard chugged to life.

Kim and Chris watched as Bill sat down on the moldy bench, wrapped the camera in his suit jacket, and placed it on the seat beside him.

"Why aren't you using the fan?" Bill asked, concern apparent on his face.

"Too late. They've got noise rules round here. I'll fire her up when we get farther out."

Bill noticed water seeping slowly under the front bench seat. "Umm, change of plans, fella. I'm going to get off at Goodland and call an Uber."

"I thought you were going to Marco Island?" Kim called out.

Chris looked confused. "You don't have any cash and the card doesn't work."

"How did you make it into college?" Bill tapped his finger on his head. "I got an Uber account for all those nights when I get lucky." Bill winked as the boat putt-putted away from the bulkhead, and the unlikely pair headed out of Everglades City. The flashlight taped to the bow barely illuminated their way.

CRANCO

Kim cursed silently. *Fuck this. I'm out of here tomorrow.* She looked over at Chris. *The kid's got his entire career ahead of him. I should warn him to get out of WBNK— now.*

<h1 style="text-align:center">CHAPTER 75</h1>

The Show Goes On

Pete exited the Albatross's men's room, tucking a Motley Crue tee shirt into the worn jeans he kept in the back of his PD Cruiser for the occasional nights he didn't go home. He clipped his shield to his belt and strapped on an ankle holster. He was dry, thinking clearly, and the adrenaline kick had subsided as he walked out to the pool deck.

He couldn't believe the carnage arrayed in front of him. Emergency responders from every service—Marco City Fire, Marco PD, Collier County Sheriff's, several ambulance companies, even Fish and Wildlife had descended on the Albatross. He could hear the whop-whop of helicopters above the scene, the buzz of drones flying around the building and the annoying whine of jet-skis. Loaded pontoon boats rafted up beyond the sandbar. The residents of the condos along the crescent beach flooded the waterfront. Cell phones recorded every moment of the unfolding event. A news crew dropped by helicopter onto a vacant lot down San Marco, and set-up camp on a balcony of the building next door. Every move made at the Albatross would be filmed, and their eavesdropped conversations recorded.

"Fucking shit show, brother." Charlie smiled as he slapped Pete on the back. "What a way to go, man—scene of a lifetime. Did you plan this? I mean look around, dead guys, fire and brimstone." He pointed to the hot woman with her boobs still visible beneath a tight t-shirt, deep in conversation with Dan. "It's even got sex, drugs, and rock and roll."

Pete stared at him. "Just tell me the numbers."

"We've got two confirmed dead. Four coronaries being worked on, the lady with the compound fracture, and about a dozen in shock."

"Sal Ferraro?"

"We're pretty sure that's him under the car in the pool."

"Lexie Ferraro?"

"Whereabouts unknown."

"Leonard Horowitz?"

"Again, unknown."

"Think they left together?"

"Her Ferrari is missing." Charlie paused. "It seems there was bad blood between Mrs. Ferraro, Sal Ferraro, and Mr. Horowitz. It was on display this afternoon. There was an episode involving the three of them."

"And you got this information from?"

Charlie nodded to a group of ladies holding on to each other on the lawn.

"They are hysterical right now, but they're the eyes and ears of this place."

Pete pointed to the far side of the pool. "Who's the guy under the coconut tree?"

"He had a passport on him. Raul Garcia, Cuban national, here on vacation. His father owns the penthouse where the Ferraros are staying."

"The sexpot? Moving on Dan? She came in with Garcia?"

"Yeah. Russian Aeroflot attendant. First name Sonja, last name, uh, mostly consonants. They arrived from the beachside. I sent some uniforms down the beach to find out where they were staying."

"Cameras? Eyes everywhere these days." Pete surveyed the perimeter of the pool and buildings and pointed to an eye above the hot tub controls.

"Got some of the squad grabbing video footage. They got a camera on the pool. Susan said most of the time it's offline. It's just there to dissuade the old folks from pulling a *Cocoon*. There's another one set-up in the garage. It's old equipment and not a priority around here. The real world hasn't encroached on the Albatross. She's one of the last of the old-school condos.

Charlie shrugged. "You never know, maybe we'll get lucky, and they were running."

Pete looked up at the high-rise next door. "We need to canvas that place: see who was watching, old guys checking out the hot Russian, nosy types seeing who's wearing what, and what kind of food was being served. Those rear condos might have had people filming the sunset." His eyes swept back and forth assessing the angle. "That might show partial views of the pool area over here."

"I'll get on it. The old guys are setting up a command bus outside the service entrance on the other side of the building. Once they're up, they'll go over whatever footage is available."

"We need to get spotlights out here." Pete looked up. The post sunset sky was spectacular. "It's going to be full dark in about thirty minutes."

"The emergency service guys are on their way. The guy under the car is going to be a challenge." Charlie looked around. "Man, this is some crazy shit right here. What do you think? Is this random?"

The smoke from the fuel was still burning off the pool surface. The EMT's were working on the old folks. The big-boobed woman was sobbing by the body covered by coconut fronds. Susan rounded up residents wandering listlessly in circles.

Pete shook his head and slapped Charlie on the back. "Well, partner. I don't think you could have planned all this. My professional opinion tells me the old lady is not a hired killer."

Charlie rolled his eyes. "In any case, time will tell."

"That's something I don't have a lot of—two fucking days left."

CHAPTER 76

Fade to Black

Lenny slid down on the passenger side of the Ferrari, the albatross still gripped tightly in his hand. The sobs came in soul shuddering inhales, exited in sputum bubbles dribbling down his chest. He moaned at his final vision of Lexie. She rose on the seat holding on to the windshield her long blond hair flying free in the breeze. She was glorious, an angel silhouetted by the blood red sky as she traveled towards the horizon.

The ground beneath him was damp as he sat hunched over on the uneven hillocks of saw grass. His legs were bloody from the razor-sharp barbs: each small movement delivered a new slice. He watched as the sky purpled. Just feet from the water's edge, he stared into the black glass liquid and saw a reflection of the first star. He breathed in deeply, willing the sobs to end. He smelled the putrid musk of the swamp. The breath from his lips was far worse. He dry-heaved with nothing left in his burning gut. He didn't care. *I did this—the Andruzzi's, those poor bastards.* Tears flowed freely. *That guy, Driggs, he told me as much. I sent those idiots to their deaths.* He trembled as he realized the depths of his depravity. *Sal. Oh my God, he trusted me. He was my only friend.* He replayed the movie of his treachery over and over. *Vinnie, David, Dominic, Louis, Garcia, Sal...Vinnie, David, Dominic, Louis, Garcia, Sal...Vinnie, David, Dominic, Louis...*

He squeezed his fisted hands harder, felt the Albatross digging into his palm. He picked up the delicate pin, letting the chain fall to the ground. *This is all I have left.* LEXIE written out in diamonds, glowed faintly in the waning light. *I still can walk out of this.* His drug-addled mind worked feverishly.

I didn't kill anybody. It was this fucking hellhole that killed them. They had choices. I didn't put a gun to anybody's head. Got to think. Okay, next move... get out of here alive...Got to find Lexie...

A shift in the air, an innate sense of danger, something brought him out of his stupor. In the last light of day, he did not see the beast as it approached from the swamp. The air around him thickened, the smell, now more acute, revealed a deeper rottenness. Blind to the vision of teeth gripping his leg, excruciating pain rocked him, sent shock waves through his body. He was screaming as the gator dragged him into the water. A single thought penetrated the horror–*Lexie's Albatross! I can't lose it!* The pin, still clutched in his fist, disappeared down his throat. His choking screams resumed as the gargantuan beast whipped him back and forth like a rag doll. He flailed. The last glimmer of life imbued him with adrenalin-fueled strength. He held his breath and punched the alligator's snout. The reptile bit down harder. The savage frenzy continued as mangrove roots, protruding from the water, tore gashes in his flesh. He was water-boarded by torrents of scum roiling the air from the violent attack. With a powerfully brutal shake, Lenny's spinal cord snapped. His eyes remained wide open. His voice was cutoff mid scream, his terror entombed in his motionless body. He no longer felt pain. His locked-in awareness made his impending death visible and unstoppable. The rancid water blurred his vision. His eyes lids froze as he tried desperately to see. Water gushed into his lungs as the gator spun him beneath the surface to drown him. Unable to hold his breath, his lungs filled with the lifeblood of the swamp.

The twelve-footer, bits of yellow and green paint worn thin by the elements visible on his back, dragged Lenny deep into the everglades. The body, bones now broken from the violent assault, was pliable and easily maneuvered into the alligator's underwater den. The rest of Leonard Horowitz, Esquire, would be enjoyed at the monster's leisure.

CHAPTER 77

Cuba - A Thrashing of Breasts

Cecilia expertly used her personal box cutter to slice open the package that had arrived that morning from Neiman Marcus. She had bedazzled the tool's handle with colored crystals. Her bright orange nails were never in danger of chipping. It was used daily as her shopping addiction had reached unprecedented heights. This new spree had a purpose. She had spent the last few weeks reading fashion magazines and cultivating a taste for refined clothes and understated makeup. She missed Raul and was excited to show him her new look. He would finally be proud to show off his mama. He avoided being seen in public with her. It hurt her deeply, but she never told him. He would be back from Florida in three days. The scars from her recent facelift should be almost healed by his return. She also hoped this effort to be sophisticated might thaw the cold hearts of the wives of her stepsons. She was lonely and missed the company of other women. With her son away, sex with Don Raul was her only human contact.

The doorbell clanged loudly. Cecilia emerged from her bedroom when it was obvious no one was around to answer. Descending the staircase, she could see uniformed Policia through the massive glass doors. Escorting them into the salon, she offered coconut water or tea.

"No, thank you, Señora Garcia." The younger of the two looked towards the doorway, "Is anyone in the house today that might join us?"

"I am alone. My family is away on business. May I help you?"

The men shuffled their feet nervously. The older officer, the one in charge, spoke quietly, "Would you please sit down, Señora Garcia?"

Cecilia had heard this tone before. Growing up in the barrio, policía showed up at your door for two reasons: to arrest someone or to inform a family of a death. She prepared herself to react with grace at the news of the demise of her husband. He was ninety-two. She knew this day would come, secretly prayed it would have come sooner. She held back a smile, knowing she would never again feel his gnarled hands scratching at her crotch.

Cecilia was engrossed in her thoughts. *Raul will know what to do. He will take control of Garcia Enterprises.*

"Señora Garcia, this morning, we received a phone call from the Collier County Sheriff's Department in Florida."

Nelson and Tito and their bitchy wives will feel how it is to be poor. My boy, she smiled, *so smart.* The word Florida penetrated her reverie.

She looked up startled. "Florida?"

"Yes." The older one sat down beside her on the sofa. "They informed us there was an accident at the Albatross Condominium on Marco Island."

"Bastardo," she spat out. "What are you saying?"

"Raul Garcia died in a freak accident yesterday in Florida. A falling coconut killed him."

"Don Garcia is in Havana today. He is not in Florida." She shook her head willing it to be the father and not her beautiful boy. "Raul works in the coconut groves in Baracoa. He was not near the groves today. He is at a party on Marco Island. His father Raul Garcia sent him to represent the Garcia family. He is *muy importante.*"

"You misunderstand, Senora." The young officer removed a notebook from his back pocket flipped to a page and began reading. "Raul Garcia, age thirty-two, resident of Miramar and Baracoa, Cuba, was confirmed deceased on the twenty-sixth of February, two thousand seventeen. Pronouncement of death was certified by the Collier County Coroner, Doctor Devon Lefebvre. Cause of death —blunt force trauma caused by a ripe coconut falling from a height of approximately thirty-seven feet. It made contact with the right quadrant of the victim's skull."

"No. No. I do not believe this. This must be a trick." She squinted as her lips formed a tight-lipped grin. "My stepsons, Nelson and Tito, they hate me. They would do this. Make up a terrible lie to get me away from their father." She nodded vigorously. "So, now you see. You are mistaken. If there is a death, it must be Don Garcia, the old man. He is dead. I know this. I pray for this." Looking at their grim faces, her hideous smile faded. She clutched and unclutched her hands, her body shaking. "Raul, he has been raised beneath the coconuts, worked in the groves since he was a child. This could never be. My boy is so smart." Cecelia's eyes welled up.

"I...we are so sorry for your loss." The young man handed her a business card with Policía Nacional Revolucionaria (PNR) and a phone number. "You may call this number and ask for División de Internacional for further instructions on the procedure for retrieving your son's remains."

She took the card and looked over at the older man. He reminded her of someone she knew many years ago. Through the veil of her tears, she saw the face of a handsome young policeman pulling her away from the pounding fists of a drunken client. He took her back to her hovel, cleaned the blood off her face and advised her not to work in that neighborhood. She never went back there, never saw that kind young man again. She met her husband, Don Garcia in a dance club the following month.

"We will show ourselves out." He spoke quietly to her as he looked to his partner. "Paulo bring the car to the front door. I will be with you shortly."

He waited until the young officer had closed the door and then he spoke, "You have done well, Cecelia. You're a strong woman. You made it off the streets. You are a survivor." He reached out and took her hand. "If Don Garcia does not react well to this news," he pressed a card into her palm, "I do not wish to again find your lovely face bruised." He let go, reached up his hand and gently traced her scar. "Adios, Señora Garcia, I am truly sorry for your loss."

CHAPTER 78

Let's go to the videotape

Dan's white board became the center of attention. The Post-its were lined up and a new row had been added - deceased.

Charlie walked in and flopped into his chair. "Looks like the assholes solved the case for you. Quite an ending, all the suspects dead, the drug cartel's new route a dead end, so to speak. No gunplay, no prisoners. It's time to party, brother."

Pete looked up from his laptop. "Not so fast, too many loose ends. I can't write this up until it's done."

"Well, let the kid do it. He deserves to put his name on the case. It should be right up there next to you and me. And the Wizened Dicks are hungry to pump up some more OT. They can work on it, too. Show the kid how it's all put together."

"Dan's on temporary assignment, and the WD*'s* write lousy reports. There is a lot we don't know. Where's Leonard Horowitz? What's the story with Lexie Ferraro? Why is the son of a Cuban drug lord dead under a coconut tree in Florida?" Pete laughed. "And if the thing with Vanessa doesn't work out...what's that Russian chick's phone number?"

"Welcome back, Captain Kirk." Charlie saluted and his voice lowered to a whisper, "I'm going to miss you, partner," he sniffed.

"Don't go getting all *P.M.S* on me. I'm not done yet."

"Okay, fuck you, Pete. Is that better?"

"Yeah. So, what you got?"

"Palm Beach Sheriff's office is checking on Alexis Ferraro." Charlie pulled up a photo of an oceanfront mansion and handed it to Pete.

"We need a statement from Mrs. Ferraro. What puts her in Palm Beach?"

"George Neuwirth, one of the original residents, old, waiting right outside death's door. Mr. Neuwirth's Rolls was seen driving off the island a few minutes after the shit hit the fan. He wasn't driving."

"Thank God. That could add to the body count."

"Traffic cam puts Preston Thayer in the driver's seat. The video from the pool deck shows Mrs. Ferraro leaving with—"

Pete finished the sentence. "Preston Thayer."

"Yep. He was leading her away from the scene."

"What's the Palm Beach connection?"

Charlie handed Pete a photo of a well-dressed man standing next to a vintage police cruiser. "Neuwirth's son, Michael, is a big developer in Palm Beach. It seems he's a cop buff—donates a ton to police charity organizations. They have their annual picnic at his oceanfront estate. Neuwirth Jr. drives around in an old Ford Crown Vic that he bought at a police auction."

Pete looked at the photo. "Every department has got their groupies. You think that's where they were headed?"

"I checked with Susan. She said Mr. Neuwirth requested any condo business be forwarded to his son's address in Palm Beach."

"Lexie Ferraro is not going to face any charges for today's blow-up. Witnesses all corroborate Sal Ferraro's death was an accident."

"She's guilty of marrying an asshole." Charlie made a note on the file. "We'll send Dan with one of the old guys to interview her. At the very least, she is a witness to her husband's death. Maybe she has something to add about his business venture down here."

"What else you got?"

Cuban guy killed by the falling coconut is Raul Garcia. He was here for the reunion. His father, Don Raul Garcia, owns the penthouse condo where the Ferraros were staying. He's a big-wig coconut exporter." Charlie laughed. "Man, there's some irony for you. I had a call with the *Policía Nacional Revolucionaria* - or PNR. They made the notification to Garcia's mother this morning. I questioned the relationship with Ferraro Enterprises and ownership of the Florida condo. Their reply was and I quote, "The Garcia Family are fine upstanding citizens, pillars of the community." Or in other words— go fuck yourself."

"No mention of their side business smuggling drugs?"

Charlie ignored him and kept reading, "Horowitz was seen leaving, no, I should say slinking, out of the pool gate. The tape wasn't kind to him. He's one ratty looking son of a bitch."

"The BBB?"

"Aah, man. I'm going to miss your acronyms. The big, boobed brunette is a Russian Aeroflot attendant, lives in the same building as Horowitz in New York. NYPD checked it out. Looks like they were big time fuck buddies. Neighbors have been complaining about the moans and screams coming from the apartment for about a year. After Horowitz left, she moved on to a quiet guy in the same building. The neighbors are happy."

Pete shivered and pushed his chair back. "How does a weasel like that hook up with the BBB? Why was she down here?"

"Sex. It looks like little Lenny was great in the sack. Her statement and demeanor support she's a nymphomaniac and Horowitz gave her what she needed. He booked her a suite at the M spa. Their relationship was a mutually satisfying fuck fest." Charlie grinned at Pete. "Her statement was witnessed by all the WD's. Dan took notes while the rest of them got chubbies."

Pete put up his hand halting Charlie's soliloquy "How did she end up with young Garcia?"

Charlie snorted. "It seems it was a random meet. Kid just got lucky...or not."

Pete shook his head. "I've got to remind Dan not to date witnesses."

"No need, he's smart. Which leads me to the next bit. The uniformed deputy found the Ferrari out on forty-one searched the area and spotted the chain the jeweler...umm Kelly Fitzpatrick, Dan's new squeeze, had hung the albatross pin on. It was laying at the edge of the swamp near the car. He also found a shoe in the water. It matches the croc Lenny was wearing at the reunion." Charlie chuckled. "Some more irony for you. One of the WDs pulled a screenshot—wait the photo's here in the file. See? He was wearing beat-up crocs."

Pete picked up the folder and shuffled through the photos. "Nobody noticed a classic Ferrari listing on the side of Tamiami?"

Charlie reached into Pete's trash and pulled out a newspaper. He paged through as he spoke. "Haven't found any witnesses yet. We're lucky some random lowlife didn't haul the car away on a flatbed. Crime Scene is going over it now. Also, Dan is reaching out to WBNK news. They were in the area filming some loopy Sasquatch story." Charlie dropped the open paper in front of Pete. "Speaking of Blink, I Missed It News, that asshole, Bill Kendall? He went missing the night of the Albatross blow-up. He was last seen heading out on the water with some itinerant homeless guy in a stolen airboat. The boat was tied off behind Everglade Irv's and was going to be scuttled for reef restoration in the gulf."

Pete scanned the page. A smiling headshot of Bill Kendall was on the thin sidebar story on page seven. The small headline read "Local News Reporter missing in the Everglades." Kendall is going to be disappointed he wasn't front page news."

'Well, that's if they find him."

"Who's got the case?" Pete tossed the paper back in the can.

"General Crimes. I figured we had enough on our plate."

"By the way, Charlie, Driggs called me. He's been searching the area around Ochopee under the auspices of Fish and Wildlife. Vanessa signed off on his contract and she had Shredder added on. They're out there now looking for any evidence that might have floated away."

"You got to love Freddy. He's really turned into quite the entrepreneur."

"We should give him a heads-up about the WBNK news asshole." Pete got up. "I need a beer right about now, but I'll settle for a cup of coffee."

Charlie blocked his path. "Sit back down and let me finish. You're going to pee your pants when you hear this."

Pete shook his head, "How can this get any worse?"

Charlie sat down across from him; his expression serious. "I got a call from the desk Officer from FFW. They have poaching cameras set up along forty-one at different locations. Our Friends, Officers Willows and Martinez, knew about the recovered Ferrari with no driver along Tamiami and they knew there was a camera near that location. It was mounted on a tree about thirty feet in from the edge of the swamp near a canal. They recovered the memory chip and downloaded it onto a computer. This is where it gets interesting."

"Okay, I'm on the edge of my seat."

"The DO says he's sitting in his office when he hears retching coming from the squad room. He looks out and sees Willows and Martinez puking into a garbage can. This is verbatim: 'They look at me, still gagging, eyes bulging, puke on their shirts, and they are pointing at the computer screen.' Charlie pauses for a beat. "So, the DO goes over wondering what the fuck is going on, and he sees the frame is paused. It was kind of blurry, but he can make out the back end of a Ferrari. Martinez looks up at him and says, 'don't rewind that thing. Just call that asshole Landry. A fucking alligator is eating a guy.'"

Pete is laughing. "How did these guys get through the academy?" He looks over at the WD's. All of them had rolled their chairs closer and were howling.

Charlie was shaking. "They sent me a copy and I watched it. Holy Shit! The gator was fucking huge. It dragged Horowitz back down the canal. You want to look?"

"Maybe later. I wonder if that could have been one of the coked-up gators? PETA is going to go nuts if one of their beloved animals is an addict." Pete reached for his phone. "I've got to call Vanessa and tell her. She can pass this on to Freddy. What did I tell you, Charlie? Right from day one—a fucking shit show."

CHAPTER 79

Crocs and Gators

"Freddy, stop." Shredder, kneeling on the front bench of the poleboat, pointed between tangles of vines at a partially obscured stream that veered off the main creek. "You see that fucker over there about 10 yards down that way? He's huge, and he's got some weird neon shit on his back. You think he rolled in some toxic waste? People dump all kinds of crap out here."

"No, man, not radioactive, but mean as hell. I've seen that one before. He's got a home around here. You up for a little adventure?" Freddy stopped the boat and looked between the low-hanging branches at the resting gator.

"No sir, Mr. Driggs. I work on dry land. This is getting too freaky for me. Let's just mark the spot and head back in."

"Is Doctor Treehorn paying you to be out here?" Freddy slowly poled the boat forward.

"Yeah. Buck and a quarter a day. I figured we would find something and then tell her."

"It doesn't work that way. You see that sum bitch? We follow him to his hidey-hole." Shredder moved back to the middle bench and shook his head. "No fucking way I'm messing with his shit."

"That's what you're getting paid for."

Shredder crossed his arms tight across his chest. "I didn't sign up for a suicide mission. No hazard pay is coming my way."

Freddy pulled out his rifle and rubbed his sweat soaked bandanna up and down the shaft. "No worries, Shredder, I got you covered. Anyhow, you're the toughest hombre in the glades, seeing as how you walked away from that gator attack. That, my little friend, took big balls. Where are you hiding them today?"

"I was young, stupid, and drunk as hell."

"Well, you lived to tell the tale, and now we are going merrily down a stream to add a chapter to your story."

"Freddy, we are so fucked."

"Just look around for anything that might be interesting." Freddy poled closer to the stream.

"Like a shoe?" Shredder grinned, his chaw-stained teeth dripping brown sludge.

"What?"

"There's a shoe, lying over there caught in a mangrove root. Aww, shit. It's got a foot still inside of it."

"What kind of shoe?" Freddy grabbed a vine and stopped the boat's slow forward progress.

"Are you shitting me? Do I look like some kind of fashionista?"

"Is it a croc? You know those rubber shoes that are ugly as hell. Wal-Mart sells knockoffs. They're real popular with the snooty crowd."

Shredder rolled his eyes. "How do you know this stuff?"

"Bonita's got a pair of them. I told her she's got to run a hose over them occasionally. They reek if you don't. Grab the net and pull it in. Doctor Treehorn gave me a special bag for collecting evidence."

"Shouldn't we call somebody?"

"We will. But first we got to pick that up before some varmint walks away with it."

"Well, keep your gun trained on that fucker. If he turns, blast him." Shredder winced at the stench as he pulled the croc closer with the gaff. The foot covered in squirming maggots was swollen and shredded. He scooped it up with the net that Freddy handed to him. "I'm thinking this guy wasn't as lucky as me. Why's the kind of shoe important?"

"The guy the cops are looking for was last seen wearing crocs." Freddy zipped up the bag. "Just like this one."

"So, we did good, right? Can we head back in now?"

"We done good, but we're not done yet. Take this orange tape and wrap it around the branch next to you. We got to mark the location of the evidence."

Shredder shook his head. "Man, you sound just like Pete."

"I thank you for that, Shredder. He's always been my role model. And now we're going to bring that mother in with us."

"Are you fucking nuts?"

The BLAM of the rifle was all the answer he got. He looked over at the gator who had traversed the distance to the boat in the time it took him to retrieve the shoe and foot. The behemoth was missing half a head.

Freddy looked over at Shredder. "You're welcome." He tied the reptile off the stern. "Now comes the fun part, little buddy."

"Oh, come on. What now?"

"We are going to take a peek inside his cozy home."

"You are. I'm going to sit right here and pretend that a piece of dead guy and a bloody monster aren't sharing my personal space."

Freddy poked around the mangrove roots with his gaff and let out a victorious hoot. "Yeah, man, that's what I'm talking about. Would you look at what Uncle Freddy found?"

Freddy wedged the gaff under the twisted roots and yanked. A bloated carcass rose from the shallows. It slowly turned, and one blank eye stared up at them through the murky water.

"That thing human?" Shredder moved up to the bow seat of the low boat.

Using a small net, Freddy dug around the roots and pulled out a shiny object. "Well, what have we here? Looks like the foot just introduced itself. Shredder, this here gentleman is Leonard Horowitz. Mr. Horowitz, meet Shredder."

"How do you know his name?"

Freddy held up the gleaming gold Rolex. "Well, besides the croc, this here watch has an inscription." He turned it over and read the words aloud, "Leonard Horowitz, Esquire. Ten years of faithful service— Ferraro Enterprise. Would you look at that! It's still ticking."

"You going to pocket that? No one would be the wiser."

"Fuck you. This is evidence. I'm straight now. It'll get turned over to Detective Landry who will show his appreciation by sending a boatload of customers to my newly formed corporation."

"You think that's going to happen? Pete's walking away from the job. His last day's tomorrow. He better get busy if he's going to help you out."

"It doesn't matter. He may be retiring, but you know Pete, tin star on his chest or not, he's always gonna be a cop."

"Driggs, think about it. It would take two years to make what this watch is worth. I know a guy."

Freddy cut him off. "You can't put a price on self-esteem, my friend. I suggest you get some." He pulled out his cell phone. "I got to call this in. First, Park Service, it's their jurisdiction, next Pete, and then I've got to call Doctor Treehorn."

Shredder picked up the rifle and searched the trees and surface while Freddy made his calls. "Never thought I'd see a day like this," he grumbled.

"Rangers Martinez and Willows are about twenty minutes away. Told us to sit tight." Freddy punched in another number. "Hi, Doctor. Yeah, it's me. Shredder and I hit pay dirt. We found another tagged alligator and as a bonus, we found most of Mr. Horowitz...Right... not far from the first attack....Yeah, I tried. His phone went to voicemail... Okay, got it." He clipped his phone to his belt, pulled out two bottles of water from his cooler, handed one to Shredder and sat next to the foot. "Now we wait."

CHAPTER 80

No Surprise – Death by Florida

"Doctor Lefebvre, heard you got my next body on the table, anything interesting?"

Pete heard the phone click and then the sounds of the lab echoed through.

"Detective, I've got you on speaker. I see you want this expedited. I get it. How many days you got left?"

"Tomorrow's my last. It would be great if this was wrapped up by then."

"It will be. No mysteries here. The victim, Leonard Horowitz, had an extremely gruesome death. His neck was broken during the struggle with the alligator. He remained alert, though completely paralyzed throughout the attack. Word is you got video of this, any chance your dedicated county medical examiner can look?"

"You are a ghoul. I'll send a copy over. I don't need to tell you it's for your eyes only. Resist the urge to share with your fellow doctors in death. When it can be released, if ever, feel free. They're going to get a real charge out of it. But the way this case is shaping up, it could be on *YouTube* tomorrow."

"You got it, Pete. I could learn a lot comparing the injuries with the actual event."

"What have you got so far?"

"The alligator executed a classic death roll where the victim summarily drowned. In the report, I've noted that his left eye is still intact. As a matter of fact, it's wide open and staring up at me from the slab. Which leads me to conclude he witnessed the event. This death is one of the most macabre I've had the pleasure to document. Cause of death is listed as drowning during an alligator attack—accidental."

"Wow, you are one sick man. I've always admired that quality in you."

"His labs returned with degraded traces of cocaine. Probably would have been quite higher if he hadn't been submerged for so long."

"Got anything else?"

"Yes, his stomach was still intact. Quite a surprise considering the animal had been feeding on him for twenty-four hours. I examined the contents and discovered an interesting item."

"Go on, Doctor Morbid."

"He had swallowed a piece of jewelry. It was an Albatross pin with the name Lexie spelled out in diamonds. I'm sure it was painful going down. I checked, and his esophagus had abrasions from its passage."

"Probably not as painful as being eaten by an alligator."

"I told you he didn't feel a thing after his neck fractured. But I'm sure the initial attack was quite excruciating."

"It couldn't have happened to a more deserving guy."

"Rendering decisions on the warranting of horrible deaths is not in my wheelhouse."

"Did you finish the Ferraro autopsy?"

Yes. You have been keeping me quite busy. Two more days and it will feel like I'm on vacation."

"Cut to the chase. We got any felonies here?"

"No. The Ferraro death was caused by the trauma of a classic older model sedan impacting his rather large frame. He did not drown. The guy was in bad shape. He would have suffered a massive coronary soon by the looks of the plaque blocking his arteries. He was a ticking time bomb. I listed the death as accidental. The woman who drove the car suffers from late-stage dementia. His head was crushed like a hammer hitting a ripe coconut." Lefebvre giggled. "That's funny, right? You see what I did there? I made a reference to the first victim I autopsied from that fateful day. The young man, Raul Garcia, died of blunt force trauma to his head caused by a ripe coconut – once again, accidental. I am looking forward to writing this report. This day is one for the books—the death trifecta.”

"Just send me the report, Doc.”

"You got it. Detective, I will see you on Tuesday night. I love a good retirement party.” Lefebvre chuckled. “Yours is going to be a killer.”

"Right.” Pete sighed and hung up.

CHAPTER 81

Blast-off

"Pete, where you been all day?" Charlie stopped Pete before he walked in the squad room. "The dicks brought in a stripper. They led her cuffed and giggling past the desk Sergeant. He thought it was an honest arrest. He remembered her from her last bust six months ago. He had no idea it was cover for your last day surprise. When you didn't come back for lunch, we gave Cindy from B-Jazz a hundred bucks and a warning to stick to lap dances. She was sad when she heard you were leaving. She said to tell you, you were always her favorite arresting officer— a real gentleman. She left this for you."

Pete looked at the business card with the words "Congrats on your retirement, Love Cindy," handwritten in bubble letters with a heart floating over the letter I. He turned the card over and saw a coupon for a free beer and a lap dance.

"Your first retirement gift. And a mighty satisfying one at that."

"Yeah, she's a sweet kid." Pete made a note on his phone. "I've got to send her a thank you card. You know she's close to finishing her master's in psychology."

"I knew she was in school. Guess she does a lot of research on the job."

"It will be good to see her move on from that hellhole."

"Speaking of hellholes. Today is your moving on day. Any last words for the ones left behind?"

"Here, Here," erupted from the WD's.

"I got nothing to say." Pete pushed Charlie out of the way and headed out the door.

Dan walked up beside Charlie. "Where's he going? He's been gone all day. I thought he wanted to write up the report."

"You and the guys better get on it. His notes are on the desk. This is going to be the last thing he signs in his career. It better be perfect. Wrap it up before six o'clock. This will be the send-off of the century. You don't want to miss it."

"Well, I hope he shows up." Dan shrugged as he picked up the file from Pete's desk.

"Me, too." Charlie said as he rubbed the tension that had taken up residence in the back of his neck.

CHAPTER 82

Parting Gifts

Vanessa entwined a flowered garland around the deck railing, while Bees hung multicolored string lights in loops around the dock pilings. A giant banner that read "GOOD LUCK PETE" was affixed to the telephone poles at the front of the Buoy Bar parking lot.

Shredder was out front, in charge of securing a wavy biker air tube dude Donna borrowed from the Harley dealership in Fort Myers. The manager, a frequent customer, agreed to let her use it after Donna handed over coupons for free pitchers of beer.

Donna had left Shredder staring at two giant promotional coconuts sitting on the lawn. A start-up rum company said she could keep them if she pushed their new product— flavored citrus coconut rum. The Styrofoam props were about three feet in diameter and permanently staked into the ground.

Shredder called out as she entered the restaurant, "I'm gonna attach this big guy to the coconuts. I don't want anybody walking off with him."

"Good idea, that'll work." Donna skipped into the bar. "Thanks, Shredder."

Bees walked up beside him as he finished tying the twelve-foot-tall frenetic biker between the coconuts. "You know what that looks like, right?"

"What do you mean?" Shredder winked.

"Hey, I got an idea." Bees pulled out his cell phone. "Take a picture of me next to it."

"You're kidding, right?"

"No. I just want to get the right perspective." Bees stood next to the wavy dude. "You get all of him in and the coconuts, too?"

"Yeah, it looks awesome."

"Hey, guys!" A woman's giggle turned them around. Two couples, clinging to each other for support were gaping up at the wavy dude.

"This is great man. Can we take a few photos?" one of the guys slurred.

Bees looked them over. "Private party, the bar is closed for the night."

"We're renting a trailer down the road for the week, heard the music, thought we'd come on down and have us some fun. We don't mean to cause trouble."

The other one straightened up as he spoke. "Our wives." He looked over at the young women now pretending to caress the dude. "Well... a picture of this would make an amazing memory."

"You see, Shredder? That's what I was thinking." Bees nodded at the girls who had pushed up their boobs in their tube tops. "Have at it. Those two beauties look like a handful," he snickered.

The women stood on either side of the floppy man as their husbands offered stage direction.

"Okay. Now one of you put your arms around it. Yeah, that's it."

"Now, honey, you should be, I don't know, thinking about a big peach ice cream cone. Show me how you'd lick that sucker."

The guys snapped the photos and high-fived each other. They turned to Bees and Shredder. "Wow, man, can't thank you enough. You think we could join the party?"

"Invitation only, cover is twenty-five bucks a head. Go see Donna. She'll be the one bossing everyone around. Tell her you are new neighbors. She might let you in." Shredder nodded towards the door.

Bees pounded an old wooden fence slat into the dirt near the coconuts. A duct taped sign, its crooked letters scribbled in black sharpie, read,

"Take a commemorative photo of Peter's Party here."

Shredder marked out the area that gave the best view. "Theme parks have these signs—'Photo opportunity.' Everybody will see this when they come in. I think it's going to be a hit."

"Pete's going to fucking love this." Shredder wheezed as he spat out half a lungful of chaw.

The roar of an approaching motorcycle drowned out the sound check from the country western band Donna hired for the party. Charlie walked the bike up the handicap ramp and onto the expansive waterfront deck. He parked it in front of the small stage at the far end.

Donna ran over, trailing an oversized neon green plastic tablecloth. "Hey, Charlie, this was all I could find. I hope it fits over the bike."

"That'll work just fine. Oh, did you see what Shredder and Bees are up to out front?"

"Yeah. I have them setting up the crazy biker guy."

His eyes twinkled. "Okay then, just checking you knew about it. Did you get the poster board we can all sign?"

"Yep. Vanessa and I had a wine and cheese party last night while we decorated it."

Vanessa walked up with an easel. "You know, Charlie, Donna is quite an artist. She did a caricature of Pete for the poster. She said she captured his best qualities," Vanessa blushed, "and exaggerated them greatly."

"Well, tell me tomorrow if I was exaggerating." Donna lips turned up in a knowing smile. "It did turn out pretty good. He looks awesome standing on the prow of his kayak, shield hanging around his neck, shirt open to his navel, a pistol on his hip, holding a python in one hand and a beer bottle in the other."

Vanessa ran her hand along the leather seat of the 1948 Indian motorcycle. "How did you manage to sneak the bike out of Pete's shed and get it fully restored in a month?"

"He was a little busy with this case. I knew he wasn't going anywhere near the shed. It's a nightmare in there. The bike was buried under his kayak, surfboard, and a shit ton of old fishing gear. It was a project he said he was going to get to—but never did. I was stuck on a gift idea, and then I remembered the bike. I figured now he's going to have free time; he can do some traveling. I even got a second matching helmet and a pair of headsets." He winked at Vanessa

Vanessa took in the big bike, its deep red paint job gleamed in the dappled sunshine, and the attention to detail was obvious. Nail head trim secured the short fringe round the seat, and the substantial wheel covers gave the bike a solid look. "I'm so glad you didn't go chopper. The fork stays true to the original design. This is a stunner, Charlie, a real showpiece."

"How do you know about Indians?"

"I've got three older brothers. They papered their walls with posters of Indians and the required teenage fantasy— bikini clad models straddling them. When they got older, they bought a junked one, cheap. They kept it in the barn, worked on it for years. They eventually got it done. I'm pretty sure they still have it." She ran her hand along the leather seat and fanned the leather fringe with her fingers. "Pete's going to love this. It must have cost a fortune. I would like to contribute something."

"No worries, you wouldn't believe how the wallets opened for Pete. I don't think he realizes how many friends he's got. They all chipped in for the total restoration. I was floored when they gave me the check. Hell, I almost want to retire." He pointed to the line of cars, golf carts and bicycles already heading into the lot. He turned and waved at a group of kayakers tying up to the dock. "I also got a lot of help from his neighbors. He's very popular with the Goodland crew."

Donna shook out the tablecloth and handed it to Charlie. "Vanessa, your being here will mean everything to Pete. I know him. He's going to be looking for you all night and after the party's over... you have my word. I'm not going to let all the assholes get him wasted. This is a momentous occasion for our boy, and I think the night should end well, you know."

Charlie sang along with the band as he covered the bike with the tablecloth and secured the ends under the tires. "Perfect."

CHAPTER 83

Let's Get this Started

By five p.m. the Buoy's lot was full and cars were parked on every narrow side street around the area.

Donna, setting up the buffet, put the orchids Bees had brought on the table and stood back to admire her work.

"Hey, you." Charlie stood close behind her. "The place looks great. Those orchids come from Bees? Are they his 'special' plants?"

"I don't know what you mean." Donna laughed and reflexively leaned back into Charlie. "Have you heard from Pete?"

Charlie massaged her shoulders. "Saw him for a few minutes this afternoon. He was acting a bit off. He must be freaking out."

"I can't believe he's doing this." She walked over and grabbed two water bottles from an oversized cooler near the bar and handed one to Charlie.

"Me, neither."

The crowd had swelled to about seventy people, all milling about and staring at the closed bar. "You think I should let them get drinks? It's hot as hell." Donna waved to the bartender.

"They want to get their money's worth. It's up to you. Can you afford an extra hour of free booze? How is twenty-five bucks a head going to cover the booze and this spread?" Charlie pointed to the mountain of seafood resting on piles of ice.

"Ronny from Keef's Seafood worked a deal for me. Pete has saved his ass a bunch of times. He gave me a huge discount on the stone crab and shrimp. A lot of local businesses made donations on everything from tacos to cheesecake. I had to turn some vendors away. All their business cards are on the tables and at the bar."

"You did a fantastic job."

Donna gave thumbs up to the bartender and within seconds the crowd in front of the bar was six deep. She tapped a waitress setting up the buffet. "Nice job on the tables. You can head behind the bar now. You got wine and beer. Thanks."

"Will do, Donna."

"Wait." The waitress stopped, as Donna continued, "Prepare yourself. This crew is ready to party. Don't get flustered and keep smiling. There are quite a few heavy hitters, so keep your eyes open and watch for problems."

Charlie shook his head. "Wow, You're good at this. I mostly see you behind the bar. Have you ever thought of opening your own place?"

"You're the first one I'm telling this to. I bought the Buoy the week after Pete and me...I guess I can't say broke up, because we were never formally a thing."

"Congratulations, Donna. This is great news! Another reason to celebrate tonight."

"This is between us. I'm going to have a grand opening in a couple of weeks. I'm thinking of making some changes."

"Whoa, not too many, I hope. You have a very loyal clientele. Though it's obvious the owners haven't sunk any capital in here for years. You know better than anyone. Folks around here don't like change."

"The owners are old. I've been running it for the last two years. Lots of people already think it's my place."

"And now it is. The Buoy has your style all over it."

"Not the Buoy—Donna's Dockside. What do you think? I want to bring in more day-trippers on the waterside."

"I love it." He hugged her. "It's perfect." Charlie gulped and continued, "The party is 6 p.m. until 10. You plan on ending the festivities on time?"

"Unless someone hands me two grand to keep open another hour, that's my plan."

"You got the cleanup covered?"

"Yeah. I just need to check there are no bodies under the tables."

"I can help with that."

"Your best friend is retiring. You aren't going to be one of them?"

"No." He moved closer. "Does that surprise you?"

"Come to think of it, I don't think I've ever seen you drunk. You've always been watching out for Pete."

"That job is done. I have other interests now. When the party's over, I was thinking of hanging out for a bit...with you." He tucked a stray hair behind her ear. "Did I tell you I love your new look?"

A voice called out from the dockside tables, "Hey, Charlie, it's time to party, brother."

Charlie looked over at the Wizened Dicks who were raising glasses and whistling at Dan and his new girlfriend Kelly.

He squeezed Donna's hand. "I'll catch up with you later."

✿

Donna watched as ever-steady Charlie greeted new arrivals. He seemed comfortable and interacted easily with everyone. *Maybe I had my money on the wrong horse all along.* She shook her head. No, he wasn't ready. And of course, there was Pete. Everything happens for a reason. She smiled and hugged herself. *This is something new... contentment.*

Freddy and Bonita Driggs walked up holding hands and chuckling. "Hey, Donna, nice turnout." Bonita's expression turned somber as she hugged her. "I'm so sorry, I heard about you and Pete." Donna laughed. "No worries, I'm fine really. Freddy, come here and give me a hug too. It's a great day!"

"You know it. Did you see the line out front at the picture booth?"

"Picture booth?" Donna looked confused as she looked towards the Buoy's parking lot.

"Out front on the lawn, the poster of Pete is hysterical. And let me tell you those giant nuts are a hit." Bees slapped his thigh and giggled. "You are something else, Donna."

"Giant what?" Donna tilted her head. "Oh, the coconuts, yeah, they're great."

"Nita was embarrassed to take a picture next to them because she says she's wearing her Sunday dress." Freddy planted a loud kiss on Bonita's cheek. "But I got a picture as we walked by."

Bonita smacked him on the shoulder. "You're a dirty old man, Mr. Driggs." She winked. "I'm going to want to get a look at that later."

"That's my girl." Freddy grabbed Bonita's hand and pulled her towards the bar. "Donna, you sure know how to get a party started."

Bonita looked back at her. "You're the best, Donna. We should grab lunch one day now that Driggs Investigations is in the black."

❧

The television behind the bar was turned to WBNK news. The bartender picked up the remote to shut it off as the band walked on stage. A voice shouted over the crowd, "Look, they must have found that dickwad from *Blink You Missed It News*. Turn up the volume a minute." Footage of an ambulance and a man on a stretcher appeared on the screen. The continuous scroll on the bottom read WBNK newsman Bill Kendall found alive South of Everglades City...

"I'm Kimberly Stamper, coming to you live from Everglades City where our colleague, Senior Correspondent Bill Kendall, has just been found near death by kayakers fishing in the Ten Thousand Islands. Let's see if Bill has any words about his three-day ordeal."

Bill attempted to grab the mic as he put a wilted version of his signature smile on his scratched and sunburned face. Through blistered lips he whispered, "This is Bill Kendall for WBNK news sign..." His eyes rolled up into his skull. His head dropped to his chest as paramedics pushed her away. "Get the AED. He's going."

The camera pulled back to Kim. "This is Kimberly Stamper. We are live at the scene of the rescue of Bill Kendall." The camera shook and swiveled over to a view of EMT's rushing the gurney into the van. As the ambulance door closed, a voice shouted from within, "Clear."

A cheer erupted from the crowd. Someone yelled, "Florida kills another idiot." The cheers got louder as the TV went blank and the band started their set with a full-bore version of Allman Brothers' "Nobody Knows."

⁂

The Wizened Dicks were crowding a four-top along the railing when Rangers Chris Willows and Rosa Martinez sat at the table next to them. They were discussing the Albatross case until one of them noticed the rangers listening in.

"I got a great idea." They all leaned in closer.

"Go for it. They deserve it, they blew chunks twice, that screams for attention."

The Dicks leaned back in their chairs. "Hey, Willows, we heard you guys were there when Driggs brought in the gator that chewed up Horowitz. He was a big sucker, had a lot of meat on him. Word is after Doctor Treehorn was done, he made a few bucks, carving it up."

Martinez looked pleased. "Yeah. We were the first ones Driggs called. We sat on the scene, kept things running smooth."

"We all admire your dedication and hard work on the case. We just wanted to show our appreciation."

Willows squinted. "No funny business, guys, we're on the same team."

"No, really, we're serious. We just want to say thank you."

A waitress arrived and slid a steaming plate of fried nuggets in front of the pair. She nodded at the table of detectives. "That's on them. Our house specialty—alligator bites, fresh caught. Freddy Driggs dropped it off this morning. Enjoy."

Martinez looked over at the snickering crew, picked up a nugget, dipped it in the blood-red barbecue sauce and smiled. "My favorite! Thanks, Dicks." She popped the dripping sauce covered nugget in her mouth.

Willows moaned. Martinez kicked him under the table. She whispered between chews, "Grow a pair or you are never going to live this down."

A pale Willows picked up the smallest bite.

"You got to dip it, man. The sauce has some kick. That fresh gator chunk is going to have some bite to it." The Dicks were doubled over.

Willows gagged and swallowed it.

"Good job, buddy. We're getting another pitcher. Want to join us?"

Willows nodded and the WD's shifted to make room.

CHAPTER 84

Old Haunts

Pete got home around five-thirty, jumped into the shower, grabbed a Diet Coke, and sat on the tiny deck behind his trailer. He bit his lip as he mulled over his day.

First stop this morning was Golden Gate High School and the school crossing he was assigned to the year he came on the job. The kids were intimidating, big boys, some taller than him, and smart-ass girls ragging on the fresh-faced young cop. He always smiled a lot, listened to their smack, and was rewarded with their trust. He mentored some, befriended a few, a couple of them went on the job. He started a community outreach program that was still thriving.

Next stop was a drive down Vanderbilt Beach Road and a left onto Gulf Shore Drive. Back in the day, he would park his cruiser and set the CCSD placard in the window. Today, he followed a similar routine. He parked his unmarked sedan, walked down a block, and sat on a bench under a Jacaranda tree. In winter, the gulf front condos and apartment buildings that lined the canals brought in thousands of snowbirds. Today was the middle of the season. The roads were jammed. Traffic congestion led to daily fender benders. The Q-tip phenomenon, old white-haired drivers unable to see above the steering wheel, had taken up the better part of three years of his career. He pounded the pavement and developed his most important cop superpower, patience.

He smiled at the memories. *My career was one long, happy hour nightmare.* To keep his sector car dent free, he would park and walk Gulf Shore past the bars and restaurants that were packed from lunch until a half hour before Alex Trebek and "Jeopardy" came on. If a rowdy senior citizen decided it was time for some excitement, dine and dashes occurred most frequently towards the end of the month. A car chase on Gulf Shore never topped fifteen MPH. He'd just jog alongside and tap his nightstick on the window. The late-night crowd was younger, affluent, and not as docile. After eight, he would take the car and troll slowly up and down the drive.

This is not much different than twenty years ago. He searched the storefronts for something familiar. All the names had changed. Nothing lasts forever.

An elderly couple clinging tightly to each other lurched out of the restaurant across from his bench.

"Where'd you leave the car, Tony?"

The old man checked his pockets for his keys and held up a valet stub. "A guy parked it for me after I dropped you off."

His wife sniffed. "Now you got to tip the guy." She pointed a red fingernail at him. "Remember. Just one dollar. We're not rich."

"Well, we're not poor either, Patrice. You just drank two Bellini's at sixteen dollars a pop."

"Hmm. Okay, give him a five. He'll know you next time and put the car out front."

Watching the couple get into their Chrysler 300, Pete chuckled to himself, different decade, same scene. Looking at the high-end shops, his hand twitched at the memory of checking for unlocked doors. He thought of the countless drunks he poured into cabs. He patted his pocket and could almost hear the jingle of confiscated car keys he had collected at the end of every four to twelve. He was so young. He leaned back and sighed, thinking of the light feather of gray he had recently noticed on his temples.

Leaving North Naples, he stopped to pick up a hoagie at an Italian deli and then drove east towards Corkscrew Sanctuary. He pulled in the lot, tinned his way past the guard, and sat down at a picnic table outside the welcome center. Peace and quiet accompanied his lunch, along with a faint odor of smoke that drifted on the southern breeze. He checked his watch, February twenty-eighth, one-thirty p.m.. Today was the first day of controlled burns set by the fire service to reduce overgrowth. He remembered…fatal fire calls were the worst. Well, Deputy Pete, you don't have to deal with that anymore. That's one good thing. He got up and tossed his garbage in the tightly covered bin. His shoulders sagged under an unseen but heavy weight: one more stop.

Pete drove into Immokalee and pulled into a small park set back from the main road. He spent the better part of an hour sitting on a swing in the rundown playground. *This place hasn't changed much.* The far end of the park now had a tennis court. *That's new.* He looked at the net torn and sagging, the asphalt was cracked; tough weeds scrabbled through the surface. *Not much grows here. Shouldn't have come back.* He looked at the place that changed his life. He rubbed his chest above his heart. His vision blurred. This was my beginning. No, the beginning of my end. His past merged with the present. Face-to-face, a young Pete and a tired old one met within the memory of a dead child.

He was young, chasing a ball like all little kids do. Pete shivered under the burning midday sun. *How do you unsee something?* Brutalized and left to die, the boy was discovered by another child. *She was eight. He was her friend. How does she deal with the nightmares?*

Charlie had stood beside him when they told the young mother her nine-year-old son was dead. They gathered her into their embrace and cried together. On the day of the arrests, they restrained each other from what they wanted so badly to do—exactly what those animals did to that innocent child. The perps, gangbangers, afraid of a little kid ratting them out, were put away for life. *It was never enough. I should have done it as soon as I knew their names. I should have waited for them. It would have been easy. The fields of saw grass so close. No one would have ever found them.* He pulled his tin off his belt. He rubbed the cold metal and roughness of the design between his fingers. He hung his head as a deep sorrow took hold.

The case took six months to solve and sixteen years later, still unable to forget. Coming out the other side, Charlie went home to the arms of Miranda. He walked away alone with the taint of suspicion coloring his world. He had an unfulfilling love life and a taste for booze that was always on the edge of becoming something else. He hid nightly in a bottle. Beer or bourbon, it didn't matter. He embodied all the platitudes—lost faith, hard as stone, cold as ice. *Charlie always said I should settle down. I couldn't. I was already married. The job was my wife, and she was a bitch.*

He returned to the present as a car pulled into the lot and a child jumped out, tossed his blue and red Elmo backpack onto the lone picnic table, and ran towards the playground. *No, it was a Dolphins backpack, bright blue, and the redwood paint on the table was peeling. It hung off the sides...long strings of congealed blood, and over there...*He looked at the bushes... *Those bushes are even more overgrown, could hide a lot more. Does anyone around here remember?* Pete's eyes filled up. The little boy smiled at him and hopped onto the neighboring swing. Pete looked over at the parking lot and saw the mother struggling to put a toddler in a flimsy umbrella stroller. She beeped the car lock and hurried towards the boy. *She's smart, watching out. She shouldn't trust anyone. She doesn't know I'm a cop.*

"Miss, I'm with the Sheriff's department. You have a beautiful family. My best advice to you—keep them close; don't let him run off like that. Things can happen in an instant."

"Thank you, Sheriff. He's a handful, and with the baby, you know, it's hard to keep up with him."

"You listen to your mama, son." Pete smiled and gave him a salute as he headed towards his car. *Pity party is over, Pete. It's a new day.*

He stood up on the deck and drained the last of his Diet Coke as the sound of traffic, a rarity in Goodland on a Tuesday night, brought him out of his head. He dragged himself out of the past. The party was about to begin. He prepared himself for what was coming next.

CHAPTER 85

The Party

Pete walked the short distance to the Buoy. He could hear the crowd's laughter and music from a block away. He was glad he had eaten lunch. His gut was in a knot. The Diet Coke was a feeble attempt to settle his stomach. *Keep moving forward man, an hour— two tops— and you can get this over with. Think about tomorrow.*

The sign over the driveway chilled him, though he had to laugh when he saw a tall air tube biker that looked a lot like a coked up, flaccid dick with huge coconut balls. As he walked under the "Good Luck, Pete!" sign all the noise stopped. At first he heard a few clinking glasses, a woman's giggle, a sneeze, and then only the gulls out over the water. He could see everyone staring at him as he walked to the deck. He climbed the stairs slowly, holding his breath. His foot hit the top step, and the band broke into "Born to be Wild." The crowd roared, and everyone started dancing and singing. Pete merged into the crowd, hands slapping his back as he passed. At the chorus, the crowd parted, the stage was in full view. Charlie, Dan, Donna, and Freddy Driggs stood in front. They stepped aside as Charlie whipped off a green tarp. The band pumped up the volume, and Bon Jovi's "Wanted Dead or Alive" blasted through the speakers. The crowd was euphoric. Pete stared at the bike in front of him. He recognized his Indian. *What the fuck? She was a rotting piece of junk last time I saw her. She's the most beautiful thing I've ever seen.* His eyes glistened as he turned and spotted Vanessa—*the second most beautiful thing.*

His heart pounded as he fought back tears. Faces from his past smiled at him, women kissed his cheeks, and men hugged him. He saw cops and ex-cons, ex-lovers, and drinking buddies, neighbors and friends, families of victims. Sitting at a table near the dock were his parents. *Everyone I know is here.*

Charlie came up beside him and led him towards the stage. "You look a bit dazed, brother. You okay?"

Pete stumbled over the words, "Charlie, I…"

"Bet you didn't know how many people love you."

"All of this, the bike…I don't know what to say."

"That's never been your problem. Look at them, just tell them how you feel. I'm guessing you didn't spend today writing a speech, right?"

"No, I didn't…" He looked around at the throng of joyful partiers. "I didn't think about any of this today."

"Get up on the stage," came from somewhere in the back.

Donna took his hand and led him up the steps. She grabbed the microphone. "You know, Pete, nobody gets dinner until you make a speech."

The crowd erupted and the chant, "Speech! Speech! Speech!" swelled around him.

Donna handed him the mic, kissed him on the cheek and whispered, "You got this, buddy." She leaned back and looked at him funny. "Whatever it is you got to say, remember, we all love you."

"I'm floored by this." He jumped as the reverb shrilled.

"Don't hold it so close to your mouth," came from the band behind him.

"I'm so…"

Another shout came from the back. "He's speechless. Told you, the man's got a heart."

"We love you, Pete," echoed from the dock.

Charlie mouthed the words, "Keep going."

"One month ago, I decided that…" Pete paused and rubbed his chin. He looked at the rapt faces in front of him. "Man, this a tough one." Donna approached him with a beer. He shook his head. "No, water, please." A waitress ran up with a glass of ice water. He took a sip and nodded at Freddy and Bonita at a hi-top near the driveway.

"The job, the entire cop thing…it's a tough life. I've seen some crazy things. And I'm being honest here, the things I saw." He took a deep breath. "Well, because of the nature of the job, they were mostly bad. The problem was, after a while, I didn't see anything or anyone as, I don't know, inherently good. I've spent thirty years looking for the bad guys. That was what I thought my job was about —getting rid of evil. I was in a losing battle." His head lowered as he tamped down the urge to pick up the beer Donna had left.

"A lot has happened since the day I decided to…take care of me." His voice grew raspy as he took another swallow of water. "Excuse me."

"Take your time, Pete. We're all here for you."

"I thought it was time to take back my life and do whatever I wanted to do."

"Time to go fishing, brother!"

He smiled and pointed to the thickets of mangrove crowding in on the open bay. "We made a choice to live on the ragged edge of the world. We appreciate the beauty and bounty that surrounds us. These last few weeks, I—no, we—have witnessed its dangerous side. It's a place where the phrase 'the strong survive' has real meaning." He looked over at Shredder and smiled. "Death came here and stayed for a while. There was no controlling it. We all had a front seat to the horror." He coughed and Donna refilled his glass of water.

"Excuse me. I'm not much of a public speaker."

"You're doing great, Pete," encouraged someone down in front.

"The familiar annoyances, ants, gators, even snakes, showed their true power. We walk among them daily. We know to be vigilant. But a lot of people think of Florida as a sanitized theme park bubble. And many down here just don't think at all." He cleared his throat and looked at the sea of faces in front of him. "The innocent, or not so innocent, are ill-prepared for the danger: not just here by the swamp, but at the malls, on the interstates, out on the water." He searched the crowd and locked eyes with Charlie. "And in rundown playgrounds." He closed his eyes, took a deep breath and looked up before he continued. "Someone must stand up for the weak. Protect them from predators."

"That's always been you, Pete."

"Here, here."

"Let me get through this, okay? This past month, I witnessed a veritable vortex of death." His deep sigh rumbled through the mic. "And today..." He took a sip of water. "Today, I figured out what is important." He paused, looking in the eyes of as many of his friends as he could... "I am not that important. What I can do for all of you—that is very important." He watched as his words hit home. The upturned faces conveyed a range of emotions. He relaxed as he saw understanding.

Pete straightened up his shoulders and stood tall. *Here goes.* "So, in conclusion, I made a decision late this afternoon. I went to Headquarters and pulled my retirement papers. I will be taking a two-week vacation and then I will be back out on the streets doing what I love to do. I am truly sorry for putting you all through this, and I will repay all of you for the gift." He looked down at the Indian. "Man, that bike is a beauty. That might have to be paid off in installments. I want to thank you all for coming and for your outpouring of love. I hope I will have your support as I continue serving all of you here in Collier County."

The stunned crowd, mouths agape, stared at Pete. His hands were shaking as put the mic down on the railing.

A voice called out, "Thank God! Pete is staying!"

Applause and whistles echoed into the evening sky.

"For he's a jolly good fellow..." swept through the crowd.

Rosa Martinez and Christopher Willows stood at the edge of the crowd. Willows grimaced. "Shit, I thought we got rid of him."

Another reveler shouted, "Here's to Pete! And the best non-retirement party ever!"

Donna ran up, hugged him, and picked up the mic. "Dinner buffet is inside! Stone crab and shrimp, fried chicken and ribs, come and get it! Full bar is open. Remember to keep an eye on your friends. They'll be no drunks driving tonight." She winked at Pete. "All the best cops are really busy."

CHAPTER 86

"Rocky Mountain High" - John Denver

Later that night, Pete drove slowly down the streets of Goodland. The Chief's engine growled and Vanessa's knees were clamped tightly around his hips. *My life took some crazy turn today. But this feels so right.* He reached down and squeezed Vanessa's hand encircling his waist. *I got one more thing to get through.* He relished the press of her body against his. *The most important one.*

The shed's open doors revealed a freshly swept and uncluttered space. A sign with "Ride- on, Pete" hand-carved into the wood was nailed to the beam above the entrance.

"Charlie did this. He's a good friend, Pete."

"I know it."

As they walked through the trailer, he cringed at the sight of dirty sheets crumpled up on the bed from the last time Donna slept over. He rushed Vanessa through hoping she hadn't noticed. "Let's sit out on the deck, it's a beautiful night."

"I love your place. It's cozy."

"Meaning small." He looked around, seeing his trailer in a different light.

She responded softly as her fingertips danced lightly across the deck railing. "I think it could work for two...in the short term."

She smiled as he plugged in a string of delicate white fairy lights. Their refection twinkled in the canal beyond the deck. "This is such a peaceful spot."

He gestured at the wicker rockers that faced the water. "Have a seat. Would you like something to drink?"

"No need to be so formal." She patted the chair beside her. "Relax. Savor the moment. You were wonderful tonight."

"I don't know how I got through it." Pete shook his head. "I need to ask you something."

"Ask me anything." She stretched her legs out in front of her and kicked off her sandals.

Pete stammered, "I'm taking my parents to brunch on Marco before their flight out of Fort Myers tomorrow afternoon. I'd like you to come. I want to formally introduce you to them. It was crazy tonight, and I didn't get a chance to do that."

"Wow. That's not what I expected." She tilted her head. "That sounds like a big step."

"It is. I've never brought anyone to meet them before." He shifted uncomfortably. "They are getting old. I thought they might enjoy that milestone before, you know."

Vanessa laughed aloud. "Shouldn't we kids date for a while before I meet them?"

"Funny. But about the dating thing, it's overrated." Pete squared his shoulders for the second time that evening. He decided it was time to dive in. He inched his chair closer. "I know all I need to know. I'm not waiting on a prescribed schedule. I found what I'm looking for. I'm happy. That's something I didn't think was possible."

Vanessa reached out and put her hand on his thigh. "I've been thinking that since the day I met you."

"About tonight." Pete stood up.

She pulled her hand away. "Don't say anything. It's okay. This was an intense evening. I think ..."

Pete watched her face closely. *I just blew it. Damn it, maybe she thinks I can't get it up. I'm all talk, no action.*

"Pete." Her voice brought him back. "May I give you my gift now? Can I use your computer? I need to open my email." She got up and headed towards the glass slider.

"The laptop is on the kitchen table." He rushed in first and shut the bedroom door before he turned back to her. "I didn't retire. You didn't need to get me anything."

"Oh, I definitely did." A mischievous gleam danced in her eyes. "Returning it isn't an option." She patted the chair she had pulled next to her. "Sit beside me."

A website opened to a scene of snow-covered mountains.

"What's this?"

"Click on the booking link." She pointed at the screen. "There."

A completed form filled the page: "This luxury log cabin high in the Rockies awaits you. You are one click way from securing your reservation."

"I thought a change of scenery was in order."

"Vanessa, wow! I've never been to Colorado."

"Me, neither. How about we explore it together?" Her hand paused above the submit button.

"Wait. I need to tell you something. I've been holding this in for a month…" He leaned in and pulled her close. "I love you, Vanessa. No frills, just the God's honest truth, I love you."

She brushed his lips with hers, inhaled his words and breathed out, "I love you, Pete."

By the time their lips parted, Pete's brain had turned to mush.

"You are going to love the mountains." Vanessa whispered as she played with the hair curling over his collar.

Nuzzling her neck, he replied, "I'm pretty sure the valleys are going to take my breath away, too."

♋︎

Two weeks later, two thousand miles west and eight thousand feet above sea level, a large mug of coffee steamed between Pete Landry's cupped palms. He stood on the deck of a magnificent ski house tucked on the side of a mountain overlooking the charming enclave of Aspen, Colorado. He breathed in the cold mountain air and took in the expansive view. His white terry robe matched the fluffy brilliance of the snow cover all around him.

The Currier and Ives valley which ranged below the cabin was bathed in muted sunlight as the clouds thickened and lowered. Curls of smoke rose from the chimneys of chalets dotting the lower slopes. The Rockies were glorious this morning. They rose on all sides and touched what he knew must be heaven. He marveled at his good fortune.

He turned to enjoy the sight of Vanessa who was luxuriating in the bubbling hot tub at the edge of the deck. She stretched her arms above her head, her perfect breasts peeked through the steam. Her nipples, blushed from the heat of the spa, were the exact color of a mountain sunset. He dropped his robe as the sky released a softly falling snow powdering his hair.

Vanessa held out her hand to catch some flakes. "Your hair is turning white." She curled her fingers beckoning him to join her. "Come in here, old man."

"I love the sound of that, Nessa." He entered the water gradually, intensifying the change from cold to hot. He sighed as he settled down beside her.

"I don't know how you do that," she giggled. "I've got to get in quick before I …" A scream erupted from the cabin. Vanessa jumped, sending a cascade of water over the rim of the Jacuzzi. "Oh my, God. Someone needs help!"

"That's Charlie's ring." Pete pulled her down and gathered her in his arms. "It can wait." His mouth covered hers and he drank her in.

CHAPTER 87

Text message

- Hey, Pete, remember that painted gator…

The End

"The Road Goes on Forever and the Party Never Ends..."
– Robert Earl Keen

ACKNOWLEDGMENTS

The moment I arrived at the Marco Island beachfront condo, the project I was going to spend the winter finishing (a novel set in Leadville, Colorado) had melted in the tropical heat. And *Florida Kills* was born.

My writing journey was not solitary. Many wonderful people walked beside me. Like signs from above they appeared, many speaking to my vision, many unaware they had made an impact on me, and there were those seen from a distance, never spoken to, that brought an unexpected clarity to the world.

Bethpage Public Library on Long Island, NY, offered me the wonders of big books as a toddler, my after-school job as a page, and the first writers' groups I attended as an adult. Not unlike the Proust Effect, the *Scent of Words* (one of my published essays) follows me with every page I turn, bringing me the joy of reading, and leading me to my passion, writing.

I want to thank Edgar Carlson, for sharing poetry and showing me how to make seeds of words bloom.

I need to mention three of the unseen and never introduced inspirations: Dave Barry, Carl Hiasson and the late Tim Dorsey. They always made me laugh and showed me that being weird, and savage could be very funny.

My heartfelt gratitude to the *Long Island Writers Guild*. I would like to thank Dennis Koch and Lorraine Conlin who tirelessly keep LIWG an inviting place where writers can learn and flourish. The gifted writers at the Guild: Florence Gatto, Rita Monte, Kathy Keevins, et al, thank you. In remembrance of Beverly Koch, butt-kicker supreme, I pray you are watching and giving a nod. Your constant battle to get me to publish finally penetrated my brain.

Author Ellen Meister, whose master class on writing has enlightened and encouraged me, and my fellow talented authors in the Meister crew: Jayne Isabel Potter, Keith Furino, Dr. Carolyn Nemec, Kate Shaffar, Fred Abatamarco, Dr Louis Carnacchia, Jeffrey Siegel, Lynn Tone and Madeline Ganis, my gratitude for hours of listening and valuable suggestions.

Thank you to the Long Beach Writer's Circle and its dedicated members who kept going through trying times and the sadness of missing Grace.

I want to express my deep gratitude to my neighbor, friend, editor, and mentor Susan Lovelace, for her meticulous edit, and infinite patience. Landing in my new home, steps from the Atlantic Ocean in south central Florida, Susan offered me the key to the next part of my journey– the *Laura Riding Jackson Foundation* in Vero Beach. Tuesday Writers and PenPoints, just two of the many writing groups under the LRJF umbrella, gave my passion a place to call home. Surrounded by talented authors, poets, essayists, and memoirists, my vision of seeing my book in print came alive.

Special thanks to Dr. Jacque Jacobs, President of LRJF, for all her advice, help, and patience, to Sara Wilson, Executive Director of LRJF, for her steady hand guiding this outstanding organization, and Ren Counts, for keeping it all running smoothly. Also, many thanks to Pete Clements, Jeanne Selander Miller, Dr. Bonnie MacDougall , Colette Thorpe, Randy Old, Jackie Grady, Dr. Crystal Bujol, Sally Boutte, Mark Hinkley, and all the extraordinary Tuesday Writer's. They are the epitome of an excellent writing group.

To the truly gifted Pen Points gang: Elaine Spooner, Kelly Marker, Theresa Morgan, Mary Hourdequin, Donna Olson, John DiMenna, and Amy Morgan , many thanks. It is my privilege to listen to your works and hear your valuable critiques.

Thank you, George Bolton for your sharp-eyed edits and suggestions.

Thank you, YaYas- Pattie Sorrentino, Susan Kasper, Jane Felsberg, Kathleen Neil, and Barbara Al Salam, forever friends are the best.

For Sean, Rachel and Jack, I love you all and thank you for believing in me. And to Sean— who encouraged me, and always made me feel like the best mom in the world. Thank you.

For my daughter, Bridget and her husband, Bryan Ford, I love you both. You inspired me with your dedication to your goals and for sharing your incredible recipes and delectable foods that graced our table. You offered me a vision for this novel's path. Thank you for sharing your *industry* knowledge, and for pushing me to move this project forward. I look forward to the next chapter in the *Florida Kills* journey with you both.

Specifically, to Bridget—you make my life beautiful.

To my husband John, always beside me on my journey. I love you, forever. Thank you for hovering over me as I type, laughing at the appropriate places, correcting my mistakes, offering your valuable expertise, and always knowing I would get this book off the ground!!!

About the Author

Ann Kenna, having spent years on the shores of Long Island, dropped her beach chair on the southwest coast of Florida and was rewarded with a front row seat to snowbird culture and a rare glimpse of old-moneyed senior citizens in high-end beachfront condos. Heading further south she found her way to the Everglades—the end of the road where exotic predators flourish.

Ann, a published memoirist, essayist and performance poet, honed her observational skills in elementary special education. Those skills, the enigmatic beauty of the Everglades, her imagination, and thirty years of writing propelled her into the world of her debut novel FLORIDA KILLS.